THE
WORD
OF A
GENTLEMAN

THE WORD OF A GENTLEMAN

PETER NIESEWAND

🔟 STEIN AND DAY/*Publishers*/New York

First published in the United States of America in 1985
Copyright © 1981 by Peter Niesewand
All rights reserved, Stein and Day, Incorporated
Printed in the United States of America
STEIN AND DAY/Publishers
Scarborough House
Briarcliff Manor, N.Y. 10510

Library of Congress Cataloging in Publication Data

Niesewand, Peter.
  The word of a gentleman.

  I. Title.
PR6064.133W6   1985   823'.914   84-40728
ISBN 0-8128-3026-1

There is no chapel on the day
On which they hang a man:
The Chaplain's heart is far too sick,
Or his face is far too wan,
Or there is that written in his eyes
Which none should look upon.

Oscar Wilde: *The Ballad of Reading Gaol.*

THE
WORD
OF A
GENTLEMAN

Prologue

The view looking down sent an unexpected tingle of fright through his body, making his legs weak, as if gravity in this deserted place had suddenly become powerful enough to collapse his balance and suck him over.

He lay quickly on his stomach, the buckle of his belt pressing hard through his clothes into his flesh, and inched forward. Seagulls floated steady on bright white wings two hundred feet down. Far beyond that, water crashed silently onto the jagged rocky pencils of grey and black which edged the sand and butted in clusters back to the granite walls of Alden Cliffs. A blur of white water reared up and hung in the air, then melted away.

The wind hit his face and filled his ears with its rushing. Behind it, he could hear the insistent cries of gulls, but mostly he was conscious of the cold wind off the Atlantic whipping round his face. When he turned and looked back over the buffeting grass and bracken sloping up to the dirt road, the noise of the wind shut off suddenly, its currents deflecting away, leaving him in a pool of seeming calm.

Montrose and Clifton were standing by the Land Rover, waiting for a signal. Even from that distance, he could tell they were nervous. They were standing very upright, close against the vehicle, as if their backs and shoulders could block out the view of the woman on the seat, and they looked around carefully, scanning the area for others.

Luther turned back to the edge, trying to ignore the unease that the sheer drop sparked in him, and carefully studied the beach below. It was late afternoon. The sun was nearing the horizon and shadows were lengthening, making it difficult to be completely sure the beach was deserted. He fumbled with a black case, pulled out a pair of binoculars and adjusted the lenses, then slowly swept the long expanse of beach and rock. He found a man, far below in the shade of a rock, his fishing rod and a box beside him. The binoculars continued their scan but the fisherman was alone. They returned to him and watched.

Montrose and Clifton were becoming jumpy at the delay. They spoke briefly, and Clifton walked towards the edge, ignoring a dirt path trampled by ramblers over the years and stepping carefully through the gorse as Luther had done. They could see Luther lying motionless, staring intently through the glasses.

Clifton dropped onto his belly and crawled the final feet. The awesome sensation of gulls gliding below, and heartstoppingly beneath them the strip of sand and rock, hit him just as it had Luther, and he feared for an instant that the lip might be eroded.

Luther pointed. "See those rocks there, where the wave's just hit?"

Clifton peered intently down. "I don't see anything."

Luther handed over the binoculars. "A fisherman," he said. Clifton adjusted the glasses even though Luther had them properly focused, and then adjusted them back. The wind rushed into their faces and Luther could feel his eyes redden with the force.

Clifton studied the rocks. Finally he saw, and said: "Shit." He lapsed into silence, the binoculars steady at his eyes. At length, he handed them back to Luther. "What do we do?"

"No sign of anyone coming up here?" Luther asked.

"Nothing."

"Then we wait. He's sure to go soon. He's not sleeping, and it looks like he's given up fishing. He's just watching the waves."

"Bastard. That's all we need."

Luther shrugged. "It was a risk. We knew that. We just have to wait for him to go. It shouldn't take long."

Clifton snorted disagreeably, and his eyes were cold in his thin, black face. Luther thought how much he disliked him, how little he trusted the man, but it was far too late for second thoughts.

Clifton rolled over and fumbled in his pocket for a pack of cigarettes. He had one in his mouth before Luther said: "No smoking."

"Fuck off." The words came in a growl.

"I mean it. We were never here, remember? No ash, no cigarette butts, no matches."

Luther turned away, knowing that Clifton was considering his position, weighing up the loss of face he would suffer by giving in against the truth of what Luther said. Luther could feel unfriendly eyes staring thoughtfully at the side of his head, and he busied himself with the binoculars, finding the fisherman again, avoiding a personal confrontation. This was not the time for conflict: everyone had become too edgy. He felt a movement from Clifton, and he knew instinctively that he had been obeyed.

Clifton lay silent and resentful while the wind whipped past and the gulls, mewling, were lifted up on currents of air. At last he said abruptly: "I'll tell Montrose about the holdup."

Luther nodded briefly but kept his binoculars trained on the fisherman. While Clifton was gone, he began another visual sweep up and down the beach. He was getting used to the height now: didn't feel so bad about lying there. When he focused back on the rock, the fisherman had moved away. He picked him up wandering slowly along the water's edge, the waves occasionally creaming over his feet in a delicate tracery of froth as their power ran out, obliterating the meandering line of prints on the yellow-brown sand. The fisherman stooped to study something: a shell maybe, or a stone, it was impossible to see, and then he straightened up and threw the object, trying to skim it on the waves. He looked in his early twenties, and Luther could tell he was a local like himself and Clifton, and not a Brit. Luther had no idea who he was.

He looked back to see what Clifton and Montrose were doing, and noticed both had climbed into the Land Rover, one in front, one behind, and were hunched where the woman lay. He waited until one of them looked up and then Luther motioned for him to come across.

This time it was Montrose, the arrogant pig, who picked his way through the gorse, his belly thrusting against his khaki shirt, bulging over his belt, but his bull neck firm and his arms thick and strong. Montrose was built like a wrestler whose gut had given up the fight and had allowed the muscle walls to distend. Montrose was Commissioner of Police, the post he had held even before Independence. Unlike other colonies, there had been many British survivors of colonialism's end on the island, and he was one of the most efficient and the most feared. Of all the white men to keep on, Luther thought, why him? Luther watched him come, wondering wryly also why it was that even in a relatively small place like St David's, he had to throw in his lot with Montrose, and with that cold bastard Clifton, but he knew the answer, of course: they had the real power, the three of them, though no one had suspected it. It wasn't the votes of the people, or the grand titles and official residences which identified the men who ruled: only those who thought they ruled, like Daniel Moorhouse. Poor Moorhouse. He was no match for Mr Commissioner of Police Montrose, with his watchful eyes and his bland, pudgy unlined face, who called him Sir, or Mr Prime Minister, and licked his ass as the rest of them did.

He was no match even for Mr Deputy Commissioner of Police Clifton either, even though Clifton was an asshole too. But Clifton was at least smart enough to realise early on who really had clout in the country. Clifton had discovered that true power came not only from the barrel of a gun, but from less obvious sources: out of beige manilla files with red diagonal stripes across the corner, which could make their subjects, no matter who or how high they were, do as they were told.

And then there was himself, Stephen Charles Luther, General in the glorious armed forces of St David's. Not just a General – *the* General, the man in command of national security, keeper of the island's integrity: a local, promoted at the time of Independence: one of the new black faces in charge. Ready to stand fast against foreign invasion with all the military might at his disposal. And that wasn't much. Thirty thousand very old FNs and half that number of submachine-guns. Hand grenades. Some armoured cars. Anti-aircraft guns which woud be useful if the enemy attacked using Dakotas. Howitzers which were probably increasing in value every year as antiques.

Train the St David's arsenal on the invading Russians and they'd laugh. But train it on the civilian population, as they had done, and no one even smiled. That was power.

3

Moorhouse never suspected, but then you don't when even your enemies call you Sir, and everyone is toadying because you're the Prime Minister and they're desperate to keep their jobs or get promotion, or they don't want to be blamed for taking an initiative which might backfire; so you, the great leader, take all the decisions, even the little ones, and you get snowed with the impression that your every word is a pearl, your every deed is in the national interest, and your fingers have just to be clicked for people to jump about. And in fact, that's how it happened for a long time. Moorhouse loved it. But as he found out, one day it just stops, everything, as suddenly as it started. And then Moorhouse came to realise that he was no more powerful than any other man: worse off, actually, because he remembered the cheers, because his head still told him he was the great leader and could demand things, when no one was paying attention any longer.

And all because of us: the men with the real power.

What a crew. Luther, Montrose and Clifton. Together, he thought, we can conquer the world. When that fucking fisherman gets out of the way.

Montrose was breathing heavily, and he flopped down beside Luther, beads of sweat on his forehead. He said nothing, but reached imperiously for the binoculars. Luther passed them across, saying nothing, hoping Montrose was on his way to a heart attack.

"Where the hell is he?" Montrose demanded, raising his voice because of the wind. He didn't seem to care about the dizzying drop.

Luther pointed: "Walking by the edge over there. You don't need the glasses now. You can see him clearly without them."

Montrose grunted and peered through the binoculars anyway. After a moment he said: "Someone we know?"

"Don't think so. A local. He was fishing."

They watched the man stroll along the sand until he rounded the projection marking the edge of the bay, and then he was gone. Montrose scrambled to his feet and looked down impassively. Luther thought how sweet it would be to stand just behind him and give one firm, sudden shove. But not today. "Let's move," said Montrose abruptly.

They walked to the Land Rover, scanning the cliff top again for strangers, the wind against their backs, giving that sudden sense of calm. Luther found to his surprise that his legs still felt shaky.

"How is she?" he asked.

"Showing signs of life," Montrose replied.

"Is that good?"

"We gave her a little bit more."

Luther grunted and hoped silently it wasn't too much more. He wanted to have her moving.

At the Land Rover, Montrose brusquely took command. Luther climbed into the back and lifted the woman under her arms. She was

4

in her early thirties, difficult to say just how old, and her eyes were closed in sleep. The smell of chloroform still hung around her. Luther put his face near her breasts and shoulders and sniffed to see if spots of the liquid had splashed onto her clothes, but it was impossible to tell. She lay heavy, her head lolling like a newborn infant, her mouth hanging half open.

They eased her out of the back seat and carried her through the gorse. The sun was a scarlet ball on the horizon now and the sky picked up pastel tones.

The men laid her on her back and stood a pace away.

"Now what?" Clifton asked.

"Let's do it," said Montrose dismissively, but Luther shook his head.

"She must get the chloroform out of her system," he said. "We have to wait until that happens. We don't want anything showing up."

"Oh fuck, Luther," Montrose snapped. "That could take all night. We can't hang about. The bitch will wake up and yell."

"No she won't," said Luther confidently. "And if she does, no one will hear her."

He moved nearer the woman and knelt beside her. He patted her face and said loudly, his voice rising against the whipping wind: "Nora! Nora! Wake up!"

The others watched intently, but she didn't stir. Luther held her wrist and felt for the pulse. It took him a while to find it, but it was there: she was alive.

"Nora! Nora! Can you hear me? Wake up!"

"Pull the cow's hair," Montrose growled.

Luther slapped her face harder. "Nora! Come on! Time to wake up!"

The woman's eyelids flickered and Luther glanced at the others. "Here she comes," he said. Montrose and Clifton moved nearer until the three of them were in a line, squatting by her side. She groaned, and her eyes opened briefly, failed to focus and closed again.

"For Christ's sake, Nora, come on," Luther urged. "We haven't got all day. Wake up!" He shook her shoulder.

This time she did look at him, at first uncomprehending, and at the other two beside her, their faces hostile. She could hear the wind without knowing where it came from.

"What happened?" she asked groggily, still not realising, and then she recognised Montrose and Luther and tried to sit up. Luther put a firm restraining hand on her shoulder. "Don't get up," he said. "Lie there a minute." He smiled, and she watched him, scared and wondering.

"What do you want with me?" she asked, her voice beginning to crack with fright.

Although Luther was smiling, his eyes were not, and the other two made no pretence at disguising their coldness.

"We don't want anything," said Luther. "It's me, remember, Steve Luther. Just relax."

"I've got a headache," she said, fighting a sudden wave of nausea.

"Bad luck," said Luther sympathetically. "It'll go in a minute. Just lie still and shut your eyes."

Without thinking, the woman did as she was told, trying to will away the dull pain, and suddenly there were hands underneath her as if to pick her up, and she felt herself rolling over onto her side. Instinctively she put out a hand to steady herself but there was nothing there. Her eyes opened and for an instant, as she wavered on the cliff edge, she saw the drop which had turned Luther's legs to jelly, and the gulls below, and heard their mewling above the wind, and, as she toppled, she began to scream. She may have screamed all the way down to the rocks, but they couldn't tell. The wind muffled some of the noise.

In the Land Rover going back, Clifton said churlishly to Luther: "Do you mind if I smoke now?"

Luther shrugged. "Do whatever you like," he said disagreeably.

He wanted a cigarette too, so he lit one up without offering the pack to Clifton or Montrose. Clifton looked at him with contempt.

They drove in silence into Port Lombard.

Chapter One

Of course it was ridiculous standing there and expecting to hear anything through the doors leading to the Prime Minister's office, and he'd know soon enough why he had been summoned. But still he did it, habit probably, pretending to study the terrible oil painting of Mount Forel which hung in the anteroom, behind the yellow velvet easy chairs and conveniently close to the doors. Who could have chosen this? he wondered idly in the silence. The artist, whose signature was indecipherable – he was sure deliberately – could surely never have had the nerve to put it up for sale. Yet here it was, in a place of honour.

It would be possible to detect raised voices in the next room: that would give him at least some indication of the mood. There were reports that Moorhouse shouted a lot these days. But nothing.

Freeman Leister cleared his throat. This painting, he decided, must be a gift from an important benefactor of St David's: the sort of thing one usually keeps in a storeroom against the day when the artist returns for a visit, and then it's dusted off and hung in a prominent place. Yet this one had been here for, what, three years? Someone liked it.

It was easy to know what was bugging Moorhouse. He had politician's menopause. He'd been in power since 1968, nearly a decade, and most of that time everyone had loved him. Well, nearly everyone loved him. Not the politicians who were out of power, of course, and who had always done what they could to cause him grief. But most of the ordinary people on the island, locals and British, had thought for a long time that Moorhouse was good news. Not any longer. Moorhouse had lost popularity faster than anyone would have thought possible. The economy took a dive and so did he. It was as simple as that.

Of course, St David's was an astonishing place. Stuck out in the Atlantic, without much going for it except its strategic position, it had missed all the usual bitternesses of post-colonial possessions.

The British hadn't been ordered off at gunpoint. They had given up the colony reasonably gracefully, but then they'd stuck around to keep the show running in much the same way as they had before. A typical Whitehall compromise. You had to admire it. Almost without exception, the British had stayed. There were some new darker coloured faces in top jobs, naturally enough, but a hell of a lot of old white faces had been kept on too, operating the same way they always did. Uncle Tom's island paradise, with Moorhouse acknowledging the cheers of the crowds and, while it lasted, loving every minute. No different from politicians anywhere. And, of course, hating it when it ended.

Leister had seen enough of them over the years – statesmen, two-bit cheats – and there wasn't one who missed being profoundly, personally hurt when those who elected them to office changed their minds and kicked them out. Naturally, they all pretended they didn't care for themselves, only for their policies. They gave out that they were pros, took the rough with the smooth, but you could tell from their eyes and often from their actions that they had been deeply stung, and that, in some indefinable way, they felt cheated.

Moorhouse was beginning to feel cheated, which was why he was suddenly shouting a lot.

Leister checked his watch. He had never been kept waiting this long before.

When the revolution comes, he thought looking back at the wall, the painting goes. He knew the Mount Forel area fairly well: in his years on St David's he had visited there maybe four times. Apart from Galloway on the north of the island where the beaches were good, and Albany of course, except that was still a bit near home, the nicest place to go for a break was up to Forel, or maybe even Mount Lyell, if you had a four-wheel drive and didn't mind making your own roads for a bit of the way.

The island was spectacular, whether you were looking at great stretches of beaches with no one around, or the lush foothills near the cliffs which forty miles inland thrust into granite peaks. A great place for a holiday, but St David's was off the usual track and expensive to get to if you lived in Europe. Worse if you had to come from the States, so there were not many Americans around, except for the navy men. They'd put in at St David's, exercising a right as much as anything else, docking at Port Lombard to pick up fresh supplies – didn't need to but it helped the local economy – unload a few hundred sailors into the bars and whorehouses to spend a few dollars, and then off through to the Indian Ocean.

Sailors hardly ever went out of Port Lombard, partly because shore leave wasn't long enough, partly because the Port Lombard bar girls did amazing things for fifteen dollars. They certainly wouldn't be tempted to make the trip inland by a painting like this. See Mount Forel and lose your perspective. Gasp at the unreal colours. Thrill to the rocks which look like bits of dough sticking to the side.

Still nothing from the Prime Minister's office. Presumably Moorhouse was around, hadn't gone off sick. Maybe he'd lost his voice.

Leister ran a hand over his forehead and felt it was faintly wet. He reached into his pocket for a handkerchief and wiped the moisture away. It was getting too hot, even for the air conditioning.

He noticed the door to the Prime Minister's office open, and Moorhouse's PPS standing there expectantly. Leister glanced round, saw they were ready for him, and instinctively decided not to hurry in, so he said, pointing at the painting of Mount Forel: "Isn't that remarkable?" His smile was amiable, and his eyes friendly.

"The Prime Minister is ready for you," the PPS said.

"I've never seen anything quite like it before. Who could have done it?"

"Would you step this way, sir," the PPS said, looking suddenly doubtful that he had been understood.

"No, I mean it," said Leister, putting away his handkerchief as a sign that he had made his point and was about to co-operate. "I've been looking at it for a long time. It's quite . . ." he smiled charmingly, "something."

He moved towards the open door. The PPS said faintly: "It was painted by the Prime Minister."

Leister blew out his cheeks. "You don't say," he marvelled, then the PPS turned to announce: "The Ambassador of the United States."

Leister stepped into the room, a cordial smile on his face, but Moorhouse did not rise to greet him. He was sitting grimly on the other side of his desk. For a second Leister wondered if he had gone too far with the gag about the painting.

"Please be seated, Mr Ambassador," Moorhouse said, inclining his head towards a chair.

"Thank you, Prime Minister."

Moorhouse wasted no time. He picked up a typewritten sheet of paper and stared across at the Ambassador.

"This is a list of names of members of your Embassy," he said. "I will read it out to you and then I will give you a copy. All these people must be off St David's in forty-eight hours."

For an instant, Leister looked as if he had been hit, but quickly his face became professionally neutral.

"My government will be surprised and saddened to hear that," Leister said softly. "May I ask the reason?"

Moorhouse chose his words with care. "The presence of these people on St David's is inimical to the national interest," he replied, leaning back in his leather chair and pursing his lips. Above his head was a framed colour photograph of himself addressing a rally, his right hand raised emphatically as he made a point and his full lips curling round some word, frozen by the camera so that they looked tinged with scorn. The Ambassador made a conscious effort to keep his eyes from straying up to the photograph.

"It has come to my knowledge," Moorhouse continued, dictating a letter rather than speaking, "that although most of them are supposed to be working for the Aid programme, which while welcome is, as you know, fairly small, many of your diplomats are actually employed by the CIA. Quite simply they are spies, Mr Ambassador, provocateurs, as you very well know."

Leister allowed his eyebrows to rise for a moment, and then he said levelly: "The United States Government cannot accept that. With respect, Prime Minister, you are mistaken. You have been misinformed."

Moorhouse smirked. "So the United States has no agents on St David's?"

"We have some security advisers, naturally. My government considers St David's to be a friendly nation, and we do not feel the need to spy on our friends. Nor do we use provocateurs. Of course, throughout the world we keep a watching brief on the activities of potential enemies, and, like every other government, we sometimes use Embassy resources to do so," Leister said. "As you very well know, Prime Minister."

"Not on this island," Moorhouse replied calmly, lifting the piece of paper off the polished surface of his desk again and making it clear the discussion was at an end. "Not any more."

Leister sat back to listen.

"John Frederick Aitcheson," the Prime Minister read. "Charles Holmes Arthur Berenson . . ."

Both Aid, both CIA, thought the Ambassador. He's got those right.

"James Walter Birkett, Vincent St Clare Burton, George Andrew Kennon.. . ."

All Aid, also CIA. As Moorhouse read on, the Ambassador had the uncomfortable feeling he was enjoying himself. Occasionally, Moorhouse would glance up to see if he was getting any reaction, but Leister maintained an outward professional calm, masking a growing feeling of alarm. It was uncanny. Moorhouse must have gone through a dozen names already, and he was right every time. How could he have been sure? Most of the men were working under covers which they'd brought with them to the island and would take to their next posting, and they did look after Aid projects to maintain these. Yet he seemed to know which were genuine and which were not. The names were apparently in alphabetical order, and Moorhouse had reached the Js, skipping Gene Gilbert and Wally Fields who were two real Aid people. That left only George Wise as the third genuine Aider. Would Moorhouse know that too?

The list began including other Embassy sections: two Defence Attachés, one First Secretary (Political), three Second Secretaries, and every one of them CIA. Even before Moorhouse reached names beginning with W and left out George Wise, Leister knew there had been a massive breach of security in the Embassy itself. The prospect of intensive post-mortems and recriminations confronted him. The CIA would be hopping mad: the State Department would be furious.

The island was strategically important not only because of its position in the Atlantic, to which the West had privileged access with the envious Soviets only able to make occasional goodwill calls at Port

Lombard, but also because it was a useful listening post. The US Government had spent millions of dollars on their communications and decoding centre at the Embassy, which dealt mainly with traffic to and from Soviet vessels in the area and computed their positions and courses for transmission to Washington. And now, inexplicably, Moorhouse was kicking out the staff responsible for the monitoring. Leister was baffled by this. The United States posed no threat to St David's: on the contrary, Aid since Independence had amounted to around $300 million, and if Moorhouse had really wanted to squeeze them for more, there'd have been some sighing and head holding, but it would have been done. St David's was too important a friend to brush aside. Friend? Leister was no longer sure.

Leister became aware that the Prime Minister was watching him, waiting for a response. He looked up and smiled gently. "Mr Prime Minister," he said at last, "I don't know what to tell you. You have read me a list of, what, twenty-five names?"

"Twenty-four. Have I missed one?"

The Ambassador's smile faded and he shrugged. "Those are not only some of the best members of my Embassy staff, but they include some of the best friends of St David's. They are also all accredited diplomatic representatives of the United States of America, which I don't need to remind you is an ally of your country's. I am urging you, with all the persuasion at my command, to reconsider your decision. You have been gravely misinformed. The repercussions if you go ahead will be profound."

"A threat? From an ally?" Moorhouse was smirking again. Leister could not remember him ever behaving like this before.

"No, Prime Minister. A threat is not a weapon of diplomacy," he said. "It must be self-evident that relations between our two nations will suffer a serious setback. You can't expel twenty-four diplomats – unjustly expel them, I might add – and expect everything to stay the same. The Aid projects, for instance, will suffer. Now I'm not saying Aid will be withdrawn necessarily. . ." Leister let the "necessarily" hang in the air for a moment before he continued: "But the men who run them will no longer be around. You will have sent them away."

Moorhouse snorted. "The amount of Aid work they do would occupy ten minutes a day, if you'll pardon my saying so, Ambassador."

Moorhouse stood up dismissively, holding out the piece of paper to Leister.

"You will not reconsider?" the Ambassador asked, remaining seated.

"Forty-eight hours, Mr Ambassador," Moorhouse said flatly. "I don't care how you do it, but I want them off this island by then."

Leister pulled himself to his feet, feeling suddenly very tired. "That is your final word?"

"It is."

Leister reached out, took the thick white paper, almost like parchment, and glanced briefly at the names. It had been done: it was now official. He snapped open his black briefcase, dropped the paper in, then locked it.

"Good day to you, Prime Minister," Leister said, bowing slightly. Moorhouse nodded curtly.

The Ambassador walked slowly out of the room. The PPS, who had been sitting behind him throughout the meeting making notes on a pad, rose quickly and opened the double doors.

The Cadillac swung left out of the entrance to the Cabinet Offices as the soldiers on duty came to attention and saluted, and headed down Constitution Avenue towards the sea front, picking up speed.

The four-lane boulevard ran from the Coast Road, which gave access to the docks and whatever industry Port Lombard could sustain, and continued on for three miles past the official buildings of St David's: the museum and library in their separate neat white single-storied colonial structures with red-painted corrugated iron roofs, which drummed so loudly when the rain beat down that anyone sitting inside next to the signs demanding "Silence" could have shouted without the librarians across the room being aware; then the Justice buildings – first the low slate-roofed Magistrate's Court, looking more solid and impressive than the library, and, next to it, the High Court and the Supreme Court. The British have always been masters at investing their colonial institutions with grandeur and often spurious dignity. Both court buildings sat solid and forbidding in the middle of palm-fringed gardens, making the neat flower beds seem out of place, as if patches of pinks, blues and yellows in such surroundings were a contempt of the solemn proceedings taking place inside.

The High Court was a Gothic structure of grey stone with windows barred in such a way that they gave the impression they were designed to keep people in, rather than out.

Separated by a high wall was the Supreme Court, whose architect early in the century had borrowed something from ancient Greece and something from the more gloomy British castles. Grey Ionic columns framed the entrance of the brooding Gothic building, and continued in dark, stately pairs along both sides of the frontage. Jets of water spurted from the mouths of angry lions rampant, and splashed heavily into large rectangular ponds where fat goldfish threaded their way through waterlilies and slime.

Surmounting both the Supreme and High Court buildings were Victorian statues of blind Justice, holding a pair of golden scales in one hand and a sword in the other. The overall impression left little doubt that the sword was frequently wielded.

Further up Constitution Avenue, and directly opposite the Cabinet Office which the American Ambassador had just left, was the Parliament of St David's: not such a threatening building, perhaps because it was white rather than grey and black, and colonial rather than Gothic, although ancient Greece once more provided the inspiration for the white marble columns along the sweeping driveway up to the Members' car park, hidden behind a high hedge at the side.

Leister was driving away from all this, onto the Coast Road. His chauffeur eased the Cadillac over into the right-hand lane for the turning which would lead them to the diplomatic quarter and the Embassy, but the Ambassador leaned forward and pressed the intercom switch beside his seat.

"Don't take me to the Embassy right away," he said. "Make a left turn and let's have a look round town."

He saw the chauffeur nod and the voice over the speaker said: "Yes, sir."

The chauffeur glanced in his rearview mirror and then over his shoulder to make sure there was no one behind them, but Constitution Avenue was virtually deserted. The Cadillac changed lanes and glided smoothly down the Coast Road towards the docks.

Leister sank back into a reverie, staring out at the waves crashing onto the shingle beach. What the hell was Moorhouse up to? None of it made sense. Maybe he was looking for a scapegoat for his own decline, but that didn't make sense either. Choosing the United States wouldn't do him any good.

The chauffeur said: "Anywhere in particular, sir?"

Leister replied: "There was supposed to be some trouble around High Street this morning. If there is, I want to see it – from a distance."

"Yes, sir."

After a minute, the car turned left up Kennedy Walk, and halted at the traffic lights on the intersection with High Street. While they waited for the green, both men checked the situation, Leister sitting forward for a better view.

"See anything?" he asked the chauffeur.

"No, sir. A few people around, but doesn't look like there's trouble."

"Drive to the end and go back towards the Coast Road along Frith Street," Leister instructed. "Take your time, and keep an eye out for problems."

For a Thursday morning, there were surprisingly few people around. Perhaps they had heard the rumours and stayed away. Shops were open. At first glance, everything looked normal enough, just very quiet. Then Leister spotted the groups of police, steel helmets buckled on, walking down High Street. There were five or six of them at a time, spread out with maybe hundred yard gaps. From the blue shoulder-flashes, he could tell they were Security Battalion men, which was strange. He looked for the red flashes of the General Headquarters police, whose beat this was and who should have been on duty, but he could see none. There were few other cars in the street, but some police Land Rovers were parked at the side, and as they crossed intersections Leister noticed police buses waiting a short distance down.

When the Cadillac reached the Stanley Road intersection, it was suddenly obvious that there had been action, and this was where it had centred. Bricks and large stones littered the road – obviously used as ammunition – and panes of glass were shattered in shop windows. There wasn't much else to see, and the chauffeur turned into Frith Street and headed for the docks.

Leister settled back in his seat. He'd hear what had happened when he got back to the Embassy, but he always liked making an on-the-spot assessment himself if he could.

Moorhouse was really heading for trouble, he thought. Today's demonstration was, what? The tenth in about a fortnight? And there was no sign of an end. They seemed to be getting worse – more violent – all the time. The opposition parties, especially the Democratic Front, had finally gained a hold on the people. They had started the unrest, but now it showed signs of gaining a momentum all its own. It was funny how people swung. In the 1972 elections – four years ago, that was all – Moorhouse and his party had wiped the floor with the opposition. They won eighty-eight out of a hundred seats, even better than the first pre-independence results. If there'd been another election even a year ago, Leister would have put money on Moorhouse's Popular National Party doing it again.

Then suddenly everything went sour. It seemed to happen very quickly, although of course it had been brewing in the background since the storms the season before last wiped out most of the crops. That had been a blow to the economy, for it meant spending foreign exchange on a lot more imports. And last season was even worse: it hardly rained at all. No one could remember crops failing for two successive years, but that's what had happened to Moorhouse. People hadn't minded him being autocratic and arrogant when things were going well: they minded like hell when they lost money, or their jobs, or couldn't feed their children properly.

The Cadillac turned right out of Frith Street, back onto the Coast Road, and Leister looked around at the dock area.

The fishing fleet was in, and one small freighter was berthed at Port Lombard, but the cranes stood idle. He had never seen it so empty. Christ, he thought, how the repercussions spread. Apart from at least two other vessels, there should have been an Italian cruise liner in round about now, bringing in twelve hundred tourists with their lire and pounds and dollars, and filling the shops and the restaurants along the seafront.

The liner wasn't going to come though, and not because the crops had failed for two years. There was plenty to eat if you could pay for it. The reason was that St David's had finally hit the world headlines.

It didn't often do that. Independence Day in 1967 had passed virtually unnoticed, because there hadn't been any lead-up violence or unrest, and the whole bonanza fell squarely into the category (d) that newspapers award to stories: that is, something neither interesting nor important.

Moorhouse, that arrogant bastard, had now sinned, and sinned grievously in political terms, which meant he'd cut corners and been found out. Years ago, the British had offered him a choice of two projects as part of their aid scheme. They would fix up the water supply of Port Lombard, which occasionally did unkind things to people's stomachs, as well as the sewage system, which was pretty antique, or they would at last come across with the project for which Moorhouse had been angling for almost seven years: a new Prime Ministerial residence. This was to be a neo-Corinthian design he had commissioned shortly after assuming office, but which had been beyond the island's resources.

For Moorhouse, there was no real choice. At the moment, the residence was being finished, and as you sailed into the Port Lombard harbour – or for that matter, if you looked out of your car window at almost any point along the coast road within a couple of miles of the harbour – it gleamed white and stately on the slope overlooking the city. It was lavish and pretentious, and it suited Moorhouse perfectly.

No one had grudged it to him in the two years the foundations were being sunk and the walls were going up, except for the Democratic Front men and supporters of the other tiny opposition groups, but no one paid attention to them. Not at that stage. The island's main newspaper, the *St David's Herald,* was almost as in love with the project as Moorhouse himself, but then the *Herald* depended heavily on official advertising and usually followed the government line. The Prime Ministerial residence was simply not a contentious matter.

This changed overnight. Maybe people had harboured secret resentments all along about the extraordinary house, and just needed an issue to bring them tumbling out, but Leister thought it more likely that when the cholera scandal broke, everyone looked around for a scapegoat and found they didn't have to look far: there it was, impossible to miss, on the hill overlooking Port Lombard – the white mansion their leader was building for himself with money which might have been spent on sewage and water.

What happened was that a Greek cruise ship had called at Port Lombard the previous December and stopped for eighteen hours. Before it reached its next port, Cape Town, six passengers had gone down with cholera. Naturally at first everyone blamed the Greeks. But when extensive tests pronounced the ship clean, the spotlight switched to St David's, and what should be discovered in the local hospital, but a whole ward of cholera cases – thirty-six in fact, and two of them British.

Independence Day on St David's had rated maybe five inches in the more serious British newspapers, a paragraph in the others, and nothing at all in the States. But the cholera epidemic ran for a week. Almost the last visitors in were journalists from London, and by the time they left, tourism – one of the main foreign exchange earning industries – had died on its feet.

This new blow sent Moorhouse's popularity into a downward spiral and the people looked for a political alternative. There was one immediately to hand. After years of ignoring the Democratic Front, the voters of St David's were riveted by the speeches of its leaders and made its slogans their own.

The new Prime Ministerial residence, with artisans busy inside plastering and decorating, became known as the Moorhouse House. Demonstrators chanted: "Get Moorhouse out of the Moorhouse House." The Democratic Front made sure all their open-air meetings were within sight of the white mansion, but it was in such a dominating position that this was scarcely difficult.

Democratic Front President, Albert Francis, would stand on a platform and demand: "Why haven't we got a decent sewage system?" He'd point dramatically up the hill. "That's why! Why haven't we got clean water? That's why! Ask Moorhouse where the tourists have gone!"

And, Leister reflected, it was all true. No matter how Moorhouse dodged and ducked, and argued in speeches broadcast over the government-controlled radio that there had been nothing fundamentally wrong with the sewage and water systems when the decision was taken to build the residence, that, although old, the systems had been working properly, he made little impact. There on the hill, jinxing his words, was the Moorhouse House, gleaming whitely.

Leister's Cadillac turned into the diplomatic enclave and through the Embassy gates. The Ambassador did not acknowledge the salutes.

Moorhouse may be in trouble, he reflected as he walked up the steps, but my Christ, so are we. So are we. Moorhouse had made an almost clean sweep of CIA personnel, missing only one man. That wasn't much to be grateful for.

Chapter Two

Moorhouse was exultant when the Ambassador left. The cancerous growth was being removed, and it had been easy. Once he had trusted Leister, but once he had done many things. Seeing the man coming into the Prime Minister's office, walking in smiling, amiable as if nothing was happening around him, not suspecting that everything was known and that the axe was ready to fall – and then the startled look on his face when Moorhouse told him his spies and saboteurs were being kicked out!

It had been a wonderful moment. Moorhouse relaxed in his leather chair, leaning back to gaze at the cream-painted ceiling, and then closed his eyes with pleasure. He would remember this for a long time, perhaps all his life: the day Daniel Moorhouse kicked out the CIA and put his country on a new course. Tonight he would issue a statement: make a speech on the radio. Perhaps tomorrow there would be a press conference. He would decide later.

The history books, Moorhouse thought, will know me as the father of this nation. A small nation, of course, but strategic! The Super Powers all clamouring for a hold, and those that got one looked inevitably for more, worming their way into the fabric and behaving not like visitors and guests, but like traitors. Trying to push the country that way or this, manoeuvring in the background, using their cash to subvert. No longer. St David's was non-aligned, and it would stay non-aligned while he was leader. There would be no interference in the island's internal affairs.

He should have suspected before what their game was. There had to be a reason for the unrest. He should have seen behind their smiles and their friendly handshakes. A Prime Minister could trust no one, Moorhouse concluded thoughtfully. Not his advisers and political colleagues, and certainly not the United States Ambassador. Perhaps not even his wife and children.

Moorhouse realised he had been taught a lesson when he was almost at the brink of disaster. But he had been saved and now he would make the people benefit from his knowledge. It would be hard. First he would have to discipline them like a stern father whose family was becoming uncontrollable, and when they had quietened down, they would see he had acted so because he loved them and because he had their welfare at heart. Once they knew that, they would love him in return and it would be as it was in the beginning.

Moorhouse expelled the breath from his lungs in a deep, long sigh and glanced at his watch. It was midday. He pressed the buzzer on his desk and waited until the PPS knocked deferentially at the door.

"I'm ready to see the Commissioner now," Moorhouse said. "Ask him to come over as soon as he can."

"Yes, Prime Minister."

The PPS paused, his hand on the door. Moorhouse looked at him impatiently. "It's just that I heard," the PPS said, "that there was a lot of trouble, and some people were killed."

There was a long silence while Moorhouse stared at him. When at last he spoke, his voice was very quiet and level, but the PPS felt at once the force of the anger behind it.

"Send the Commissioner of Police in to me," he said. "The Prime

Minister requires a first-hand report, not office tittle-tattle."

The PPS flushed deeply and went out, closing the door quietly behind him. In the outer office, he leaned against the wall and took a deep breath, rolling his eyes heavenward. Christ, he hadn't deserved that. He only wanted to help. It was impossible to tell what Moorhouse's mood would be these days, couldn't fathom him at all, not his changeable humours, nor his swings in policy. He was under strain, of course, but still . . .

The PPS dialled a number on the ivory internal phone and it was answered almost immediately. "Mr Montrose," he said, "this is the Prime Minister's PPS. Could you step over right away, please?"

He heard the grunt at the other end, and the line went dead. The PPS stared blankly at the receiver in his hand. He thought: perhaps it's me. There's something wrong with my tone. Maybe I rub people up the wrong way.

Then he smiled ruefully. He had dealt with Montrose for years, and today the man was only marginally more crass than usual. The Prime Minister, whom he personally admired, even on bad days, had a facility for surrounding himself with third-raters. The PPS had never been able to understand why he did it. Montrose was certainly efficient, if one wanted one's business performed by an efficient pig. The PPS had always felt the Commissioner would have been more at home in some banana republic where he could have headed a really oppressive torture squad. He had a bland, cruel, piggy look about him: there was no other way to describe it. His eyes were small and watchful in a smooth podgy face, and he strutted on short, muscular legs. Stories were told about the suspect confessions that were produced from the cells of the Central Police Station near the docks. A couple of prisoners had blurted out in court that they'd been beaten up and ill-treated until they signed statements, but they were never able to show any marks of this, and so they were sentenced to imprisonment in the island's main gaol, where, from all accounts, Montrose's influence was also considerable. The PPS presumed that Moorhouse had heard all the stories about his Commissioner of Police, although the matter had never been mentioned in his presence, and he wasn't going to bring it up himself.

Certainly, it would be hard for Moorhouse not to know: it was common gossip. The PPS grinned. But then Moorhouse wasn't interested in tittle-tattle; only in first-hand reports, so unless the Commissioner had confessed, perhaps he didn't know after all. He shrugged dismissively and turned to check through the correspondence which had come in on the morning delivery, sorting it into piles which he or other Ministers could deal with. The much larger pile was for the attention of the Prime Minister himself. Moorhouse was a one-man band: God knows why he even bothered to appoint a cabinet, except for appearance's sake. He did all the important work himself, while the Ministers who were supposed to be responsible sat in his office and said: Yes, sir, no, sir, like schoolboys before the headmaster. They all put up with it, because they knew they had been elected on Moorhouse's personal ticket. The PNP was his preserve, almost a private limited Moorhouse company, and the electorate had followed the man, not the policies. If Moorhouse sacked a Minister, and then dropped him from the PNP list of candidates in an election, the man's political career would be effectively at an end.

The door swung open and Montrose barrelled in, nodded brusquely at the PPS and headed straight for the Prime Minister's door.

The PPS felt unaccustomed anger. Very loudly and distinctly, as if talking to the elderly deaf, he said: "Take a seat please, Commissioner. I'll see if the Prime Minister is free."

Montrose paused in his stride, almost as if he couldn't believe what he'd heard, and he glanced at the PPS with undisguised scorn. For several seconds the two men stared at one another. Finally Montrose capitulated. He shrugged and found a chair.

The PPS said: "Thank you." He went across to knock at the connecting door and let himself in, closing it firmly behind him.

In the anteroom, Montrose said: "Little prick."

Standing before Moorhouse, the PPS found his heart was thumping, and he couldn't make up his mind whether it was from anger or fear.

"The Commissioner of Police is here, Prime Minister," he said.

"Show him in," Moorhouse replied, still looking unfriendly.

The PPS paused: "Would you like me to sit in on the meeting and take a note?" he asked.

"No."

That was it. No explanation, not even a "thank you".

"Very well, sir," the PPS said with dignity. "Shall I organise tea?"

Moorhouse shook his head.

The PPS opened the door and motioned to Montrose. "The Prime Minister will see you now," he said.

The Commissioner pushed past him, his eyes already seeking out Moorhouse, but he deliberately passed so close to the PPS that his body brushed hard against him, forcing him out of the way.

The PPS returned to his desk and sat down. He found that his fists had been so tightly clenched that the nails had cut into the palms of his hands. I am a career civil servant, he told himself as calmly as he could. I will outlast them all, the whole bunch. When they are has-beens, I will still be here.

The thought comforted him.

Inside, Montrose settled himself on a gilt chair, upholstered with yellow velvet, his fat policeman's bulk looking ridiculous and precarious on the delicate seat. He composed his face and stared directly into the Prime Minister's eyes.

Moorhouse sat back silently, watching him. Finally he said bluntly: "So?"

Montrose wasted no words. "Three dead," he replied. "Twelve in hospital, one of them critical and not expected to live out the day. Twenty arrests."

The Prime Minister digested this. "God," he said slowly. "No one's ever been killed in a demonstration on St David's before."

"There's never been a situation like this before," the Commissioner reminded him.

Moorhouse exhaled heavily. "I suppose you're right," he said. "Still, that's not much comfort. How did it happen?"

"We knew there'd be trouble," Montrose spoke carefully. "I told you that three days ago, Prime Minister, if you remember. The demonstration had been fixed to turn violent. They'd got the hard men in, the anti-social elements. We're isolating them: we know who they are and where they hang out. I ordered the security battalion onto riot standby round the High Street area and, sure enough, stones and rocks started being thrown into shop windows, and the looters were out, grabbing what they could. The ordinary people and the shop assistants were trying to get away, but they were trapped. About four hundred people shouting and chucking rocks. Then we saw one of the mob had a gun, and looked about to use it. I gave the order to fire, and try to take out the ringleaders. So that's what we did."

Moorhouse stared at him. "What about the man with the gun? Did you get him?"

"Unfortunately no," Montrose said dismissively. "That particular element got away. But I think we know where we can find him."

Moorhouse leaned his elbows on his highly polished desk and put his head in his hands. There was a long silence. Montrose watched him with his bland, piggy eyes. When he judged the moment was right, he said: "I'm afraid there's more to come."

Moorhouse looked up. "More what?" he asked.

"Violence," said Montrose regretfully. "I've just had an intelligence report – same source as before – that they're going to be looking for another confrontation in the port area the day after tomorrow. After the shootings this morning, it'll probably be a fierce one. If it is, we'll have to consider opening fire again."

There was another pause, while Moorhouse stared at him. The Commissioner met his eyes and allowed the silence to drag out.

At last the Prime Minister said: "I saw the American Ambassador this morning and gave him the news."

Montrose looked sympathetic as if he had learned of another man's tragedy. He nodded: "An unpleasant business, but I'm sure you were correct, Prime Minister. It was in the national interest. The latest intelligence bears that out. Until these people are off St David's, the trouble will go on."

Moorhouse sighed. "We have to stop it, Commissioner. There's no getting away from the fact – this is the moment for hard decisions and hard action."

Montrose nodded. "You can count on me, sir."

The Prime Minister glanced gratefully at him. "Thank you," he said. He clapped his hands together once, as if signalling the start of a new, businesslike phase, but when he spoke, his voice was soft and serious.

"Right. Now I want from you by this afternoon a list of the anti-social elements, with an explanation of what they've done and what they're planning. I don't care who's on the list, as long as there are cogent reasons. But I do want it to be comprehensive. When I give the order to pick them up, I want to be sure that the trouble will stop."

"I'll do my best, sir," said Montrose.

"I'll get the legal department to prepare the documents declaring a State of Emergency, and emergency powers we'll need to call a halt to this nonsense."

"When do you intend making the announcement?" Montrose asked. "It ought to be soon if we're going to have the chance of defusing the next demonstration."

"There's no reason why it can't be tonight," the Prime Minister said. "There are precedents we can draw on. I just need to get the President's signature. There won't be any problem about that."

"May I suggest then, sir, that we meet at, say, four o'clock, to agree on the list of detainees? Then there's the job of rounding them up. Perhaps if you delayed making the announcement until tomorrow morning, we could pick these blighters up before dawn. The whole thing will be over before they know what's hit them."

Moorhouse nodded approvingly. "Excellent," he said. "Let's get on with it, shall we?"

The Commissioner rose from the gilt chair, and half bowed to the Prime Minister. Although his face was bland, his eyes were bright, and if Moorhouse had not been so preoccupied, he might have thought that his Commissioner of Police was enjoying himself.

Chapter Three

Moorhouse's PPS took his lunch as usual on the veranda of Chez Kay, a seafood restaurant overlooking the harbour. The day was very humid and close. From the moment he walked quickly out of the air conditioned cabinet offices, Stephen Ayer felt the wet heat surround him, and, as he drove his elderly Morris Oxford down Constitution Avenue, the perspiration soaked through wherever his shirt touched the fabric of the car seat.

By the time he parked at Kay's, his whole shirt, except for a rectangle around the buttons at the front, was damp, and a trickle of water rolled from his hairline down his cheek. Ayer could feel his legs starting to sweat too. Jesus, it was a bloody awful time of year, he thought as he peeled off his jacket and slung it over his shoulder, an index finger hooking around the collar. He realised he had made it much worse for himself by not driving in shirtsleeves, but he so badly needed to get out of the office that he had gone straight to his car and driven away without even thinking – and then it didn't seem worth parking on Constitution Avenue to take off his jacket when it was only a five-minute drive. He knew there would be a cooling sea breeze on Kay's veranda, underneath the canopy of coconut matting, and there were always a couple of powerful electric fans to help it along.

Ayer climbed the restaurant's cement steps and, because he was tall, ducked his head as he went through the entrance into the cool gloom. He stood for a second, enjoying the refrigerated air of the main dining-room, and he unselfconsciously lifted his arms slightly so that it could circulate round his sweating body.

The dining-room was about half full. Ayer recognised most of the people there as regulars. Kay had built up a faithful clientele, based on really fresh fish, cold alcohol and swift service. The restaurant did not have the pretensions or the prices of Franco's, three hundred yards along the seafront. There was little organised attempt at décor. Here, the tables were simple and sturdy, covered with faded red gingham tablecloths, or white ones when they ran out, and the walls were whitewashed and peeling. Anyone could see that things needed doing at Kay's, but she didn't seem to care, and nor did her customers.

Ayer could not see her, but her husband, who was opening a bottle of wine on the other side of the room, noticed him and smiled a welcome. Ayer waved back, then walked through to the veranda where Joe Rana and Tilak Kataria were drinking iced beer at the usual table.

Ayer joined them, slumping into a chair, his coat still dangling from his finger as he relaxed. He only half-heard their greetings and joking remarks as he savoured the moment, feeling the cool breeze from the sea on his face. It was good to be out of the office.

He twisted round to drape his jacket over the chair, and saw the waiter already coming with his usual lunchtime gin and tonic. That was another thing about Kay's: they knew what you wanted.

Ayer looked across at Rana and Kataria, and shook his head slowly, making a low grumbling noise in the back of his throat.

"Is it that bad?" Joe Rana asked sympathetically.

"It is," said Ayer with feeling.

Tilak Kataria grinned at him: "The boss man doesn't like being unpopular." It was a statement, rather than a question.

"Who does?" Ayer replied. "But especially not the boss man. He chewed my ear off this morning – I mean, really chewed it off. Nothing half-hearted."

The men stopped talking while the waiter poured Ayer's drink and dropped ice cubes and a slice of lemon into the long glass.

"Thanks," said Ayer gratefully. "Get some plates of prawns would you? And more beer for my friends."

The waiter nodded and turned away. Ayer took a gulp and set his glass back on the table with a sigh. "A bad day," he said.

"You heard what happened at the demonstration this morning?" Tilak Kataria said.

Ayer made a wry face. "Not officially," he replied. "Only office tittle tattle."

Kataria looked surprised. "Well, officially, three people were shot dead by Montrose's goon squad and a dozen are in hospital with bullet wounds," he said. "But how come you don't know this?"

Ayer shrugged. "I wasn't with the boss man when Montrose made his report. Today I'm being frozen out. I wish to God I knew why."

His friends glanced at one another. Joe Rana said: "Oh, he'll get over it. He's just not used to being hated."

"Who is?" Ayer asked. "It's hard for me too."

Ayer stared past the others towards the port area. There was hardly anything to see there these days, except for the small fishing fleet. But it was good to listen to the rhythmic crashing of the waves onto the beaches and against the concrete sea walls. The three men sat in a companionable silence.

They met for lunch at Kay's virtually every working day, and had done so for years. Ayer, Rana and Kataria had all been born on the is- land – Ayer of a British father and a St David's mother, and the others of purely local stock. They had joined the civil service at about the same time, and had seen each other sporadically over the years – at first, sitting in the civil service examination rooms, and later at official functions. A friendship had built up gradually, and now all of them were in their late thiries, and they shared the same seniority.

Because of his position as Moorhouse's PPS, Ayer saw most of Joe Rana, who was the Cabinet Secretary. Both attended weekly cabinet meetings, and their offices were in the same corridor.

Tilak Kataria headed the St David's political desk, and was responsible for reports on international developments affecting the island on which Moorhouse was supposed to base his decisions. No one knew on what Moorhouse was actually basing his decisions lately. It might as well have been the state of a chicken's entrails.

Stephen Ayer sipped his gin. His shirt was drying out and his mood had marginally improved.

"What do you think of the American decision?" Ayer asked, breaking the silence.

Rana and Kataria looked at him so blankly that Ayer knew no one else had been told.

"I give up," Kataria said finally. "What American decision?"

"The boss man is expelling twenty-four US diplomats."

Rana looked surprised, but Kataria's mouth dropped open in disbelief. "You're joking," he said faintly.

"I wish I was," Ayer replied. "He called Leister in this morning and read him out the names. Most of them are Aid chaps, or supposed to be anyway. He's given them forty-eight hours to get out."

Kataria was suddenly angry. His eyes blazed, but he tried to keep himself from shouting. "Jesus Christ, why?" he said urgently.

Ayer shrugged. "National interest," he answered, "whatever that means these days. The boss man thinks they're all CIA, and he says he doesn't want spies on the island. He suspects them of causing all this trouble."

"Oh that's bullshit," Kataria said. "He can't really believe that. And so what if they *are* CIA? We've known a lot of them weren't Aid. Christ, it's obvious they're here to watch the Russians. Moorhouse knows that. A five-year-old kid knows that."

"Of course he knows," Ayer said. "But he's decided to get rid of them anyway."

Rana asked casually: "Any idea why?"

"None."

"What did Leister say?" Rana poured himself another beer, then refilled Kataria's glass until the froth spilled over the edge and spread damply over the cloth. Kataria was still staring at Ayer as if his friend had developed leprosy.

"Not very much," Ayer replied. "He was as surprised as anyone. I didn't even know why Moorhouse had called him in. I was just sitting at the back, taking notes, and it all came tumbling out. Leister tried to get him to reconsider, but the boss man wasn't having any of it. He just said their presence was inimical to the national interest, and he wasn't having spies around. Or saboteurs. That was it. No other explanation. It was very brief and to the point."

Kataria leaned forward. "But to what point?" he asked. "Where the hell is he leading us?"

Ayer shook his head slowly and made a helpless gesture with his hands. The waiter arrived with plates of prawns, and they sat quietly as he served them.

In Port Lombard, a tug was pulling the nose of a small freighter away from the wharf, and the three men watched it move gradually out towards the harbour entrance, seagulls wheeling and mewling around its derricks.

24

The men began eating, saying nothing, each wrapped in his own thoughts about Moorhouse's actions and the implications. Their mood was sombre.

Kataria, with the dark curly hair of a local, and an ancestry which, through the centuries, had encompassed Portuguese, Dutch, French and British colonists, was the most morose of all, as he considered first his own position, and second, what counter-attack – if any – might be mounted by the Americans. Even though the United States needed St David's badly, it was too much to hope that they would escape all retaliation.

Joe Rana, apparently least affected of all, ate his sea food slowly and delicately with his fingers, twisting the heads off the grilled prawns and unpeeling the shells so that the sweet white meat was exposed, then lifting off strips to eat. Rana's ancestors must have missed some of the generations of interbreeding, for he was almost ebony in colour, as against Kataria's milk-coffee-coloured skin. But he too had the shining curly hair of a local.

Both men were stocky and short, like most of the islanders – about the average five and a half feet. Beside them, Ayer, who topped six feet, could have passed for a Brit – at least among other locals. The British on St David's would never have been fooled, despite his Scottish father and his public school accent.

Although Ayer's skin was light and his build rangy, there was something in his facial structure which suggested his mother, and of course, the texture of his hair, its thickness and slight glossiness, told its own story. When he was at boarding school in England, Ayer had often been mistaken for a Briton. At home, never. The St David's Brits knew. at a glance who he was.

But that had not stopped Ayer from marrying a British girl, who cared nothing for local prejudices, and from fathering three children. One of them – a girl – had her mother's auburn hair and grey-blue eyes, a triumph over Mendel's theory of genetics. Even on the island, this girl could pass as a Brit, although there was never any doubt about her brothers.

By the time the men had finished their prawns, and Ayer had ordered his second and last gin, the tugboat had released the freighter half a mile out and was butting back through the swell. The freighter's engines were full ahead and, underneath its bows, white water rose as it headed out to sea.

Apart from the local fishing fleet, Port Lombard was deserted.

Chapter Four

Montrose sat fatly behind his large oak desk. Despite the air conditioning, which hummed softly in the corner of the room beneath the crest of the St David's police force, there were beads of sweat on his forehead and damp patches around his armpits.

The Commissioner of Police smiled grimly at the neatly typed lists in front of him, and he shuffled through the papers until he found the one he wanted. He read and re-read it carefully, and it seemed in order. He leaned across to an office intercom box and pressed the button marked "2".

The Deputy Commissioner of Police answered almost immediately. "Yes, Claud."

"Alec, come through," Montrose said.

"Right away."

Montrose settled back to wait while Alec Clifton walked the short distance between offices. There was a knock at his door and the reception sergeant looked in.

"Mr Clifton's here to see you, sir," he said.

"Send him in."

He stood aside and the Deputy hurried through, his thin face showing the strain of the last few weeks. The door closed behind them, and Clifton drew up a chair.

"How do you feel?" asked Montrose, his voice showing concern, but his bland face and small eyes none.

"I'm all right," said Clifton defensively.

Montrose made no comment but tossed the file across the desk. "Read it," he instructed.

As he watched his Deputy scanning the papers in the file, his face lined and worried, Montrose felt growing contempt. At one point, Clifton's eyebrows raised, and he said: "Huh?" in surprise, but then shrugged and read on.

Montrose watched. A small trickle of sweat ran down the Commissioner's cheek and he pulled out a handkerchief to mop it away. Shit, the man was a slow reader. Bloody locals.

With difficulty, Montrose suppressed annoyance, and set his face into an expression which he hoped showed comradeship and understanding. Another trickle of sweat started at his hairline and unhurriedly coursed its way down his forehead until it stuck in his eyebrow. If he noticed this time, he gave no sign. His face was

26

unmoving, his small eyes alight with feigned interest and enthusiasm, which would turn into hostility the moment he relaxed.

At length, Clifton laid down the file and looked up.

Montrose was about to ask: "What do you think?", but he changed his mind and instead said firmly: "All of this is necessary. Every name is there for a purpose. *You* may not like it. *I* certainly don't. But we have no choice."

Clifton nodded slowly, glad of leadership.

"Will he buy it?" Clifton asked anxiously. "It seems a little . . . comprehensive."

"He'll buy anything we're prepared to sell," the Commissioner said positively. "He's in the right mood."

"Even so." Clifton looked away, frowning. "We don't want him asking questions."

"He can ask whatever he bloody well likes," Montrose said. "I know the answers. But if I understand my man, there's only one question he'll ask, and that is: when can we do it?"

Clifton sighed in an involuntary expression of resignation. "Tomorrow," he said.

Montrose's eyes were alight, this time genuinely. "Tomorrow," he echoed confidently. "That's when we move. I've sent the order out cancelling all leave, and I've called a briefing at ten p.m." He smeared his forehead with a big, muscular hand. "I've thought of a code-name, by the way," Montrose said.

Clifton waited expectantly.

"Operation Tiger." Montrose paused for applause, but none came. Clifton looked bewildered. The Commissioner fought to keep his face good-humoured. Before Clifton could say: "I don't understand", Montrose explained: "If you catch a tiger by the tail, he turns round and savages you. You're dead. We're going to catch a tiger, and when it turns round, it's not going to be us who's holding the tail."

"Oh, I see," said Clifton faintly.

Montrose could no longer keep the hostility from his eyes.

"For Christ's sake, Alec," he said sharply, "brace up. It's not the end of the world. It's the beginning of the world. Do you want me to remind you what the alternative is?"

Clifton shook his head.

"Then fuck off out of here and practise being cheerful. You're supposed to be a leader of men, not the chief bloody mourner."

The Deputy Commissioner of Police left without a word. Montrose sat fuming behind his desk for a few moments, then he glanced at his watch. Time to go.

He pressed button 3 on his intercom and the reception sergeant answered. "Yes, sir."

"My car at the front, right away."

"Sir."

Montrose gathered up the file which Clifton had been reading and flicked quickly through to make sure everything was still in order.

The intercom buzzer sounded. "Your car's ready, sir."

Montrose grunted and walked to the door.

The drive to the Cabinet Offices took less than ten minutes, but by the time the Commissioner stepped out he was sweating heavily and his temper was even more frayed. He walked into the foyer and stood taking deep breaths of the cooled air.

He glanced at his watch again: five minutes to four. He would wait down here: not up in that prick's office. He needed to prepare himself. This was the key meeting. If this one went smoothly, the trap was sprung.

Montrose settled himself quietly on a sofa in the foyer, watching the leisurely activity. His body began to cool and he wiped the perspiration from his face with his damp handkerchief. Just before four o'clock, he moved across to the lift and pressed the button for the third floor. The door closed silently, and a fan blew warm air against his face. Montrose held his black briefcase containing the file tightly in both hands.

When the doors opened, he stepped confidently out into the green carpeted corridor and walked down to the Prime Minister's suite. This time he knocked on Ayer's door, once, before entering.

The PPS looked up and Montrose could see the hostility flicker across his face.

"Good afternoon, Commissioner," the PPS said. "I'll tell the Prime Minister you're here."

Montrose nodded curtly and went across to stare out of the window at the concrete courtyard below, fringed with the coconut palms which grew in profusion throughout the island.

Ayer reappeared at the door.

"Please come through, Commissioner."

Montrose turned and walked into the Prime Minister's office. Moorhouse was sitting behind his desk almost as if he had not moved since the morning, his Savile Row suit and silk shirt still immaculate, and a silk handkerchief to match his tie tucked into the front pocket. Montrose was uncomfortably aware of his own sweaty turnout, and he hoped the starch in his uniform gave at least an illusion of smartness.

At Moorhouse's invitation, he sat in the flimsy gilt chair and opened his briefcase. He was about to begin when an instinct made him glance round and he saw Ayer seated a short distance behind him, a notebook on his lap and his fountain pen ready.

Montrose's mouth opened once like a fish, and closed. Moorhouse noticed his surprise and explained: "I've asked my PPS to sit in on this meeting and take notes. I may need them."

The Commissioner leaned forward earnestly, his face flushing pink, and said with a subservient smile: "Prime Minister, I really do think that this meeting, above all, should be conducted totally in private."

Moorhouse considered the request for a moment, then he nodded.

To Ayer he said: "All right, you can go. I'll call if I need you."

The PPS half bowed and left the room. Montrose waited until the door closed behind him before he said: "Thank you. I'm sorry to ask you that, Prime Minister, but you'll see why in a minute."

Moorhouse inclined his head. His expression gave away nothing.

Montrose held the typewritten sheets of paper in his thick fingers and spoke softly and urgently.

"Everything that's on these, Prime Minister, comes basically from the same source. Naturally we've checked and double-checked each fact, and every allegation, as far as we can. It all stands up. Now I'm not saying we have enough to charge these people and take them to court. Anyway, that's probably inadvisable because of the sensitive nature of these things. And we all know how often sharp lawyers can get criminals off on some technicality or other. God knows, it's happened here often enough. We don't want it happening now. Our source, as you know, is highly placed in the United States Embassy, and his information so far has been of the highest calibre. I think you would agree with that, Prime Minister."

The Commissioner looked inquiringly at Moorhouse, who, after a pause, nodded agreement. "Go on, Commissioner," he said.

Montrose continued: "As we suspected, the conspiracy is both deep and widespread. In an attempt to destabilise our elected government, the Americans have recruited not only rabble and anti-social elements as you'd expect, but some top men in the administration."

The Prime Minister's eyebrows raised slightly in surprise. "In this administration?" he asked. "Who? And why?"

"Why?" said Montrose. "To provide information on yourself, Prime Minister, on how you're reacting, what the possible weak points are, what plans you have to combat the dissension. Now I'm sure you've suspected for some time that there may be one or two disloyal elements in your government . . ." Again a pause, and the Commissioner was gratified to see Moorhouse nod and prove right his intuition, before he continued: "I have thought so myself, but I gave strict instructions that no allegations should be made – no smears – until we had proof. We had to be one hundred per cent sure before I was prepared to come before you with the names of the guilty men. Today, Prime Minister, I have come to you. I am sure."

"Who?" asked Moorhouse simply.

Montrose handed over the sheets of papers, his face set in a mask of pain and sympathy, as if he was being seared by the awfulness of the treachery. His small eyes watched.

The Prime Minister began reading, but the Commissioner interrupted immediately. "The first list, sir, is of those I recommend being detained right away if we are to avert a national crisis. The second list – the longer one – is really a supplement. If the first dose of medicine doesn't work, then we should go on to the second, and sweep up those elements too. At the back, you'll find extracts from the police files on each of these subjects, outlining the evidence against them. Naturally, there's a lot more back at Headquarters."

Moorhouse said: "I see, yes." He began reading the names, scanning them quickly to pick out the really bad news, stopping, clicking his tongue in disbelief, reading on, then his eyes flicking back to the beginning and going slowly down the page, from time to time turning to the annexes for details of the allegations.

Half way down the list, the Prime Minister paused and said ponderously: "Are you sure, Mr Commissioner?"

Montrose knew which name he had stopped at. "Yes, sir," he replied positively. "I would stake my career on it."

The Prime Minister looked across at him speculatively. "You *are* staking your career on it," he said quietly. "I hope you realise that."

Montrose felt himself beginning to flush. "I'm not worried, Prime Minister," he said defensively.

Moorhouse shrugged and gazed at the wall above Montrose's head.

"We have worked together for several years," he said. "I have found him sometimes irritating, but mostly invaluable. I never doubted his loyalty."

The Commissioner stared sadly across the desk at him.

"That's always the way," he commiserated gently. "Those are the ones that really hurt – the Judases. But we need to take action now. Three people were killed today. Unless we move, more will die the day after tomorrow. These measures may seem draconian, but they will save lives, not waste them."

Montrose sat back and waited while the Prime Minister studied the list and the annexes again.

As the silence grew, Montrose knew he had won.

Chapter Five

A north-westerly wind gusted into Port Lombard with the dusk. Scudding clouds blotted out the stars. Moonrise was not until two a.m., but no one on the island would see it. Even at night, the buffeting air was hot and wet and not seeming to cool. It would soon rain. The coconut palms, silhouetted against the lights of the port, swayed in the wind, their slender trunks aslant and twisted by the roughness of years of winds harsher than this, and on the air was the musky, decaying salt scent of the sea.

The Brides of Dracula was playing at the Port Lombard Odeon. *The Godfather* was in its fourth and last week at the Star Cinema. Both films, savagely censored, were watched by half full houses. They ended at almost the same time, and Stanley Road and the High Street were crowded with people, mostly locals. The demonstrations and killings of the morning had not discouraged them, as if they knew these were set-pieces which did not affect the ordinary citizen. The broken glass and bricks had been cleared away around the Stanley Road intersection, and the shop fronts were empty and open to the wind. Armed police stood guard to prevent looting. At intervals along High Street, policemen were posted in pairs, armed with batons but paying no attention to the late-night strollers, who stared without fear or hostility. By midnight, the streets were deserted, except for patrolling policemen.

The wind had finally cooled. The port itself was quiet. The $15 prostitutes had mostly gone to bed alone, their art unpractised. A few of the more persistent loitered in doorways round the dock area, talking quietly and smoking, the red glows of their cigarettes identifying their territory. But no one came.

At midnight, the first convoys of cars set out quietly from the police headquarters, headlights flashing briefly across the walls of buildings as they turned into Haddon Walk and headed for the Coast Road. They went without haste, as if on routine patrols. First three cars together, then, after a gap of several minutes, a further three, and four, then another two – eighteen separate groups left Claud Montrose's briefing. He himself stayed behind: a Commissioner of Police does not soil his hands. Not on things like this, anyway.

Montrose brought out a bottle of whisky and drank it with mugs of black coffee, while Clifton sat morosely across his desk, declining the coffee and swallowing the whisky as if it was evil-tasting medicine which would, he knew not how, do him good.

The telephone rang once. The caller said: "Steve here."

Montrose replied carefully: "How are things?"

"Fine. Just waiting."

"Okay," said Montrose. "I'll call you if I need you, but I think we're all right." Then he hung up the phone on General Stephen Luther, head of the island's armed forces, and poured himself another whisky.

Montrose shoved the bottle across his desk. "Come on, laughing-boy," he said jocularly. "Have a last drink before they come and get you."

Clifton glanced at him resentfully, but accepted the whisky.

The police cars moved along the Coast Road and split up, some turning right into Kennedy Avenue, and then along High Street, before heading off into the lower-middle-class suburbs beyond the first groups of corrugated iron shanties: others going further up the Coast Road towards the diplomatic quarter, past the guarded Embassy residences to the expensive areas for upper-bracket islanders and Brits. The night was dark and the smell of the sea gusted on the wind.

The cars cruised past their targets without pausing, and halted a distance away. Policemen, some uniformed, some in plain clothes, got out and strolled casually back, checking which lights were on, which garages had vehicles in them, who was around. But Port Lombard had shut up for the night.

All were near their targets by 12.30, smoking in their cars, talking quietly, maintaining a listening watch on the radio, while the north-wester whipped around them. At two a.m., the time they were scheduled to move in, the moon rose invisibly behind the scudding banks of cloud. Montrose himself called them up on the radio to begin the operation, his pudgy face glistening with a mixture of heat, whisky and anticipation.

"All stations," Montrose said, his voice professionally neutral, "Tiger, over."

And they came back to him like clockwork. "One, Tiger, out."

"Two, Tiger, out."

"Three, Tiger, out."

On through every vehicle ranged round their target houses, until all had answered.

Montrose could visualise the police cars starting up and moving quietly through darkened streets the few hundred yards to the suburban gates and the silent houses, then the sounds of doors slamming, and the men walking quickly to cover front and back entrances, the doorbells ringing or chiming, fists banging on wood or glass, rousing the sleeping occupants. Maybe even the fucking occupants, Montrose thought with grim humour. That would be even better.

The house at Number 34 Nelson Avenue had a light burning in the hall – the sort of light which alerts burglars to the fact that everyone has either gone out, or is asleep. No one lives in hallways. Three policemen went to the front door, and two to the back in case the occupants tried to make a run for it. The Inspector in charge waited until he was sure his men were in position. There was no sound from the house. He nodded to those with him and his finger pressed the bell, holding it down for several seconds while it shrilled inside. He released it and began knocking hard on the wood.

For several seconds, nothing happened. The hammering on the door sounded obscenely loud. Then a light clicked on inside one of the rooms, and the Inspector could see through a frosted glass panel that a figure was coming towards them, pulling on a dressing-gown. He stopped knocking.

A man's voice called: "Who's there?" The voice held a hint of apprehension.

"Police! Open up!"

A chain rattled and a key turned. The door was pulled slightly ajar and the man was silhouetted against the hall light, peering out into the darkness at the strangers.

32

"What do you want?" the man asked, doubtfully.

The shadowy figure in front pushed an identification wallet at him. The man took it, but his brain was working too fast now, too confused, and he could make no sense of the information on it.

The policeman said: "I am Inspector Manley and these are my men. Are you Stephen Vincent Ayer?"

"Yes I am. What do you want? Perhaps you'd better come inside."

Moorhouse's PPS stood aside and let the three policemen into his hallway. Beyond the open bedroom door, he could see his wife tying a floral dressing-gown around her and putting on her slippers. Ayer turned on the living-room lights and motioned with his hand to the others. "Would you like some tea or coffee, gentlemen?" he asked.

The Inspector smiled at him, not unkindly. "No thank you, sir, that won't be necessary."

"Sit down, Inspector," Ayer said, but the man remained standing. Ayer sat down himself, feeling somehow it was expected of him. He looked inquiringly at the three men: the Inspector directly in front of him, a sergeant standing barring the door, and a constable a little to the right with a notebook open and a pen ready. Ayer felt a chill of fear, but when he spoke, his voice was firm.

"What can I do for you?" he asked.

The Inspector reached into his pocket and pulled out a folded piece of paper. "Stephen Vincent Ayer," he said, "I have here an Order, signed by the President, detaining you in terms of the St David's State of Emergency laws."

Ayer looked at him with amazement. "What do you mean?" he asked. "What emergency? What laws?"

"A State of Emergency has just been declared," the Inspector said. "You are under arrest."

"On what charge?"

The Inspector consulted the piece of paper. "It is considered expedient for public safety and public security," he said. "Here, this is your copy. And this –" he handed across a second sheet "– you have to sign as having been duly served on you."

Ayer read the detention order, taking his time, forcing his mind to concentrate and understand the words before him, while the policemen watched. His wife came into the room, looking around bewildered, but not yet frightened.

"Stephen, what's wrong?" she asked.

He held out a hand to her and she took it and sat beside him. He handed the paper across.

"It seems I am to be arrested," he said. "Moorhouse has declared a State of Emergency and he thinks I'm a danger to public safety."

His wife's face registered shock. "That's preposterous," she said, scanning the detention order. She looked angrily at the Inspector, who shifted his weight onto his other foot.

"Are you sure you've got this right, Inspector?" she asked sharply. "You realise my husband is the Principal Private Secretary to the Prime Minister himself."

"I do, Madam," the Inspector replied calmly.

"Well!" said his wife indignantly, but she could think of nothing else to say. After a pause she added simply: "This is crazy."

Ayer felt suddenly calm: remote from everything.

He asked: "Can I call a lawyer?"

"No." The Inspector shook his head. "You are not allowed to contact anybody. You shouldn't even be speaking to your wife." He caught her eye and said hurriedly: "But of course I won't stop you unless you talk politics."

Ayer nodded briefly. "Where will I be taken?"

"To the Police Headquarters tonight. After that to the Central Prison. You will be held there."

"For how long?" Ayer inquired.

The Inspector shrugged. "I'm afraid I don't know. That's up to the government."

He reached into his pocket again and pulled out another typewritten sheet of paper. "This is a warrant to search your house," he said, handing it over, "and we propose doing that now. When we have finished, you can pack a suitcase with some clothes and toilet requirements and then you must come with us."

Ayer reached over and squeezed his wife's hand. She sat shocked and immobile. He kissed her cheek gently.

"I'd love a cup of tea," he said. "Would you mind?"

She shook her head and went quickly through to the kitchen. The constable put away his notebook and followed her. From the kitchen, her voice said: "Oh for God's sake, get away from me," but the constable did not reappear.

Ayer spread wide his hands in a gesture of submission and said to the Inspector: "Where do you want to start?"

"In the bedroom, if you don't mind. And I'd like you to be present while we search."

Ayer nodded and they went through. He sat on the bed while they rummaged among underwear and shirts, and felt in the pockets of his suits hanging in the cupboard. They pulled out his wife's pants and brassières, and squeezed the rolled-up stockings to see if anything was concealed in them. They showed interest in her pack of birth control pills, reading the instructions. They looked carefully through a pile of private letters, once glancing up at him in amusement, and inspected the St David's telephone directory beside the bed for special numbers or names that might have been written on it. The policemen stripped the double bed and peered under the mattress, then went to the bookcase and sorted carefully through every volume, looking for subversive titles, incriminating pieces of paper concealed between the pages. They found nothing. When they had finished, they moved to the living-room.

Tea was ready, and Ayer sipped it as he watched. His wife did not offer the policemen a cup, but sat silently close to him as the men searched through their possessions.

"Now the other bedrooms," the Inspector said.

"The children are in there," Ayer protested. "They're asleep."

"Then we'll have to wake them, won't we?" the Inspector said.

Ayer and his wife looked at each other helplessly. It was useless to argue. They went and quietly opened the door of the boys' room, lifted them up, heavy and limp in the sleep of children, and carried them into the master bedroom. They laid them in the double bed, pulled the sheets off the floor to cover them, and Ayer went back for his daughter. She too did not stir.

At last the Inspector said: "I think we're finished now. You'd better get a bag packed."

Ayer nodded and went off to do it. It was difficult to know what to take to prison, or what he would be allowed. As his children slept, he chose a couple of changes of clothes, his shaving kit, soap, toothbrush and a comb, and selected some books and writing material. He sat on the bed beside his wife. The Inspector hovered watchfully in the doorway.

Ayer kissed her and ran his hand down her shiny hair and the smooth skin of her cheek. "Don't worry, Nora," he said gently. "This has got to be a mistake. Moorhouse can't have flipped that badly. Telephone a lawyer and see what he can do."

She nodded and smiled brightly at him. He could see she would cry in a minute.

Ayer stood up and said to the Inspector: "Shall we go?"

They walked out into the dark garden. The north-wester had died away. It was four in the morning and Ayer was a prisoner.

As he was driven off, he did not look back.

Chapter Six

When he was sure the first stage of Operation Tiger had been completed successfully, Montrose caught four hours' sleep on the sofa in his office.

The detainees – eighteen men, bewildered or arrogant, some scared – had been locked into the cells in the basement of Police

Headquarters, and additional armed patrols were out in the city centre and in towns throughout the island, waiting for dawn; there not because immediate trouble was expected, but to reinforce the awareness of the people that a new emergency regime had come into force while they slept.

The Commissioner of Police, snoring gently, missed Moorhouse's nationwide broadcast announcing the steps he had taken overnight and blaming American imperialist agents for the unrest, accusing them of trying to destabilise the elected government of St David's for their own political ends. He confirmed the front-page story in that morning's *Herald* which reported rumours of diplomats being expelled. The CIA was being driven out, he declared, and their locally recruited spies and provocateurs were now behind bars.

"This island," Moorhouse said sonorously, "will maintain a policy of strict non-alignment. In the next few weeks or months, if we seem to be moving closer towards the Soviet bloc, it is because we are redressing the balance, nothing more. For too long we have tilted towards the United States, and they have repaid our trust and friendship by attacking us in this cowardly fashion. Now the scale is swinging the other way. We extend the hand of brotherhood and co-operation to all nations, without favour."

Leister, in his office at the American Embassy, heard the announcement with growing dismay, and settled down to draft another urgent telex to the State Department. The implications of what Moorhouse had said were enormous and unwelcome. The treaty allowing the US navy access to Port Lombard might be in jeopardy, but even if it were not, Moorhouse seemed to be opening the door to providing identical facilities to the Soviets. The refusal value of St David's to the Russians was by itself great.

And what about the satellite tracking station and the communications base? Would they be allowed to continue?

Leister snorted: American imperialist agents, Moorhouse had called them – wheeling out the clichés to explain away his own growing unpopularity. He would have to do better than that if he wanted to stay in government.

Elsewhere on the island, little changed immediately. Important events in the lives of nations are usually greeted with silence. People do not read the newspapers or listen to the radio, and then pour spontaneously onto the streets to demonstrate or riot. Rather, political opponents gather quietly to plot. Ordinary citizens have their breakfast, kiss their kids, go to work, keep out of trouble: even those who may be inwardly angry sniff the air first, like animals, trying to gauge what others feel, how those with guns are reacting. Only the insane and the fanatic immediately confront whatever new authority has come out onto the streets, risking the bullets or the beatings.

There were none of those on St David's.

Others bide their time, waiting for an opening.

When Montrose woke, sweating, and sat up rubbing his hand over his eyes, it was nine a.m. His head felt thick and the taste of whisky was stale in his mouth. He waited until he was sufficiently confident he could get across to his desk without staggering. Once there, still groggy, he pushed the intercom button.

"Good morning, sir," said a voice.

"Tea," he said shortly.

"Right away, sir."

Montrose sat heavily behind his desk and rested his head in the palms of his hands. He stayed like that until he heard a knock at the door.

"Yes?" Montrose called. The reception sergeant came in with a pile of brown folders, pausing just inside to salute. The Commissioner glowered at him.

"Here are the morning reports, sir," the sergeant said, placing them on the blotting-paper in front of him.

"Where in fuck's name is the tea?" Montrose asked in a low voice.

"Brewing, sir. I'll bring it through the moment it's ready."

"You do that."

The sergeant hurried out and Montrose began flicking listlessly through the folders. Reports had come, as he had requested, from all major centres on the island, giving police dispositions. There had been no incidents. Montrose yawned and threw the files into a corner of his desk.

The reception sergeant knocked again. This time he brought in a wooden tray covered with a plain white cloth, and on it the white tea service emblazoned with the police crest.

"Shall I pour, sir?" the sergeant asked.

Montrose looked at him with contempt. "What do you think, laddie?"

The sergeant poured.

The Commissioner felt better when he had finished his first cup. Alone in his room, he had a second, and noticed that his hand was shaking only slightly. Today was going to be busy but productive, he thought. There were things to do, people to see, and every step of it would be profitable.

It was about time too. They were all in a bad way: himself, Clifton and Luther. The cash returns had fallen virtually to nothing as the island's economy weakened. After the failure of the first harvest, a few shopkeepers had cut down the amounts they were paying for the special protection Montrose provided, explaining they could afford no more. When the rains failed the second year, almost everyone reduced their payments by more than half, and some stopped completely. Then came the cholera scare and massive tourist cancellations. The whole network which Montrose, Clifton and Luther had painstakingly set up in the first year after Independence, trading on people's uncertainty about how life in the new island Republic would work out, that whole beautiful, lucrative operation collapsed. The trouble was, they had been too gentlemanly, Montrose thought. Did shopkeepers really need "special protection" for their premises? They thought they could get away without it. What would happen to them if they didn't pay? they reasoned. And the answer was, they didn't think anything would happen.

And hardly anything did.

Without even deliberately banding together in opposition, the major shopkeepers on the island, from the general merchants who catered for locals, to the general manager of Maxwell's in Port Lombard High Street, all felt secure enough to call Montrose's bluff. Of course, some retaliation was tried. Luther organised a group of army sergeants to smash up two stores in different areas, but there was a limit to what they could do without starting rumours and calling Moorhouse's attention to their business dealings. There was no genuine unrest on St David's then. It only built up later, but by the time it had, the water-tight operation was effectively dead. Now conditions had changed, and it was time to resurrect it.

Montrose was proud of his plan. From the beginning, he had involved Clifton and Luther. Luther was most important, because he was both a local and a potential threat. But once the heads of the army and the police were co-operating, it was difficult for the government to move unexpectedly against any of them. At least one of the three would have warning of what was coming. Also, they had been careful not to be too greedy, and they dealt only with the top people. The owner of a big general store would be asked to pay $50 a week: not an exorbitant sum. At the top end, Maxwell's contributed $100.

It was a personal service the three men provided, calling on their clients sometimes once a month, occasionally once every two months in the case of businesses in the more remote towns. Between them, Montrose, Clifton and Luther had sixty regular customers – twenty each on whom to make a short social call during their normal tours of inspection or their days at Headquarters. It was not taxing work. The three men shopped at some of the bigger local stores anyway, and at one time, the managers used to make them gifts of the items they had selected, but that generous habit too had long stopped.

As corruption went, theirs was petty. But for the three men, averaging $80 per client, it meant more than doubling their salaries, tax free, which made an enormous difference to island living. They could not – they did not see why they had to – adjust back. Without knowing where the extra money came from, nor did their wives and children. In fact, their family spending was as high as it had ever been, and the three men – Clifton in particular – had gone deeply into debt. Now, thanks to an unexpected security windfall, the disasters which had befallen St David's could be used for their benefit – and this time to even greater financial advantage. There was no question now of store managers refusing to pay up.

Moorhouse's unpopularity meant a genuine groundswell of dissatisfaction existed for the three to harness. If a demonstration led to a riot, and a shop was smashed up and looted, everyone would know it was caused by the general unrest. A manager who defaulted on payments might be suspicious, but could he point a finger at the protection racket? Christ, there was a state of emergency, after all. And behind it was the CIA, as Moorhouse would be the first to point out. Paid agents were fomenting trouble. In those circumstances, who would accuse Montrose, or Luther or Clifton, and expect themselves to be taken seriously?

Besides everything, of course, there *was* a genuine element of protection in the scheme. Every one of the paid-up clients really did get policemen stationed outside their front and back entrances every night. This cost Montrose nothing beyond ordering a revised duty roster, and none of the stores had suffered a burglary since Independence. By itself, that must have been worth the money. Yet their troublefree lives had given the managers a false sense of security. Now was the time to show them exactly what they had been paying for.

Montrose drained his cup of tea, getting half a mouthful of leaves in the final gulp and spitting them back in disgust. He took a clean uniform from his cupboard and went down to the shower room at the end of the corridor, where he stood, fat-bellied and pink, underneath the needle spray. After several minutes, he dried himself briskly with a rough, official-issue towel and, as he did so, he felt the beads of sweat breaking out again on his back. By ten o'clock he was ready. Everyone would be in their offices, the first of their morning chores out of the way, and they would have had time to digest the news of the emergency.

Montrose ordered his official car to take him straight to the High Street, and it parked outside the entrance to Maxwell's store. He was in an affable mood, ready to do his public relations best.

He took the lift up to the administration offices on the third floor, and asked the receptionist to tell Mr Maxwell senior the Commissioner of Police was waiting to see him.

She reappeared quickly and motioned him to step through.

Martin Maxwell had been head of the firm for twenty years, having inherited it from his father. He was due to retire in three years, and his son was ready to step into his place. After that, who knows? Perhaps his grandson too.

Martin Maxwell had been brought up in the old tradition of service and quality. His father had made him start in the store at the age of twenty-three in the despatch department, and after a year promoted him to salesman in the shoe department. It was a decade before Maxwell had worked his way up to the administration offices, but by that time he knew everything there was to know about life on the shop floors. He took over the store on the death of his father, and for many years it functioned as it had always done.

After Independence – within a week of the Union Jack being lowered for the last time – an unpleasant element entered his life in the shape of the Commissioner of Police with a rather baldly phrased invitation to contribute a cash amount every week in exchange for a protection service which really ought to have been given automatically. There had been an implied threat behind the Commissioner's invitation, and those were unsettled days anyway, so, like others, Maxwell had reluctantly agreed. But it annoyed him, particularly when life on St David's continued as peacefully as usual. As time passed, business grew more difficult, and the arrangement had lapsed. Clearly the Commissioner had not been happy about this, but he had seemed to accept the situation.

And now Montrose was back: freshly shaved and with a shine on his bland face.

Maxwell rose courteously and shook the Commissioner's hand, peering at him through his thick, rimless spectacles.

"May I offer you some coffee?" he enquired.

"That's very good of you, sir," Montrose said jocularly.

After the receptionist had gone out, he added with a smile: "Business doing well?"

Maxwell looked at him carefully, hiding his dislike. "Unfortunately not," he said. "As you know, there's not much money around these days, what with the weather and the cholera scare. Still, we get by, Commissioner."

Montrose nodded sympathetically, but his eyes were bright.

The girl brought back coffee which had been brewing in a Cona machine in the reception area. Montrose put three spoons of sugar in his cup, stirred it vigorously, and stared pointedly at her legs as she walked out, his tongue flicking briefly around his lips. Maxwell watched with distaste.

"Very worrying about this state of emergency," the Commissioner said conversationally, turning back to the desk. "But you can understand the reason for it, I'm sure. I take it you saw yesterday's demonstration just down the road?"

"I heard it more than saw it," Maxwell replied. "There seemed to be quite a lot of gunfire. I read in the *Herald* this morning that three people were killed."

Montrose inclined his head as if he had been congratulated on reaching a certain score.

"And a dozen wounded," he said. "There'll probably be a lot more of that."

"Oh, I do hope not," said Mr Maxwell.

"Come on," Montrose said conspiratorially. "They were only locals, *and* they were troublemakers. Agents of the CIA."

"They were people, Mr Montrose. I don't care about anything more than that."

The Commissioner appeared to concede defeat. "I daresay you're right," he said. "It was a great shame. But, as I say, it won't be the last. We expect another big demonstration in this area tomorrow – quite near your store, as a matter of fact. Could be trouble. I'd watch out, if I were you."

Maxwell sipped his coffee and looked dispassionately across at Montrose. He knew what was coming.

"Well, Commissioner," he said, "we shall all be relying on you and your men to do your public duty and protect our lives and property."

"We'll do our best, as always," Montrose said. He paused and added sombrely: "I just hope it will be good enough. The trouble is, with this emergency on, there are just too many calls on us: too many buildings to protect, too many shops. We don't have the manpower to go round. We have to pick and choose where we station our forces. I'm sure you understand that."

"Perfectly," Maxwell replied. "Nevertheless, I hope you'll manage to station a few round our store. As you know, it is the biggest on the island."

Montrose looked doubtful. "I'm not sure I can do that," he said. "Times are hard. Manpower's short. Our forces have been badly stretched, as I say. Now is when there's likely to be a lot of trouble too: looting, buildings on fire, that sort of thing. To give special protection to a place like this would mean bringing men back from leave, or from their days off. You follow me?"

Maxwell looked calmly at him. "I understood from my *Herald* this morning that all police leave has been cancelled on your orders. So you should have no worries on that score."

Montrose felt himself begin to flush. Jesus, he hadn't expected such a hard time. "Not all leave," he said levelly. "The press exaggerates as usual."

Maxwell stood up to indicate the meeting was at an end. "Well," he said, "we shall all have to trust in your good offices, won't we?"

Montrose gazed at him dumbly, then felt anger mount. He rose and came straight to the point, his voice suddenly harsh.

"It will cost you, Mr Maxwell, two hundred dollars a week from now on, to protect your store in these difficult times. That is a bargain rate, considering the trouble that's going on. Two hundred dollars cash, paid to me in the usual way."

A few seconds passed before, unbelievably, Maxwell shook his head. "I can't do that, Commissioner. These are hard times and the price is too high. I'm not even sure I *should* do it. After all, police protection is a right. It's one of the reasons I pay my taxes. I'm sure you would agree with that."

Maxwell was aware of the hostility radiating out from Montrose, and he felt a surge of alarm. For an instant, he thought perhaps he should just pay up. But his resolution hardened and he held out his hand. After all, this was St David's, not Chicago.

Montrose stared coldly at him.

"No doubt you're right," he said. "You as a shopkeeper know better than anyone that you get what you pay for. I wish you luck."

Montrose turned and walked angrily out of the office towards the elevator. Well, the gloves were off. Maxwell would have to learn a lesson. Anyone who didn't pay would be taught a lesson.

The money must start coming in, and quickly. There was no question about that. Clifton was in a bad way: his wife had expensive tastes. Luther wasn't much better, although Christ knew what he spent his money on. And Montrose himself – well, the bank had made it clear when they increased his overdraft last month that there would be no more loans: that the time had come to start paying back the money.

And shit, he owed them thirty thousand dollars. On his Police Commissioner's salary, he didn't have a hope. If they foreclosed on him and took him to court, there was no doubt he would lose his job. No country had a bankrupt as Commissioner of Police, not even a piss-hole like St David's. There was no way out but on. It was them or him: the bald choice, and he didn't even have to think about it.

Montrose walked down the street to the next shop on his list – a large general dealers, catering mainly for locals.

He was appalled to find himself facing a similar refusal, and from a local too.

The third store paid without demur. Perhaps it was the barely suppressed rage in Montrose's face which decided the manager not to stand his ground, and he handed over one hundred dollars.

As he left, Montrose thought viciously: if I pay that into my bank account, I'll only owe $29,900, not including interest.

By the end of the morning, Montrose had visited ten stores. Only two of them had gone back on his list as clients.

He felt as if his rage would overpower him.

Chapter Seven

Stephen Ayer sat on the hard narrow metal seat of the prison van, peering out through the slit window in the side. He was locked in a tiny metal cell, one of twenty or thirty so caged. If he put his hand out in front of him, it touched the green steel door before his elbow had room to unbend. There were perhaps two inches on each side of his shoulders if he sat squarely on the seat.

A metal box, barely big enough for a man.

It was hot, God, so hot. The van was not moving and he could hear no sounds of a prison driver or escorts about to board.

On the ceiling, four inches from his head, was a small air vent. No breeze came through it. The perspiration ran down Ayer's face and the sweat from his body soaked his clothes until he felt he was sitting in sticky warm water. Around him he could hear the uneasy, uncomfortable stirrings of the other prisoners, bodies knocking against metal, a low murmur of voices as some struck up a conversation through the walls.

Ayer's mouth was dry, and his eyes stung from lack of sleep and the saltiness which trickled into them from his forehead and hair.

They had been taken from the filthy Central Police Station cells with nothing to eat, not a mug of tea or a glass of water, and loaded into the van. That was just after dawn. Ayer couldn't be sure of the exact time now because after his arrest the police had confiscated his watch, wedding ring and what little money he had brought with him. They listed it in a book and made him sign it over.

Men around him – people he did not know, had never even seen before – also handed in their valuables, victims of similar detention orders.

Then in the remaining hours before dawn they were all herded into cells which stank of urine. Ayer shared his with four others. There were two bunks, but Ayer looked at the state of the blankets and did not compete for either. Instead he squatted on the concrete and tried to relax, to rest. Dawn was a long time coming.

When the sky lightened, there was sudden activity, doors crashing metallically open, voices shouting, orders being given.

Three armed policemen opened Ayer's cell door, hurried the prisoners out into the bleak courtyard and ordered them into the van. The individual cell doors were locked, then there was a much louder crash as the rear entrance door was sealed, and they waited for the van to move. But nothing happened. Inexplicably, the policemen just went away and left them, and the sun rose higher.

Hours passed, or seemed to pass. The heat became unbearable. Ayer tried first to sleep, but where his body touched the metal, pools of water quickly collected and his flesh began to itch so he had to keep shifting his position.

He tried remembering poems, then nursery rhymes he had taught his children.

Down the police van, someone cried out in anguish. Ayer felt that his eyes were filling not only with sweat, but with tears too, tears at the unfairness, the inhumanity of it, and he fought to check himself. Jesus, he had been under arrest for less than a day and already he was cracking up.

Less than a day. It seemed like a week.

As time went on, some prisoners began to shout, to cry out, trying to attract attention. They beat on the metal sides of the van, first rhythmically, then with increasing desperation. From the other side of the metal partition, Ayer could hear a man retch, and eventually the sound turned into a combination of groaning and sobbing.

Suddenly from just outside, a military voice screamed: "YOU FUCKERS SHUT UP!"

There was a shocked silence within the hot metal cells, but only for a few seconds. One prisoner, his voice raw with outrage, yelled back: "YOU FUCKING SADISTS! LET US OUT OF HERE!" and others immediately took up the cry, banging on the walls with their fists, kicking with the heels of their shoes. The noise built to a crescendo.

Ayer felt swept away by it, by this unexpected solidarity among strangers, and he too smashed the side of his fist against the metal and shouted: "Bastards! Bastards!" until the dryness in his throat made him gag and he collapsed weakly onto the metal seat.

Around him, the beating of fists and shoes against metal reverberated through the van but the shouts were difficult to understand, the words indistinct, just inarticulate rage and suffering.

Without warning, the engine of the police van burst into life and the prisoners raised a ragged cheer. Victory! Now the van would move and air would be forced through the vents. Perhaps the temperature would drop a degree or two.

But in any case, at least they would be going somewhere, not just sitting roasting.

Ayer watched through the window slit as the van rumbled through the Central Police Station gates and turned right into Haddon Walk, heading for the prison. He knew the drive would take about fifteen minutes, and they would not see the town.

The van moved slowly. Hardly any air seemed to circulate. Putting his hand against the ceiling vent, Ayer could not detect a breeze. If anything, it seemed to be getting hotter.

The shouting had exhausted him. Ayer became aware of a buzzing in his head and a feeling of dizziness. Sweat streamed down his face and his clothes were soaked, then suddenly, inexplicably, a chill ran through his body. He felt his muscles relax and he slumped lower on the metal seat.

He thought suddenly of James Bond – clad in a towel – locked in a steam room in a film he had once seen. He couldn't remember who the villain had been. It didn't matter. But Bond had been locked in the steam to die, left until his blood began to boil. Yet he'd got out. He smashed into the door with his shoulder and it gave way. That's what I should do, thought Ayer groggily: hit that metal door and watch it buckle and bend.

Another shiver of cold went through his body. His muscles felt so heavy. He wondered if he could still move, if his limbs would obey an order passed down from his brain, but although he thought about it, he couldn't seem to persuade his brain to issue any commands.

Only his mind was working, and his memory. There was Bond, free, gasping on the floor as he regained his strength. Ayer, still trapped in the steam room, watched, unable to move, his body alternating between fevered wetness and a delicious icy chill.

It was not an unpleasant way to die, Ayer thought, immediately wondering what had made him think that, whether he really was going to die, and then feeling not only undecided about it but totally neutral. He didn't care.

The buzzing in his head increased its pitch.

As the van rounded a corner, he was aware of toppling slowly onto the floor, but of feeling nothing. It was almost as if someone else's body was crumpling into that small space, while Ayer sat on the metal seat, observing.

Then he decided he had to sleep, and immediately that decision was made, his mind shut off and he fell into blackness.

It was a wonderful sleep, broken by Daniel Moorhouse bringing him tea as if Ayer had suddenly become the Prime Minister himself, and by James Bond smashing his shoulder against the steam bath door again and the wood splintering in slow motion as his body barrelled through to safety. There may have been a high speed car chase, but Ayer couldn't be sure. He was certainly on a mountain top because he could feel the cool air, and although he knew he was going to be sick very shortly, the prospect did not distress him and he felt no pain.

There was something inside him his body knew must be rejected and it was doing it in the most effective way it could. When it came, he was surprised at the independent power of the muscles in his slack body as they squeezed the contents from his stomach, and he drifted off again, aware as he did so that his head was on a cool white pillow; that he had been ill – had had a nightmare; but that he was home again and in the morning he would go to work.

Hours later, Ayer's eyes flickered open and after a while of lying motionless, he wondered why his bedroom window had been barred. He noticed also the mattress was different – lumpy and hard.

Remembrance came in a sickening wave, bringing with it a weak feeling of panic. He realised miserably that he was trapped. Home was a thousand miles away and a hundred years ago. When would he see it again?

He turned his head and gazed across the prison hospital ward. All the beds were full. He recognised some of the faces. Two warders with truncheons sat at the end by the door and paid no attention to him.

Ayer lay back and, without realising it, began to practise that most skilled of prison occupations: learning how to wait.

An hour passed. Was it more? Or only ten minutes? It didn't matter. A doctor came into the ward and strolled across to Ayer, reaching for his wrist to feel the pulse. He carried a truncheon on the belt around his waist.

"How do you feel?" the doctor asked.

"Okay."

"You've had heat exhaustion," the doctor said. "You've lost a lot of salt and you need to make it up. I'll send you some tablets and something to drink. You can get out of here this afternoon." The doctor caught his eye. "I mean, out of the hospital," he explained. "Not out of prison."

Ayer nodded slightly. "Thank you," he said.

The doctor turned away.

Chapter Eight

Montrose positioned his men with care, showing on a diagram where they ought to be at different stages, and then sending them off in pairs to check out the area themselves and make sure of their escape routes.

There were ten of them, six from the police – selected himself from those whose conduct would have rendered them liable to substantial terms of imprisonment had their cases ever been presented before a court – and four seconded by Luther as an alternative to being courtmartialled and sentenced to a military prison.

Two of the army men had worked as a team before, and Luther had enough evidence for them to be jailed for fifteen years for rape. The others were felons of varying sorts – pilfering army or police stores to sell on the black market, breaking into shops and then investigating the crime themselves. The usual things.

Montrose was using them regularly now at meetings of the opposition Democratic Front, cheering on Albert Francis and his crew, shouting anti-Moorhouse slogans, and taking part in demonstrations.

It was Montrose's men who had begun throwing bricks in the last High Street demonstration, and smashing store windows. They were an efficient crew and there was nothing particular to distinguish them from the other locals. They looked rather ordinary: young and fairly rough, but not aggressively so.

Montrose was impressed at the way they operated in the crowds, and at how quickly the group mood could be changed by a series of contrived events. He had never seen anything like it: the technique had certainly never been used on St David's before, but really all you needed was a handful of men in the crowd operating in concert with the police, and you could order up a riot as easily as if it were the dish of the day in a restaurant.

And the really funny thing, Montrose thought, was that he'd been taught the technique by an American fairy. He'd never have believed fairies knew such things, but you learn all the time. It worked like a charm, and soon it would be helping make money for Montrose.

Two hours from the scheduled start of the demonstration, Montrose briefed his men. He was again using his security battalion units. They were tougher, more disciplined. They knew him of old.

They sat on the hard-backed wooden chairs of the briefing room, relaxed and talking among themselves until Montrose and Clifton walked in. Everyone stood to attention until the Commissioner settled himself, his small eyes flicking about the room as if to check who was there.

"At ease," Montrose said finally, and with much scraping of chairs the men sat down.

Montrose waited until he had their attention.

"Right," he said. "There's a demonstration today, scheduled for eleven o'clock as you know. It's supposedly being held by the Democratic Front. Our friend Mr Francis will be speaking, or at least that's what's rumoured. This is completely illegal." He paused for emphasis. "The state of emergency regulations clearly ban all demonstrations and public meetings. Nevertheless, it's been decided to let it go ahead."

Montrose could sense the disappointment among the men.

"It can go ahead," Montrose said, "unless it turns violent."

The room was very still now.

"We are going to start off keeping a very low profile." He emphasised the words "start off".

"We are staying right out of the way."

He got up and pointed to a map of the central area – the same map he'd used to brief his ten men earlier.

"The demonstration's starting here," he said, pointing to Jubilee Park at the western end of the High Street, "and we're going to be waiting out of sight down these roads here." He hit at the areas with his swagger stick. "We've got plain clothes boys in the park, and they'll call us up on the radio if we need to go in. Now you'll all be armed – twenty rounds of ammo per man. No one will fire – I say again, no one will fire – until I give the word. Is that understood?"

He stared fiercely around.

"Anyone who fires early had better be shooting at me, because I'll have that fucker's balls before he knows what's hit him."

There wasn't a man in the hall who believed Montrose was incapable of sudden terrible revenge. He glared at them, and they looked back silently.

"Now that we understand each other," the Commissioner continued, "let me say that when I do give the order to shoot – correction, *if* I give the order to shoot – then you must shoot to warn, and not to kill. Fire over their heads. If you really have to, fire at their legs. I don't want the thing to turn into a bloodbath. Do you understand? If some element or other has a gun and is shooting at you, then when I give the order, you can certainly take him out."

Montrose let another silence drag out. His piggy eyes narrowed to slits and he said softly: "But he'd better have his finger around that fucking trigger when I come across to look at his body, or I'm going to have some questions to ask, and none of you will like answering them. Is that clear?"

It was.

"Any questions?"

Silence.

"Okay. Get out of here and draw your weapons."

Clifton, with his haggard black face, watched dispassionately as the men hurried to get out of the room, away from Montrose. Chairs scraped back immediately and they crowded into doorways like schoolchildren on the last day of term, jostling and pushing to get through. They feared Montrose, and he could see some of them even hated him.

Clifton didn't like him much himself, but Montrose was his last hope. He had no choice now but to back him, and back this risky scheme with its elements of revenge and spite.

When my finances have pulled right, Clifton promised himself, when I've got a bit extra put by, then I'll get out. Nothing will stop me.

He followed Montrose from the room and into his office, trying to shake off the sick depression which had dogged him over the last few weeks. They were set on their course now: it could not be altered. He just had to put as good a face on things as possible, and he made an effort to do that right away because he knew how infuriated Montrose could get at the display of anything less than full confidence.

But this morning, sitting behind his desk, Montrose was beaming and expansive. The plan had been decided, the dispositions made. Soon the money would come rolling in. Even Clifton, trying too hard to be cheerful, his anxious face belying his words, could not shake the Commissioner's mood.

They drove towards Jubilee Park an hour before the demonstration, and took a quick walk around. Everything was quiet. It was shady but still hot. Coconut palms fringed the lawns.

They checked the security battalion's positions, well out of sight of the park and the High Street. After that, they waited.

At eleven o'clock, small groups of people who had been walking around the park perimeter, or window shopping in the High Street, began to collect nervously around the white wrought-iron bandstand.

There was no sign of the police, and, as their numbers grew, so did their confidence.

After ten minutes, a man brought out a green and red Democratic Front flag and hoisted it up a palm, tying the flagstaff in place with string. There were about a hundred and fifty people present, including Montrose's ten.

Albert Francis arrived nearly half an hour late, obviously waiting until he had been given word that the police were keeping a low profile, and that it was safe to make an appearance.

The crowd swelled to three hundred. Montrose's men began the chanting and more men and women came off the surrounding streets, appearing as if from nowhere.

By the time Francis was ready to start his speech, it was a respectably sized demonstration of about a thousand, and still growing.

One of his party workers handed him a megaphone. "My friends," Francis declared importantly, "today we are proving that the people of this island will not be intimidated by Moorhouse's bullying tactics. I ask you! *A state of emergency* on St David's! Why, we didn't even have a state of emergency when we fought for our Independence. We didn't have one under the British, so why should we have one today?"

He looked around him. "Is it because of the CIA as Moorhouse tells us?"

Cries of "No!" from Montrose's ten.

"You're wrong!" Francis contradicted. "I say to you frankly, my friends, yes, I believe it is! Pin the blame where it's due. It's all the fault of the CIA! I hate to admit it but for once in his life, Moorhouse is right! The CIA did it!"

As his words echoed across the park, Francis looked around at his audience again, who waited expectantly, keeping a sideways watch for the approach of the police.

He judged his moment. "After all," he said, taking them into his confidence, "who decided not to use British aid on cleaning up the water supplies and fixing the sewage? Why we all know who that was: it was the CIA, that's who." The laughter rose round him. "Who decided to build that white elephant up the hill instead?" Francis demanded. "The CIA decided to build it, damn them. Who ruined our tourist industry? They did – the CIA! Are we going to let them get away with it?"

From the audience, more laughter and shouts of "No!"

"Of course," said Francis, "these CIA fellows are pretty smart these days. They don't come out in the open, oh no, sir. They creep around in disguise, so no one knows who they are. They perform their deeds in the darkness and behind locked doors. But the Bible says: 'By their deeds shall ye know them.' So let's just look at the deeds, my friends, and see if we can unmask the CIA traitor who's brought this country to its knees. I ask you: name the man who said No to clean water!"

Montrose's ten were first off the mark: "Moorhouse!" they shouted back.

"Name the man who said Yes to keeping filthy sewage!"

Everyone joined in: "Moorhouse!"

"Name the man who spent the Aid money on himself!"

"Moorhouse!"

Francis worked himself up: "Name the CIA agent!" he cried, almost in a religious fervour.

"Moorhouse!"

His eyes blazed, a fist held up at the heavens, like Lenin. "Name the villain!"

"Moorhouse!" they roared in return, becoming delirious.

"Name the man we've got to get rid of!"

"Moorhouse!"

"Name the coward who detained our countrymen without trial or charge!"

"Moorhouse!"

"Name the traitor who's brought this island to ruin!"

"Moorhouse! Moorhouse!" The shouts dissolved into cheers, and Montrose's men knew their moment had come. They began chanting slogans, the ten of them together, and within seconds the others picked it up.

"Moorhouse out! Moorhouse out!"

Albert Francis tried to quieten them, to make himself heard over the megaphone, but no one was listening any longer. Party marshals attempted to control the crowd, motioning them frantically to sit down, but the police were nowhere around and the demonstrators had been infected by the spirit of Francis' remarks.

There were now more than two thousand of them, and the numbers were still growing.

Montrose's men, who had moved towards the edges of the audience, began motioning and pushing people outwards, towards the gate leading to the High Street, and soon the shouting crowd was showing signs of becoming a procession, ignoring the marshals and the megaphone entreaties of Albert Francis.

Montrose's men circled around the side and seized the unwilling politician, lifting him onto their shoulders and carrying him along. With Francis being taken, shoulder-high, to the gate, the procession got under way, unstoppable. There was nothing for the marshals to do but follow.

When they had him well into the High Street, Montrose's men set Francis down and moved off, leaving him smiling uncertainly to walk with the surging, chanting people.

There was still no sign of police. The demonstrators shook their fists and chanted: "Moorhouse out! Moorhouse out!"

Montrose's men split up, spreading themselves along the fringes of the crowd, ready for the moment when they came near Maxwell's store.

A few blocks away, out of sight, the security battalion units waited in their buses for the word to move. The Commissioner himself followed the progress of the demonstration from radio reports by plainclothes men, and he was in no hurry. He lit a cigarette and relaxed in his car, his face amused and his body flooded with the feeling of well-being which came from teaching that fucking Maxwell who was in charge.

In the High Street, his men neared their objective. They reached into their right-hand pockets, one after the other – or at least to where their pockets had been before they were cut away at the American's suggestion – and detached from the sheaths round their thighs the slender, solid steel bars with which they would perform their main task.

These were not their only weapons. The men had also made sure that, overnight, a few neat piles of bricks had been left on the pavements, and they were still there, attracting no attention. Bricks are associated in the minds of most people with order and building: not with destruction.

Now was the time for Montrose's men to act.

The first sounds of shattering plate-glass as they struck out were lost in the chanting of the people, but some women near them began screaming and a fever of expectancy passed through the demonstrators. Whatever happened, they were part of it. With so many around, it was difficult for individuals to control where they went. They were trapped.

Although one or two pockets of chanting remained, the sound generally became confused, a mixture of shouting, yelling and the noise of smashing windows. Bricks arced through the air towards shop windows, first lobbed by Montrose's men, but soon hurled by others too.

The demonstration reached Maxwell's store just as security officers struggled to lock the doors, and were overwhelmed in the spill of people pushing through. One of Montrose's men brought his metal bar down on the side of the head of the first security officer who tried to stand his ground, and the man crumpled, blood pouring down his face. The others retreated immediately.

The demonstrators swept on, and the fallen man was lost beneath their feet, tripping them up until a pile of screaming bodies grew.

Inside the store, shoppers and assistants ran in panic, looking for safety but not knowing where to go. Some started scrambling up the stairs to the administration offices and others followed automatically.

The first rioters in, led by Montrose's men, moved quickly through the store, smashing display counters and dummies, breaking open cash registers and pushing handfuls of notes into their pockets. Behind them, the mêlée on the floor had somehow sorted itself out. The security officer lay motionless, pushed out of the way on one side. No one realised he was dead.

More demonstrators were pouring in, infected by the violence and eager suddenly to get their share of the pickings. Some ran up the stairs to the first and second floors, but the more distance they put between themselves and the main body of rioters, the less comfortable and confident they felt, and they soon turned back.

The looting took place almost entirely on the ground floor. Every cash register was emptied. The electrical department was ransacked. Radios, tape recorders, piles of records and tapes, entire stereo sets were carried off.

On the third floor, frightened shoppers and assistants locked themselves in the administration offices.

Martin Maxwell, his lips trembling with alarm, was on the phone to the police for the third time. His emergency call was being dealt with, he was told. The Commissioner himself was on the spot and had been informed. They couldn't explain why no police had yet arrived: probably they were tied up elsewhere, but they would get there shortly.

Maxwell felt his heart sink. Well, he thought despairingly, I've saved my principles and two hundred dollars. Not caring who saw him, he covered his face with his hands.

The sounds of shouting and destruction carried clearly up the stair-well.

The attack on the store had been going on for ten minutes before Montrose's men were loaded with all the booty they could decently carry, and were ready to get out.

They headed for the emergency exit, pushing open the doors and walking twenty paces to where they had parked a closed van. They locked their radios and stereo equipment in the back and had a brief argument about going back for more, but decided it was now too late and too risky. The time had come to get clear.

The van's engine burst into life and it moved off, down a service lane running parallel to High Street, and turning right, away from the trouble, heading towards the industrial area.

At the pre-arranged time – ten minutes after the attack on Maxwell's began – Montrose gave the order to move in. The armed police buckled on their steel helmets, collected up their riot shields and headed for the trouble.

The Commissioner positioned himself at the front, the growing shouting and sounds of destruction pleasing to his ears.

When they came in sight of the riot, it was all he could do to maintain his purposeful stride forward at the head of his column of men, rather than stand silently in admiration. The rioters were mobbing Maxwell's, and every plate-glass window was shattered, every showcase looted. Whole bolts of imported silks had disappeared. Montrose could see people carrying away bundles of clothing and electrical equipment. He knew that most of them would still be inside the store.

A quick glance up and down the High Street showed that six other shops leading to Maxwell's had also been attacked, but not badly, and the rioters were now moving on to the next.

Time to stop them, Montrose thought, before they touched one of the clients.

Despite the scrum and the shouting, the first rioters noticed the arrival of the police almost immediately, and for an instant stood frozen like animals in a spotlight's glare. Then they began to run.

Montrose took out his own pistol and fired a shot above their heads, aiming in the general direction of the third floor administration offices where that bastard Maxwell would be cowering.

The blast echoed through the street and some of the rioters shouted in panic. Others began tumbling out of the store, trying to get away, many still laden with loot, unwilling even at that stage to let it go.

Montrose ordered his units in, and they went, truncheons flailing, pulling people at random from the crowd, grabbing handfuls of hair, twisting and tearing, punching faces, beating chests and stomachs and hauling away cowering bodies.

Bricks began hurtling across the street towards the policemen, crashing onto the pavement or the walls opposite and splitting into pieces. One caught a constable squarely in the middle of his forehead and glanced off as he crumpled. The police retreated, riot shields up, warding off the missiles.

Montrose picked up a megaphone and shouted into it: "SURRENDER OR WE SHOOT! SURRENDER OR WE SHOOT!"

Bricks and stones curved through the air and crashed short in front of him.

Montrose turned to his units: "Remember what I told you, you men," he ordered. "In your own time – fire!"

The first salvoes made a deafening sound, reverberating between buildings, drowning the sounds of screaming.

The rioters began to pour back into Maxwell's to get away, not realising that the bullets were being aimed high. One man was hit by shrapnel as a window pane on the first floor shattered and sent splinters of glass flashing down into his face. As blood filled his eyes, he hunched motionless and uncomprehending, too terrified to move, unable to see where to go. Nobody helped him.

Those back inside Maxwell's began to dump their loot, flinging it behind counters, into corners, as they searched for a way of escape. In the earlier panic, no one had thought about the emergency exits, but now they were found and rioters fled through them, down the service lane to safety.

The crowd thinned quickly, vanishing back into the store and not reappearing. The police advanced again, but the riot was over. Nearly one hundred people had been arrested, one was dead, a dozen had been hurt, and the ground floor of Maxwell's was a wreck.

Montrose looked about him with satisfaction as he made his way to the administration floor, flanked by a team of men.

He found it hard not to laugh when he saw the anxious faces staring at him through the glass partition windows of the fragile offices into which the staff and some customers had uselessly locked themselves. Christ, Montrose thought, a five-year-old kid with a hammer could have smashed that lot up in a minute.

"All clear," Montrose shouted, knocking on the wooden partitions. "You can come out now."

They emerged timidly, still obviously scared and shocked, but feeling faintly foolish too now that the danger had passed. Behind them, Montrose could see the tall, thin figure of Martin Maxwell staring at him. For a second, he thought Maxwell still looked defiant, and he felt a surge of irritation, but then the man's shoulders slumped.

Maxwell came slowly towards him.

"Couldn't you have stopped it, Commissioner?" he asked softly.

Montrose nodded dispassionately. "Yes."

The men stared at each other, not with hatred or hostility, but for Maxwell, with exhaustion and defeat and for Montrose with the knowledge that he had done only what his circumstances required.

Finally Montrose broke the silence. "I warned you," he said seriously. "You were the first person – the very first – I came to. I told you it was a question of priorities."

"You didn't say that you wouldn't come to my aid at all."

Montrose shrugged. "We did come to your aid, as soon as we could. Here we are, as you can see. There were other things we had to do first, that's all. You have to take your turn now."

Maxwell sighed, the long sound of an old man. "It's too late," he said. "It's all finished. It doesn't matter any more."

"Oh, I wouldn't say that," Montrose replied encouragingly, putting an arm round his shoulder. "The ground floor is a mess certainly, but the first and second floors still look okay. You've got insurance. There's other stock in your warehouse. You could be open for business again tomorrow if you move quickly."

He paused and looked shrewdly at Maxwell. "This time you were lucky," he said softly. "You could have lost everything, you know – the whole building could have gone up in flames. The lot of you sitting up here would have been roasted alive."

Montrose smiled at him so kindly as he spoke, that Maxwell knew it was a threat. He bowed his head in submission and gave the small laugh of a defeated man.

"I think we'd better go through to your office and talk," Montrose said gently. "We don't want this sort of thing to happen again, do we?"

As they passed through, the Commissioner of Police called to the receptionist: "Bring some coffee would you, please? I think Mr Maxwell needs it."

Chapter Nine

Montrose had never seen the Prime Minister in such a mood. He was standing behind his desk, obviously holding himself in check, his knuckles showing white as he grasped the back of his chair.

He stared coldly as Montrose came into the room and sat down, murmuring a greeting which was not returned. Montrose felt a spasm of alarm. The Prime Minister's face was pale and strained, and he seemed to be having difficulty sleeping. Under his eyes, the flesh was puffy, and the light chocolate of his skin was darkened there.

After a long silence, he asked suddenly: "What is the explanation, Commissioner?"

Montrose could see that round his jowls and in beads on his forehead the Prime Minister was sweating almost as badly as he was himself.

"I want to know what went wrong."

Montrose decided to brazen it out. "Nothing went wrong, Prime Minister," he said calmly. "Everything went as we expected."

Moorhouse turned away abruptly, facing the wall now, and the Commissioner could see his fists were clenched.

"It did not go the way *I* expected, Commissioner. You assured me that if I detained the people on your list, the trouble would stop. I agreed, although privately I had reservations. Now what's happened? The trouble is as bad as it ever was. Worse probably."

"In fairness, Prime Minister," Montrose said, "I did point out that those on the first list were the main culprits. There were others. I told you we might have to expand the number of arrests later if the trouble didn't subside."

"You want me to order more detentions?" Moorhouse asked, turning angrily.

Montrose shook his head and replied without rancour: "No, sir."

The Prime Minister hesitated, caught off-balance. "No?" he demanded. "Why not? Surely if we take your thesis to its logical conclusion, we need to pick up all the suspects you've named, and probably more."

"If it were necessary, yes. But I don't think it is necessary. Personally, I'm very satisfied with the way things have worked out."

Moorhouse stared at him strangely. At last he pulled out his chair and sat down.

"All right," he said, suddenly calm. "A security guard has been killed. Another dozen people are in hospital. Our police have opened fire again. We have detention without trial for the first time in St

David's history. One of the island's biggest stores has been looted, and others have been damaged. Tell me, Commissioner, why are you satisfied?"

"We're over the hump, Prime Minister," Montrose said simply. "Everything you've told me is quite right, and if you list them like that, it doesn't look good. But there's a positive side too, and we can see it if we don't panic." He leaned forward and his small eyes were earnest. "When did the CIA men leave the island? Only last night. We've got their main local operatives behind bars, so they're out of action. Who's going to plan their next violent demonstration?"

He waited for an answer.

"I give up," the Prime Minister said tetchily. "Who?"

Montrose shrugged. "No one that I know of. No one my American source can point to at the moment either. Perhaps they have someone in reserve, and we'll find out about it later, but frankly I doubt it. Our action has been comprehensive. It hit them without warning. I think their structure on this island has collapsed, and that demonstration today was the final fling. There's nothing more to come."

Moorhouse considered the matter in silence. He pulled the navy blue silk handkerchief from his jacket pocket and mopped his brow.

"I hope you're right, Commissioner," he said finally. "Frankly, if this goes on for much longer, I shall have to consider going to the country for a new mandate."

Montrose said softly: "You'd lose, Prime Minister."

Moorhouse looked startled, then affronted. "Perhaps not," he said defensively. "Not everyone is taken in by propaganda. I have great faith in the wisdom of the electorate."

Montrose stared at him coolly. "All I'm saying – no, more than that, what I'm urging – is that we keep our heads. Let's wait and see what happens. Personally, I don't think anything will happen. I'm not saying there won't be any more demonstrations, but I don't think we'll see this sort of violence again. It was an aberration and it is over."

The Prime Minister sighed and glanced at the ceiling in supplication. "Please God," he said. "But what do we do about the detainees?"

"They're safe where they are," Montrose replied. "Let's leave them there for the time being and reconsider the situation in a month's time. If everything is peaceful and they give us undertakings that they won't engage in illegal activities, perhaps you could think of freeing them."

"At the first possible moment," said Moorhouse fervently. He leaned back in his seat and looked distantly at a point behind Montrose's head. "You know, Commissioner," he confessed, "I have found these last two days very difficult. I never expected to. I'll tell you frankly, it surprised me. Ever since I asked the President to sign the detention orders on those men – particularly poor Ayer – I have been in . . ." he chose the words carefully ". . . an agony. What if we are wrong?"

Montrose did not interrupt, but let the Prime Minister unburden himself, making his expression as understanding as he could, although he found this an increasing strain.

Moorhouse continued: "We have acted with the best of motives, believing our information was correct. Still, we must consider: what if it was not? What if Ayer and his family and the others are suffering unfairly – I'm not saying all of them unfairly, but let's say some of them; swept up in our understandable desire to cover every eventuality, to be a little too efficient? Do you understand what I'm getting at?"

The Commissioner nodded doubtfully. Moorhouse caught his eye and held it, until Montrose wanted to shift uncomfortably, but he forced himself to stay still and stare levelly back. He realised he was holding his breath.

"Commissioner," Moorhouse said simply, "if we have done a wrong, it is not too late to undo it. Let us be men enough to admit that we have made a mistake. Now, I accept completely your own good faith. You have received information from a highly placed and trusted source within the Embassy of the United States. He disclosed to you the names of CIA agents who were fomenting trouble on St David's and he told you the reasons why. Now I must say I am perfectly satisfied with his information up to this point. The protest made by the Americans has been muted, to say the least. They haven't even expelled any of our diplomats in Washington in retaliation. They've said nothing about cutting off economic aid. To me, all this indicates a guilty conscience. So that part is fine. But your Embassy source went further, Commissioner. He also gave you names of locally recruited spies who were helping the CIA. These are the men – some of them – who have been detained. Would you agree with my assessment so far?"

Montrose inclined his head.

"Good. Then we come to the next point: how did your source know? I accept that he would know about the CIA agents in the Embassy, or at least be able to find out. In certain circles, it would be gossip. But the names of local agents could surely never be gossip. The overall CIA design for the island also would not be gossip. It would be a Top Secret. So how did our man know? Did he actually find out from some authoritative source? Or did he guess?"

Montrose shifted uneasily. It hadn't occurred to him. "I don't know the answer to that," he admitted.

"Exactly!" Moorhouse broke in, triumphant.

"But I must point out that we ourselves investigated every single allegation as carefully as we could in the time available."

"And there wasn't much of that! A couple of weeks, that's all."

Montrose was defensive. "The ones that stood up to my total satisfaction were on the first list. Those still under suspicion I put on the supplementary list. Investigations about them are going on."

"Not much point now, is there," Moorhouse said agreeably. "The Embassy agents have all gone. The link has been broken."

"That's true," agreed the Commissioner, and then he added quickly: "at least it's true to the point that we're unlikely to catch them red-handed at some rendezvous. But there are other areas we can look at: their financial situations, for example. Were they living beyond their means? Are there unexplained payments into their bank accounts? That sort of thing."

Moorhouse conceded the point, but pressed his attack. "And here's another thing," he said. "When I ordered the detentions, I understood your lists had simply been divided into, shall we say, the first team and the second team. Now today you tell me you weren't even sure of the names on that second list. In fact, you're still not sure. Investigations are continuing."

A flush crept up the Commissioner's neck and spread over his fat cheeks. "I was working on information provided by my source," Montrose replied, a slightly hard edge to his voice. "He told me which were the important local agents and which were not. Naturally our investigations started at the top."

The Prime Minister considered this, and Montrose could hear faintly that he was making a "Hmmmmm" sound.

"Very well, Commissioner," he said finally. "However, I'm still not convinced we haven't unwittingly cut too many corners. I want you to order a new investigation on all the detainees and let me know the results as soon as you can. And I want you to go back to your American source and ask him to recheck his information. But for God's sake don't make him feel that he's got to stand up his information at all costs. I would be happier if he came back and said sorry, I was wrong about these two people, or however many It is. There'll be no recriminations. He won't lose face, and he won't be out of pocket. What are we paying him, by the way?"

Montrose was taken by surprise and his mouth opened to say "Nothing", but instead he replied quickly: "Rather a lot, I'm afraid," and he felt his hostility to the Prime Minister begin to evaporate.

"How much?"

"Ten thousand dollars." The Commissioner's eyes were watchful.

Moorhouse whistled. "That is a lot. Out of your budget?"

Montrose shook his head slowly. "There's no provision in my budget for special payments like this," he said. "I was going to take it up with you at an appropriate moment. Perhaps it could come out of your special contingencies fund. Of course, it will have to be paid in cash and there won't be any receipt for obvious reasons, but it will be quite safe. I'll handle it myself."

The Prime Minister looked thoughtful. "What does an American diplomat want with ten thousand extra dollars on St David's? Why

58

doesn't he ask us to pay it into an overseas bank account? We could do that easily enough."

Montrose's cheeks began to burn again. "That's what he asked for," he said gruffly. "I didn't question him. Anyway, it saves us foreign exchange."

The Prime Minister nodded. "Still, it's very curious," he remarked. "No doubt he has his reasons. When are you seeing him next?"

"I'll try to get to him today," Montrose said.

"Fine. When you do, don't forget to ask him to recheck. Ten thousand dollars is a lot of money. We want to be sure his information is completely right. But please assure him that he won't suffer financially if he finds he has made a mistake. Whatever happens, he'll be paid."

"Perhaps," Montrose suggested, "we ought to give it to him immediately to prove our bonafides."

The Prime Minister looked doubtful. "It will take a day or two to organise anyway," he said. "What about giving him half then, and the rest when he comes back with the answers?"

The Commissioner couldn't stop himself smiling slightly. "I'm sure that will be all right," he said. "I'll tell him this evening." He rose to go. "Although it does seem a large amount, Prime Minister," he added pompously, "it isn't really if you consider that it's saved democracy on St David's. It's a bargain price."

Moorhouse looked at him directly. "No doubt you're right," he remarked. "I just thought somehow that spies were paid rather poorly. I don't know how I got that impression."

"Not at this level," the Commissioner said earnestly. "This is the big league."

Chapter Ten

Clive Lyle lit a cigarette and sat on the sea wall in the semi-darkness. The air was hot and damp against his face. Palm trees and a bougainvillea creeper growing thick over an archway blocked out much of the sky. On the other side were the rocks, battered and eroded by the waves, and beyond them a few feet of coarse sand. The tide was coming in and the constant crashing of the water was loud. There was a faint smell of decay.

On the horizon, the sun was setting, falling fast, a huge scarlet ball, still too bright to look into, its shafts of light brilliantly hitting the edges of clouds and fading into a musky rose glow. Beams, as if from powerful spotlights, illuminated a section of the sea near the horizon, turning it silver. Most of the sky was a delicate blue.

The lower edge of the sun touched the horizon, sending out an orange pathway of light across the sea, and in a few seconds it had dropped out of sight. Even with it gone, the sky glowed and changed for twenty minutes before fading into blackness.

Lyle felt he ought to applaud. He lit another cigarette and looked at his watch. Six-fifty. No sign of Montrose, but it was early yet.

Lyle was waiting three miles out of town on the Coast Road towards Albany. The Port Lombard authorities had built up this area as a picnic spot, and during the weekends a small restaurant sold ice-creams and pies. On weekdays it was closed, and hardly anyone came near. But late almost every night, couples would park their cars in the darkness under the palms. In the morning, there would usually be empty beer bottles lying around, and a few condoms, their ends knotted. The rubber dried in the sun and every Friday, before the families came out for weekend treats, sweepers would go around getting rid of the evidence. Port Lombard was good that way.

But now it was deserted.

From his position on the wall, his back against a concrete post, Lyle could get a clear view of the road and nearly 180 degrees around.

The lights of a car flashed briefly as it curved along the path through the palms, and he watched it approach. It was too dark to recognise the silhouette, but he was sure it was Montrose's Rover. He took a draw at his cigarette and waited. The car stopped a hundred yards from where his own was parked, off the road, and a door slammed.

He saw the bulky figure of the Commissioner walking confidently over to the wall, their usual meeting place, and he shielded the flame of his cigarette with his hand so Montrose would not be able to see it.

Lyle watched quietly. In the humid darkness of the evening, under the palms and the bougainvillea, he could not easily be spotted. Montrose's step faltered. Lyle saw him stop and scan the darkness.

"You there, Lyle?" His voice was low and cautious.

"Hi," he said. He sucked at his cigarette and Montrose headed for the glow.

"Jesus," Montrose complained. "What are you doing sitting in the dark like this? Why not somewhere I can see you, for Christ's sake?"

"Your eyes get used to it. I've been watching the sunset. Very nice."

Montrose fumbled for the edge of the wall and sat down, not too close. You didn't want to sit too near a fairy. You never knew when he'd make a pass. Montrose lit a cigarette. He was adjusting to the gloom, and he could make out the American clearly now, although he could not see his face.

"How did it go?" Lyle asked.

Montrose shrugged. "It went fine. You must have heard."

"No," said Lyle. "I've been busy."

"We had a riot, that's what happened. One man got killed. Maxwell's got smashed up and looted. That's it."

There was a silence while Lyle considered this. Finally he said softly: "Good for you."

Montrose grinned at him suddenly in the darkness. "Where did you learn that stuff?" he asked. "It really works."

"I picked it up," Lyle replied offhandedly. "I've been around a bit. I had a good friend who used to organise it in South America. We shared an apartment for a couple of months. He showed me how it was done."

"Jesus," said the Commissioner rudely. "Not another fairy."

Lyle drew at his cigarette and said nothing. They listened to the waves crashing onto the beach and the rocks.

For an instant Montrose considered apologising, but then thought: shit, that's what he is. So instead he said: "Moorhouse was asking about you today. That's why I called you here."

Still no reply.

"He wanted to know how you could have found out the names of the local agents."

"What did you tell him?" Lyle's voice was calm and even.

"I said I didn't know. He thinks you made them up. He wants you to go back and check."

"The ones that were made up were made up by you," Lyle said softly.

In the darkness, he could see Montrose shrug dismissively.

Montrose sat in a comfortable silence, not feeling the need to explain his actions. After all, he was the master and Lyle the servant. One word out of place and a copy of the police file would be sent around to the Embassy, detailing the American's recent activities on the island. He'd bet they didn't have that sort of personal information on their files. Lyle would never have got his job if he had, and he'd be sacked once they knew. Worse for him, they'd put him in gaol for the rest of his life if they ever found out what sort of information he'd been passing on. Lyle might be queer, but he wasn't a fool.

"The point is," the Commissioner pressed on, "how did you know who the agents were? That sort of stuff's top secret."

"Yes it is," Lyle agreed. "I borrowed a set of keys and looked at the files."

"Christ. Whose keys?"

"Berenson's. He was in charge."

"How did you get them?" Montrose was curious.

"I took them out of his pants pocket." There was a long silence while Montrose watched him speculatively. "Now I suppose you want to know where his pants were at the time?" Lyle asked calmly. "Well they were hanging over a chair in my room." There was another pause. "Do you want to know how they came to be hanging over a chair in my room? Or what he was doing without them?"

Montrose gave a scornful laugh. "Jesus, don't tell me. What sort of fucking Embassy are you people running anyway?"

"At the moment, a pretty empty fucking Embassy."

Montrose laughed again, genuinely this time. Sometimes he almost liked Lyle. Then he said: "I thought Berenson was married."

"He is. We were in my apartment."

Lyle could see Montrose shaking his head in disbelief. He stubbed out his cigarette on the side of the sea wall and lit another.

"What else did Moorhouse want to know?" Lyle asked.

"He wanted you to double check the names."

"I can't do that," Lyle said. "The files have been destroyed. Shredded."

"Oh shit."

"But there's no doubt about it," the American added. "I copied them out myself, the twenty I gave you. The other names are yours."

"Well for Christ's sake, at least pretend to double check them. Moorhouse has this bee in his bonnet that he's been unfair, particularly to that bastard Ayer."

Lyle asked: "What did you tell him about me?"

"Not a lot. He knows your name and position at the Embassy. I wrote them down on a piece of paper to show him, then I burnt it, just as you said. We don't talk about you by name. Does that make you happy?"

"Yes. What else does he know?"

"Nothing."

"Why does he think I'm doing this? Did you tell him I'm being blackmailed?" There was no hint of recrimination in Lyle's voice. He was merely stating a fact.

"No," said Montrose shortly. "He thinks you're a freedom-loving democrat. How the hell do I know what he thinks?"

"Didn't he ask?"

"Moorhouse has other things on his mind."

Lyle let the matter drop. After a pause he said: "Listen, you can't call me again like that – not at the Embassy."

"I can do anything I fucking well like, laddie, and don't forget it," Montrose replied sharply.

"No." It was a simple statement, made without fear. Lyle held up his hand before the Commissioner could threaten and bluster. The American said: "Look, it's insecure. Anyone could be listening in, particularly now. We've got a couple of new guys coming over from Washington, and they'll be trying to find the leak. They haven't got many people left to investigate and I'm one of them. So it just isn't bright to have the Commissioner of Police call my office."

"Well how the hell do I get you if I want you?" Montrose asked impatiently.

"Write me a letter," Lyle said. Montrose made a scoffing noise, but Lyle interrupted. "Not a long letter, and don't sign it. Just write the time and the date you want a meeting on a piece of paper and leave it in my post box." He reached into his pocket and pulled out a small key. "You know the private boxes around the side of the Stanley Road Post Office? This opens number 122. It's mine. I rented it today."

Montrose took the key and looked doubtfully at it.

"You can pick up messages from me there as well," Lyle said. "You start work at 8.30 – right?" Montrose nodded. "Well on your way in every morning, drop by the box. If there's anything in it, anything at all, it'll be for you. If you want to leave something for me, then I'll check the box at about 9.45. I don't have to be in the office until ten. How does that sound?"

Montrose shrugged. "It sounds all right," he said, "as long as you do check it every morning. If you don't turn up for a meeting, then watch out. I'll phone you at your office. I might even come around in person for a chat. Tough shit for your security check."

Lyle heard the threat without comment, and watched Montrose pocket the key. Finally he got up and dusted the back of his trousers.

"Good night, Commissioner," he said. "I have another appointment now if you don't mind."

"I'll bet you do," Montrose said, his lips curling in a half-smile.

The Commissioner watched the American stroll into the darkness, and shook his head in wonderment. You wouldn't suspect it, looking at him, he thought, but that was why he'd got so far. And he was cool all right, although the Commissioner had seen the mask slip just once.

Right at the beginning, at their first meeting when Lyle had been claiming diplomatic immunity and protesting against his arrest in a raid on a gay bar – hell, the only queers' bar on the island as far as Montrose knew. Then the American had been close to panic. It was in his voice. He had asked if there was any way the incident could be kept quiet, from everyone and not just from diplomatic circles. The note of pleading was right there.

Montrose loved it. If it cost money, Lyle had said, he would pay. Montrose listened to the diplomat trying to bribe the Commissioner of Police and smiled thinly at the crime being compounded.

But there was little danger of exposure, although Lyle couldn't have known that. Montrose was jumps ahead of him. He had been trying for a line into the American Embassy for weeks, and now that he had one, he would not surrender it easily.

First he got a tip that a US diplomat was spending time in that bar. Then it was just a matter of keeping watch and ordering a raid at the right moment. The fish was on the hook. It would cost Lyle all right, but not cash. Montrose had other plans.

The Prime Minister had always been uneasy about the Americans, and had become paranoid about the unrest on the island. The two had to be brought together. And once they were, they could be used to make money.

Montrose had given the matter hours of thought and had discussed it with Clifton and Luther. They were not much help at first, although

Luther later came up with some pretty good and imaginative ideas. Funny what locals could do if they put their minds to it, and thought there'd be a big pay-off at the end.

Everything fell into place once Lyle had been hooked – easier than the Commissioner had dreamed possible. At first, Montrose hinted that a full dossier of his activities had been kept, including photographs the State Department would be revolted to see. Of course it was the Commissioner's duty to turn the whole serious case over to the Ambassador.

Lyle looked a beaten man.

However, Montrose remarked doubtfully, after letting the message sink in, there might be another way . . . and he knew without even looking across his desk that he had the American's full attention.

Montrose didn't ask for much. He wanted a couple of low-classification internal memos on local staff postings, just to get the ball rolling. Lyle gave him these within hours at their first meeting next to the picnic ground.

He and Lyle had sat on the sea wall, at just about the exact spot Montrose was now smoking a cigarette and watching the American's car pull away. They spent an hour talking about the Embassy, about who was who, and about the CIA men there. Then Montrose laid one card on the table. He wanted a list of the spooks, he said – a full list.

Lyle was doubtful at first: scared. But after two days, they met again and he produced it. A typewritten sheet with twenty-four names.

It was time for Montrose to lay down his second card. He had information, he said, that the CIA was behind the trouble on St David's and was using locally recruited agents. He wanted the names of these other agents.

The Commissioner had expected Lyle to protest, to raise some objection about the risk involved, but none came. The American just nodded slightly, showing no surprise, only acceptance.

It was a week before that second list was delivered. Montrose hadn't questioned Lyle on how he'd got the information: frankly, it hadn't mattered then. It gave him the names of those on whom immediate checks could be run to bulk out their files, and then, with some personal additions, these could be presented to Moorhouse as candidates for detention. Most would stand up to inspection, and any doubtfuls would be carried along by the authority the others conferred

It was then that Montrose had casually mentioned the anti-Moorhouse demonstrations taking place, and the conversation moved naturally to the general subject of violence and crowd control. Lyle seemed perfectly relaxed. He began talking about how easy it was to foment a riot and gave examples.

Montrose listened with surprise, then with attention. His own plans were not nearly as well laid as these. In fact, the minor incidents which had already taken place showed up for what they were: small-scale stuff, clumsily executed. The principles of disruption, enunciated by Lyle, represented a new world. At Montrose's insistence, they went to Lyle's car and the American drew diagrams to illustrate what he meant. When they parted, Montrose took these with him.

But he still had his doubts. It was an interesting theory, all right, but would it work?

That night, Montrose went over their conversation and decided to try the technique with his men. The demonstration he chose coincided with the expulsion of the CIA and it turned out to be a cracker. Three dead, a fair bit of damage, Moorhouse in a panic. Then there was the riot at Maxwells, and the whole trap was sprung, courtesy of a fairy at the United States Embassy.

Even now, sitting alone on the sea wall, when he thought about it, Montrose couldn't help smiling.

It was a funny world.

Chapter Eleven

The mosquitoes whined persistently around Ayer's face but he kept his eyes closed and tried to ignore them. Beneath him, he could feel the scratchy fibres of the blanket, pricking even through the thick loomed cotton of his prison shirt and irritating the exposed skin on his neck. He lay on his back, willing his body to relax, to accept without resistance the discomforts of the gloomy cell.

Two mosquitoes made low passes, one over his forehead, the other lightly brushing his cheek, and a muscle in his face jumped spasmodically. He thought: I must relax.

He flexed his toes and moved his feet, and concentrated on those, willing the tension out of them; then his calves, thighs and fingers.

His hair was damp with sweat and so were his clothes.

He felt the muscles of his forearms become heavy. His back began to itch with perspiration and the scratchiness of the blanket, but he tried to blot all that from his mind.

The mosquitoes went suddenly silent, watching from the white-painted concrete ceiling, or from the sill of the steel barred window. Ayer wondered if he should open his eyes, seek them out and try to crush them. But he told himself: relax, they're only mosquitoes and there's plenty of time to get them.

In the distance, a mosquito began to whine again, and another, then a third. Ayer listened to them, seeming a long way off, but he knew they could not be more than a matter of six or seven feet away in his claustrophobic cell.

He refused to look.

The high-pitched whine was at his ear and it cut off suddenly as a mosquito landed on the lobe to feed. Ayer could feel the itch begin around its bite. His body stayed motionless.

The second mosquito was close now, just above his forehead, with the third around his cheek. They landed lightly and fell silent.

In the distance, he could hear a fourth, and a fifth, and the areas where his blood was being sucked began to torment him. He was aware of more high whines around his ears. In the background came the sound of still others, and his neck began to itch unbearably again. Ayer fought to keep his body relaxed but a trickle of sweat coursed from his forehead slowly past his eyelid before sliding languidly down his cheek, tickling his skin until his muscles began to tense, while the prison blanket stuck small needles through his sweaty shirt, and suddenly Ayer could stand it no longer and his hands lashed out, hitting at his face where he felt the mosquitoes, trying to smash them to pulp as they fed, while his body writhed, released at last, rubbing and scratching itself hard against the blanket.

The mosquitoes whined angrily around the cell, out of reach of his flailing hands and the fingernails which clawed his face and neck, leaving red welts.

Ayer was raving, shouting and clawing at himself until he saw the blood on his hands, too much to come from dead mosquitoes, and the sight quietened him. He rubbed his face gingerly with his hands, feeling the stinging as he touched the wounds. He was panting and his heart pounded.

He ripped the blanket off the bed and hurled it into the corner of the cell. He lay exhausted on the lumpy mattress, stuffed with horsehair, pressing his face against the filthy cotton covering while a wave of desperation engulfed him.

Boots echoed loud on the concrete corridor.

Ayer lay motionless as they came closer. Whose cell would they stop at? His? Someone else's?

The key turned in the heavy steel door of his cell and the lock opened with a crash. Ayer sat bolt upright, staring at the burly figures silhouetted against the light.

"YOU FUCKING BASTARD! STAND UP WHEN WE COME IN!"

Ayer got to his feet, trying not to scramble, but failing. His lower lip trembled and he knew there was panic in his eyes. He brushed ineffectually at the blood with his hand, smearing it over his cheeks.

The scream again: "OUT ONTO THE LANDING, CUNT! MOVE!"

Ayer hurried towards the light of the corridor. Globes burned bright behind wire grills. There was no way of knowing if it was day or night. Even from his cell window, he could see not a corner of sky, just a high grey wall opposite, and the light which filtered through was the same, day and night. He measured time according to the meals pushed through his door. Ayer calculated he had been in prison for three days, and it was somewhere between lunch and dinner.

Lunch had been a disgusting, muddy-tasting fish of a sort Ayer had not known even existed, so it was probably Friday. And it must be about five o'clock in the afternoon.

His brain was working, clear and acute, sharpened by fear.

The air in the corridor seemed wonderful: cool and clean. Ayer had not realised how fetid his cell had become. He had not been allowed out since his arrival from the prison hospital. Even his bucket lavatory had not been emptied.

"MOVE YOU FUCKER!"

Everything the guard said was in a parade-ground shout, heavy with loathing: a scream almost. Ayer felt himself becoming increasingly unnerved. He walked quickly along the corridor, the two guards behind, their boots crunching on the concrete, seeming to chase him, faster and faster, past lines of identical steel cell doors with spy-holes.

Were there other prisoners in there, or were they empty? Apart from the noise of the boots and his own shuffling steps, there was silence.

Ayer wondered what was going to happen to him, and his mind raced through the possibilities. Perhaps he was going to be interrogated, or tortured. What would they want to know? What could he say to satisfy them?

At the end of the corridor, he hesitated, uncertain whether to go left or right. A cane came down sharply on his arm.

"LEFT YOU SHIT-HEAD!"

A few paces ahead there were steel bars, floor to ceiling. Ayer halted nervously.

The lead guard smacked his cane against the steel and roared: "GATE!"

Another warder, unconcerned by the noise and the shouting, strolled casually towards the bars, searching through a bunch of keys. A door inset swung open, at least eighteen inches from the ground and so narrow that only one man at a time could use it. Ayer squeezed through and waited for his guards to follow.

They were in an administrative block. Leading off the corridor were office doors, wooden, without spy-holes. Further along, a sign said "Superintendent".

Ayer began walking without being told and, as he passed the Superintendent's office, the guard yelled: "WHERE DO YOU THINK YOU'RE GOING?"

He wasn't swearing any more. Ayer concluded they had reached their destination.

"Stand outside the door," the guard ordered. Ayer did so, and the man knocked smartly, three times.

"Yes," a voice said.

The guard opened the door. "Prisoner Ayer, sir!"

"Thank you."

The guard hissed: "Get in there, you bastard, and fucking well behave yourself."

Ayer walked in, licking his lips nervously. The Superintendent was a white man, about forty, almost bald but with a thick bush of black hairs thrusting from the top of his open-neck khaki shirt. He was strongly built and obviously in good condition. Ayer recognised him: Simon Norwood, one of the Brits who had not only kept their jobs after Independence, but had been promoted as part of Moorhouse's policy to operate only on merit. Ayer had seen Norwood at one official reception, mixing easily with the other guests, but he found it hard to reconcile that personality with the man who sat staring neutrally at his filthy, blood-smeared face.

A chair was positioned across the desk from the Superintendent, but Ayer was not invited to sit in it.

He waited uncomfortably, meeting Norwood's eye once and then glancing away around the room, to the air conditioner humming in a corner by a small potted plant, and then to the clock on the side wall, which incredibly gave the time as 1.15 pm. Out of the barred window, Ayer could see a green lawn and coconut palms, and he knew from the shadows that the clock was not wrong. He looked back at the Superintendent, and this time met his gaze.

Norwood's voice was quiet and without emphasis.

"What happened to your face?"

"I scratched myself."

"SCRATCHED MYSELF, SIR!" the guard roared suddenly behind him.

"I scratched myself, sir."

Norwood considered this statement in silence, for a moment.

"Why?"

"Mosquitoes. I mean," Ayer amended hurriedly, "mosquitoes, sir. There are a lot in the cell," he concluded lamely.

"Don't do it again," Norwood said calmly. "It will look bad if ever you get a visitor."

Ayer felt his heart sink. What did he mean, if ever he got a visitor? Surely his wife would be allowed to see him? But he said: "Yes, sir."

"And another thing: even though you're a detainee and not a convict, it makes no difference to us. You're subject to prison regulations just like everyone else. Do you understand?"

"Yes, sir."

"If I see you scratch yourself like that again, I'll have to assume you've attempted to commit suicide. Suicide is against the prison regulations, and you will be punished severely for it. Understand?" There was no hint of humour in Norwood's quiet, measured voice.

"Yes. Yes, sir."

"Now, a word of advice. I don't know how long you're going to be

68

here. No one knows. It could be years. So just take each day as it comes and try not to get excited. If you get upset, you'll behave badly. If you behave badly, you'll be punished. You can't win. So do yourself a favour and keep calm. That's all."

Ayer looked at him nervously. "What about the mosquitoes, sir?"

"What about them?"

"They're all over my cell. I can't sleep. I'm not allowed out, not even to empty the lavatory bucket. I don't see anyone, or talk to anyone."

Norwood regarded Ayer for several seconds, neutrally, without compassion. Then he said, "Mosquitoes are endemic on this island. I sometimes think they all come from this prison." For the first time, he smiled thinly. "I'll see if we can get some spray, but I don't hold out much hope. Is there any spray, Mr Marshall?"

Behind Ayer, the one guard said: "No, sir."

Norwood shrugged. "There you are," he said. "As for getting you company, there's nothing I can do about that either. You're a detainee, so you're not allowed to associate with anyone." He looked beyond Ayer at the guard again. "Oh, Mr Marshall, let the prisoner slop out tomorrow morning."

"Yes, sir!"

"That's all."

"PRISONER! A-BOUT TURN!" The guard yelled the command, and Ayer instinctively followed instructions. "NOW GET OUT OF HERE," he shouted. "MOVE!"

They hurried along the concrete corridors, through the barred gate into the cell block.

The stench of Ayer's cell hit him as soon as he stepped into the gloom, and at once his stomach began to heave.

From the corridor, the guard said: "You won't worry about mosquitoes once you've seen the size of the lice and the bed bugs."

He grinned at Ayer, and then the cell door crashed shut. The lock turned and the boots of the guards, Marshall and his silent friend, echoed hollowly as they left.

Ayer lay on his bed, fighting to control his nausea. When he thought he had, he closed his eyes and tried again to relax.

From the corners of his cell, the mosquitoes whined into the air again in search of food.

Chapter Twelve

A ripple of laughter and applause greeted the club secretary as he handed out the ritual "fines" to members at the weekly lunch – money which would go to charity.

"To our honoured guest, for accepting the invitation to address us today," the secretary declared, "there will be no fine."

A mock groan went through the audience.

"But for refusing our invitation six months ago," the secretary declared triumphantly, "I fine him fifty cents."

He waited for the burst of approval to die away, one thumb in the belt of his trousers, the other hand holding a list of club "miscreants".

"To our chairman, for laughing at that joke, a fine of one pound!"

Loud cheers.

"And from everyone who's just enjoyed his misfortune, fifty cents each!"

Loud groans.

The waiters passed silently, balancing trays of drinks. Tilak Kataria summoned one by clicking his fingers and placed an order in a low voice. The club secretary spotted him from the top table.

"And to my old friend Tilak Kataria over there in the corner, for ordering drinks instead of listening to me with respectful attention, twenty cents!"

It wasn't much. Kataria smiled and shrugged, but the secretary wasn't finished yet.

"And, because I have to maintain the moral tone of the club: for having external affairs, Mr Kataria is fined another pound!"

It was a bad joke and Kataria made a wry face. The secretary was almost at the end. Two other fines, the last and biggest against himself, and he sat down to applause.

The waiter returned with their drinks. Kataria raised his glass to the two other men at the table.

"Good luck," he said.

One of his companions smiled sadly. "I think we all need that," Martin Maxwell said, and, on his left, Steven Khanna nodded his bald head in agreement.

The buzz of conversation rose around them. There were a few minutes to go before the speech would begin – enough time to let everyone refill their glasses. The Imperial Hotel ballroom was packed: a much bigger turnout than usual, and the ceiling fans, whirling slowly, lost the battle to keep down the temperature.

At the top table, in the place of honour, waiting to begin his speech, sat the Commissioner of Police, looking bland and benign, beads of sweat glistening on his face.

Kataria turned to Maxwell: "I haven't been in to your store since the attack," he said. "I hope everything's back to normal."

"More or less. As normal as anything can be in St David's these days."

Kataria was surprised at Maxwell's defeated tone. Even when others were complaining, he was usually an optimist. "I suppose business is pretty terrible," he said sympathetically.

"Oh, I'm one of the lucky ones in that respect," Maxwell admitted. "There's been the recession for more than a year now, of course, but you know, it hasn't really affected us so badly. We cater for a different market. People still want luxuries, and we're the only ones who provide them. From the point of view of the recession, men like Mr Khanna are undoubtedly worse off."

Steven Khanna placed a thin, slightly damp hand on Kataria's arm. "For us it's really terrible," he said. "Our trade has always been with the ordinary people, the workers, and they've never had much money. Now they're having to cut down even on necessities. I tell you, Tilak, it's meant our turnover dropping by almost a quarter."

Kataria grinned: "So it's going to take you an extra year to become a millionaire?"

Khanna smiled wanly. "It's no joke," he said. "A lot of my old customers have started living on credit. I let them do it. What's the alternative? I don't know if I'll ever be paid, but I can't let kids I've known since they were this high go without food, can I? But even so, unless things get better soon, I just won't be able to afford to keep going myself."

Kataria was surprised. "I can't understand why it's that bad," he said. "You've got the biggest of the general provisions stores in town. Well, maybe not *the* biggest, but one of the top five."

"Ah yes, but for us the recession's been on for nearly three years – ever since the first crop failure. It's my customers who get hit first, and hit hardest I may say. And my overheads are going up all the time. Particularly recently." Khanna shot an instinctive look of venom at the top table, where Montrose was deep in conversation with the club president.

Maxwell interpreted the gesture at once. "You too?" he said simply.

The two men stared at one another with sudden empathy.

"Me too," Khanna confirmed. "I'd assumed you'd have been pulled in. I couldn't imagine that bastard passing by such a rich picking. I hate to think what it's costing you."

Kataria looked from one to the other, bewildered.

"What's all this?" he asked. "What's going on?"

Khanna was about to answer, but Maxwell raised his hand to silence him.

"It's a shopkeeper's problem," he said evasively. "To do with insurance."

"Oh, I see," said Kataria. "Your premiums must be pretty steep, Martin, particularly after the attack. But at least you were insured: that's something to be thankful for."

"Well, I wasn't insured then," Maxwell said. "But I am now."

Kataria was appalled. "Jesus," he said. "I can't believe that! A place like Maxwell's not being insured? You must have lost a fortune."

"Oh, I had ordinary insurance," Maxwell replied primly. "I hadn't realised I needed something extra as well."

Kataria was baffled. Maxwell was obviously holding something back, but he couldn't imagine what. Still, that was his business.

It was almost time for the speech. Kataria looked gloomily over at the Commissioner of Police and shook his head slightly. "I don't know why I came today. I can't stand that man."

"Who can?" said Maxwell.

"He was the bastard who put the finger on poor Steve Ayer. No one can explain why, except for this idiot story that he was spying for the Americans. Hell, I've known Steve for years. I know that's rubbish. I'd love to see what proof Montrose had dug up."

"Probably nothing," Khanna said. "Since when did Montrose need proof? He is the law."

"And he's also above it," Maxwell broke in sourly. "He does what he likes. Acts as if St David's was Chicago."

"Do you think the Prime Minister knows?" Khanna asked.

Maxwell shrugged angrily. "Who can say? Perhaps not. They're rumoured to be very close, but whatever faults Moorhouse has, corruption was not supposed to be one of them."

The word was out before Maxwell realised it.

"What do you mean, corruption?" asked Kataria immediately. "Who's corrupt? The Prime Minister or the Commissioner of Police?"

"Sssssh," Maxwell said, nervously glancing across at the tables nearest them in case anyone was listening. He looked suddenly harassed. "We can't say anything. Please understand. It will just make matters worse."

"Oh come on," Kataria persisted, his tone bantering. "You can't just drop a juicy hint like that and leave it. What's been going on?"

Maxwell's distress showed clearly. He mopped his forehead with a large white linen handkerchief, shaking his head and mumbling: "No, no please, don't ask me. I can't say anything."

Kataria felt he detected a hint of real fear. He looked at Khanna, but the thin bald shopkeeper sat quietly, showing no emotion and looking fixedly at some point across the Imperial ballroom.

At the top table, the chairman rose and thumped the gavel three times for silence. Maxwell was relieved at the intervention and sat bolt upright, concentrating earnestly.

"Fellow Rotarians," the chairman said, adjusting the microphone's

72

position as he spoke, "we are honoured today to have as our guest and principal speaker, the Commissioner of Police, Mr Claud Montrose, OBE. As we all know, OBE stands for 'Other Bugger's Efforts' [laughter], or at least it usually does. But Claud Montrose has a reputation for doing things himself. Where the action is, there you'll find the Commissioner of Police."

At his table, despite his nervousness, Martin Maxwell snorted derisively.

"A policeman's lot is a pretty thankless one," the chairman continued, "particularly in difficult times such as St David's is now passing through. Too often the ordinary people don't really understand the policeman's view of things. But today, we have a chance to hear their side of the story, and so it is with great pleasure that I call upon Claud Montrose to address us now."

As the applause briefly swept the room, and the smoke from cigarettes and cigars curled lazily upwards towards the fans on the high ceiling, Montrose got to his feet, his face shiny with perspiration, and began to talk.

His first words were inaudible, and immediately from the back of the hall came shouts of "Can't hear you!"

Montrose grappled with the microphone, helped by the chairman, who half-rose in his chair to push it across the tablecloth, and his cheeks flushed pink.

"Is that better?" he asked, his voice booming through the speakers, and someone shouted back: "Now it's too loud!" There was laughter again, and the Commissioner's flush deepened. Kataria felt himself beginning to enjoy Montrose's discomfort.

But the Commissioner rallied. "As you can see," he said gruffly, "when I do things myself, they tend to go wrong. Perhaps I should listen to my subordinates and delegate more."

There was laughter and applause. Montrose had won most of the audience onto his side. He mopped his face with relief.

"The subject of my talk today," he said, "was going to be The Citizen and the Law. But I think I'll change it and risk another fine." He smiled slyly at his companions on the top table. "What about The Citizen and the Lawless? Because that, too often, is what it's about. I suppose most people feel we're over-governed."

Montrose launched into some anecdotes about petty clerks and big businessmen whose fiddles had been uncovered, usually by himself, and he spoke about the growth of computer frauds in the world.

"From that point of view," he said, "we in St David's are lucky to be out of the mainstream, otherwise rather more of our annual budget would have to be spent on law enforcement than is now the case.

"But we have our own particular problems, too, as you gentlemen in business and the professions know as well as anyone. We have the state of emergency. Everyone regrets this: the Prime Minister, the Honourable Daniel Moorhouse, regrets it bitterly, and so do I. We want it lifted as soon as humanly possible.

"But when will that be? No one can say. It depends on so many imponderables. It depends on the security forces receiving the wholehearted co-operation of the civilian population. It depends on stamping hard on the anti-social elements who are threatening our way of life and even our democracy. It depends on stopping these riots which have scarred our capital city, although I'm glad to say that on that score, the danger is receding."

Montrose caught sight of Maxwell and Khanna sitting in the corner and added: "It hasn't gone completely, however, and perhaps it never will. We must all take extra care. There is an additional price we have to pay these days for our security."

He glanced elsewhere in the room. There were more of his clients.

"But I say to you gentlemen" – he addressed them directly – "it is a price well worth paying."

He saw their faces expressionless, and he grinned inwardly. "The alternative is chaos," he told them. "Ruin. Anarchy. More people dying. No one wants that. But if we pay the price, if we do as we're told . . ." he paused, looked around and continued forcefully ". . . if we obey the law, then we will *all* prosper. St David's will continue to give us all the peace and the quality of life which we have taken for granted until now. Thank you very much."

A wave of applause swept the room. Kataria joined out of politeness, but noticed that neither Maxwell nor Khanna were clapping. Two tables away, another man sat stonily, and he recognised him as Samuel Laksha, who ran a big grocery chain on the island. The Commissioner didn't seem too popular with shopkeepers, Kataria thought.

Then his eye was caught by a group of four, sitting nearer the centre of the room. The tall man was ostentatiously not applauding, but smoking and looking angry. The others were bringing their hands together in such a slow and deliberate way that it looked not even minimally polite, but actually antagonistic.

In the general noise of approval, these isolated pockets of rebellion went unnoticed, except to Kataria. He tried to identify the men at the centre table, but they meant nothing to him.

As the applause ended, Kataria leant over to Khanna and said urgently: "You see those four at the table just underneath the chandelier . . . there, they're just standing up, tall bloke in a light brown shirt just shaking hands now . . ."

"Oh yes, that's Brian Philips," Khanna said, staring across, and rising to get a better view as those around scraped back their chairs and prepared to leave. "He's with Luke Davies and, if I'm not mistaken, the man half-hidden behind him is David Joshi. Do you want an introduction?"

"Not especially. I just wondered what they did."

"Same as me. They own general stores. Brian Philips is probably the number one man on St David's. He's got branches all over the island. I hate to think what his turnover is. A lot more than mine, anyway. Davies and Joshi are also pretty big."

"About the same as you?" Kataria asked.

Khanna made weighing motions with his hands. "More or less," he conceded.

"What's your interest, Tilak?" Khanna asked. "Thinking of going into competition?"

Kataria laughed. "Christ no," he said. "I just noticed they weren't very impressed with Montrose's speech. They could hardly bring themselves to applaud. Just like you two. And it was the same with Sam Laksha. Montrose certainly didn't get the shop-owners' vote."

Martin Maxwell touched Kataria's arm and said earnestly: "I must talk to you seriously. Let's all go somewhere a bit quieter. You come too, Mr Khanna."

The men joined the throng around the exit, remembering to drop their "fines" into the box at the door, and they crossed the foyer of the Imperial to the residents' lounge. It was filled with overstuffed chintz sofas and armchairs. Wine-coloured velvet drapes hung at the high windows, while sepia photographs of he early days of St David's, and old oil portraits of past governors, were mounted in ornate carved frames on the walls. The room was cool and empty. The men settled themselves in a corner near the air-conditioner.

Maxwell began, clearly nervous. "Tilak, my old friend," he said, "I want to ask you a favour."

Kataria shrugged: "I'll do what I can."

"For personal reasons which I can't go into, I'm not very fond of our Commissioner of Police."

"I can understand that," Kataria said. "You suffered pretty badly in the attack."

"That's true," Maxwell replied, grateful to have been presented with an easy avenue of escape. "I think he was simply inefficient. We could all have been killed by the time he got there. As it was, one of our security men did lose his life as you know. We're all angry about it. You know how close we shopkeepers are." He smiled briefly. "But we have to keep a sense of proportion about this, and we can't afford to let the impression get around that we're antagonistic to Montrose. There is a state of emergency, after all, and anything can happen. We just have to watch our steps and hope for the best."

"Okay. So what's the favour?" Kataria asked.

"Please don't mention anything about what happened at lunchtime today. Not to anyone. Forget what we said. I was particularly . . ." he hesitated ". . . injudicious . . . in my choice of words."

"Corruption."

Maxwell almost flinched. "Whatever I said," he added hastily, "please wipe from your mind. I was wrong. I'm still a bit overwrought. You understand?"

Kataria looked doubtful.

"Please," Maxwell said urgently. "If anything like that ever gets back to Montrose, heaven knowns what will happen. Promise me you'll keep it a secret."

His old man's hand, blotched with brownish spots, fastened round Kataria's forearm with surprising strength.

"Okay, okay," Kataria agreed finally. "Your secret's safe with me. I just wish I knew what the hell was going on."

Maxwell's relief was almost tangible. "Thank you," he said simply. "If there's anything I can do for you in return, you just have to say. Anything you want from the store, perhaps?"

Kataria laughed, embarrassed. "Forget it, Martin. It's not important."

"To me it is," he said.

Steve Khanna had sat quietly watching, and if he felt relief at Kataria's agreement, he did not show it.

They walked slowly out through the foyer into the sunlight, Maxwell talking almost compulsively about trivial matters, and parted on the pavement.

Maxwell and Khanna turned left into Jubilee Avenue, heading towards the centre and their respective businesses, while Kataria went down Kennedy Walk to fetch his car. It was 2.30 and he was due back at the Cabinet Office, but there wasn't much on his desk and no meetings were scheduled.

The curious conversation with Maxwell and the strange, hostile behaviour of the other store owners nagged at him.

Kataria crossed into Jubilee Park and headed for an empty bench, shaded by a clump of palms. The humidity wasn't too bad today, he thought, and it was fairly pleasant in the park.

Kataria could understand Maxwell's bitterness at the attack on his store. It must have been a frightening experience, and people caught in situations like that tended to be ultra-critical of the police, believing that somehow they ought to have superhuman powers of prediction and response.

But what about the others, and their behaviour? And why was Maxwell so scared? Criticism of the police was hardly an uncommon occurrence on the island, and anyway what could Montrose do if he heard someone was unhappy with his performance? Detain him?

This thought gave Kataria pause. Steve Ayer had been detained, after all. But old man Maxwell? It was too improbable.

The Commissioner had some hold over the shopkeepers: that much was obvious. Maxwell had used the word "corruption". Perhaps he was getting a rake-off somewhere.

Kataria shrugged. It was none of his business anyway.

Chapter Thirteen

Kataria acknowledged the salute of the doorman with a nod, and strolled through the carpeted foyer of the Cabinet Offices, glancing briefly at the huge, dominating portrait of the Prime Minister, flanked by an array of luxuriant potted shrubs.

The wood-panelled lift was waiting, and he took it to the first floor instead of using the stairs. As he reached his office, he could hear an electric typewriter chattering inside as his secretary transcribed his report on the state of relations with the United States after the expulsions.

"Any messages?" he asked as he walked in.

"Only one, sir," the secretary said. "Mr Rana wanted you to look in at his office."

"Hmmmm, okay. Did he say why?"

"No, sir. It sounded important, though."

"Well I'd better go and see what it is. I'll be on the third floor if anyone needs me."

Tilak Kataria retraced his steps to the lift, but grew impatient after waiting a few minutes and climbed the stairs instead.

Joe Rana's office was down from the Prime Ministerial suite, and Kataria knocked briefly.

"Come!" Rana's voice commanded.

Kataria put his head round. "My master called?" he asked innocently.

Rana grinned a welcome. "I certainly did. And called and called. You're taking pretty long lunchbreaks these days. Where the hell were you?"

"More business than pleasure, I'm afraid," Kataria said, easing himself into an armchair. "I went to listen to Montrose blowing his trumpet at Rotary."

"And?"

"I didn't actually throw up, but it was close."

"What did he say?"

"Pretty much what you'd expect. That everybody ought to obey the law and do as they're told, and then the emergency would be lifted. He couldn't say when, of course." Kataria took out a pack of filter cigarettes and offered them across the desk.

When they had lit up, he said: "So, what can I do for you?"

Rana grimaced. "I wanted you to see something." He opened a safe beside him and pulled out a beige manilla file. He held it up so Kataria could see the red diagonal stripes and the TOP SECRET stencil. "As you can see," he said, "it's the real thing. Now I ought to warn you, you've no right to look inside, so if you don't want to, now's the time to say so."

"Bloody hell," Tilak Kataria said. "Are you sure *you* ought to be doing this in the first place?"

Rana nodded. "I'm sure. It's about Steve Ayer."

"Then I want to see it."

"I thought you would." Rana took a plain-coloured cardboard folder from a desk drawer and covered the file with it. "In case anyone comes in," he explained, handing it across.

Kataria settled down to read. "Jesus, there's not very much is there?" he said, flicking his thumb through the few sheets of paper, numbered and attached inside. "Considering he's detained without trial on the strength of this."

"Just read it."

The top document was from the Superintendent of Port Lombard gaol, certifying that Stephen Vincent Ayer was lodged in his custody under an Order signed by the President in terms of the State of Emergency Regulations 1976.

Next came a copy of the detention order served on Ayer, with his signature on the bottom as having duly received it. Kataria felt a slight shock at seeing the familiar writing: it brought home the reality of what was happening to their friend. The signature was shaky, as if Ayer had been pressing the paper on his knee or on a soft surface, or as if his hand had been trembling. Kataria bit his lower lip.

The third document was a typewritten extract from the police file on Ayer: obviously the evidence on which the detention order had been based.

Kataria read it with care.

TOP SECRET
Authorised access only: G1 and above.

EXTRACTS FROM FILE INTEL/SN/414/28/CM

NAME: Stephen Vincent Ayer
DATE OF BIRTH: 2 January 1944
PLACE OF BIRTH: Port Lombard
NATIONALITY: St David's
OCCUPATION: Civil Servant: Grade 2A (PPS to Prime Minister)
FATHER: Walter Vincent Ayer, born London, England, 12 March 1902, died Port Lombard 10 November 1966.

The subject married British citizen, Nora Stephanie Cannon, in February 1966. The family resides at 34 Nelson Avenue, Port Lombard. There are three children: Ronald Vincent Ayer, *b* 8

October 1967; Charles Vincent Ayer, *b* 3 September 1969; Laura Stephanie Ayer, *b* 22 March 1972.

The subject was recruited as an operative for the Central Intelligence Agency of the United States Government shortly before taking up his position as Principal Private Secretary to the Prime Minister in January 1970. His control was Charles Holmes Arthur Berenson, listed in the Diplomatic Register as an Aid Affairs Officer. Details of recruitment unknown. Confirmation of recruitment from INFORMANT Q. (NOTE: ACCESS ON Q IS RESTRICTED TO PRIME MINISTER AND COMM. POLICE.)

Subject's duty was to keep his control informed of Prime Ministerial plans and alternatives being debated in confidential cabinet committees and meetings, with particular reference to activities of other governments accredited to Port Lombard. Later, subject provided information useful to US destabilisation campaign.

Informant Q reports that payments to subject were in cash into numbered Swiss bank account, details unknown.

Meetings between subject and his control, Berenson, were sporadic, arranged usually at subject's instigation by means of two evening telephone calls to control's residence, the first allowing the phone to ring twice before replacing the receiver, and the second, immediately afterwards, terminating the call when the telephone was answered. Rendezvous was one hour after receipt of second call, near the bandstand in Jubilee Park, Port Lombard.

Extracts from surveillance records INTEL/SN/585 et seq:
12 JANUARY 1976: Tues. Subject left 34 Nelson Avenue 2130 hours and drove to Jubilee Park, arriving 2144. Subject walked past bandstand and stood in shadows until arrival of man, identified as Charles Holmes Arthur Berenson. Subject lit cigarette as Berenson approached and contact was made. Men walked in park, keeping to dimly lit sections, for 35 mins. Subject left first at 2220 and returned to residence.

7 FEBRUARY 1976: Sun. Subject left 34 Nelson Avenue at 2200 hours, driving light grey Morris Oxford (PT 415-633). Parked vehicle in High Street and walked two blocks to Jubilee Park. Man k.a. Berenson met subject near bandstand. For first eight mins, they sat on bench in unlit area and attempt was made to approach them from behind. Words "Moorhouse" and "cabinet" heard clearly but rest indistinct. Impossible to get closer undetected. At approx 2228, subject and Berenson left bench and walked slowly through park. Meeting terminated 2236. Subject returned to residence.

26 FEBRUARY 1976: Fri. Subject left residence in Nelson Avenue at 2115, driving quickly and arriving Jubilee Park 2123. Waited

near bandstand until 2215. Observed frequently checking his watch and smoking constantly. No contact made. Returned home 2225.

27 FEBRUARY 1976: Sat. Subject drove from 34 Nelson Avenue in car registration No. PT 415-633, leaving 2014, arriving High Street 2030 approx. Walked to Jubilee Park and waited near bandstand at point where bench is situated beside beds of tall shrubs and palm trees. When on bench, subject's presence detectable only by glow of cigarette. At 2045, contact k.a. Charles Berenson arrived and after short discussion, the two men left using Berenson's car which was parked on perimeter. Unable to follow as surveillance vehicle some distance away in High Street. Waited near subject's car. Subject reappeared at 2150, walking from direction of Jubilee Park. No sign of Berenson. Subject drove home immediately, arriving 2213.

Tilak Kataria glanced up from his reading and saw Rana watching him closely.

"It looks bad, doesn't it?" Kataria said quietly.

Rana nodded. "It *looks* terrible. How far have you got?"

Kataria checked the file. "To March the fourth."

"Notice anything funny?"

Kataria shook his head. "Don't think so," he said.

"Look at the entry for February the twenty-seventh."

Kataria scanned it again quickly. It was the first report of Ayer and Berenson leaving the park and driving off together.

"It was a bit stupid of Steve to go off in an American Embassy car," Kataria observed. "Did it have a diplomatic licence plate, do you know? This doesn't say."

"I've no idea, but I don't think that matters," Rana replied, stubbing out his cigarette. "Does anything strike you about the date itself – February the twenty-seventh?"

Kataria put a hand over his eyes while he thought. Had anything happened on 27 February? At length he gave up.

"Hit me with it," he invited.

"I wish I could. The date rings some kind of a bell in my head, that's all. As soon as I read that entry, I thought to myself, hold on. I felt I knew something about it, but I couldn't remember what it was. I'd hoped it might strike a chord with you."

"Well let me think while I go through the rest of this. Perhaps something else will jog my memory."

Tilak Kataria settled back to study the file, reading slowly, weighing up every sentence to see if it had particular significance. The contacts between Ayer and Berenson became more frequent in April and May, and at one period of June – just before the state of emergency – they were meeting in Jubilee Park every second or third night.

At the end, Kataria sighed and closed the file. "Jesus," he said, "I'd never have thought it of Steve. No wonder the boss man ordered his detention."

He handed the file back across the desk, and Rana replaced it in the safe. When he had locked it, Rana said simply: "There's something about that date. I wish I knew what it was."

"February the twenty-seventh. What was happening then?"

"I've looked at the cabinet minutes for that period. Shit, I've even been through back copies of the *Herald*, that's how desperate I was. Nothing."

"You ought to have a look at Steve Ayer's office diary. But I suppose Montrose has taken that."

"Probably." He thought for a moment, then picked up the internal telephone. "But maybe not. Worth a check, anyway."

Rana dialled the number of the Prime Minister's PPS. It was answered immediately.

"Hi, Bob," Rana said cheerfully. "Joe Rana. Listen, I wonder if you can help. When you took over the hot seat, did you have to get a new diary? . . . No, not the boss man's official book, the other one. . . Oh I see, great. Look, there's something I want to check on. Would you mind if I came through and had a quick glance at it? . . . Okay, be along in a minute."

Rana put the phone down and shrugged. "Well, it's still there," he said. "Now to find it doesn't have anything in it."

"Shall I wait here?" Kataria asked.

"Probably better if you do. I don't want Bob to think there's something special going on. I'll be two minutes."

Rana pulled on his jacket in case the Prime Minister happened to see him – Moorhouse was a stickler for formality – and walked down the corridor to the PPS's office.

He looked cautiously in, but Bob Sehai was alone.

"Come in," the PPS invited. "The Prime Minister's in conclave with the British High Commissioner. They'll be a while yet. Anything special you were after?"

The red leather-bound diary was by his elbow and he made no move to pass it across.

Rana said casually: "I want to refresh my memory about a date in February. I've been through the cabinet minutes, but I can't find what I'm looking for. There's just an outside chance Steve Ayer noted it down in there."

"Help yourself." The PPS pushed the diary across his desk.

"Thanks." Rana flicked back through the pages. Ayer's neat handwriting listed events and appointments in his thin-tipped fountain pen, not only the Prime Minister's engagements to cross-check the official book, but his own as well.

February the 27th had six entries: a busy Saturday. Moorhouse was seeing the US Ambassador that morning, and he had three separate meetings scheduled with cabinet ministers. Perhaps there was some significance in those? Rana pulled out a slim notepad and began copying the entries for the day. The fifth was a reminder from Ayer to himself on redesigning official stationery, and the sixth simply said "Nora".

"Lovely," Rana said, pushing the diary back to the PPS. "I don't know if this helps me, but it's a start. Thanks very much."

"Any time."

Rana reread the list as he walked back to his office. Tilak Kataria looked up enquiringly as he came in.

"Well?" he asked.

"Nothing leaps out at me," Rana said. "Let's go through it. Ten a.m. the United States Ambassador. Would that be significant? A reason for Steve to meet Berenson?"

"Probably not. Didn't he try to organise a contact the night before anyway?"

"Yes, that's right. Berenson didn't turn up."

"Then the reason should be earlier than that. February twenty-sixth, maybe? Did you have a look at that?"

"Oh shit. No I didn't. I could go back, I suppose."

"Well, let's go through the rest and decide later. What came after the Ambassador?"

Rana consulted his notes. "Ten forty-five, Minister of Tourism. That must have been a jolly meeting. But a pretty short one by the look of it. At eleven, the boss man saw the Minister of Finance, and at eleven-thirty that fool Webster in Water and Natural Resources. Do you make anything out of that lot?"

Kataria shook his head slowly. "Not a thing," he said.

"Then it says: 'Arrange new design PM's stationery'. That's straightforward. And the last entry just says 'Nora'."

"Nora? Steve's wife?"

"I suppose so. It could be someone else, but it's not a very common name."

"No other hint?"

Rana shook his head. "Just the one word."

Tilak Kataria turned to gaze out of the window. The day was hazy and humid and there were two hours to go before he could go home. At last he said: "Give her a call and ask her."

"What do I tell her?"

"God knows. Nothing much. Just ask how Steve is and see if the date rings a bell with her."

"Okay." Joe Rana opened his address book, found the Ayer's home number and started dialling.

"For Christ's sake don't give her any hope," Kataria urged. "She's under enough strain as it is."

Rana nodded, listening to the Ayer's number ring. He put his hand over the mouthpiece and said: "What's the betting this call is being tapped?"

"All the more reason to be cautious."

The number answered, and Rana said: "Hello, Nora? It's me, Joe. How are you?"

Her voice was cool and composed. "Joe," she said. "How nice to hear from you. I'm pretty well in the circumstances."

"What about Steve?"

There was a pause. "I haven't seen Steve since he was detained three weeks ago," she said, her voice level. "They won't allow me in. I don't suppose there's anything you can do about that? Any strings you can pull?"

"Nora, that's awful," Rana said, appalled. "I'll do what I can. Can you send him anything? Food, books, that sort of thing?"

"No, nothing."

"Letters?"

"Well, I write every day, but I doubt if they're getting through to him. I certainly haven't had a letter out."

"Look, I'll try and get to see the Prime Minister. I can't believe he knows about that."

The hostility was clear in her voice suddenly. "That may be," she said coldly, "although how can one tell? He ordered the detention, didn't he? What grounds could he have had for that?"

Rana sighed. "Oh God," he said, "I just don't know. It's such a mess, isn't it? Listen, Nora, I wanted to ask you something. Does the date February the twenty-seventh mean anything to you? Is there any chance you can remember what you were doing on that day?"

There was a silence. Finally she said: "Is this an official inquiry?"

"Jesus, no," he said emphatically. "I can't go into it now, but please trust me. Tilak and I are wracking our brains to try and make sense of this mess."

"Tilak's there?"

"At my elbow."

"Give him my love. He and his wife have been so kind since Steve's detention."

Rana felt himself beginning to flush. His own family had made no attempt to contact Nora Ayer after the arrest: not as a deliberate, discussed policy. They had just instinctively stayed clear, in case there was dirt around which might rub off on them. "Fine," he said, "I'll tell him."

"As it happens, I can remember perfectly what happened on February the twenty-seventh. You ought to be able to as well, and Tilak, too, because you were both there."

"We were where?"

"At our house. It was my birthday."

Rana was exultant. "Oh Jesus, how stupid of me! Of course it was.

We had a marvellous party. Nora, thank you. That's just what we wanted to know."

"I wish I knew what it was for."

"I'll tell you as soon as we work it out. Meanwhile, why don't you and the kids come round and spend Saturday with us?"

There was another short pause. "That would be nice," Nora Ayer said, accepting the olive branch.

"Great. Come around about midday and get the kids to bring their swimming costumes. We might go down to the beach in the afternoon. Meanwhile, if I hear anything about Steve I'll let you know right away. Or Tilak will."

Rana hung up the phone, grinning.

"It was her birthday," he said. "We went to her party, don't you remember? That's why the date rang a bell."

"I'm hopeless at dates," Kataria said. "But I do remember that evening. It was good fun."

Rana fumbled with the safe combination and pulled out the dossier on Ayer. He leafed through until he came to the intelligence report for 27 February.

"Listen to this," he said. " 'Subject drove from 34 Nelson Avenue in car registration No. PT 415-633, leaving 2014, arriving High Street 2030 approx.' He fucking well did not. He was at 34 Nelson Avenue at eight o'clock, because that's when the guests started arriving, and he was there all evening. This . . ." he held up the manila file ". . . *This* piece of bullshit claims he was out of the house for two hours starting at eight-fifteen. Now we can get twenty independent witnesses to prove that was just not so."

Kataria stared at him thoughtfully. "Maybe they made a mistake over the date," he said. "Maybe it was the day before."

"But maybe it bloody well was not. This is the evidence on which Moorhouse ordered his detention, and it is wrong. At least on this one major fact, it is wrong. We haven't checked out any of the others yet. But surely this one monumental mistake taints everything else?"

Kataria was still cautious. "So long as there isn't a reasonable explanation for it," he said.

"What explanation?" Rana was beginning to get irritated.

"A transcription error. Some secretary typed the wrong date. You can bet it was put together in a hurry. That's why everyone was taken by surprise."

"Well, maybe," Rana conceded grudgingly after a pause. "I don't believe that myself, and if you think about it, I'll bet you don't really either."

"What I'm saying," Kataria said, getting up from his chair and walking across to the window, "is that we need to go carefully. We've got one fact. Or we think we've got one fact. Let's see if we can check any of the others. Let's get at least one more before we go to Moorhouse."

"How are we going to do that?"

"Ask Nora. She might remember some other dates. Have a longer look at Steve's office diary. There could be more clues in that."

It was Rana's turn to hesitate. "We're dealing with a Top Secret file," he said seriously. "I don't mind asking her about one date, but we could be in big trouble if she found out we'd got hold of Steve's dossier. I reckon she'll use any information she can lay her hands on if she thinks it will help him."

Tilak Kataria thought about that. If anything went wrong, the penalties were certainly high. They could both be gaoled for thirty years under the Official Secrets Act for possessing and distributing such information. But on the other hand, they couldn't just leave Steve Ayer sitting in gaol if there was a reasonable doubt about his guilt: in fact, more than that – if there was a possibility he had been framed. It was just the sort of thing that bastard Montrose would do, Kataria knew. If Steve had crossed him in some way, the Commissioner would have his revenge.

"Listen," he said. "Let's sleep on it overnight. We'll talk again in the morning when we've had a chance to think what we should do. My own feeling is we can't just leave it now. We have to follow it through. The question is, how do we do it?"

"Okay," Rana said. "What about lunch tomorrow at Kay's?"

"Fine. We'll draw up a battle plan then."

Kataria left the cabinet secretary's office, and Joe Rana sat motionless behind his desk, deep in thought. After several minutes, he opened Steve Ayer's file and re-read it.

At last he made a decision.

There was a photostat machine in the corner of his office. He went over and began work.

Chapter Fourteen

It poured through the night, a squall gusting the sheets sharply against windows and drumming deafeningly on the older tin-roof buildings. In the shanties on the outskirts of Port Lombard, families huddled together while their rickety wooden-frame homes, covered with coconut matting and polythene bags, leaked steadily. Dirt streets became muddy, fast-flowing streams, and water bubbled and seeped through cracks, under rough brickwork and into doorways, soaking bedding and clothes. Palm trees bent to relieve the strain from their bases, where the roots had only a tenuous hold on survival. Sheet lightning illuminated the night, but there was no thunder: just the sound of water.

By breakfast, the storm had died away, and gradually the clouds cleared.

When Joe Rana ordered his first beer on the veranda of Kay's, it was a fine day and, best of all, still cool. The humidity would rise later in the afternoon, but for the time being, it was perfect.

A hand came down heavily on his shoulder, making him jump in fright and swing round.

"Bastard," he said, seeing Kataria. "You took a year off my life."

"Why? Did you think it was Montrose coming for you?" Kataria asked cheerfully.

"For that, you pay for the lunch."

"Okay," Kataria said agreeably. He settled himself comfortably at the table and signalled to the waiter for another beer. "Listen," he said, wasting no time, "I've been thinking about Steve. We're just going to have to take a chance. The only person who'll be able to tell us whether he kept going out at nights will be Nora. God knows, it's the sort of thing a wife would remember. Maybe she suspected he was having an affair. Or he could have been going out for a drink. Either way, she'd know."

"So we show her the dossier?"

Kataria shook his head. "We don't need to. We just tell her we have to trace some of Steve's movements because we think it could help him. She trusts us. I'm sure she'd co-operate. We don't have to say why we've chosen any particular date."

"She'd guess, of course. She's not a fool."

"Guessing's one thing. Proving is another."

"Who needs proof these days?"

The waiter brought Kataria's beer. "With that pleasant thought," he said, raising his glass to Rana, "cheers."

"Cheers." Joe Rana wiped a smear of foam from his mouth with the side of his thumb. "Okay," he said. "I suppose we don't have any option. But for Christ's sake, not on the phone. Montrose will know about it in twenty-four hours. Actually, I'm a bit worried about my call yesterday. If he sees a transcript, do you think he'll guess what we're doing?"

Kataria shook his head. "He'll be suspicious all right. Hell, he's suspicious of everything. But I doubt he'll make a connection with the dossier."

"I wish I was convinced," Rana said. "I think we ought to move quickly, just in case he does decide to give trouble."

"That's fine with me. You've still got the dossier?"

"No. I had to return it yesterday. But I took a photostat."

"Kept in a safe place, I hope?"

"In a very safe place. Not in the office either."

"Well then, let's go and see Nora straight after work. The sooner we start, the better. Have you ordered lunch?"

Rana shook his head. They called a waiter over and in ten minutes two of Kay's special seafood salads were placed in front of them: heaped plates of prawns, oysters, lobster claws, mussels and sea urchins, their black shells cut in half to expose the thin slivers of meat inside, while their needle-sharp spikes continued to wave almost imperceptibly.

As they ate, Kataria spoke about the Rotary lunch, and the curious reception Montrose had been given by the store owners. Then he said: "Now listen: for God's sake don't tell anyone, because Maxwell swore me to silence, but there's something very funny going on. You know what a cautious old stick Maxwell is? Well, he said Montrose was corrupt. It's not the sort of thing a man like that would say unless he really meant it. It just came tumbling out. Maxwell was sorry later, and he made me promise not to repeat it."

Rana puffed out his cheeks in surprise. "Jesus," he said, "I wonder if that's true? Did he give any details? Any hints?"

"Nothing at all. But don't forget, none of the other store-owners liked Montrose. I could see that, especially at the end."

"Everyone else was applauding?"

"Sure. Just as if Montrose had announced he had six weeks to live."

"Very strange."

"First I put it down to bad feeling over the riots," Kataria said. "After all, the shops took the brunt. Other businessmen weren't affected. And you remember the complaints about the police reacting slowly when Maxwell's was attacked? It's pretty understandable that Maxwell's cronies would be cross about that. It could be their turn next if Montrose dawdled inefficiently somewhere."

"No, it's still strange. Surely if they thought they might need Montrose in future, they'd be going out of their way to be nice to him?"

"You'd have thought so, wouldn't you?" Kataria squeezed a quarter of lemon onto an oyster, and forked it out of its shell. "Maxwell might hate Montrose, but he's scared as hell of the man. It's as if the Commissioner of Police was the most dangerous man on the island."

"Well?"

Kataria grinned. "Emotionally, yes, I'd agree with that. But intellectually – do you really think so?"

"It may seem far fetched," Rana agreed. "But what about the dossier? Is that a mistake or is it deliberate?" He poured the rest of the beer into his glass and signalled the waiter for more.

"If we can discover that, we'll be laughing," said Kataria.

Joe Rana, still half-turned in his seat, quickly scanned the diners. As he expected, the man he was looking for was at his regular table, lunching with two others Rana had not seen before.

He felt his stomach tighten as it always did, then he turned back and began talking easily about mutual friends: the ordinary gossip of the island.

As he spoke, his right hand under the table carefully unfastened the clasp of his watch, and slid it around so that the face was on the underside of his wrist. He refastened it securely.

A few minutes later, Rana excused himself. He walked through the restaurant towards the lavatories, pausing for a word with Kay, who was serving behind the bar. Rana's shirt sleeves were rolled up, his left hand at his side.

The one CIA agent who had not been on Clive Lyle's list, and so had been missed in the Montrose purge, glanced casually up, saw the watch, and continued his conversation without a flicker of recognition or interest.

Two minutes later, when Joe Rana came out of the lavatory, the man's elbows were on the table and he was grinning at one of his companions recounting a story.

The American's watch was also swivelled on his wrist, and the gold strap glinted slightly as Rana passed by.

The meeting was on.

Chapter Fifteen

Rana and Kataria drove to Nelson Avenue straight after work and arrived unannounced. They rang the doorbell. The house was quiet and it seemed as if Nora Ayer might have gone out. But after a pause, there was a movement of colour behind the frosted glass and a voice called: "Who is it?"

"Hi, Nora," Kataria said, his face close to the crack. "It's Tilak and Joe."

There was a scraping as the chain was unfastened and the door swung open.

Nora Ayer was genuinely glad to see them, and Joe Rana again felt a pang of guilt for not calling on her before when she must have felt acutely isolated and anxious.

"Hello!" she said. "Come on in. It's so nice of you to drop around. The place is a mess, I'm afraid. I'm just getting the kids bathed and fed."

She led the way into the living-room, where children's reading books and pieces from a Lego kit were scattered over the furniture and around the carpet. "See what I mean?" she said apologetically, gathering up books and making space on a sofa. "I'm afraid I've rather been letting them have their heads, which is probably the wrong thing to do. I suppose I should have made sure ordinary discipline was maintained." She made a wry face. "But it just seemed easier this way."

"God, you should see the mess my kids make," Kataria said cheerfully. "But of course, you have. So you know what I'm used to."

They sat down, and Nora Ayer perched gracefully on the edge of a chair, looking at them with steady green eyes. She was a woman who improved with age, and now, at thirty-six, she was starting her best years. Her body was slim and firm, her breasts full and her skin clear. She needed little makeup, and wore hardly any. Her auburn hair hung loose, touching her shoulders. Rana was always surprised when they met at how attractive she was. At other times, he could recall her as good looking, but his memory somehow never took account of her warmth and intelligence. He felt the extra impact only when they came face to face; and he reflected how lucky Steve Ayer had been.

"I'm so glad you came round," she said. "It's the high spot of my day, and it gives me the bonus of an excuse for an early drink. Tilak, will you organise, please? I'll have a gin and tonic."

Kataria went over to the drinks cabinet and began sorting through glasses and bottles.

"What news about Steve?" he asked.

She shook her head. "Nothing. Did you get a chance to speak to Moorhouse?"

"Not yet, but we will."

"Oh please. You can't imagine how important it is to us. I have no idea what conditions Steve faces, or how he is. The fact that they won't let me see him – well that's pretty suspicious, don't you think? Are they interrogating him? I don't know. Is he being tortured?" Her voice had risen slightly, and she glanced quickly at the door to make sure none of the children were near.

"What does your lawyer say?" Rana asked.

Nora Ayer shrugged. "He's made representations, of course. He's a good man. I think he tries hard. But we're up against a stone wall. The Emergency Regulations don't say anything about lawyers or prison visiting. There's a provision for a judicial review of the detention order. By which judges, though? When? No one will tell us. Under the regulations, they're obliged to look at Steve's case within six months. Six months! Even the lawyer can't get in to see him yet. The prison people won't say anything, not even whether he's allowed letters. I went down myself and saw the Superintendent."

"Who's that?" Kataria asked, handing her a large gin. The ice cubes were already causing condensation around the glass.

"Simon Norwood. Thinks he's God's gift to St David's. A smug Londoner: very cool and calm, but you feel that underneath it, he's really enjoying himself. A closet fascist. You know the sort?"

Kataria nodded sympathetically. "I certainly do. Like Montrose."

Nora smoothed her hair away from the side of her face. "There's nothing closet about Montrose. Norwood is a blander, more civilised version. Probably more dangerous because of it." She mimicked Norwood's low, measured tones surprisingly well. " 'I'm sorry I can't help you, Mrs Ayer, but you must realise my hands are tied by prison regulations. I can assure you that your husband is being well looked after.'

He is such a bastard. Of course he could help me if he wanted to. I've read the prison regulations, and there's enormous discretion for any superintendent who wants to use it. I said: 'Can I write letters to my husband?' " She mimicked him again. " 'Mrs Ayer, I can't stop you writing letters.' 'Ah, but will you see my husband gets the letters?' 'That depends on what the letters say, and what the Regulations allow me to do.' 'Well, Mr Norwood, what do the Regulations allow you to do?' 'Not a lot, Mrs Ayer.' I had to force myself to sit calmly and not cry. To have me in tears would have been game, set and match for him."

"That's awful," Kataria said shocked. "What a bastard."

"Oh he is that all right, and proud of it."

Kataria handed Rana a glass of iced beer, and took one for himself. He settled on the sofa and raised his glass: "To happier times," he said.

She drank to that. "And quickly too."

"Listen, I don't want to raise your hopes in any way," Kataria said earnestly, "but Joe and I are trying to help Steve and we think we've got a lead. We can't say what it is at the moment – forgive us for that. It's all pretty sensitive. We don't want to go to Moorhouse until we're sure of our ground."

Nora Ayer looked reluctant, but intrigued. Kataria could see her assessing the two of them, wondering instinctively if they had ulterior motives. Finally she shrugged: "Okay," she said. "I can't see that we can be in a worse position than we are right now. What do you want?"

"To ask you some questions."

"Fire away."

"Some of them are personal questions."

"Then you'll get personal answers."

Kataria grinned at her admiringly. "Thanks," he said. "If it wasn't important for Steve, we wouldn't be doing this. So, number one: did he go out at night much?"

"With me, or by himself?"

"By himself."

"Once or twice. He'd go off to the club occasionally."

"How occasionally? Once a week? Once a month?"

"Gosh, I never kept track. It certainly wasn't a Friday night with the boys thing. Maybe once a month, and never for very long. Only a couple of hours."

The men glanced significantly at one another. Nora intercepted the look. "Did I answer wrongly?" she said. "What is it?"

"No, that's fine," Kataria replied, knowing he sounded evasive. "Was there any pattern to it that you remember?"

She shook her head. "I don't think so," she said. "He'd arrange to meet someone there for a drink. Or he'd decide he needed a couple of hours out."

"How did he arrange the meetings? Did he phone people from home?"

"Sometimes. Other times, he'd organise it at the office, and just tell me when he got in after work."

"You didn't mind?"

"Not at all. Everyone needs time by themselves."

"Forgive me for asking this, but did you suspect Steve might be meeting another woman?"

Nora began to laugh. "No," she said, "I didn't suspect that. Unless I gravely misjudge him, Steve's not the type. Do you have other information?" Her eyes were amused, so sure was she of the answer.

Kataria grinned back disarmingly. "No, not a thing. We're just covering possibilities."

"Well, anything's possible, but I don't think this is a starter. I know my man. And anyway," she pointed out, "St David's is too small for that sort of thing. Word would be round in a month, and you can't tell me that one of my dearest friends wouldn't have dropped me a hint or two by now."

"True enough," Joe Rana said. "We could all name a dozen examples to prove that. So Steve would go to the club, maybe twice a month. Did he drink a lot?"

"Not much."

"Never came home drunk?"

"That wasn't his style."

Kataria asked: "Did you notice that over the last month or so before he was picked up that he went to the club more often?"

She shook her head. Rana and Kataria exchanged glances again.

"Are you sure of that?" Rana persisted. "Particularly in the last couple of weeks. Did he go out at night by himself?"

Nora Ayer sipped her drink while she searched her memory. Finally she said: "Actually, I don't think he went out at all in the last couple of weeks. He used to come home pretty tired and worried. Moorhouse was riding him hard for some reason. We'd just talk, listen to music, have a drink and go to bed."

"Could he have slipped out without you knowing?" Kataria asked.

"For five minutes, you mean? Yes, it's possible."

"For an hour or so."

"Not a chance."

"And telephone calls? Did he make any from home?"

"Of course. I couldn't say how many, or when they were. But it wasn't unusual."

The sound of children's voices could be heard, arguing heatedly. Soon the four-year-old girl came running in in tears, complaining about a fight with her brothers. She was almost a carbon copy of her mother. Nora Ayer took her by the hand and led her away to sort out the problem. Rana and Kataria waited in silence. At length, Kataria got up and opened some more beers.

After a few minutes, Nora returned. "Sorry," she apologised. "You know what kids are like. Where were we?"

"Talking about Steve's telephone calls," Kataria said. "Did he have a lot of trouble getting through to people?"

Nora grimaced. "Don't we all?"

"Wrong numbers? Crossed lines? That sort of thing?"

"You've just given a description of the St David's telephone department. How often do you get a wrong number?"

"Quite a lot," Kataria admitted.

"That's right," she said.

"But was there any pattern you noticed? I mean, did Steve try a couple of times, and then give up and not make the call after all?"

"Oh, he'd always get through in the end, even if he had to go through the operator. You know how he is. Never gives up."

Kataria sighed. "Jesus," he said. "What do we make of it all?"

Nora shrugged. "Sorry," she said. "I can't help you there. I don't even know what you're looking for."

Joe Rana passed her across a sheet of paper, on which he had written the dates and times specified in Steve Ayer's dossier.

"This is a hard one," he said, "but have a look at these dates and tell me if you remember Steve going out on any of them."

They watched as she scrutinised the list.

"Well, there's my birthday," she said. "He was home then. So were you, so you know that's right. But the other ones . . ." There was a long silence. "Sorry, they don't mean anything to me. He could have gone out on some of them. Not on the ones at the end, though – just before his arrest. I definitely remember he was home in the last couple of weeks. We had dinner out once, I think, with the Fletchers. That would have been on the Sunday before, but it's not marked here. Otherwise, nothing."

She handed back the piece of paper. Rana folded it and put it in his trouser pocket.

"When do I get to hear what all this is about?" Nora asked.

"As soon as we make sense of it ourselves," Kataria promised. "Thanks for putting up with our Perry Mason imitation."

"Can I ask you both a question?" Nora's green eyes looked frankly from one to the other.

"Go ahead," Kataria said.

"Do you think Steve was a spy for the Americans? That's what Moorhouse was implying."

Kataria shook his head slowly. "If we thought that, we wouldn't be putting our own necks on the block."

Rana nodded agreement.

"Are you putting your necks on the block?" Nora asked candidly.

Kataria drained his beer and stood up. "It's starting to look that way," he said cheerfully. "Thanks for the drinks."

The men left the house and drove off towards the centre of Port Lombard, the route Steve Ayer was supposed to have taken for the meetings with his control. Neither spoke for several minutes. Kataria turned left along the Coast Road, and then left again up Kennedy Walk.

The sun was setting and a soft warm light filled Jubilee Park. He stopped the car at the kerb and switched off the engine.

"Well?" he asked, "what do we tell Moorhouse?"

"There's no point giving him anything we can't prove. And we've still only got one fact: Nora's birthday."

"We could get a sworn statement from her that he didn't go out in the last couple of weeks."

"Worthless," Rana said dismissively. "Moorhouse would never look at something uncorroborated like that. And from his wife, too. We have to have independent proof."

"What about the club?"

"What about it?" He took out a pack of cigarettes and offered it to Kataria. His cigarette-lighter flared briefly, and the white smoke drifted through the car.

"If he was there, people must have seen him."

"Who? When?"

"Christ," said Kataria defensively. "Whoever was around on those nights."

"And how do we find them? Show our list of dates to the bar flies and set the rumours going? Do you want to take a bet on how long it would be before Montrose came around asking what the hell we were doing?"

Kataria blew out his cheeks. "Oh God," he sighed. "I'm no good at this sort of thing. How the hell did we get involved?"

"Montrose got our friend arrested. Montrose is a crook. Our friend is not. Therefore we were involved."

Kataria smiled amiably and inhaled a lungful of smoke. Suddenly he gave a gasp, as if he was about to say something urgent, and began to choke, hunched over, coughing, tears springing to his eyes.

Rana clapped him on the back. "Is this your first cigarette, sonny?" he asked pleasantly.

Kataria fought to speak. He leaned back in the car seat and, despite his choked throat, grinned in triumph.

"Jesus," he said, his voice faint. "It's so easy." He turned the key in the ignition and the engine stuttered into life.

"Where are we going?"

He cleared his throat desperately. "To the club. To find out."

"Oh Christ. How? What?"

The car pulled away from the kerb and turned into High Street. The St David's Club was a few blocks along, in Stanley Road.

Kataria began to laugh. "So simple," he said. "Members have to sign in. Remember that ridiculous rule they were trying to scrap a couple of years back but finally kept on because it was tradition? We just look at the Members' Register. If Steve was there when he was supposed to be meeting Berenson, his name will be in the book in his own writing."

"Of course!" Rana exclaimed. "Man, you're wasted on the political desk. That's brilliant! You should be a policeman. I understand there'll be a vacancy around here soon."

"Please God," grinned Kataria. "I'd love to nail Montrose."

The St David's Club had premises in one of the modern blocks which had sprung up in Port Lombard. Rana and Kataria walked the one floor up to the club entrance. It was deserted. The porter who should have been on duty was nowhere to be seen, but the leather-bound Members' Register was open on an antique William and Mary desk, and a pen stuck out of an old china inkwell.

Rana pulled the piece of paper from his pocket, while Kataria flicked back the pages.

"What's the first date?" he asked in a low voice.

"January the twelfth."

"January the twelfth . . . right, here it is. Now let's see . . ." He ran his finger down the names. "No. Not here."

"Try February the seventh."

Kataria turned the pages, scanning the dates recorded in the margin. "February the seventh . . . no Ayer on the first page. Let's look over . . . Herbert . . . Miller, Khanna . . . yes, here it is," he said, trying to keep the elation from his voice. "S. Ayer. And his signature."

Rana peered over his shoulder. "That's him, all right. Okay, I'll tick that one as a positive. Now February the twenty-sixth."

They searched through the register. Ayer had not visited on that date.

"There's no point looking at the twenty-seventh," Rana said. "We know where he was that night. The next one is March the fourth."

Towards the end of the members' names for that day was the neat, precise handwriting of Stephen Ayer. Rana ticked off a second date on his list.

They worked methodically through. Ayer had also visited the club on 20 March, once in April and twice in May when he was supposed to have been in Jubilee Park. No visits were recorded for June.

Kataria straightened up. He was smiling, but curiously; behind it was an indefinable feeling of apprehension. Now they had no choice. They would have to go to Moorhouse. Their necks were truly on the block.

"How many does that make?" he asked.

"Six," Rana replied.

"So with the birthday party, we can prove that the dossier is wrong on seven separate occasions. Christ, that's not bad. Let's sign in. I think we deserve a drink."

But Rana shook his head. "I'd love to, Tilak, but I've got to get off."

"Oh come on. I'm buying."

"No, really. I said I'd be home by seven, and I'm late as it is. We'll celebrate another day."

Kataria shrugged, disappointed. "Okay. You want me to drop you back at the office to pick up your car?"

Rana hesitated. He hadn't thought of that. "No thanks," he said easily. "I've got to pick up a friend near here. We'll go in his car."

"Are you sure? It's no trouble."

"I'm sure. Thanks for the offer."

Rana squeezed Kataria's shoulder and walked quickly from the club, leaving his friend to sign in. Outside, he glanced up and down the street. It was dark now, and the lamps had come on, leaving puddles of yellow light bordered with pockets of shadow. Further along, illuminated shop windows spread a glow on the pavements.

He headed for Jubilee Park, then skirted round it, along Kennedy Walk to the Coast Road. He waited for a break in the traffic and crossed over, walking casually now, into the cover of palm trees.

He stood, staring back, in case anyone was following him. He could make out some figures in Jubilee Park, but they seemed to be concerned with their own business. Otherwise, the pavements were deserted.

Rana walked along the sand, listening to the crashing of the waves and smelling the sea.

The American was waiting for him.

Chapter Sixteen

Rana and Kataria met in the morning to draft a letter to the Prime Minister, asking for "an urgent appointment on a matter of national importance". They took it by hand to Bob Sehai and watched as he read it.

The PPS' expression did not change. "Wait here," he said quietly. "I'll go and ask him."

The two men sat in the anteroom, dressed in their most sober jackets and ties. Kataria's palms were sweating and he rubbed them on his trousers. It was like waiting for a job interview, he thought. Joe Rana sat quietly, staring intently out of the window, although there was nothing to see except the cloudless sky. If he was nervous, he gave no sign, and Kataria envied that. In fact, Rana had reached the point where he was feeling numbed, and strangely empty. The elation of their discovery was gone, and they would now have to take whatever consequences there were. He had no doubt they were on safe ground as far as Steve Ayer was concerned, but knowing Moorhouse, the Prime Minister could be equally interested in the fact that a Top Secret dossier had been illegally seen by two of his officials.

Bob Sehai was with Moorhouse for a long time. The men caught each other's eye but said nothing. Rana continued staring out of the window.

Kataria again felt his palms begin to sweat and he rubbed them surreptitiously on the fabric of the chair.

Suddenly the double doors to the Prime Minister's office opened, and Sehai stood framed in the light from the large windows at the other end. "Would you come through, gentlemen?" he asked.

They rose automatically, Rana feeling as if he was in a dream: Kataria realising his mouth had gone dry. Whatever happened, after this interview nothing would be the same again.

Moorhouse's office seemed even quieter than the anteroom, perhaps because it was so large. There was not even a hum from the air conditioners, but the temperature was pleasantly chill. Underfoot, the grey carpet was thick.

Although both men had been in many times before, this morning it felt alien and indefinably hostile. Moorhouse was behind his desk, head down, signing letters. They approached tentatively and paused behind the visitors' chairs, waiting for the Prime Minister to acknowledge them. The sensation of being schoolboys in front of the headmaster was over-whelming.

The silence in the office grew. Moorhouse read carefully through a document, his face expressionless, and at the bottom he signed his name. The Prime Minister's signature was like the man himself: assertive and flamboyant. Even from that distance, Rana could see how the stroke of the thick fountain pen nib curved up through the last line of typewriting.

The Prime Minister turned the page to scrutinise the next document. Kataria shifted his weight from one leg to the other and swallowed to try and rid his mouth of the dryness.

Moorhouse was still reading when he spoke: "Sit down." They could detect nothing from his voice: good mood or bad, it was impossible to say. He had not looked up.

They settled themselves in the gilt-framed chairs and Kataria spread his palms on his thighs, trying to relax. He dared not glance at Joe Rana, but focused his eyes on the portrait above the Prime Minister's head. Suddenly he knew how cabinet ministers felt every day in the boss man's presence: it was discomfiture he had observed often before without fully understanding what it was like being in the direct line of fire. Christ knew how Steve Ayer had stood it. Moorhouse had a way of unsettling people, of making them feel unimportant and slightly stupid, and he exercised this power almost as a reflex.

The Prime Minister crossed out an entire paragraph of a letter and filled the margin with writing. When he had finished, he closed the leather-bound folder slowly, and Bob Sehai was instantly moving, silent and unbidden, to his desk to take it away, rather like an efficient waiter who lurks watchfully a few paces off and carries out plates the moment they are empty. Moorhouse deigned not to notice him.

At last he was looking curiously at Rana and Kataria.

"Well?" he said.

"We apologise for taking your time, Prime Minister," Joe Rana began, "but we thought we ought to come to you immediately."

"Gentlemen, I can do without the preliminaries," Moorhouse broke in tersely, flicking up the silk cuff of his shirt and glancing at the slim gold watch on his wrist. "My next appointment is in . . . seven minutes. Is that correct, Mr Sehai?"

The PPS' voice came from a position behind them and to the side. "Yes, Prime Minister." Kataria sneaked a look over his shoulder and saw Bob Sehai on a chair, notebook open, pen poised.

"So let's get straight into it. A matter of national importance. What is it?"

Rana took a deep breath. "Stephen Ayer has been unfairly detained," he said, and watched Moorhouse's face freeze. Rana started to falter under the hostile stare but he said hastily: "This isn't a moral criticism, Prime Minister, it's an objective fact. We believe the decision to detain Mr Ayer was taken on the basis of certain assumptions – facts which were put before you. We have discovered that many of those facts are wrong."

Now Moorhouse was becoming incredulous. "I do hope you're not wasting my time, Mr Rana," he said evenly. "I am a very busy man."

"No, sir, we're not wasting your time."

"How can you possibly know what evidence I had before me when I decided on the detentions?"

Rana stared him straight in the eye, unrepentant. "We've looked at the dossier relating to Ayer. We've studied the extracts from the surveillance records," he said.

Moorhouse considered this admission for a moment. "Are such dossiers normally available to you?" he asked, surprisingly mildly, considering it was *prima facie* a serious breach of the Official Secrets Act.

"No, sir."

"But somehow you got hold of this one?"

"Yes, sir."

"I see. And?"

"It's bullshit, sir." The words came tumbling out. "The whole thing is rubbish from start to finish . . . it claims Ayer was meeting his control in Jubilee Park when he wasn't doing anything of the sort. He was with his wife, or at a party, or having drinks in the club . . ."

"Stop!" Moorhouse held up his hand and his eyes were flashing dangerously. Rana felt his heart sink. Now the Prime Minister spoke slowly and distinctly. "From the beginning," he said. "Facts only, please. No theories."

Rana began, taking him through the dates, explaining about Nora Ayer's birthday party and giving names of guests who could vouch for Ayer's presence; then onto the evidence of the Members' Register. When he had finished, Moorhouse picked up his telephone, consulted a list and dialled a number.

"This is the Prime Minister," he said. "Bring to my office

immediately the Intelligence File on Stephen Ayer."

He replaced the receiver and glanced again at his watch. To Bob Sehai he said: "Hold him out there for a few minutes, please, then come back inside."

"Yes, sir." The PPS rose quickly and went through the double doors, closing them behind him. The Prime Minister seemed lost in thought, an elbow on his desk, chin in one hand, staring down at the highly polished woodwork.

Rana and Kataria sat motionless. The minutes ticked by, agonisingly slowly. Kataria wanted to cough, but turned it into a clearing of the throat which sounded both impossibly loud and made it obvious how ill at ease he was.

Kataria longed to say something, anything, to relieve the tension and make contact with the man sitting silently behind the desk, but the problem was, what? There was nothing more to say until the dossier arrived. And better not talk about how they had got hold of the file. Not that he really knew. It had actually been obtained by Rana, who had never specified how.

At last, Sehai came back, the beige manilla folder in his hands. Moorhouse ended his reverie abruptly and went across to meet him.

"Right," he said, taking the dossier and bringing it to where Rana and Kataria were sitting. The Prime Minister pulled up a chair near to Rana. He flicked through until he came to the extracts from the surveillance record. Rana leaned over to look.

"Well, Mr Rana," Moorhouse said. "This *is* the file you've seen? Good. Then let's go through it from the beginning."

The men went minutely over the dossier, and Moorhouse made pen marks beside the dates which were being challenged.

"You say his wife claims he didn't go out at all in the last two or three weeks?" the Prime Minister asked.

"Yes, sir," Rana confirmed. "We didn't make much of that because it's only her word. There's no independent proof."

"Quite so."

"But it seemed to us that there were so many proven errors that the dossier had become a suspect document."

"We'll see about that," Moorhouse said shortly. "All right, Mr Sehai, I think we're ready now for the Commissioner of Police. Call him in."

Kataria's heart lurched in panic, and he thought despairingly: *Oh Jesus.* His hands immediately began sweating again. Rana's face had gone pale, but otherwise he looked composed.

The PPS walked to the doors again, while Moorhouse went round to his side of the desk and sat, his face expressionless, waiting for the confrontation.

"The Commissioner of Police," Bob Sehai announced formally, and Montrose appeared in the doorway, pink-faced and angry. Kataria suddenly understood how people could faint with fright: he himself was feeling suddenly dizzy, and he wished more than anything to be able to avoid this confrontation.

How much did Montrose know? Was he angry at being kept waiting, how long? . . . Kataria looked furtively at his watch . . . fifteen or twenty minutes? But he must have seen the Top Secret file going in. And he probably knew whose it was.

"Prime Minister," Montrose acknowledged curtly with a nod of his head.

Moorhouse smiled at him in a friendly, expansive way. "My apologies, Commissioner, for keeping you waiting," he said charmingly. "I know how busy you are. Won't you sit down? You know Mr Rana, my cabinet secretary, and Mr Kataria from Foreign Affairs?"

Montrose ignored the two men and took the seat just vacated by the Prime Minister.

"I'm afraid, sir, that my business with you is strictly confidential," Montrose said brusquely, while his face summoned up the ghost of a humourless smile. "I can't possibly talk in the presence of third and fourth parties."

"We'll try to be brief," Moorhouse said smoothly. "I'd like Mr Rana and Mr Kataria to remain here while we clear up one or two outstanding matters." He held up Ayer's file. "Do you know what this is, Commissioner?" he asked.

"Well I can see it's a Top Secret file," Montrose said resentfully. "Obviously I don't know which one."

"Stephen Vincent Ayer."

"Ah." Montrose's voice was disapproving.

"Mr Rana has just been taking me through it, pointing out what seem to be errors in the Intelligence Reports."

Montrose glanced at Rana in fury, his lips tight and bloodless. "And how would he know?"

"How?" asked Moorhouse. "Because he says he checked. On February the twenty-seventh, for example, this dossier has Mr Ayer meeting an American agent in Jubilee Park and going off with him in a car, whereas these gentlemen – and others – can tell you he was at home, hosting a party to celebrate his wife's birthday."

Montrose stared in disbelief for a second. Then he said quickly and defensively: "Quite simple, quite a simple explanation probably. A typing error in the date. It should have been the seventeenth, or the twenty-eighth. Something like that. Perfectly easy for me to check the original. Proves nothing."

"Quite right, Commissioner," said Moorhouse. "That's probably it. But what about February the seventh?"

Montrose was on his feet, pink with indignation. "Prime Minister, this is intolerable," he said. "What *about* February the seventh? I haven't committed the whole file on this one man to memory. It is a distillation of information collected scrupulously over many months. Hundreds of man-hours have been spent. Thousands. I really cannot be expected to account for every single fact without due and fair warning."

"Sit down, Commissioner." The Prime Minister's tone was still friendly, but when Montrose failed to obey at once, he repeated himself, an edge of steel in his voice. Montrose sat.

"February the seventh has Mr Ayer going to Jubilee Park again to meet his CIA colleague," the Prime Minister continued equably. "Whereas Mr Rana has evidence that in fact he went for a drink at the St David's Club in Stanley Road. What have you to say about that?"

"What evidence?"

"The Members' Register. Mr Ayer signed in."

There was a pause. "The signature's been analysed I suppose?" Montrose demanded.

Moorhouse looked enquiringly over at Rana.

"No, sir," Rana replied. "But we know Mr Ayer's writing well enough to recognise it."

"Oh splendid, Sherlock Holmes," Montrose sneered. "You could tell whether or not it was a forgery, couldn't you?"

"Who'd want to forge Steve Ayer's signature in the Members' Register?" Rana asked.

"I could think of several people," the Commissioner said, turning on him again. "Anti-social elements, that's who. People out to discredit the forces of law and order on this island. How about that for a start?"

Rana turned away in distaste, but Moorhouse said: "Well what do you have to say about that, Mr Rana? Could the signatures have been forged?"

"Well I suppose so, Prime Minister," Rana said. "But I can't think why. Still, let's put aside *who* might have done such a thing: anti-social elements, or myself perhaps, or Mr Kataria . . ."

"Exactly!" chimed in Montrose.

"And let's look instead at *when* they might have done it. The forgeries are in the Members' Register, in a particular date order. They are among lists of names, with signatures both before and after them. So either the names of genuine members were erased for those particular dates and the forgeries substituted – in which case, we ought to be able to see some signs of that – or else they were forged on the actual days involved. And this would be impossible. It would mean the forger knowing what dates would appear in the official dossier weeks or even months later. No one could possibly foresee that."

"Well, Mr Montrose?" The Prime Minister was almost like a tennis umpire, turning to the Commissioner of Police for his return shot.

"I don't suppose this famous Register records the exact times Ayer went to the club?" he said gruffly.

"No, actually it doesn't," Rana admitted.

Montrose was triumphant. "Well there you are," he declared. "So what does it prove?"

"Yes that's true," the Prime Minister said thoughtfully. "How do we know he wasn't there earlier in the day?"

Rana felt his heart sink. He cursed himself silently for not having thought of that earlier. But this time it was Kataria who came to the rescue.

"That's not a fatal flaw in the argument," Kataria observed. "Not necessarily fatal, anyway. If you'll look at the Register, the presumption must be that he came during the evening. His signature appears towards the end of the list for the day. We can check with those who signed in just before him, and see if they remember when they were there."

"What do you think your chances are of getting some Port Lombard drunk to remember when he got to his Club on a particular night last February?" Montrose scoffed. "We have a hard enough job getting sober citizens to tell us about the day before yesterday."

"Not all people who belong to the St David's Club are drunks, Commissioner," the Prime Minister said icily. "I myself am a member. So is the Chief Justice and every senior member of the judiciary. In fact, I am not aware of any drunks there at all."

Montrose looked flustered. "I apologise, Prime Minister," he said. "I didn't intend to imply . . ."

"Indeed not," Moorhouse replied calmly. "Continue, Mr Kataria."

"Well, sir, we can check the time. Not just on February the seventh. That's only one of the dates he was signed in at the club when he was supposed to be in Jubilee Park. There are half a dozen others. We should be able to get somewhere on that. For example, the barman might remember. According to Nora Ayer, he only went there at nights."

"What about lunchtimes?" Montrose demanded.

"Well, we usually had lunch together, the three of us, down at Kay's on the seafront."

"Every day?" the Prime Minister asked.

"Almost every day," Kataria said. "There were very few exceptions. At the moment, I'm just talking about the balance of probabilities. It was probably not lunchtime, but we should be able to prove that definitively by asking a few questions."

There was a pause, then Kataria continued. "Excuse me, sir, but I wonder if I might be allowed to ask a question of the Commissioner? It might help clear the matter up."

The Prime Minister smiled. "Please do."

Kataria turned to Montrose, who glared at him with contempt. Kataria suddenly felt completely calm and in control.

"Were you surprised to hear that Mr Ayer might have been visiting his club rather than making contact with his CIA controller?" he asked.

Montrose laughed shortly. "Certainly I was surprised," he said. "Shocked. Amazed. Flabbergasted."

"It hadn't occurred to you before?"

"No."

"Nothing you saw in the surveillance reports indicated he spent time at the club?"

"Nothing."

"You went through the surveillance reports yourself?"

"Yes."

"So if there had been anything there, you'd have seen it?"

"Certainly I would."

"And there was twenty-four-hour surveillance on Mr Ayer, I take it?"

"Yes." Montrose stopped, realising at last that he was talking himself into a dead end. "Well, twenty-four-hour surveillance for some of the time. Not all. Our budget – " he smiled humourlessly at the Prime Minister " – does not permit luxuries. But we do what we can."

"When did twenty-four-hour surveillance start on Mr Ayer?" Kataria asked.

"Offhand, I can't remember."

"But approximately. From the beginning of the year?"

Montrose appealed to Moorhouse, who was listening interestedly. "Prime Minister, I think this has gone far enough."

"Do you?" Moorhouse said, pleasantly.

"I am the Commissioner of Police," Montrose insisted. "I cannot allow myself to be interrogated in this fashion by a . . ." he hunted for words ". . . a civil servant."

"No of course not," said Moorhouse. "I understand it's very difficult for you, particularly as you had no warning. Please don't let it upset you."

The Commissioner settled back in his seat, tight-lipped.

"However," Moorhouse continued, "matters of great importance have been raised. The accuracy of this dossier is in question, and answers must be found urgently. Commissioner, I would like you to go personally to the St David's Club, straight away please, and bring the Members' Register here to my office. We will go through it together." He turned to Rana. "You looked through the Register," he said. "When was that?"

"Yesterday, sir."

"What was its condition?"

Rana caught on immediately. "Oh, very good. It's a stout, leather-bound volume."

"Do the pages come out easily?"

"No, sir."

"None of them are likely to fall out during the move?"

"Absolutely not."

"I'm glad to hear that. Then I should have it on my desk in perfect condition within . . . what? Twenty minutes, Commissioner? Half an hour at most. Mr Sehai, cancel my appointments for the rest of the day." Then to Rana and Kataria: "Gentlemen, thank you for bringing this matter to my attention. Please hold yourselves ready for further meetings this afternoon. Oh, and Commissioner, please don't feel defensive. We're all on the same side. You and I are only interested in justice. If mistakes have been made, then we must find out who made them, and why. I understand very well that we function mainly on the evidence fed to us by our subordinates. And if that evidence is mistaken or tainted, then our decisions might be mistaken or tainted. I think I've spoken to you before about this. We must not be afraid to admit our mistakes, particularly when a man's liberty is at stake. If the dossier is wrong, then the fault lies with the people who supplied the information. It need not reflect on you personally."

"Yes, Prime Minister. Thank you."

Montrose stood up abruptly, half bowed to Moorhouse and ignored the others as he strode quickly through the doors. As soon as he had gone, much of the tension left the office, and Kataria heard himself giving a long sigh. He glanced at Rana, who motioned with his head that they should go.

They looked uncertainly at Moorhouse, but he had his back to them, so they left quietly, Bob Sehai last of all, closing the double doors.

Moorhouse gazed through his window across acres of palm trees stretching towards the buildings which marked the northerly edge of Port Lombard. The concrete office and apartment blocks quickly gave way to single-storied buildings, and then to the shanties which spilled into open land.

In the distance, Moorhouse could just make out a single watchtower on the perimeter of the Central Gaol. The rest was hidden, but he stared at the tower for a long while.

Chapter Seventeen

The two men in civilian clothes listened silently to Montrose. He was sweating as usual, but for the first time they could see he was rattled, and they detected an edge of fear.

The bottle of whisky which Montrose had opened before Alec Clifton and Stephen Luther gathered in his office was now virtually empty. About an inch remained in the bottom, and as Montrose splashed it into his glass, they saw his hand was unsteady.

It was hard to believe the game was up: or if it was, they reasoned to themselves, it need only be up for Montrose. If they were careful, they could carry on, although perhaps not as aggressively as before.

"That FUCKER made me go and get the Members' Register from his snotty little club," Montrose raged. "And I had to get it back to his office in half an hour! Like an errand boy! I could have killed him with my bare hands! Sitting there, smug little shit!"

The Chief of Staff of the St David's armed forces said gently: "But you didn't, Claud. You went and got the Register. What was in it?" Stephen Luther lit a cigarette casually.

"Ayer had signed in!" he complained. "Jesus, I couldn't believe it! Those times I had reports of him going out alone at night, he wasn't even shafting someone! The little turd was going somewhere he could actually *sign in*!"

From the side of the office, the Deputy Commissioner of Police gave a dry chuckle, and Montrose wheeled on him angrily.

"What are you laughing about, you stupid cunt!"

Alec Clifton drained his whisky and said solemnly: "I was just thinking: what bad luck. You don't happen to have another bottle hidden away, do you, Claud? We seem to have killed that one."

Montrose reached reluctantly into his desk drawer and pulled out a replacement. He dropped the empty into his wastepaper basket.

"We ought to kill Moorhouse," Montrose brooded. "That's what we should do."

"I don't think that would solve anything," Clifton said placidly, pouring himself a half glass. For the first time for months, he felt calm and clear-headed. It was partly the sheer pleasure of seeing Montrose cracking, and partly the new flow of adrenalin caused by the changed situation. "Anyway, it was bloody stupid of you to start paying off private scores," he observed. "You should have stuck to the list the American gave you."

"Who are you to tell me I'm bloody stupid, you ignorant bastard!" the Commissioner raged. "What fucking help were you? Mooning about, snivelling! What did you contribute to the plan? Fuck all, that's what!"

General Luther said calmly: "I don't think swearing's going to help us, Claud. We need to make a new plan. But first, you have to tell us exactly what happened. So you brought the Members' Register back to Moorhouse. Then what?"

"I told you. Ayer's bloody name was all over the book."

"What did that mean? How many of the intelligence entries were discredited?"

"Six or seven. I forget. But they're still not discredited, bloody hell they're not! They've just been questioned. I'll explain them away tomorrow."

"Oh no you won't." It was Clifton again, speaking calmly. "They're discredited, Claud, and if you try to justify them now, you'll be discredited too."

"Don't you tell me what do do! Who planned this whole operation, tell me that?"

"You did," said Clifton. "And now you're in trouble. We'd like to help, but you have to calm down and listen. Otherwise you're going to finish up out of a job. Or in gaol," he said, almost as an aside.

"Alec's right," Luther said. "You're out on a limb. You can't afford to stand on your dignity now. Let's have the rest of it. What did Moorhouse say?"

"He said Ayer would be released tomorrow unless there was a good explanation. He wants a full investigation into what went wrong, and whose fault it was. But there've got to be some answers for ten o'clock tomorrow morning. He also wants a complete check on the dossiers of the other detainees."

Clifton sighed. "Looks like you need a scapegoat, Claud," he said. "Who do you particularly hate in the office these days?" He noticed Montrose staring at him peculiarly. "I mean, apart from me." Clifton smiled disarmingly, and the wrinkles on his thin, ebony face deepened. "It seems to me that you're on a loser with the Ayer case. My advice is: retreat and live to fight another day. What do you think, General?"

Luther nodded. "I agree," he said. "Claud could probably spin some fantastic story around the Members' Register if he really tried, but who would believe him? One mistake in a dossier like that is pretty bad. Six or seven are fatal. I'm afraid, old man, if you stick by the dossier you'll go down with it. Moorhouse will suspect your motives. As it is, you can claim you were acting in good faith."

"But you have to *prove* that good faith now by taking the initiative in getting Ayer freed," Clifton urged. "You have to go in there and say: 'This dossier is complete balls from beginning to end. I didn't realise it before because . . .' And that's the hard bit. Filling in what comes after the 'because . . .' ."

"Now think carefully, Claud," Luther said. "What precisely did you tell Moorhouse about your part in putting the dossier together? What does he think you did?"

"Oh fuck, how the hell should I know?" Montrose grumbled, pouring himself another drink. His hand was still shaking, and the beads of sweat shone on his forehead, although the office was cool. It was 9 p.m. and out of the windows the lights of Port Lombard glittered. Luther and Clifton exchanged glances.

"Think, Claud," Luther urged. "If you want to keep your job, you have to remember."

"It's *your* job too," Montrose snapped pettily. "And yours, Alec."

Clifton shook his head slowly. "No," he said gently. "This is your show. We had nothing to do with putting Ayer in gaol. That was your decision, Claud, your revenge. If there's a rap to be taken for it, either you take it, or you set someone else up. But it won't be the General, and it won't be me. You're out by yourself. It's only because we're your friends that we're just trying to help."

Montrose stared at him in disbelief, then across at Luther, who nodded agreement. "You're on your own, Claud," the General said. "So concentrate, for God's sake. What part does the Prime Minister think you played in compiling that dossier? I mean, you didn't tell him you went on any surveillance missions yourself, did you? Nothing dumb like that?"

"Jesus, of course not."

"Good. So you were working off the reports of subordinates. How many others were involved?"

"I don't know. I don't think I said. There was supposed to be twenty-four-hour surveillance so it would have been a couple of dozen."

"Those mistakes – could they have been the work of one team? Say, every time these two idiots came up on duty, they falsified their report? Christ knows why."

"I'm not sure it could have been just a couple of men. Maybe two different teams, or three."

"Okay. Four or six guys could have done it. Why?"

Alec Clifton suggested: "Part of a CIA plan to get the honest Ayer out of the Prime Minister's office, and their own man in?"

General Luther considered that for a moment then shook his head. "No, Moorhouse wouldn't fall for that now," he said. "Anyway, it would mean falsifying a whole lot of new records to get Ayer's replacement on the hook. Too difficult. It must be something simple and uncomplicated."

"What sort of car did Ayer drive?" Clifton asked.

Montrose shrugged. "A heap of some sort."

"No chance of it outdriving a surveillance car?"

"No chance of it outdriving a horse and cart. It's old and slow."

"So we can't say they lost him and made something up to avoid getting hell from the office?"

"No."

The men sat in silence. It was certainly a problem. The more people who were thought to be involved, the more difficult it became. Framing half a dozen intelligence men meant finding people who had actually been on duty on the nights in question, and doctoring their official records. This had its own dangers. The men might still be able to produce alibis – other intelligence officers could remember being with them, any number of permutations could upset the whole story.

A sudden thought: except for Montrose's ten. That group might do. It was Clifton who remembered them first. The ten who had led the attack on Maxwell's were certainly expendable. But how to use them without having them confess about the riots and involve Montrose? And, worse still, involve Luther and himself?

That was the problem, and the more they discussed it, the less simple it seemed. The discussion went on late into the night. The second bottle of whisky was finished, and Montrose produced a third from another drawer of his desk. Clifton wondered mildly what size supply he had back there.

The Commissioner became drunk and abusive, but around midnight his mood changed and he felt sorry for himself, his small eyes showing their first signs of softness.

Clifton found that the drink was hardly affecting him at all. He must have consumed a good half bottle of neat whisky – Montrose was having two to the others' one – yet he felt surprisingly clear-headed, and his speech was normal, no hint of a slur. General Luther, too, acted as if he'd been on orange squash all night, although his mood was slightly abstracted as he considered the problems facing them.

It was important that the first hurdle tomorrow be overcome to buy time. Moorhouse had to be placated: he needed to be assured of the basic honesty of his Commissioner of Police, who was at that moment slumping in the chair behind his desk, giving a rambling, self-justifying explanation of why Ayer was a threat to them all.

Once they had the breathing space, they could plan an explanation.

But finally, if this failed, both Luther and Clifton knew instinctively Montrose would have to be sacrificed. Perhaps Montrose himself realised this, which was why he was suddenly falling apart, having been for so long the aggressive team leader who brooked no argument.

Still, it would be both better and safer to keep the team together, and that was the goal they would aim for at first.

When at last Montrose reached the end of his monologue, he looked across at the others with his face no longer bland, but suddenly hurt and on the point of crumpling, pleading silently for support and encouragement. For once, his defences were down.

Luther sighed in disgust. "Oh shit, Claud, you've had too much to drink," he said, his patience running out. "Now this is important, so for Christ's sake pay attention. What are you going to say to Moorhouse tomorrow morning at ten o'clock? Give us a quick run-through."

Montrose looked beseechingly at him for a few seconds, before giving a disappointed grunt – "Huh!" – and with an effort of will re-assembled his defences. He straightened up in his chair, and stared into the whisky which he swilled round and round in its glass.

There was silence for a full minute. Clifton thought of prompting him, but caught Luther's eye and settled back, waiting.

"I will say," Montrose began with dignity, "Prime Minister, I was wrong. I was misled by my subordinates. It will take some time to find out who was responsible, but I *will* find out. I will also find out why. I recommend, meanwhile, that you release that bastard Ayer..."

"MISTER Ayer," said Luther.

Montrose gave a thin, sycophantic smile and his eyes were hard and shining: "I beg your pardon, MISTER Ayer. I recommend you release him from detention without a moment's delay. At once. In fact, I myself will drive straight off to the prison and set him free. Furthermore, I will shake his hand and ask his forgiveness. I will kiss his bum if I have to. He will sit beside me in my official car while I speed him back to his lovely wife and family. I will avert my eyes during the reunion. I will buy toys for the kiddies. I will stop tapping their telephone. I'll even call off that idiot who sometimes watches the house, and tell him never again to look through the bedroom windows to see the action. I will join Rotary. I will even ask him to sponsor me at that fucking club, so I too can sign in every time I want a fucking drink. I will..." he stopped suddenly, and the others could see his face had gone deathly pale. "Oh shit," Montrose said. "I'm going to throw up."

He rose unsteadily from his chair, groped round the desk and out of the door with surprising speed. It slammed behind him.

Luther and Clifton looked at each other in exasperation.

"What do you think?" the General asked quietly.

Clifton shrugged. "He'll pull round. We just need to watch him through tomorrow morning, then he'll be all right; he won't say anything too stupid to Moorhouse. His instinct for self preservation is too strong."

Luther took a cigarette from his pack and lit it thoughtfully. "That's what I'm worried about," he said finally. "In trying to preserve himself, do you think he might put the blame on you? Or me?"

Clifton considered the proposition. "I think he would if he knew he'd get away with it, but he's smart enough to realise he can't. Both of us know enough to send him to gaol for the rest of his life. He needs us."

"But if he's for the high jump because of this Ayer thing, the court case might pull us down with him anyway. You know how those things can go."

The Deputy Commissioner of Police sipped his whisky. "I wouldn't worry about that. It'll never happen. Moorhouse won't put him on trial just for this. Imagine the political scandal! The government would probably have to resign, and if it did, Moorhouse knows he wouldn't have a snowball's hope of ever getting to live in his new mansion. No, he has to hold on and hush things up as best he can. I think he'll settle for Claud's resignation."

The General asked softly: "And what will Claud do then?"

Clifton smiled mirthlessly. "You know as well as I do. He'll blackmail us, that's what. He has no other choice. Who'll give him a job? Who'll keep him going? You will, old friend, and so will I. *We'll* collect the protection money, take the risks, and we'll have to give Claud his share."

Luther drew on his cigarette. "That's not too bad."

"Oh yes it is. After a while, he'll want more. He won't be able to live on his share because, don't forget, he won't be drawing a salary any longer. And we'll have to pay up or he'll expose us. As time goes on and he gets desperate, he has less and less to lose."

"So what will we do?"

Clifton made an expansive gesture with his thin arms. "Oh," he said, "that's all a long way off. But maybe he'll get depressed and commit suicide. People would understand. It's an honourable way out for a disgraced Commissioner of Police."

General Luther grinned amiably across at him. They understood each other so quickly.

They could hear Montrose cursing as he came back down the corridor and into his office. His face was still pale, but he no longer seemed drunk.

"Fuck off out of here," he said briefly. "I need some sleep."

Clifton looked at Luther and shrugged. "You going to stay here, Claud?" he asked, standing up.

"What does it look like?"

"Sweet dreams, then. I'll see you before you go off."

Montrose grunted, and turned away, stripping off his khaki jacket.

Luther and Clifton walked into the corridor, closing the door behind them. It was deserted.

"You'd better get here in good time tomorrow and check him out," Luther said. "If there's trouble, call me straight away."

"It'll be fine," Clifton assured him. "I know Montrose. He's almost back to normal already."

The men parted in the car park of the Central Police Station. Both of them smelled of whisky.

Clifton drove to the darkened house, not far from Ayer's, where his family had long gone to sleep. His wife did not stir as he climbed in beside her, and she was still asleep when he rose at his customary 6.30 a.m. His head felt terrible.

He was in uniform and at his desk an hour later, swallowing aspirins to clear his hangover. Clifton knew better than to disturb Montrose too early, so he waited until 8.30 before going through to the Commissioner's office.

As soon as he opened the door, he knew they were in trouble. Montrose had been up for some time, and he was drinking again.

The Commissioner sat behind his desk, staring balefully at Clifton. A quarter-full tumbler of whisky was in his hand, and the bottle (how much of it had they drunk the night before? Clifton wondered suddenly, but he could not remember) was almost empty beside him.

They stared at each other.

"Have a drink," Montrose offered finally, and there was a slight slur to his voice. The office reeked of whisky and stale cigarette smoke.

Clifton suppressed a surge of irritation. "Is this your farewell party, Claud?" he asked, his thin hands clenching by his sides but his voice level.

"Moorhouse's fucking farewell." The Commissioner was drunker than he'd thought. "Today, I'll tell him where he can stick his investigation, and his fucking Members' Register."

The Commissioner poured himself another half-tumbler of whisky, unsteadily.

Clifton crossed to the telephone and dialled General Luther's office. He was through in a matter of seconds, and the conversation was laconic. Then Clifton went across and opened the office window to clear the smoke. The air conditioner had gone off: Christ knew why. The air blowing in was warm and humid.

Montrose watched impassively, saying nothing but occasionally snorting derisively as at a private joke. Gradually the smoke cleared. Clifton checked the air conditioner and found that the plug had been pulled out of the socket – presumably by Montrose tripping over the cord. He pushed it back into place and the machine hummed into action.

Clifton went to close the window.

As he looked out, he could see Luther's car arriving at the main gate and being waved through by the guard. Behind him, there was the clink of bottle against glass as Montrose topped up his drink.

"You are a stupid bastard, Claud," Clifton observed quietly. "Today of all days. You realise you could be out of a job by lunchtime?"

"Not me. Him."

"Oh bullshit. A fat drunk versus the Prime Minister. What a contest."

"Jesus, you skinny black runt," Montrose shouted, half rising from his chair. "You talk to me like that and you die!"

"Oh really!" Clifton said crossly. "Grow up, Claud. The first sniff of trouble and you collapse. Now just pull yourself together and throw that bloody whisky away."

"It's my whisky. I bought it and I'll drink it when I like."

Clifton shrugged helplessly and sat down to await Luther's arrival. The General entered without knocking. He had gathered from the telephone conversation that formalities would not be necessary. He sized up the situation in a few seconds.

"Well, Claud," Luther said in a deceptively friendly voice. "You ready to do battle with the Prime Minister?"

"Fucking sure I am."

"Great. What are you going to say to him about the dossier?"

"I'm going to tell that shit every word is true. That bastard Ayer deserves to be locked up and he's going to stay locked up."

"And what do you think the Prime Minister will say to that?"

Montrose was aggrieved and defensive. "How the hell should I know?"

Luther moved over to the desk and took the whisky bottle and the half filled glass. Montrose saw them going. His hand jerked out to grab them, but then he had second thoughts. Even in his drunken state, he recognized that there was something in Luther's manner which ought not to be challenged. The General was fitter than he, and better trained. Luther took the whisky to a cupboard across the room and locked it inside. He pocketed the key.

"What if," Luther persisted, "the Prime Minister says to you: 'What about the proof that my civil servants have brought me, which shows that your dossier is nothing but a pack of lies?' What then, Claud?"

Montrose was less certain now. "I'll tell him to fuck himself," he said without conviction.

"No you won't. What will you tell him?"

A long silence, then grudgingly: "I'll tell him we need more time."

"What if he won't give you more time? What if he says he's going to release Ayer right away?"

Montrose shrugged, and his shoulders slumped. "He's going to anyway," he said, soft and resigned. "I don't have a hope. I've got no reason to give Moorhouse. I thought about it last night after you left. There's nothing. What the hell can I say?"

"Just buy time," Luther suggested. "You could do what we were talking about last night: admit something has gone wrong and promise to find out what it is. And meanwhile plead for Ayer's release."

Montrose nodded tiredly. But then he said: "I don't think I can do it. Not today."

"It has to be today. In fact . . ." Luther checked his watch. "It has to be in exactly one hour. Now, you bastard, I'm going to get you into shape in the next forty minutes. You're going into the lavatory and you're going to put your finger down your throat and get rid of all that booze."

Montrose groaned. "Oh Jesus, no. Not again."

"Otherwise I'll punch you in the stomach until it all comes up anyway," Luther said pleasantly, knowing they were both aware he had the ability to carry out his threat. "And then you're going to get showered and changed. You can have a couple of Alka-Seltzer and a cup of coffee, and Alec Clifton's going to go along with you at ten o'clock to hold your hand. Okay, Alec?"

Clifton's eyebrows raised in surprise, but it was a sensible idea. Montrose needed someone to back him up, to catch the ball if he faltered. And it wasn't a bad plan to let Moorhouse think the police hierarchy had been burning the midnight oil trying to find out who'd cooked the intelligence reports on Ayer.

He waited in Montrose's office while the Commissioner and the Chief of Staff were in the bathroom at the end of the corridor, and when he thought it was almost time for them to get back, he pressed the intercom button and ordered black coffee. Then he walked quickly along to his own office to find the Alka-Seltzer.

When Montrose emerged, showered, shaved and freshly uniformed, he looked reasonably presentable. His face was pale, however, and his eyes were bloodshot. He had stopped slurring his words.

"What do you think?" Luther asked.

Clifton stared at the Commissioner critically. "I've seen him look better, but he'll pass. If Moorhouse thinks we spent the whole night going through the files on Ayer, that'll account for the fact that he's got roadmaps for eyes and looks like he needs a blood transfusion in his head."

Montrose glanced at his deputy with contempt.

They waited until he had finished the Alka-Seltzer and the coffee, and took him downstairs to his official car. It was 9.45.

Montrose and Clifton completed the journey in silence, but again Clifton was surprised at how calm and composed he now felt, even though they were to confront the Prime Minister from a position of considerable weakness. And Moorhouse was never a man to appreciate weakness.

The Commissioner said nothing as they entered the Cabinet Offices, or went up in the lift, or while Clifton explained to Bob Sehai that he would also be attending the meeting with the Prime Minister. His silence began to worry Clifton. Perhaps Montrose intended remaining mute through the whole interview? Christ, how could that be explained away?

Suddenly they were in the Prime Minister's office, settling themselves in the gilt chairs which made Montrose's bulk look so precarious, and Moorhouse was staring across his desk at the two of them, looking from one to the other. Clifton waited for Montrose to begin, but the silence grew. He stared expectantly at the Commissioner, just as the Prime Minister was doing, yet the man did not move. Clifton felt a surge of alarm and prepared to start himself.

Then suddenly Montrose's voice came; calm and low, and tired.

"Prime Minister, I must personally apologise to you" he said. "We spent all last night, Mr Clifton and myself, going through every intelligence report relating to Stephen Ayer, breaking them down to see which officers said which things. We have come to no firm conclusions. I would be deceiving you if I pretended we were on the verge of a breakthrough. Something is clearly wrong, but precisely what it is will need considerable research. A few weeks, certainly. There is a rottenness in the organisation . . ." his voice rose " . . . which must be found and destroyed. If I had had the time to check every detail myself, double-check each report which was submitted – in fact, put intelligence officers onto watching other intelligence officers – this would never have happened."

Montrose cleared his throat and looked straight into the Prime Minister's eyes, his fat, cruel face seeming curiously repentant and sincere. "If I had known a few weeks ago the things I know this morning," he said, "the name of Mr Ayer would never have been on the list submitted to you. He would have been watched, certainly. There are one or two things about him which are unexplained but, I hasten to add, which might easily have reasonable and convincing explanations. In our country, a man is innocent until proven guilty, even if we're just proving it to ourselves. Therefore Mr Ayer must be considered innocent, and I urge you, Prime Minister, to take steps for his immediate release."

Clifton felt the tension go from his body. Montrose was brilliant.

Now it was the Prime Minister's turn. He touched the tips of his fingers together, almost in an attitude of prayer.

"Thank you, Commissioner," Moorhouse said quietly. "It is always difficult for a man to admit that he was wrong. As I said earlier, we all make mistakes. The important thing is that we should never try to hide them. Rectify them – yes. Pretend they had never happened – that is the road to disaster. I will see that Mr Ayer is released immediately and sent with his family on a holiday at government expense to recover from what I'm sure must have been an ordeal."

"An excellent idea, Prime Minister," Montrose said. "I would like to volunteer to collect Mr Ayer from the Central Gaol myself and take him back home, as soon as the appropriate order is ready."

"That would be a handsome gesture, Mr Montrose. In fact, I have the papers for his release right here, signed by the President last night." The Prime Minister gestured to a file on his desk. "I too was working late."

So, Clifton thought, this morning had really been an exercise to test the Commissioner of Police. He saw Moorhouse glance over at him, so he nodded approvingly.

Clifton said: "Prime Minister, we are all very conscious of the deplorable situation we are in, and we are determined to make amends. The investigation will proceed with vigour. No stone will be left unturned."

"I'm glad to hear it, Mr Clifton. It's a sad day for St David's when we uncover something of this magnitude. Now go and get Mr Ayer and take him home. Please tell him I will call on him personally this evening at six. Meanwhile, I shall issue a press statement saying that he has been totally cleared of all suspicion, and is a free man. If he wants to return as my PPS, I would welcome him back. But if he wishes to do something else – another branch of Government perhaps – then I will understand. I'll do all in my power to accommodate him."

"Very good, sir," Clifton said, and Montrose bowed his head submissively.

"And, Mr Montrose, I shall want a daily report from you on the progress of the investigation. In particular, what other detainees are being held unfairly in our prison? By tomorrow morning, I shall require a preliminary list. If I don't get it, I shall release everyone. Is that understood?"

The Commissioner of Police nodded sadly, but all things considered, it had gone quite well.

He was living to fight another day.

Chapter Eighteen

Ayer slept, exhausted. He hardly noticed the stink of the cell any longer, and the days passed – if days they were – faster than he had believed possible. He slept or dozed for most of the time. He hardly thought about his wife and children any more. Perhaps they had never existed. It seemed impossible that life had ever been different from this. His memories were as insubstantial as dreams, and when he tried to pin them down to specific incidents or people, they fled away. Sometimes he did actually dream, but, as he awoke, these too disintegrated into fragments, and then into vapour.

He noticed the mosquitoes no longer. Perhaps they had left, but he doubted it. They fed while he slept, which was most of the time.

He tried to remember how long he had been inside, but the effort was too much, and he pressed his face into the matted blanket which no longer seemed rough, or smelly, and drifted into sleep.

He awoke, still tired.

Breakfast again, and he drowsed in the gloom. Then lunch and he slept.

Dinner. So soon. Hard to believe. The boots on the concrete, the key at the door. The eye glimpsed through the spy hole.

Ayer struggled to stand. The plate, the dinner plate and mug, they'd want those. He picked them up and stood ready for the ritual exchange.

The door opened and he held out his plate.

"Outside!" a voice ordered suddenly. "Leave that stuff behind."

Ayer felt his pulse race in panic. He did not want to leave the safety of his cell and face the terrors outside. There were tortures and interrogations! Oh God. But his legs, driven by other fears, took him forward into the corridor, and into that blessed air again, so cool and clean as it swept over him that it was hard to imagine anything so fine.

He breathed deeply and gratefully, but then his anxieties crowded in on him again and he looked quickly around, from one warder to the other, eyes bright with fright, and to the third man.

Montrose! Oh Jesus, Montrose had come for him! Ayer's lower lip began to tremble.

When Montrose spoke, there was dismay in his voice. "Oh shit," he said slowly. "What have you done?" He was talking not to Ayer, but to the warders.

The defensive reply: "Followed orders, sir."

"Fuck-ing hell." Montrose drew the words out. Then he said, softly and resigned: "Okay, get him cleaned up."

They moved off, along the concrete corridor with the lights shielded by metal grilles, turned right at the end, along another corridor and into a courtyard. There was grass, green and freshly mown, and shrubs. Above was the sky, and the sun, still high as if it was early afternoon when Ayer knew it must almost be night.

Across the courtyard was another block, in which were showers and flushing lavatories. The air inside still smelled good.

"Strip off," a warder said. "Throw your clothes over there." He pointed to a long wooden bench against a wall. Ayer looked around, but Montrose had gone.

As he took off his prison clothes, he realised how filthy they were, and how both they and he were stinking. He had not changed or bathed since . . . well, since however long he'd been in.

The warders watched without interest, and finally he stood naked on the concrete, waiting for an order.

"Take a shower," the warder said. "Make it a good long one. You look a mess. There's soap in there."

Water, icy, stinging his body. No doors on the shower stall. No doors on the lavatories either. The warders lighting up cigarettes, keeping an eye on him. The filth falling off and gurgling down the drain at his feet, and his heart still thumping with the prospect of the unknown. A hard, brown scrubbing brush found in the corner, and soap, smelling of disinfectant and making a white lather. He had never before felt such luxury.

The water streamed down his face over his closed eyes, and splashes filled his ears. He checked to see if the warders were growing restive, but they showed no signs of wanting to hurry. He soaped himself again. Heaven knew how long it would be before the next time.

At last he was finished. His skin was hurting with the pressure of the water. His hands, rubbing over his rib-cage and shoulders, told him that he had lost weight. He turned off the water, and stood in the stall, dripping.

"There's a towel here," the warder said. Was this the same man who used to scream at him?

The towel was rough but clean, and when he had finished, Ayer waited passively.

"Okay," said the warder. "Let's go."

Ayer walked naked before them along a corridor to a storeroom. The second warder unlocked it, and flicked on the light. Piled along the walls were flat brown cardboard boxes. They searched through them while Ayer stood nervously in the doorway.

"This is it, I think. Okay, get dressed."

A box marked 179886 AYER was placed before him, and the lid removed.

The clothes were beautiful and strange, but as he picked them out, he realised they were his own. They seemed so new and so luxurious.

Fresh panic gripped Ayer. Suddenly he understood that he was being taken to court. Oh Christ, why? he thought. He dressed quickly under the watchful eyes of the warders.

There were clothes left over in the box: ones he had brought from home the night he was detained. One of the warders lifted them out.

"Right," he said. "Let's go."

Ayer fell in behind the first warder, with the second taking up the rear, and they re-crossed the courtyard to the administration block. They halted at the door marked "Superintendent". The lead warder knocked.

"Come in!" Norwood called and, as they entered, he said: "Ah, Mr Ayer. Nice to see you again. How have you been keeping? Sorry I didn't have the chance to look in on you."

Ayer stared at him, bewildered. "I'm . . . I'm fine, sir," he said.

"Glad to hear it. You know Claud Montrose, of course." He waved his hand to the chair in the corner, and the Commissioner of Police smiled subserviently.

"I saw Steve a few minutes ago," Montrose said.

Steve! He's never called me Steve before!

"Well, this is an unexpected turn of events in an unfortunate affair," Norwood said, bafflingly. "Do you have any complaints? Apart from the mosquitoes, that is." He turned ruefully to Montrose. "Mr Ayer was being disturbed by mosquitoes. We all are, of course: it's the area around here – pools of water just left lying. We keep making representations about it but nothing is ever done."

Then, looking back at Ayer: "But otherwise, everything all right?"

Ayer stared at him dully. "Yes, sir."

"Food all right? Enough to eat? As you probably guessed, we pride ourselves on our kitchen. Good grub, hey?"

"Yes, sir," Ayer agreed without enthusiasm.

"Do you know, Claud, some of the prisoners don't want to leave here when they've finished their sentences? They beg to be allowed to stay. The meals are better than they get at home. Costs them nothing, on top of it. Wish I could say the same for the poor old taxpayer."

"That's always the case," said Montrose breezily. "Isn't it, Steve?"

"Yes, sir."

"Well," said Norwood. "Have you got all your things?"

"Not his valuables, sir," the warder said behind him. "We've still got to pick those up."

"Right. Well go and do that now. Claud will wait for you here."

Ayer plucked up his courage. "Where am I being taken, sir?" he asked, his voice low.

"Taken?" Norwood looked surprised. "Claud, what's this? Haven't you told Mr Ayer the good news?"

Montrose's face went pink. "Well, actually I thought I had: at the cell. But I was taken a bit by surprise, so it may have slipped my mind."

"Well I never! Mr Ayer, the good news is, you're a free man. The detention order against you has been revoked. You're going home. Unless our food has tempted you to stay on."

Ayer stared at him dumbly, suspecting a joke, but Norwood had an encouraging smile on his face. Montrose too was smiling, in a clenched-teeth way.

Going home. Inexplicably, Ayer felt panic again, then quickly numbness and unreality. He found it difficult to grasp what it would be like.

The warders escorted him along the corridor to another office. There, a large brown envelope was opened in his presence, and out of it came the things that had been his: a wristwatch with a black leather strap. It had run down and the hands had stopped at ten minutes past eight. A narrow gold wedding band which felt strange as he put it back on his finger, as strange as it had on the day of his wedding, and he suddenly remembered Nora. A leather wallet with his official identification card and pass to enter the cabinet offices, some money. A small overnight case.

Ayer signed that all had been safely restored to him. The second warder packed his clothes into the case, and they walked back to the Superintendent's office.

Montrose stood up at once. "Well," he said. "No offence to Simon Norwood or his excellent cooks, but I'm sure you can't wait to get out of here."

Ayer nodded wordlessly. The Superintendent reached out a hand in farewell and Ayer found that in a wave of gratitude and forgiveness, he was shaking it warmly.

"I'll see you again, I hope," Norwood said. "In happier circumstances, of course."

"Yes," Ayer replied, managing a smile.

The steel gates of the prison – three separate sets of them – were opened as they progressed through, and locked behind them. The warder carried the overnight case.

Montrose's car was parked just outside, and his driver sprang out to open the doors. As they left, the warder saluted.

One last hurdle: the guards at the final checkpoint before the road. Montrose presented a piece of paper, the barrier went up, and they were waved through.

Freedom.

The tarmac road stretched ahead, with the shanties of Port Lombard being reached quickly and the buildings looming beyond them. A beautiful, clear, hot, cloudless day: the sun scorching through the glass. Ayer wound down the window and felt the wind on his cheeks, carrying with it the smell of the distant salt sea. Behind him, beyond the high grey walls and the barbed wire and the watchtowers, prisoners were already locked into night. This was real: this day, this road, the sun. Had the other been real too? Did the two conditions really exist side by side, unknown to one another, with only a few men in uniform moving between them, keeping the daily secret?

Montrose was speaking. "It's been a bad business," he said. "I can't tell you how hard I've been working on your case. I was up all last night, going through the files, the intelligence reports. No sleep at all. As soon as the element of doubt crept in, we got to work. The Deputy Commissioner was with me until all hours. You've no idea what trouble you caused! Of course, there's going to be a full inquiry into how it happened. You don't know anyone with a grudge against you, by any chance?"

"No."

"It must have been hard for you. A nightmare."

"Yes."

"But all's well that ends well. Forget about it as quickly as you can: that's my advice to you. The Prime Minister will be coming to see you this afternoon. You can imagine how he feels. You're being sent off on holiday with your family to recuperate. At government expense, of course. Any idea where you'd like to go?"

"No."

"The north is very nice. You should try Galloway. You've been there, of course."

"No."

"Oh well, that's it then. You must go. Born on the island and not been to Galloway! This is your chance." Montrose's face was shiny with sweat, and his small eyes watched Ayer shrewdly.

"Lovely beaches," Montrose went on. "Your kids swim, do they? Very nice for a family holiday. Quiet: you know what I mean?"

Ayer did not respond and Montrose lapsed into silence. Ayer watched the cars coming in the opposite direction. No one paid them any attention. There were shanties on both sides of the road now, and hundreds of coconut palms; urchin children playing with home-made wire toys, roadside stalls selling fruit and vegetables, groups of men sitting idly ignoring the traffic.

"Does my wife know I've been released?" Ayer asked suddenly.

"I don't know," Montrose admitted. "Perhaps she doesn't. It all happened very quickly. I made my recommendation for your release at ten o'clock this morning, and here you are."

"What's the time now?"

Montrose consulted his watch. "Eleven forty-seven," he said.

"God, I thought it was later. What day is it?"

"Good gracious, don't you know that? It's Thursday, of course. Thursday July the fourth. 1976, in case you've forgotten," he added with a laugh.

"How long have I been in gaol?"

"I'm surprised at you asking," Montrose said jovially. "I thought that was the one thing every prisoner knew. Didn't you scratch the days off on your bedroom wall?"

"It wasn't a bedroom. It was a cell. And I didn't write on the walls."

"Well, you obviously don't have much feeling for tradition, then," Montrose's smile faded slightly. "Now let's see," he said. "The President signed the order for your detention on June the fifth, and you were picked up that night, so that makes it just a day short of four weeks."

The journey seemed interminable, and Ayer felt the urge growing strongly in him to get away from Montrose, to get rid of this dangerous man who tried to mask his hostility, and failed.

At last they were in Nelson Avenue, a road which seemed so familiar, so ordinary, that it was almost a disappointment, and stopping outside his house, a suburban home smaller than he remembered. It was as if he was revisiting old haunts from childhood, to find everything smaller, drabber and changed.

Things looked strange inside, too. He recognised the individual pieces of furniture, of course, and the children's books scattered over the living-room floor. But it was the overall impact which took him by surprise. For years he had known the house and the furniture so intimately that day by day he had noticed nothing. Suddenly he walked into it with new eyes, and what he had expected to be familiar and special was suddenly – ordinary. That was the only word to describe it. Ordinary. And lived in by other people, not by himself.

"Nora!" he called, moving from room to room, checking.

Montrose waited in the hall.

At last Ayer came back to where he was. "She must have gone out," he said. "I'll wait for her. Thank you for the lift."

"I'll stay with you."

"No!" The vehemence in his voice surprised them both. He collected himself and said it again, more calmly. "No. I'll be all right. I'd prefer to wait by myself."

The Commissioner's eyes were hard and watchful, but he managed a thin smile. "If you're sure," Montrose said.

"I'm sure."

Montrose nodded curtly and held out his hand. This time, Ayer had to overcome great resistance before he could bring himself to reach out and touch the other man. The Commissioner's hand was large and muscular. It fastened on him in a tight vice grip. The Commissioner held him for a long time, until Ayer's hand began to hurt and he felt a flush mount on his cheeks.

Then Montrose released him, but remained standing close, his face about a foot away. Ayer desperately wanted to take a step backwards, but he was frozen in his tracks.

The Commissioner stared hard at him, deep into his eyes, and Ayer tried to force himself to meet his gaze but his eyes began to water.

The seconds ticked by. Ayer swallowed. What was he trying to do? Was he building up to say something? Or was he trying to pass a silent message? Ayer's mouth had gone dry and his right hand ached from the Commissioner's grip.

At last Montrose said coolly: "I've no doubt we'll meet again."

He turned and walked to his car, leaving Ayer feeling weak. He knew it was a threat. He closed the front door quickly, and locked it.

Chapter Nineteen

Montrose's car accelerated along the Coast Road, while he stared grimly ahead. It had been a bad day, and he was feeling sick. He couldn't remember when last he'd eaten: it must be twenty-four hours anyway, and an ache throbbed rhythmically in his right temple. He needed food and aspirins.

Montrose rapped on the front seat with his swagger stick.

"Drop me off in the High Street," he ordered, "then go and have lunch. Pick me up outside Maxwell's at two-thirty. Understand?"

"Yes, sir," the driver affirmed.

Montrose watched his car move off before walking into a chemist for a pack of aspirins. He ate four on the spot, chewing them slowly without water. It would be a while before they took effect, and he wondered whether he wouldn't be better off with a drink, a Bloody Mary or a beer, to clear his head properly. He wrestled with his conscience for a while, but in the end his instinct for self-preservation won. This morning's shave with the Prime Minister had been too close for comfort, and at the end of it, he'd only managed to get an extension of time. He couldn't afford anything to go wrong now. They still had to decide on an explanation for the dossier cock-up, and that wasn't going to be easy. In fact, God only knew how they'd do it.

Montrose realised his own position was disintegrating round him, not just because of Moorhouse's suspicions, but because Clifton and Luther would support him only to a certain point. If it became clear he was finished, he would be abandoned without compassion.

He paused outside Maxwell's. There were no signs that there had ever been a riot, or that the store had been looted. The windows were again featuring expensive imports, tastefully displayed, and when he stared in the main door, most of the counters were busy. With the mark-ups he put on his goods, old man Maxwell must be coining in the money, Montrose thought.

The security officers just inside the door saluted respectfully, and he returned their greeting as he entered.

Montrose took the lift to the administration floor and, immediately he stepped out, noticed appreciatively the rich man's smell of fresh ground coffee beans. As usual, the Cona machine near the receptionist's desk was ready filled.

The girl looked up inquiringly, and gave a professional smile of recognition.

"Good afternoon, Mr Montrose," she said. "Have you come to see the General Manager?"

She was a pretty local: skin of light chocolate and eyes that flirted discreetly. Early twenties, he guessed. No rings on her fingers, but a fine chain of gold round her wrist and a heart-shaped gold pendant, which swung slightly between her breasts when she leaned forward. She was obviously aware of Montrose's stare, because her hips swung slightly more than usual as she moved towards Maxwell's office.

She was back within seconds.

"Please come through, Commissioner," she said, meeting his gaze briefly and glancing demurely down. She stood beside the door as he passed through, and although he did not look at her again, his left hand brushed, as if by accident, across the tops of her thighs, ruffling her skirt. He caught the scent of her perfume – obviously expensive and probably French. Bought on staff discount, he thought automatically. Or stolen.

The girl looked quickly round to see if anyone had noticed, and returned to her desk without a backward glance.

Maxwell rose to greet Montrose, fumbling to put his spectacles into their velvet-lined case, and tried to manage a smile.

"Good day, Commissioner," he said. "Won't you sit down?"

"Thank you, Mr Maxwell. And a cup of coffee too, if I may."

Maxwell was immediately flustered at having the initiative taken from him so early in the conversation, and his eyes darted uncertainly around the office. A feeling of helplessness came over him.

"Of course, of course." He collected himself and dialled the girl. "Sheila, bring a cup of coffee for Mr Montrose, would you?" he said in his quiet, precise voice. "No, just one. I won't join him right at the moment."

Montrose's head was still aching, but not quite as badly as before. He gave Maxwell a thin smile. "I see you're doing well downstairs," he said. "No shortage of customers."

"Appearances can be misleading," Maxwell observed stiffly. "Don't forget, it's not all profit. There's the cost of the goods, and shipping and customs duties. Then we've all the overheads: staff salaries, electricity, that sort of thing. A lot of people have to be paid before we make any money."

"You're breaking my heart," said Montrose quietly, looking away.

The receptionist brought in a tray with a coffee cup, a small jug of cream and a bowl of sugar. She placed it on an occasional table near the Commissioner, making sure she stayed out of range. His eyes were on her.

"Cream," ordered Montrose. "And three sugars." When she passed the cup to him, he said curtly: "Fine."

She gave him the flicker of a smile as she left. Montrose stirred his coffee, enjoying the silence and Maxwell's unease.

At last the old man spoke. "Well," he said in an attempt at cheerful conversation, "what's happening on St David's?"

It was the wrong question. The Commissioner closed his eyes in irritation and noticed that his headache had suddenly got worse. Maxwell watched anxiously.

"What you read in the paper," the Commissioner said at last. "That's what's happening. Have you got the money ready?"

Maxwell was startled. "Yes of course. It's in my desk." He reached down to unlock a drawer and brought out a brown envelope. Montrose stretched across to take it. It felt bulky.

"It's all here?" he asked.

"I counted it myself. Eight hundred dollars. That's for a month, of course," Maxwell added hastily.

Montrose pocketed the envelope. "Then I won't bother you any more right now," he said. "You finding the security arrangements satisfactory?"

His tone was aggressive, like a Sergeant Major asking his troops if they had any complaints about the food.

"Yes. Perfectly. Thank you."

"Good. I'll see you next month."

"As you wish."

"I do wish."

Walking past the receptionist's desk again, Montrose's large hand ostentatiously ruffled her hair, thick and silky, and she swung round in alarm, but he gave her not a backward glance as he strolled to the lift.

From his doorway, Maxwell watched bleakly.

Out in High Street again, Montrose went down to Pioneer Stores, his next client, and then on to the St David's Provision Company. He was in and out of each within five minutes. His last business call of the day was at Philips and Company, conveniently near the bank.

He had milked only one-fifth of his allotted stores. It had all become so easy.

He deposited $2,300 in cash in his account.

The visit to the bank was the link in the chain he liked least, but there was no way round it. He had an overdraft to clear. He handed the money directly to the manager in the privacy of his walnut-panelled office, and they spoke about gambling: he jovially, the manager in respectfully disapproving tones.

The Commissioner pretended he was heavily involved in horse racing and a weekly poker school. He had needed some sort of story to explain the large amounts of cash which were suddenly finding their way into his account. Montrose wasn't sure the manager entirely believed it, but it was a convenient fiction and, beyond that, none of the bank's business. His overdraft was being substantially reduced, and that was all that mattered.

Montrose's headache was almost gone, and he felt hungry. He decided to eat in a small restaurant up Stanley Road. On the way, he dropped in at the private post boxes to check Clive Lyle's Number 122. He had made it a routine to call in on his way to the office every morning: but this particular day had been chaos.

The private boxes were in an enclave at the side of the main Post Office building: rows of small green metal doors fronted with brass numbers, stretching in decks along three walls.

So far Montrose had never used the boxes to call a meeting, but he accepted that it was a handy and fairly secure method of communicating with the American. The small key turned in the lock, and Montrose swung the door open.

A white envelope lay face down inside. He fished it out, slightly surprised, and saw the name "Claud" written in pen on the front.

Montrose tore it open and on a single sheet of paper was written simply: "7.15 p.m."

He walked slowly into the sunlight, wondering why Lyle wanted to see him. Still, another meeting would be useful. Maybe Lyle would be able to come up with some ideas on how to explain away the Ayer dossier.

Montrose worked late: sitting in his office until nearly seven, looking through the scanty intelligence files on Stephen Ayer to see if anything in them suggested itself as a story he could use to involve his group of ten.

But every possible scenario was so complex that for it to be believed required an effort of will he knew the Prime Minister would not be prepared to make.

At last, in a mood of depression, he drove through the dusk along the Coast Road towards the picnic ground. Lyle's Chevrolet was parked off the side of the road, and he drew in alongside.

He could see the American's silhouette against the sea wall, but as he walked up it was impossible to tell whether Lyle was watching him come or looking out to sea. Then Montrose saw the glow of the cigarette at his side. He raised his hand in a brief greeting.

"Enjoyed the sunset, sweetie?" Montrose asked, unable to suppress a sneer.

"I always do. That's why I chose this place." Lyle held out the cigarette pack. "Smoke?"

Montrose took one and Lyle lit a match, cupping it against the sea breeze. The Commissioner leaned towards him and, for an instant, touched Lyle's hands to steady himself. Then, remembering what the man was, he moved away lest his gesture be misinterpreted.

"I got your message," Montrose said shortly.

"Yes."

"So? What do you want?"

There was a silence as Lyle took a drag of his cigarette and considered how to begin. "The new spooks are in from Washington," he said. "Ten of them so far. It's not good news."

The Commissioner shrugged in the darkness. "Don't tell me they're on to you already?" he said unsympathetically. "Perhaps your lover boy's been talking."

Lyle refused to rise to the bait. He said coolly: "No, I don't think so. Naturally, everyone's being checked, and I wouldn't be an exception. Even the Ambassador will get a going over. But I've no reason to think they regard me as anything special." He inhaled a mouthful of smoke. "I think they're on to something local."

Montrose grunted. "What sort of thing?"

"It's difficult to say," Lyle admitted. "My links with them are pretty weak since Berenson left. I mean, I do get some access, but not much. Enough to tell me something's going on, but not enough to be sure just what."

"Jesus, that sounds exciting," Montrose said dismissively. "How much can ten new boys find out in, what – a fortnight?"

"That's just it," Lyle said evenly. "They've been here less than that –

eight or nine days, that's all, but you've never seen a bunch of guys more pleased with themselves."

"It's got to be pretty low calibre information, whatever it is," Montrose said. "Perhaps it's a trick of some sort, to see if they can flush out the informer. And maybe they have. You sure you weren't followed?"

Lyle shook his head. "Positive," he said. "You could be right about the trick. I'll be pretty careful in future. Maybe it would be better if we didn't meet again for a while."

"Oh no you don't," Montrose said swiftly, his tone derisive. "You don't sneak out of it that easily. If I want you, I'll call you."

Lyle stubbed out his cigarette on the sea wall, and a shower of glowing red ash dropped. "I wasn't trying to sneak out," he said. "But let's at least keep meetings down to a minimum: essential ones only. That's reasonable."

"Sure," said Montrose. "I certainly don't want to troop out here just to have a cosy chat in the dark with you, sugar plum. I'll call you if I need you."

The American shrugged. They sat in hostile silence for a moment, listening to the crashing of the waves behind them.

"Actually, I'm not convinced it is a trick," Lyle said at last. "I think maybe I missed out some agents on the list I gave you. Anyway at least one. And he could have a whole local network we don't know about."

"For Christ's sake," Montrose said. "Surely you know who's a fucking spook around your place? Your friend Berenson would have known anyway."

"Not necessarily," Lyle said. "It's mostly on the need-to-know basis. If there was a deep cover agent around, maybe even the Ambassador wouldn't have been told. I just don't think the latest information can have come from the new guys. And anyway, it's obvious there's a basic St David's source still operating."

"What is the information?"

"Hard to tell. A list of names is all I've seen. People who apparently know things we think should be made public quickly. I just had a glance at the list. I wasn't able to copy it all out." He felt in his pocket. "Here, light a match. I wrote down the three names I remembered. They don't mean a thing to me."

Lyle unfolded the paper, and Montrose again found himself standing close to the man. The match flared and the flame settled down.

"Gallo," Lyle read, "Molvi. Guntur."

Montrose stood frozen, not bothering to move away from Lyle. The match went out. The atmosphere was electric.

"Gallo, Molvi, Guntur," he said softly, almost to himself. He felt a chill of fear creeping up the back of his neck.

"What's it mean?" Lyle asked.

"Now listen, Clive," said Montrose, addressing him by his Christian name for the first time, his voice friendly. "How many names were on the list?"

"Hell, it's difficult to say. I was only able to get a look at it for three or four seconds. Those were the top names. I suppose there were nine, maybe ten altogether."

That chill again. Montrose felt his stomach contract.

"Now what were your boys saying about the names?"

"They were excited. Someone had discovered these people had important information, and it was in America's interests that it should be made public."

"The people on the list were ready to talk?"

Lyle thought for a moment. "No, not exactly," he said carefully. "At least, I don't think so. They had information, that's all. I got the feeling they might need to be persuaded to talk. It was getting their names that was the important thing for us. That's what turned everybody on."

Montrose asked as casually as he could: "Any idea where they might have got the names from?"

"None."

"Even the general area? From government, maybe? Or the police even?"

"No, nothing. The idea is to give the names to someone in authority and let everything run from there."

"Who? Who would they tell?"

"I don't know. The Prime Minister probably."

After the studied calm of his earlier questions, Montrose suddenly raised his voice in anger. "What makes you say the Prime Minister, you stupid bastard!" he shouted. "Why not someone else? Why not me, for example?"

Lyle was unmoved. "Because there was a suggestion they might bring the Ambassador himself in," he said calmly. "The Ambassador doesn't talk to the Commissioner of Police. He talks to the Prime Minister."

"Moorhouse wouldn't listen to Leister," Montrose scoffed. "He doesn't trust the Americans."

"Maybe not," Lyle agreed. "Maybe they'll ask someone else to tell him. Their source, whoever he is. He might have access to the Prime Minister."

Montrose fell silent, but he could hear his heart thumping loud under his khaki jacket. At last he said: "Jesus, I wish I knew what was going on."

Lyle replied equably: "So do I, Claud. But I know even less than you do. Who are these three guys?"

"Ten," said Montrose bitterly. "If my luck's running true to form, that list has all ten of them. They're the bastards I taught *your* disruption lessons to. They're the ones who've been leading the demos."

"The one against Maxwell's?"

"That, and the other one."

Lyle gave a low whistle. "Poor old Claud."

"Poor old Claud, nothing. If those buggers say one word about it, they're dead."

Lyle lit another cigarette and exhaled slowly. "But so are you," he said quietly.

Defensive: "Not necessarily."

"Correct me if I'm wrong, but I seem to remember three people died in the first riot, and another one in the attack on Maxwell's." Montrose's silence was his confirmation. "And if your ten do talk, they'll say you put them up to it. It'll be a murder charge, Claud."

"They won't say anything."

"I hope you're right, for your sake. It would be pretty embarrassing to be mistaken over a thing like that. What sort of people are they, anyway?"

"Dregs," Montrose said scornfully. "Cheats and thieves and a couple of rapists."

"And you don't think they'd sing like canaries?"

Another silence.

"They'll sing, Claud," Lyle insisted softly. "You know it. If they thought it would help them, they'd tell on their mothers. No wonder the CIA is laughing."

"I'll stop them," Montrose said flatly.

"How?"

Montrose shrugged. "There are ways."

Lyle waited expectantly, but the Commissioner of Police was in no mood to offer explanations. He gave a low groan deep in his throat. "Oh fuck it," he said savagely. "This whole thing is going out of control. Now listen, Clive, you keep your eyes and ears open around that Embassy, and I want to see you here tomorrow night, same time. I don't care if you're being followed by every CIA man on the island. I want you here, and I want to know more about this whole deal."

"I don't know if I can help you," Lyle said evenly. "I told you: I don't have links with the new guys."

"Then make some. Blow kisses at them in the men's room if you have to. I've got to find out who leaked the names of my ten. And I have to know if Moorhouse has been told."

Lyle shrugged. "I'll do what I can," he said, "but no promises."

"You'd bloody well better," Montrose said, his parting shot. He stalked off without another word, a fat, cocky figure quickly lost in the darkness.

Lyle watched him go.

Chapter Twenty

Montrose pushed his foot hard onto the accelerator and the rear wheels spun in the sand as the car leapt forward, careering to the right. He swung the steering to correct it, and it straightened and sped along the dirt road, the corrugations beating abruptly underneath and the headlights picking up the slanting trunks of palms which fringed the track. Ahead was the tarmac Coast Road.

An oncoming pair of headlights forced him to give way and the wheels skidded in the dirt as he braked. Montrose cursed loudly.

Then he was off, foot flat, engine racing. He caught up with the other car within thirty seconds, and was doing eighty-five miles per hour when he passed it, flashing his lights.

Montrose's lips pressed together, tight and thin, but his small eyes stayed thoughtfully on the road. He now felt calm, even determined. He was not certain precisely what it was he was determined to do, but he felt released from the impotence which had gripped him after the confrontation over the dossier.

It was clear that that problem had simply been a diversion. A lot had been at stake, it was true, and he had been out on his own, unprotected, with even Clifton and Luther prepared to let him sink. He could have lost his job and been disgraced. But it was nonetheless a diversion.

Now it was war. They were all in it together, and if they lost, it would not only be their careers at risk, but their lives too. They still hanged people in St David's, and Lyle had been right: the charge would be murder.

The lights of Port Lombard came up, and Montrose checked his speed, then reduced it further as he came to the turn. He swung left into Constitution Avenue, tyres squealing, and accelerated again along the four-carriage highway past the library, the court buildings and Parliament, until at the end, he saw the turn-off to Luther's house.

Another two hundred yards, and the wheels skidded to a halt.

The lights were on, and Montrose could dimly see through the net curtains at least two people in the living-room. As he climbed out, he could smell hot rubber from his car. He walked quickly up the path.

Montrose beat loudly on the door and rang the bell simultaneously. After a few seconds, it opened suddenly with General Luther's muscular figure, braced ready for trouble.

When he saw who it was, he said: "Jesus, Claud. What's wrong with you? You sick?"

Montrose shook his head. "We've got to talk," he said. "Get Clifton round right away. This is an emergency."

Luther stared at him blankly for a moment, then stood aside. "You need a drink," he said.

"No," Montrose replied, stepping into the hallway. "No thanks. There's work to do."

Luther shrugged. "You're right. It is an emergency."

"And it isn't fucking funny, either."

"I never said it was, Claud. Now come and sit down, for Christ's sake. Have you eaten?"

"No, but I'm not hungry."

"Okay, well we've just finished. I'll call Clifton while you have some coffee."

Montrose went through to the living-room, and smiled thinly at Luther's wife, a slender girl of twenty-six, wearing jeans and a tight tee-shirt. Although he disliked her, he tried instinctively to pull in his stomach.

She looked at him over the top of her brandy balloon. "Hello, Claud," she said. "What a noise you made. We thought it was the police. Do you want a drink?"

"Good evening." He tried to smile, but failed. "Sorry to break in like this. We've got important work to do. No drink, thanks, but I could take a cup of coffee."

Montrose sat on the large modern sofa, covered in a grey synthetic fabric shot with silver thread. Behind his head were framed photographs of Luther taking the salute at a parade, Luther posed near an old Sherman tank, Luther being presented with a medal by the Prime Minister, and Luther smiling between two of his military colleagues. On the other side of the room, near the stacked stereo equipment and the pile of records, most of them out of their jackets, was an illuminated tank where tropical fish glided through pale green ferns, and a plastic diver sent up a stream of bubbles from a floor of coloured stones.

Priscilla was stretched on the carpet, her back against an armchair. The wall behind her was midnight blue, and hanging in the centre was a portrait of herself in pastel chalk.

She finished her brandy and walked casually over to the tea-trolley. She half-turned to Montrose: "Sure you won't change your mind?"

"Coffee's fine."

Luther came back in, picking up his drink from a side table and sitting in the chair next to his wife. "He'll be along in three minutes," he said to Montrose.

"Who's that?" Priscilla asked, looking round.

"Alec Clifton. I've asked him to come over."

"An old boys' reunion. Do you want me to organise sandwiches or anything?"

Luther touched her shoulder affectionately. "No thanks, darling. I think everyone's eaten."

Alec Clifton lived just up the road, and within a few minutes the doorbell sounded. Montrose had never thought the day would come when he'd be glad to see Clifton's anxious, lined black face: although of course, it wasn't looking so anxious these days. A change had come over the Deputy Commissioner. Perhaps he'd suddenly grown balls, but Montrose felt the answer was more mundane than that: he had the uneasy sensation that Clifton had begun to smell power, to imagine that he, Montrose, was on the way out and that the desk of the Commissioner of Police would soon be his own. Clifton was being fuelled by ambition, and it had made a man of him.

Well, thought Montrose bitterly, let's see the smile fade when he hears the latest news. See how he feels when his new balls get kicked.

Clifton was composed and cordial. He gave Priscilla Luther a kiss on both cheeks and exchanged pleasantries. To Montrose, there was a brisk nod and an "Evening, Claud."

The bastard still obviously thought he was finished. Montrose began to take a grim pleasure in what he would soon have to say.

When Clifton was settled with a drink, Montrose stared pointedly at Priscilla, who took the hint.

She looked at her watch. "Goodness," she said. "Look how late it is! Eight-fifteen! Time I was in bed. I hope you gentlemen will excuse me."

Montrose glared at her coldly. Luther said apologetically: "I'm sorry about this, darling, but we've got something important to discuss." He had the air of a husband who knew he'd be made to pay later.

"No, no," she replied. "I've been meaning to get an early night for ages, and now I can. Goodnight, darling." She touched her hand lightly on the top of Luther's head where the hair was thinnest, and turned to the others. "Goodnight, Alec. Nice to see you again." To Montrose, an inclination of the head and a slightly mocking tone: "Commissioner."

Montrose watched her steadily, his face fat and bland.

When she had gone, the others looked expectantly across. Montrose took his time. He chose a cigarette from his pack, and lit it slowly. From the corner of his eye, he saw Clifton and Luther exchange wry glances.

"I've met Lyle," Montrose began. "There are new CIA men in the Embassy. They've got the names of the ten idiots we used for the riots. They're going to tell Moorhouse." He paused to let the news sink in. Their faces betrayed nothing. They waited for him to continue.

"Lyle says he might have missed a deep cover agent, which means that there'll be a local cell we don't know about."

Still no reaction from the other two. They watched silently. Montrose felt uneasy, then resentful.

"Fucking hell," he said, raising his voice. "Don't you shitheads understand what I'm saying? They know we organised the riots! They know how we did it! Who we used! Those bastards have got enough to hang us!"

Clifton sighed and took a sip of his whisky. "How can they know,

Claud?" he asked. "Are you sure you're not making this up?"

Montrose's face went puce, but with a mental effort he controlled himself. When he spoke, his voice was calm, but clipped with anger.

"Point one," he said. "It doesn't matter two shits how they found out: at least, not right now. It only matters that they know. Lyle saw a list of names – ten names, he says. He saw it for a couple of seconds, that's all, and he remembered only the top three names. Gallo, Molvi and Guntur. Gallo and Guntur are yours, General. Molvi is one of ours."

Luther went across to pour himself another drink. He spoke with his back towards them.

"What about the other names, Claud? How do we know they're part of the ten?"

"We don't. We have to presume they are. We have ten people; they have ten names. Three of the ten are on the list. The other seven aren't going to be fucking washerwomen, are they?"

There was the chink of ice against crystal and Luther turned round, his face thoughtful.

"Claud's right," he said to Clifton. "We have to make that presumption. Any chance of Lyle having another look?"

"I've asked him to find out whatever he can. I'm meeting him again tomorrow. But he isn't hopeful. He isn't having it off with any of the new guys. Not yet, anyway. So his links are restricted."

"But what are they going to do with the information?" Clifton asked. Montrose noticed with irritation that he was remaining calm.

"They're going to stick it up their arseholes, Alec," he said unpleasantly. "They're going to eat the piece of paper and forget all about it. What in the name of Christ do you think they're going to do?"

Clifton stared at him with contempt. "For example," he said, ignoring the response, "are they going to try and take it directly to Moorhouse? That would make it easier to discredit. Moorhouse still hates the Americans: even after the collapse of your dossier, Claud, he's still suspicious of them. Probably marginally more suspicious of them than he is of you."

Luther could see the exchange was about to deteriorate into a slanging match. "Listen," he broke in, "let's keep calm. There's a lot of work to be done, a lot of planning. We can't afford to waste time. Claud, it'll probably be easier if you take us right through the conversation with Lyle, as accurately as you can make it."

Luther and Clifton listened quietly while the Commissioner talked of the meeting by the sea wall. Occasionally the General asked a question. Clifton remained silent, sipping his drink.

"So that's as much as I know," Montrose concluded. "They're going to get the information to Moorhouse somehow, and we don't know when."

Luther selected a cigar from a box nearby, and sliced off the end with a silver cutter. The others watched. Clifton and Montrose knew instinctively he was about to take control, and that he was the only one who could.

Luther lit up, the match flaming high against the tip of the cigar, and a cloud of smoke wreathing his face.

Finally he said: "On a scale of one to ten, how do you rate the danger to our position, Claud?"

Without hesitation: "Ten."

"Alec?"

A pause. Then: "If it's correct, ten."

"Yes," Luther said, "I agree. Ten. Claud must have his meeting with Lyle again tomorrow, and Alec, you'll go along with him."

Montrose started to object, but then he shrugged. He had nothing to hide.

"With any luck, we'll be able to find out how far the information has gone," Luther observed. "There's nothing we can do to stop the Americans now. I don't think there's any point in trying to get the Prime Minister to expel the new CIA men: there isn't enough time and the moment is bad psychologically. So we must expect they'll get the news out."

He puffed at his cigar. "We just have to be sure it makes no difference."

Chapter Twenty-one

There was almost an election atmosphere in the offices of the Democratic Front. The old, high-ceilinged house, with its corrugated iron roof and the wooden strip floor which creaked underfoot, had once seemed empty and unjustifiably large for the party's activities. But gradually, as the people turned against Moorhouse, the Front's importance had grown. More members were recruited: then others began joining of their own accord. A temporary secretary was employed to cope with the additional work. Before long, she became permanent, and extra staff and volunteers were brought in.

Now the house was filled with people. It hummed with the noise of talking, of telephones constantly ringing and, in the background, the rhythmic sound of a duplicator throwing out two pieces of printed paper every second into a growing pile inside a metal basket.

The one oasis of calm was the office of the Democratic Front President, Albert Francis. He was alone, frowning as he read through a document. Behind his desk was the flag of St David's, and the walls were hung with photographs of himself, of well-attended rallies and with party posters, most of which were personal attacks on the Prime Minister.

On one of these, the neo-Corinthian lines of the controversial official residence, etched strongly on a bright orange background with a cartoon of the Prime Minister beside it, were followed by the words: "Moorhouse makes us Sick." In the corner was the Democratic Front logo.

Another showed a gloating Prime Minister in front of his white house, with the scornful legend: Minister of Tourism.

A third had large white letters on a black background and was laid out like an official warning poster. It said: "CAUTION: MOORHOUSE IS DANGEROUS TO YOUR HEALTH."

They were, Albert Francis was prepared to acknowledge breezily, crude and cheap propaganda, but, he felt, they went right to the heart of the problems confronting St David's and, most important of all, they worked. The activity in the Front's headquarters proved that.

The Prime Minister had spent money on an opulent residence for himself, rather than on the sewage and water supplies of Port Lombard, and a cholera outbreak had destroyed the tourist trade. Those facts were enough to wreck Moorhouse's political career, and the more starkly they were presented to the electorate, the better for the Democratic Front.

But, at the moment, Francis was concerned with another matter. In the morning's post had come an anonymous letter, addressed to him personally and marked "Urgent".

Usually anonymous letters were written in capital letters or in felt-tipped pens of different colours, and they went straight into the rubbish bin. This one Albert Francis had read carefully, and was now going through a second time, his brow wrinkling thoughtfully.

It was on a single sheet of thick, good quality paper. From the clear, precise handwriting and the phrasing of the sentences, the author was an educated man. He had used a fountain pen, which further appealed to Albert Francis, who personally disapproved of ball-points for correspondence, even anonymous correspondence.

The tone of the letter was low key: no sign of hysteria, just matter-of-fact statements:

Dear Mr Francis,

I felt I should draw to your attention the existence of corruption in the St David's police force. The Commissioner of Police, Mr Claud Montrose, is running what can only be called "a protection racket". He demands from major stores in Port Lombard – and possibly elsewhere – weekly payments to ensure their security from attack. One of these stores is my own.

Recently, Maxwell's refused to pay, and you will recall what happened to it soon afterwards. I realise that the riot stemmed directly from a Democratic Front procession led by yourself – in fact, that is why I am writing to you now. You have, of course, condemned the violence in the strongest terms, and I accept your assurances of innocence. But were there professional trouble-makers in the crowd? If so, on whose orders were they acting? You will remember that Commissioner Montrose took a considerable time to reach the scene of the trouble, and Maxwell's suffered much damage. Subsequently that store, and others who had similarly hesitated, resumed their weekly payments to Commissioner Montrose, since when there has been no trouble. Is this a coincidence?

I doubt there is anything you can do about this, because of the state of emergency and the extraordinary powers now possessed by the Commissioner of Police. However, I thought you ought to know what was going on.

As for those of us who are victims of the protection racket, I wish we could help you further, but we fear for our livelihoods and, indeed, for our safety.

Therefore I regret I cannot sign this letter. I apologise for something which must seem to you to be an act of cowardice.

Albert Francis stared thoughtfully at the letter. If it was true, no wonder the writer wanted to remain anonymous. Claud Montrose was a feared figure on the island. Even before the Emergency, people had been wary of him, but now he was probably the most powerful person around. More powerful than the Prime Minister, some said.

Francis picked up the telephone on his desk and dialled an internal office number.

"Sam?" he asked. "Have you got a few minutes to spare?"

He leaned back in his chair, staring at the anti-Moorhouse posters on his walls, and waited for the arrival of his party vice-chairman, Sam Wallace. He needed to talk this over, and Wallace had a sensible head for problems and an instinctive feel for what would work to the party's political advantage. He was young – only thirty – but Albert Francis had come to respect his judgment and lean on him more than he cared to do with the older office-bearers of the Front.

There was a brief knock and the door swung open.

"Come in, Sam," Francis said cheerily, waving him to a seat on the other side of his desk. "Oh – and close the door."

Sam Wallace was straight British stock, although he had been born and brought up in Port Lombard, and he considered the island his home. He was of medium height and wiry, with glasses which he needed mainly for reading but tended to keep on all the time. This gave him a quiet, studious air.

Albert Francis passed the anonymous letter across and waited silently while he read it. Wallace's face betrayed no expression, and, at the end, he put it back on the desk.

"Well?" asked Francis. "What do you think?"

"I don't like anonymous letters."

"Nor do I. But?" he prompted.

"I don't recognise the writing either. I know quite a few of the store-owners around here through my father."

"He was in import-export, wasn't he?" Francis remembered.

"That's right. All of them have been round at the house at some time or another, and after Dad died I went through his old files to sort things out. This handwriting is pretty distinctive. I think I'd have remembered if I'd seen it before."

"Do you still have any of those old files?" Francis asked.

"Some," Sam Wallace replied. "I'll have to look through them tonight. I'll take the letter with me for comparison."

"Okay. It would be interesting to know who sent it, although I don't suppose it'll help us much. He's obviously not prepared to say anything publicly."

"I can understand why," Wallace observed wryly. "Montrose is a bad man to tangle with."

"But is he corrupt? That's the question."

"There've been rumours, nothing more than that. Some people say he's the finest Commissioner of Police money can buy."

Albert Francis grinned. "Thanks. I'll use that in a speech some day."

"But not yet, Al. For God's sake, let's not go into this thing at half-cock. It could explode in our faces. As it is, we're sailing pretty close to the wind. We don't want Moorhouse to ban the Front and shove us all in gaol. Before we make charges, we have to be sure they'll stick."

"So what do we do? Investigate?"

"Why not? I'll take it on myself, if you can spare me for a couple of days. I'll go and have words with some of Dad's old friends and see if I can get any worthwhile line. I'll start with our friend the anonymous letter-writer if I can discover who he is. Otherwise, I'll go to old man Maxwell."

"He's such a nervous old codger, I don't think you'll get much out of him," Francis observed. "Anyway, it's worth a try."

"After that, I'll work my way down the High Street. Someone's sure to let something slip, even if it isn't for publication."

"Well, if it isn't for publication, it won't be much good to us, will it? I want something I can shout from the rooftops. I want to prove that Moorhouse isn't only running a stupid, inefficient and self-seeking administration, but a corrupt one too."

Sam Wallace paused thoughtfully. "If we can do it that way, fine," he said at last. "But my guess is we won't find anyone prepared to come out and repeat publicly what's in that letter. Don't forget, the man who sent it obviously suspects Montrose is crooked enough to put professional trouble-makers into the crowds at our meetings and to bust up the stores of people who won't pay protection money. The other thing we shouldn't forget is that a man got killed in the riot at Maxwell's, so we could even be talking about murder. And if that's true, we're mixing with the big league. Still, that doesn't mean to say we should be frightened into silence. There *are* things we can do. And we can make sure the Front benefits, at least indirectly."

"What things?" Francis asked.

"Take the whole case privately to Moorhouse," Sam Wallace said simply.

Albert Francis groaned. "That's a terrible idea, Sam," he said. "You can do better than that."

Wallace smiled at him, unflustered. "No it's not. Think about it, Al."

"What if Moorhouse himself is involved? Maybe he's getting a cut."

"Anything's possible," Wallace conceded. "That would be a risk. But I don't think the Prime Minister's corrupt. Foolish, yes. Pig-headed, arrogant and a bad judge of men. All those things I'd go along with, and a lot more. But corrupt? I wonder. Look at how he released Stephen Ayer. It was a massive climb-down, but he did it. I hear he had to walk all over Montrose to get Ayer out."

"Well that was a disgrace anyway," Francis said. "He couldn't have left him rotting in prison if the man was innocent."

"Of course he could," Wallace said cheerfully. "It's done all over the world. Gaols are full of innocent men. It hurt Moorhouse politically to release Ayer, at a time when he could have done without more bad publicity. And it could get worse. I meant to tell you: I hear Moorhouse might release all the others today unless the Commissioner can convince him otherwise. From the sound of things, the two of them are on a collision course."

Francis whistled. "That would be something," he said.

"Wouldn't it? And if we could prove the Commissioner of Police was running a protection racket, and is at least an accessory to murder, then Moorhouse is as good as dead. He has to resign."

"So," said Albert Francis. "That brings us back to my earlier point: it has to be a bad idea to take the corruption charges to Moorhouse."

"Not if he isn't corrupt himself. Not if he's a man of principle, Al."

"Oh come on! You sound like you might be designing posters for him next."

"I kid you not. It was a principled thing to let Ayer go when he must have known it would hurt him politically. It will be even more principled to set the others free as well. So I think we can count on the Prime Minister's good offices. And as I said, we can do ourselves a favour at the same time."

"How?"

"We prove to Moorhouse that the Commissioner is a crook. Moorhouse suspends the Commissioner and starts an inquiry. With Montrose out of the way, our friend the anonymous letter-writer, and all the others, suddenly find it's okay to come out in the open and make their complaints. Goodbye, Montrose. Now we don't get the immediate benefit of announcing it all in public, but the truth that it was the Front who exposed him should come out about the time the general election gets underway. And Moorhouse will still have to have an election, because his Commissioner of Police – a kingpin in the Emergency saga – has turned out to be a criminal and a killer."

"Hmmmm," said Francis reflectively. "Maybe."

"I knew you'd see it my way." He grinned across at the party leader. "By the way, how do you like the speech?"

"Not bad. I thought we might thump the Ayer case a bit harder. I've made some amendments."

"Fine. They're all ready to run it off as soon as the final draft comes through. I think it will be a good meeting. We've had a couple of teams out today putting up posters." Sam Wallace stood up to leave. "Should be a good crowd tomorrow. I think the people are ready for a really big protest rally."

"A really big – peaceful – protest rally," said Francis fervently.

"We'll have more marshals in the park this time. There shouldn't be a repetition of the last incident, whatever Montrose might do."

"Let's make sure there isn't. We don't want the Democratic Front becoming associated in people's minds with violence. That's not our image at all."

"We'll do what we can. It should be all right. If you ask me, the thing we ought to worry about is the police breaking up the meeting because of the emergency regulations. We might all be in gaol tomorrow."

Francis shrugged. "Maybe," he said. "That wouldn't do us any harm electorally. We'll become a party of martyrs. People love that sort of thing."

Sam Wallace laughed. "How do the martyrs feel about it though?" he asked.

"That's not usually recorded. It's probably a bit like childbirth: awful for the woman while it's going on, but she forgets the bad parts pretty quickly afterwards. Triumph is a great healer. Which reminds me – stay away from the rally tomorrow."

"What?"

"Yes, keep well away. If we get arrested, we need someone to hold the fort here, send us in cakes with files in the middle, that sort of thing."

"Are you sure?" Wallace asked.

"Positive. There's no point your sitting in prison as well when you could be getting the evidence to nail the Commissioner and topple Moorhouse. How you handle things will be up to you," Francis said.

"That makes sense, I suppose. I hope it won't come to that, though."

"So do I. But we got away with holding a rally once, and I've got a feeling Montrose won't let us get away with it again."

Chapter Twenty-two

Montrose was in his office by seven a.m. having snatched only a few hours sleep, but he felt alert and grimly confident. The adrenalin was pumping through his body. They were back as a team: he, Clifton and Luther, and they had gone onto the offensive.

For hours the night before, they had discussed tactics, making plans and discarding them, until finally they had agreed on a scheme which could be operated in stages. If it was ever followed through to the end, Montrose thought, it would shake up St David's as the island had never been shaken up before. It might even make them rich, but that would be the reward for the risks they had to take.

The important thing now was to seize the initiative from Moorhouse, who thought he was so smart ordering the release of Ayer and demanding a full investigation into what had gone wrong. The Prime Minister might think he still had the ball; and they'd let him believe that for a day or two yet, but in fact it was an illusion. Not only was the ball out of his hands, but the game was changing totally while he slept.

One day he would realise this, and it would be too late.

Meanwhile there was work to be done and not many hours left before the Democratic Front held their illegal meeting in Jubilee Park. Montrose walked through to the briefing-room and drew a map in chalk on the blackboard.

As he was finishing, he heard a noise behind him, and he swung round to see his group standing in the doorway: tough, young, sure of themselves. No flicker of emotion crossed the Commissioner's face.

"Get in here and sit down," he said quietly, before turning back to complete the map.

There was a scraping of chairs, and by the time Montrose was ready, his ten were watching silently.

He wasted no time on preliminaries. "This is a map," he said, hitting the board hard with his swagger stick so that the sound was almost like a pistol shot, "of Jubilee Park, here . . ." smack " . . . with the bandstand round here, and the Imperial Hotel . . ." smack " . . . just here. Jubilee Avenue runs along there to the West and East. Everyone with me so far?"

He glared round, his small eyes cold.

Silence.

"Right. The Democratic Front, who brought you stereo sets and cash last time, are meeting again. Starting time, one o'clock. Lots of people on the streets for lunch hour, so should be a big crowd. Now it begins just like last time, build them up, help Mr Francis along, get everything going. Then we – that is, the uniformed police – are going to move in. We're closing off three sides like this, so the crowd's going to have to run in this direction. We'll funnel them into Jubilee Avenue through this gate here . . ." smack " . . . and that's when you get to work."

The men glanced surreptitiously at each other, grins quickly stifled, except Molvi, who began whispering to Gallo on his left, refusing to be silenced immediately by the Commissioner's glare. Montrose watched coldly. Molvi would pay for that.

"There are a couple of pretty nice plate glass windows in the front of the Imperial Hotel," Montrose said finally. "They'll do for a start. No one will be able to get into the Imperial, by the way. We'll see to it that the doors are locked and there'll be police on duty to arrest anyone trying to go in through the broken windows. So the crowd gets pushed down Jubilee Avenue to these shops along the north side. Smash 'em all up, get things started there. You'll find this one, the second from the end, is a radio and television shop. There's only one of them so you can't make a mistake. Give it your special attention. They have portable televisions, by the way. Who wants one of those?"

There was a moment's hesitation before one man – Kayaban – put up his hand.

"Right," said the Commissioner. "That's what you'll take, Kayaban. Anyone else? What about you, Molvi? Or you, Gallo?"

Gallo looked sheepish.

"I already got a television," Molvi said, clearing his throat.

"Me too," Gallo agreed.

"Well," said Montrose, "as it happens, I want a portable TV. So you, Molvi, are going to pick one up for me. Understood?"

Molvi looked sullen. "Yes, sir."

"If you want anything yourself, one of the others will have to help because you won't have a chance to go back. Your vehicle, the same van as last time, will be parked up the side street here . . ." smack " . . . which is Connaught Street, so you don't have far to go. If you get there early enough, you'll find a parking space nearby. Any questions?"

Silence.

"Good. Now for your getaway, you'll act on a signal, and you'll act together. You can collect what loot you want but do not – repeat do not – leave the shop until you hear a volley of shots. That means it's time to move. You get out of there, stash your things in the back of the van, and drive like hell. From the first volley of shots until we move in properly, you've got three minutes."

He saw the men exchange glances again. It was long enough for them to get clear if they parked the van near the corner.

Montrose took them through the plan once more, making sure it was imprinted in their minds, then threw the van keys across and ordered them to get out.

They went to drive the unmarked van from the vehicle pool to

Connaught Street while they could still choose from rows of empty parking spaces.

The Commissioner returned to his office and called for a tray of coffee and some rolls. When he had eaten, it was time to brief his Security Battalion men on how they should handle the Democratic Front meeting, and he picked up Alec Clifton on the way.

It was extraordinary how Clifton had changed, how assured he was becoming, even though this morning Montrose could detect a lurking sense of apprehension, of nervousness at the new course on which they had embarked. But it was nothing like the depressed, scared figure the Deputy Commissioner had presented a few days earlier. Montrose wasn't sure he welcomed the change, but there was nothing he could do about it: at any rate, not immediately.

When the briefing was over, the men went to draw their weapons and ammunition. They were in position, out of sight of Jubilee Park, just as the crowd began assembling. Placards were in evidence this time: "Now Release The Others," they read. "Moorhouse Out." "Bring Back Democracy." "End the Phoney Emergency." The Democratic Front flag was unfurled around the bandstand.

It was obviously going to be a well attended meeting. By one o'clock, there were two thousand people in the park, and the numbers grew steadily. Ten minutes later, Albert Francis arrived, to cheers and applause. He clasped both hands over his head in acknowledgement, rather like a prize fighter, as party marshals escorted him to the bandstand.

Before he began his speech, Albert Francis took a good look around. One solitary police car was parked a couple of hundred yards away, but there was no other evidence of an official presence. Francis wondered if his earlier fears had been misplaced. Perhaps Montrose would leave them to get on with their meeting after all.

He lifted the loudhailer. "My friends!" he said. "I see we have a police car parked over there watching us."

Heads craned round to look. There was little nervousness because the crowd was large and still growing and in the numbers there seemed to be security.

"I welcome them!" Francis declared. "I welcome the police watching our little meeting here this afternoon, and I hope they enjoy it as much as we will because on this entire island, this is the only place where democracy is still being practised! Everywhere else there is the rule of the dictator!"

There was a cheer of agreement.

Montrose, watching with Clifton from the police car, picked up his radio microphone and gave the order for his forces to move in.

"The gaols are full of political prisoners!" Francis said. "Fellow-islanders are being held without trial, without charge! Their lawyers are not permitted to see them! Their wives cannot see them! Other wives can visit the lowliest thief or the vilest murderer, but such privileges are refused to the families of those who have committed no crime! This is nothing less than a disgrace!"

The people, led by Motrose's ten, applauded and shouted encouragement.

"A disgrace! And now the tattered fabric of the excuse which Daniel Moorhouse has given for the detentions is exposed for the shameful, threadbare thing it is! Stephen Ayer, Moorhouse's faithful Personal and Private Secretary, arrested at midnight by a whim of the man for whom he laboured, is released after a long and terrible ordeal in solitary confinement! We rejoice in Stephen Ayer's freedom! But we are appalled – appalled, my friends – at the reason for it! Stephen Ayer was released because Moorhouse suddenly found he had been wrongly and unjustly accused!"

Cries of "Shame!"

"The time to find out is before an arrest like that is ever made!"

Lines of police emerged from side streets and into the park, fanning out quietly along the perimeter. No one noticed them.

"Shameful!" roared Albert Francis. "Disgusting! An affront to freedom and civilised standards! Moorhouse's panic when the people found out what he was really like turned into an orgy of hasty and undemocratic action. The state of emergency! What a disgrace! The furtive detentions! What a crime! And now the shabby second thoughts! Well, my friends, I am not a man to say to Daniel Moorhouse, thank you for releasing Stephen Ayer. No! I will not say that!"

Out of the corner of his eye, Francis saw the lines of police snaking out to surround them. He felt his heart skip a beat and for a second he lost his concentration. Then he recovered himself and inside he felt burning anger and contempt.

"I say to Daniel Moorhouse: you poor – pathetic – blind – miserable – stupid – greedy little man! HOW DARE YOU ARREST STEPHEN AYER WHEN YOU HAD NOT A SHRED OF PROOF AGAINST HIM!"

Francis' voice was edged with rage. The crowd roared agreement.

"HOW DARE YOU ARREST THE OTHERS IN THIS SHABBY, ILLEGAL WAY! RELEASE THEM AT ONCE! RELEASE THEM!"

The people shouted back: "RELEASE THEM!"

"MOORHOUSE, GET OUT! GET OUT NOW! THE PEOPLE WANT YOU OUT!"

"OUT! MOORHOUSE OUT!"

Albert Francis lowered his voice, as if exhausted. "But Moorhouse is a coward," he said. "A bully and a coward and a cheat! Now, my friends, he seeks to bully us! Look around you! Look what he has sent to put an end to the one bit of democracy which still survives on this unhappy island! Look!"

Heads turned, and there was a perceptible restless movement in the crowd. There must have been three or four hundred policemen lined up blocking the exit to Kennedy Walk and the Coast Road, and along the third side fringed by a wire fence. The policemen were starting to move forward, like beaters flushing out game from an area of bush: a semi-circle, closing.

A wave of murmuring and apprehension swept the audience and Montrose's ten began to shout and push and jostle those around them, who were forced against their neighbours until the effect of the movement became increasingly violent as it went on, and people began to stumble.

"Run!" "Get out!" "Here they come!" the ten yelled, and others, beginning to panic, took up the shout. At the edges, people started heading for the exit into Jubilee Avenue, along past the Imperial Hotel.

Albert Francis tried desperately to keep order. "Stay calm!" he implored. "Don't let them panic you! They can't arrest us all!" But the wave had already begun and there was no stopping it. Only Francis himself and a handful of party marshals and supporters stood their ground by the bandstand, waiting to be seized, but when the police reached them, their line simply parted and they moved past, arresting no one.

Francis and his men watched in disbelief. The khaki ranks closed and walked steadily on, keeping a distance from the stragglers at the back. The crowd siphoned in a shouting jumble through the double gates which led to Jubilee Avenue, while some climbed over the fence and went running off; then, seeing that they had escaped, they paused and waited to watch what would happen next.

In the park, the police fell back slightly. After a minute, they began withdrawing to the far end.

By this time, the first of Montrose's ten had reached the Imperial Hotel, and from their pockets came the slender iron bars. A huge plate-glass window shattered, then another. Sounds of the violence drifted over to the police but evoked no reaction from them. They waited.

Around the hotel, people tried to scatter, but they were too densely packed and those at the front had virtually stopped moving.

The ten pushed their way along the edges of the crowd to the first shop, and the crash of breaking glass was followed by the screams of the women shop assistants fleeing through the rear emergency exit. Molvi grabbed a pile of dresses and pushed them into the arms of a woman demonstrator. She began to protest, but then clutched the garments tightly to her and moved off. Others began entering the shop, sorting quickly through the goods.

The ten went on to the next. It took several minutes to reach the radio and television shop, which had been locked as a futile precaution. Through the window, just before he smashed it, Kayaban could see the owner and an assistant scrabbling to open the fire exit and get to safety. Then they were in, feet crunching over broken glass.

Molvi and Kayaban headed for the display of television sets, as others packed in behind them. Electrical shops were where the best pickings usually lay, and they would have to claim their loot quickly. Molvi and Kayaban grabbed two portable televisions and took them to the side.

Molvi spoke urgently: "Look, I'm going to put this in the van and come back for something else. See if you can find me a stereo cassette recorder."

"Jesus, Montrose will have your balls!" Kayaban warned over the din.

"Fuck Montrose! He'll never know. I'm not going to carry out a television for him and nothing for myself! I'll be back in a couple of minutes."

Without waiting for a reply, Molvi moved away, pushing against the crush of people who were still climbing through the broken display window, glass slippery under their shoes, to join the looters.

It took a few seconds until he could fight his way onto the pavement, and he went as quickly as he could the few yards toward Connaught Street. The TV set was not particularly heavy but it was difficult to carry because of its bulk. Molvi paused at the corner, holding the set with one arm and bracing it under his chin, while he fumbled in his pocket for the key to the van.

When he had it, he moved on again, almost at a run, calculating he would have time to dump the set and still get back for more. The key jingled against its chain in his hand.

But the van was gone.

Molvi felt first bafflement, then indecision. Perhaps they had parked further up. He ran quickly on, but there was nothing there. He stopped and looked back, in case in his hurry he had overshot the parking place.

A wave of irritation passed over him. Christ, it would be just their luck if the bloody van had been stolen. It would mean leaving behind their loot, or maybe storing it somewhere – in a garbage can perhaps – and coming back for it later.

He looked for a safe place to stash the television, but all the street garbage bins were small, fastened onto lamp posts. Steal another car, that was the answer.

Molvi jogged over to a family sedan and tried the door. It was locked. He went to the car parked beside it, but that was also locked. He reached into his pocket for the metal bar to smash the car window and, as he did so, out of the corner of his eye caught sight of a line of khaki-clad policemen, rifles at the ready, moving purposefully down Connaught Street towards him.

Molvi's mouth dropped open. The police were walking quickly, maybe twenty seconds away.

Jesus, where was the volley of rifle shots, the signal for them to get clear? He couldn't have missed it. Even with the noise of the riot, a single shot would dominate everything.

The policemen were nearer now, obviously prepared for business. There were no riot shields or batons in evidence: just steel helmets and rifles.

Suddenly Molvi knew. Montrose you fucker, he muttered to himself, dropping the television set behind the car and crouching ready to run. Montrose, you double-crossing *bastard*.

The policemen were ten seconds off. Two streets away, but sounding inches from his ears, a volley of rifle shots signalled the others it was time to get clear.

Behind the first wave of armed police, Molvi – peering over the bonnet of the car – recognised the fat, strutting figure of Montrose, and he heard his voice shouting commands: "Right, you men, get ready to fire. If you see any looters, I want them dead! Shoot on sight!"

Molvi took off, crouching low and running for his life across the road to the entrance of the building opposite. He slammed against the glass doors with a force which drove the breath from his body, but they opened and he tumbled in, falling onto the cool marble floor, then terror catapulting him up again, he raced up the stairs three at a time, looking for an emergency exit which would give on to the fire escape at the back.

Suddenly he was out of the building, and the metal stairway sounded loud under his feet. He tore down to the sanitary alley and began to run. At the end he could see more khaki-uniformed figures, so Molvi climbed the next fire escape he came to, clambering up until he found an open door, and then into the sanctuary of the next building.

Here he paused, gasping for breath, his heart pounding and the blood throbbing loud in his ears. He could run no more.

Inside the electrical shop, the remaining nine stopped wrecking display counters and overturning drawersful of electrical components immediately they heard the rifle shots. They picked up their loot and headed for the street.

The sound of the rifle fire had caused panic and it was more difficult now to get clear. People were bunched around the shattered entrance to the shop, but the nine barrelled through, using their weight and sheer power to force a path. Around them, people stumbled and fell but they pushed on. There was not much time.

They broke into a run when they came to the intersection of Connaught Street, choosing the middle of the road rather than the pavements because of the congestion.

"Who's got the keys? Who's got the keys, for Christ's sake?" someone shouted.

"Molvi's got them!" Kayaban called back. "He should be at the van!"

Almost simultaneously, the nine realised that their vehicle was gone and that a line of armed policemen, stretching across the road, were raising their rifles. Their forward momentum faltered and stopped, and they stood open-mouthed, feeling simultaneously foolish and heart-stopping vulnerable, the television sets and stereo systems piled in their arms.

They were still standing silently like that when the first bullets ripped into them, smashing through the boxes and the metal, chrome and wood. The force of the impact knocked them back and they crashed with their loot onto the tarmac to twitch and bleed and finally lie still.

Behind them, others caught in the fusillade lay wounded or dying and the streets rang with cries and screams, but quickly the crowd thinned. The police, having boxed them in, now stood aside to let them disperse.

The rifles fell silent.

Montrose walked briskly forward, Clifton at his side, towards where the men lay. With the toe of his shoe, he turned the first one over and saw the open, blank eyes and the trickle of blood from the side of the mouth.

Kayaban.

Montrose smiled grimly. Next to him was Guntur, his arm flung carelessly over the chest of Gallo.

The Commissioner avoided the widening pools of blood. The shooting had been accurate. He must remember to compliment the men. Montrose gave a grunt of satisfaction. It was a job well done.

"Claud! Claud!" Clifton's voice was urgent. He turned and saw the black face wrinkled with anxiety. Jesus, what was it this time?

"What do you want?"

Clifton, almost hissing at him, mouth near his ear: "There's one missing!"

Montrose frowned, suddenly uncertain.

"What do you mean?"

"There should be ten. There're only nine!"

The Commissioner looked swiftly around, counting the dead. Nine.

In Jubilee Avenue, he saw more bodies. "Over there," he said. "Check that lot."

They moved swiftly towards the intersection, but there were only a woman and two men they had never seen before.

Montrose and Clifton looked at each other for a long moment. Finally Montrose said: "Do me a favour, Alec, and just don't panic. We'll find out who it is and deal with him later. Okay?"

Clifton nodded dumbly, wondering why nothing seemed to go right any more.

A few buildings away, Molvi, slumped on a staircase landing, had heard the shots and knew instinctively that his comrades were dying and that he was meant to have been there with them. The firing seemed to go on and on, and he could visualise their bodies flinching under the bullets.

He pulled himself to his feet and, despite his trembling, forced himself to walk down the staircase to the main lobby of the building. He looked out into the street, but apart from people running in panic, he could see no policemen.

Moving was an effort, his body sluggish with shock, but he took a few steps and then found he could increase his speed.

By the time he reached the intersection, Molvi was running for his life.

144

Chapter Twenty-three

Sam Wallace started at nine o'clock, waiting by the main doors of Maxwell's for the security guards to raise the padlocked steel shutters. Inside, he could see shop assistants taking positions behind their counters, checking the cash floats in their tills and idly gossiping. No one even glanced at the small crowd on the pavement.

Wallace checked his watch. Maxwell's was running a couple of minutes late. A middle-aged woman restlessly shifted her weight from one foot to the other and stared fixedly through the glass as if to attract the attention of someone in charge.

Wallace's efforts the night before searching through his father's papers to find a handwriting to match the anonymous letter to Albert Francis, had been futile.

By itself, this proved nothing. He had burned a lot of old records in the few weeks after his father died: things which had not then seemed important and which were cluttering up the study he intended taking over as his own. Wallace, who had a sense of history, kept only those documents which he thought a researcher might later find interesting. Now he was sorry. Why was it, he wondered, that the piece of paper you throw out always turns out to be the only one you really want?

Behind the main doors, two blue-uniformed security guards appeared to fumble with the locks, and the steel shutters clanked sluggishly upwards until the baseplate fitted flush against the overhanging concrete.

It was a strange sensation being first into a large store like Maxwell's: the silence and the emptiness of the customer gangways made him feel uncomfortable and conspicuous. Sam Wallace walked swiftly over to the lifts, and rode one to the second floor administration offices.

They were clearly not yet ready for business. He felt an intruder, as if he had arrived early at a party to find the hostess in a housecoat and curlers, and the host still soaking in a bath. The reception area was empty, but in the offices behind he could see people moving, carrying files, opening cabinets – with the sluggishness of those who were still in the process of waking up.

Wallace waited uncertainly, trying to spot old man Maxwell. The receptionist came in, carrying a glass container filled with water.

She noticed him and said: "Can I help you?"

"Er, yes please. I wondered if I could see Mr Maxwell?"

"Do you have an appointment?"

"No, I'm afraid not. I'm an old friend though – Sam Wallace. Perhaps he could spare me a couple of minutes. It's rather urgent."

The girl nodded. "Please take a seat, Mr Wallace," she said. "I'll ask him."

He settled himself on the expensively upholstered settee while she set the water down next to the coffee stand and knocked on the door of Maxwell's office.

When she reappeared, she asked: "Would you mind waiting a few minutes, Mr Wallace? He's a little tied up at the moment but it shouldn't be too long."

Wallace gave her his most charming smile. Funny that old man Maxwell should have chosen a beautiful girl like this as his receptionist, he thought. The last one had been a painfully thin maiden lady from London who had come out to the island in her early twenties for reasons no one could remember and had grown old and bitter in the service of the firm. He'd heard that she had recently retired and was spending the grim twilight of her years in solitude somewhere on the island.

This girl, with the pendant swinging between firm, full breasts and eyes which instinctively flirted, must be Maxwell's way of making up for the barren years of having a dragon guard his door.

The smell of fresh ground coffee wafted towards him.

Wallace picked up the morning's *St David's Herald* and glanced quickly over the front page. The release of Stephen Ayer had obviously had its day and was no longer being mentioned. He detected government pressure. The press statements issued yesterday by the Democratic Front and the other opposition parties condemning Moorhouse and calling for his resignation were apparently being ignored, unless they were tucked away on one of the *Herald*'s seven other pages. He flicked quickly through, but there was no sign.

A one-paragraph story on the back page did catch his eye, however: "The Prime Minister, the Hon. Daniel Moorhouse, is still considering the cases of the remaining men detained in terms of the State of Emergency, official sources said today. The Prime Minister has decided that no precipitate action should be taken, and that the review of detentions might last another two or three days."

Sam Wallace grunted. He wished he knew what Moorhouse was up to, and he didn't like the sudden delay. It looked as if the Prime Minister, recognising the personal political threat, had begun dragging his heels.

"Can I offer you some coffee, Mr Wallace?" The girl was standing close to him, a cup in her hand. Fresh ground coffee and French perfume.

"Thank you." He grinned and sat forward, holding her eye until she glanced down, a couple of seconds too late to be considered demure. She served him cream and sugar, and then took a tray in to Maxwell's office.

Wallace drank his coffee, staring thoughtfully at her through the half-glassed partition which separated the reception area from the office. He could not see Maxwell, who was obviously at his desk, but he watched the girl's profile, and the long silky black hair which swung round her shoulders.

It was nine-fifteen. Wallace began feeling restive. He had many calls to make today, and none of them would, he imagined, be easy. There was an increasing sensation, which he could not account for, of time running out.

"Would you come through now please, Mr Wallace?" The girl again, posed against the office door.

He stood up, folding the newspaper hastily, and walked in to confront old man Maxwell.

The store-owner came round his desk to greet him, shaking his hand warmly and ushering him to a comfortable armchair.

"Well, Sam, what can I do for you?"

Wallace leaned forward confidentially. "Mr Maxwell, I come to you with a problem."

"Oh dear. Personal or professional?"

"Professional. You know I'm working for the Democratic Front?"

"Yes I did hear something of the sort. Doing rather well, I understand."

"Not too bad, sir," Wallace conceded with a brief smile. "The thing is, we've reason to believe the Commissioner of Police is running some kind of protection racket."

He was aware that a sudden stillness had come over Martin Maxwell, and that his eyes were cautious, watchful and – was he imagining it? – a bit scared.

"I wouldn't know about that," Maxwell said, offhand.

Sam Wallace thought: Oh God, don't back yourself into a corner right at the beginning. He said quickly: "Please don't say anything right head on the block if we can help it.

Maxwell inclined his head briefly.

"Firstly," Wallace said, "this isn't a straight party political matter. We're not looking for cheap points to score. We're deeply worried about it, and we realise only too well what a dangerous man – a potentially dangerous man – Claud Montrose is. We don't want to put anyone's head on the block if we can help it.

"We were sent an anonymous letter apparently signed by one of the people who've been pulled in on the racket. That's why I was going through my father's old files yesterday – to see if I could trace the handwriting."

"And could you?"

"No, unfortunately not. But I threw away hundreds of documents after he died, so that doesn't necessarily prove anything. Anyway, the anonymous letter said Montrose asks the stores for weekly payments to protect them from attack. It claimed that you, sir, had refused to pay but that after the attack here, you were forced to knuckle down, along with all the others. The implication was that Montrose had deliberately staged the riot to terrorise you all. Now if this is true – and I'm going to go to all the major store-owners today to ask them – then it's something we must stop. The question is: how?"

Maxwell, motionless and watchful, waited for him to continue, offering no encouragement.

"Albert Francis agrees that it would be pointless to make allegations at a public rally, for example, or in a press statement, and give Montrose a chance to cover his tracks or intimidate people into silence. Heaven knows he seems to have the power these days. So the answer would be to take the whole story direct to the Prime Minister and let him deal with it in his own way."

"The Opposition would offer something like this to the Prime Minister?" Maxwell seemed academically amused. "If it were true, the scandal would be an amazingly effective stick to beat Moorhouse with, don't you think?"

"Undoubtedly. But between you and me, the Front would still collect a political dividend later by using the indirect route. When it's all over and the Commissioner of Police is behind bars, we can claim credit for uncovering the whole thing. And of course, we'd demand Moorhouse's resignation. We'd probably get it, too. But we feel at the moment that the important thing, in the national interest, is to root out this corruption . . ."

"If it exists."

" . . . If it exists, as you say, and leave the politics for later. We think Moorhouse is inept and wrong, but we don't think he's corrupt. We can't believe he has a hand in anything as sordid as a protection racket. Basically, we think he's an honourable man, just politically misguided. But not a crook; not like Montrose."

When Sam Wallace had finished, there was a long silence while Maxwell considered how to respond.

At last he said softly: "I'm sorry, Sam. I can't help you at all. I don't know anything about this. I certainly wouldn't want to be associated with anything said against the Commissioner of Police. Now you must forgive me." Maxwell rose to his feet. "But my work is piling up and I'm due at a meeting in a few minutes. It's been good to see you again, my boy."

Wallace stared at him in dismay. Was that all? "You mean you're not being blackmailed by Montrose?"

"No."

"You're not paying him any money at all?"

"No, I am not."

"So there's no protection racket?"

"That's what I said. Give your dear mother my best wishes when next you write to her. Is she still in Devon?"

"Yes she is. I . . . well . . . I don't know what to say. I was sure . . ."

"Scurrilous rumours, nothing more. Let me see you to the lift. Did you bring anything in with you? No?"

A friendly but firm hand on Sam Wallace's shoulder, and Martin Maxwell ushered him through the reception area to the lifts and pressed the "Down" button.

"One final thing," Maxwell said. "I would urge you most strongly, as your father was my friend, not to pursue this inquiry further. If word of it got back to the Commissioner, you might regret it. He can be a harsh and cruel man. That at least is what people say, and I have no cause to doubt them."

The lift door slid silently open. Maxwell shook his hand, less warmly this time, and turned away, walking quickly back to his office.

Wallace watched him go, holding the lift door open with one hand. The receptionist gave him a warm smile.

A blank. Not only a blank, but a brush-off. He stepped into the lift. Perhaps it was true there was no protection racket: but the temperature in old man Maxwell's room seemed to drop as soon as he mentioned it, which indicated that at least a kernel of truth lay there. Maybe.

Oh well, he thought. On to the next.

The sun was higher in the sky now and the heat enveloped him as soon as he left the air conditioned cocoon of Maxwell's. He glanced up and down the street. There was no point trying any of the smaller stores: they couldn't afford to pay much, so Montrose had probably left them alone and, anyway, they would feel too small and powerless to complain even if he hadn't. The clue, if there was one, had to be among the top ten.

In the next block was a possible candidate: Pioneer Stores, part of an island-wide grocery chain. Wallace had met the owner, Samuel Laksha, several times: both at his own house and at the Lakshas' rambling colonial residence which boasted its own billiard-room and a sprung dance-floor.

The windows of Pioneer Stores were crammed with as many goods as could be fitted in, with little attempt at display. Each item carried a large, clearly marked price tag. Inside the store, ceiling fans whirled. Crowds of shoppers, all locals, milled around the display counters and, in the background, Wallace could hear the ringing of cash registers.

He pushed his way through to the administration offices at the rear, separated by old brown wooden partitions and frosted glass windows.

A receptionist, middle-aged and plain, wearing too much make-up, gave him a toothy smile in which there was a glint of gold.

"Good morning," Wallace said. "Is Mr Laksha in? I'd like to see him for a few minutes, if I may?"

"Certainly, sir. Who shall I say is calling?"

"Sam Wallace."

A look of guilt passed over her face, then confusion. "Oh I'm sorry, Mr Wallace," she said, "but I've just remembered Mr Laksha is out. I don't know when he'll be back."

Wallace glanced over her shoulder at the frosted glass of Samuel

Laksha's office and through it he felt he could make out the owner's bulky shape behind his desk.

"Are you sure?" he asked, still cordial. "I think I can see him through the glass."

She darted a quick glance behind her, then said firmly: "No, sir. I'm afraid he is out."

"Perhaps I could wait."

"There would be no point. I couldn't say when he'll be back. He might not come back at all today."

"Has he left town? I could call him at home."

"I don't know where he is, Mr Wallace. I'm sorry I can't help."

Wallace looked again through the frosted glass. The blurred, indistinct shape behind the desk had not appeared to move. Perhaps he was mistaken.

"Look," Wallace said. "Let me leave my telephone number and Mr Laksha can call me when he gets in. Please tell him it's urgent."

The receptionist nodded doubtfully and accepted the visiting card. On the back, Wallace had written: "I'd appreciate a call on a matter of national importance."

He smiled at her and left, threading his way through a crowd of shoppers, who were watching a demonstration of a new cooking aid.

The Port Lombard Suppliers' Company was diagonally opposite and was almost a carbon copy of Pioneer Stores. Wallace wondered sometimes how the two, so close together, managed to survive. But Port Lombard Suppliers' was almost as full as its competitor.

Sam Wallace took the stairs to the administration floor where Luke Davies ran his expanding empire.

A secretary looked up inquiringly. "Can I help you?" she said, sounding as if she would not be able to.

"I'd like to see Mr Davies, please, on a matter of some urgency."

"Mr Wallace, isn't it?"

He looked surprised. "Yes, that's right."

"I'm sorry. Mr Davies is out of town at the moment. He won't be back for a few days."

Wallace stared at her doubtfully, but she stared back impassively.

"Do you know when he will be back?" Wallace asked.

"No, I'm sorry."

"Or where he is at the moment?" Wallace realised he was playing a game with her.

"I've no idea."

"So if the store burns down, you wouldn't know where to contact him."

"That's correct."

"You surprise me."

The secretary prepared to resume her other business. "I'll tell him you called."

"I think he knows that already," Wallace said.

She shrugged and he turned away. As he walked out into the street, his mind was racing. First Laksha, then Davies. It was too much of a coincidence. Someone must have tipped them off, and he knew who it was: Martin Maxwell's telephone must have been busy from the moment Wallace left, presumably covering each store in the order he'd reach them.

By now it would probably be too late: everyone would have been alerted, all doors would be shut, right down the High Street.

Wallace checked his watch. It was about ten minutes since he'd seen Maxwell.

Perhaps . . . just perhaps, if he skipped all the intervening stores and went straight to the last one on the street . . . maybe he'd get there before old man Maxwell had time to phone.

Right at the end was the St David's Provision Company, six blocks away.

Sam Wallace began to run, covering the first block before he even noticed the sweat breaking out on his body, dodging through pedestrians, across intersections, racing between cars until finally, his breath coming in heaves, he reached the entrance.

Without pausing for breath, Wallace ran up the stairs into the old stone building. Inside it was quiet and cool: more an old-time company than a supermarket, smelling of spices and oils. He raced towards an iron-grilled lift which was waiting – amazingly – an attendant standing idly beside it.

Wallace catapulted in and leaned panting against the wood-panelled sides. "Administration floor," he gasped. "Quick as you can."

The iron door clanged shut and, with a jerk, the lift began its slow ascent. Wallace tried to collect himself. The sweat had soaked through his shirt, and ran in rivulets down his forehead and cheeks. His hair was wet.

The door opened and the attendant stood aside.

"Thanks," said Wallace briefly. Hurrying now, not running, he moved towards the reception area.

The secretary in charge looked up in surprise. She was an elderly woman, almost at retirement age, Wallace guessed, but her face was kind and humorous.

"Goodness me," she said, looking him up and down. "We must be having a heat wave out there."

Despite himself, Wallace grinned. "I've been running," he explained unnecessarily. "I'd like to see Mr Khanna urgently if I could."

"He has someone with him at the moment," she said. "Would you like to take a seat, and I'll tell him you're here. What name is it?"

"Sam Wallace."

He waited for the look of caution and the refusal, but there was none. It seemed he might have made it in time.

"Very well," she said. "Make yourself comfortable. He shouldn't be too long."

She picked up a telephone and pressed a button. "Mr Khanna," she said, "a Mr Sam Wallace is here to see you. He says it's urgent . . . very well, I'll tell him."

Wallace's heart sank, but she replaced the receiver and said: "Two minutes, and he'll be with you."

Wallace sat, regaining his breath and praying that the telephone would not ring with Martin Maxwell to warn Khanna off. Time passed slowly, but at last a thin, bald-headed figure stood in the doorway.

"Good heavens, Sam," Steven Khanna said, amused. "Have you been in some sort of race?"

Wallace stood up at once, smiling sheepishly. "In a manner of speaking, yes," he said. "I'll tell you about it in a minute."

"Come on through."

Wallace walked into his comfortably furnished office, while Khanna said: "I think our visitor could do with a cup of tea, Mrs Mac. So could I."

"Right away, Mr Khanna."

The door shut and Khanna moved back to his desk. Wallace settled into an armchair.

It was time for attack, he thought, although from a slightly different angle.

"The reason I was running," he admitted, "was to get to you before Martin Maxwell phoned and warned you not to see me."

"Why would he do that?" Khanna's face was inscrutable.

"Because I know that Maxwell's, and a lot of other major stores, are being blackmailed by Montrose into paying protection money. Now I don't want to make trouble for anyone, or score any cheap political points, but I do want a sensible talk with someone involved to try and work out what the hell we can do about it."

There was a long silence. Finally Khanna said: "So – talk."

Wallace felt absurdly off-balance. "About the protection racket?" he said.

"If that's what you came to talk about."

"It is." He took a deep breath. "Point one: Maxwell is being black-mailed. Correct?"

"Correct."

"So are you."

A pause. "Correct again."

"By the Commissioner of Police."

Khanna nodded.

"And if you don't pay, your store will be smashed up, just like Maxwell's was a couple of weeks back."

"Just like that."

A sudden thought struck Wallace. "Was it you who wrote an anony-mous letter to Albert Francis?" he asked.

Khanna shook his head. "I don't know anything about an anony-mous letter. What did it say?"

"It just outlined what was going on, but whoever sent it obviously didn't think anything could be done. He was scared."

"We're all scared, Sam," Khanna said. "Every one of us. Montrose is a powerful and ruthless man."

The telephone on his desk rang. "Hello? . . . Yes, put him on." He glanced across at Wallace, and gave a sudden grin. "Maxwell," he explained.

Wallace felt a wave of relief.

"Good morning, Martin . . . Yes, I'm fine, thanks very much. And yourself? . . . Glad to hear it . . . What can I do for you? . . . Yes, he's with me now . . . That's right, he's sitting across the desk from me as I talk to you. Do you want me to put him on?" Khanna winked at Wallace. "Oh I see, I see." There was a long silence while he listened. Then he said: "I appreciate all that, Martin. Thank you for calling me. I'll get back to you later. Perhaps we could have lunch? . . . Fine, see you then."

The door opened and Mrs Mac brought in a tray of tea, setting it down on the desk and pouring two cups. When she had gone, Wallace asked: "What did he want?"

"Just as you thought," Khanna said. "He was warning me off. He said it could cost us our lives if Montrose ever found out. I'm inclined to think he's not exaggerating."

"But there must be a way. We can't be powerless, surely? I thought if we could get enough evidence together, we could take it straight to the Prime Minister."

Khanna sipped his tea. "What makes you think the Prime Minister isn't getting his cut?" he asked.

Wallace said cautiously: "Do you have any evidence that he is?"

Khanna shook his head.

"Our feeling," said Wallace, "is that Moorhouse is a fool but not a crook. We think if we presented him with enough evidence, he'd do the right thing. Suspend Montrose, have him arrested if the evidence is good enough – and we'd have to make sure it *was* good enough – and Bob's your uncle."

"Sounds too easy."

"It *ought* to be easy," Wallace insisted. "Hell, Montrose is just a common criminal who's worked himself up into a high position of trust. You just have to short-circuit him and that's it. There are others who can complete the investigation."

Khanna smiled wryly. "Who, for example?" he asked. "The Deputy Commissioner of Police?"

"Exactly!"

"He's in it too." Khanna spoke in a matter-of-fact voice, but Wallace was appalled and showed it.

"You're joking!" he said.

"I wish I was. Montrose collects from some stores. Clifton collects from others. Guess who collects from the rest?"

Wallace felt suddenly drained of energy. "I give up," he said. "Who?"

"Luther. The Army Chief of Staff. He's got the stores around the barracks area. Some of them are branches of ones in the High Street – Pioneer, for example. Phillips and Company. They have to pay twice."

Wallace's mouth opened in disbelief. "Bloody hell," he murmered faintly. They sat in silence. At last Wallace said: "But that's even more reason to go straight to Moorhouse. It's got to be stopped before it goes any further."

"You won't find anyone to help you," Khanna replied with certainty. "They're all too scared."

"You'll help, though?"

Khanna shook his head slowly. "No," he said.

"But why not? You must!"

His voice stronger: "No!" He smiled wearily at Wallace. "I've worked all my life in this business, building it up from nothing. Thirty years I've spent on it. Montrose could destroy it in thirty minutes. Don't underestimate him: the man's vicious, a killer. Look what happened to Maxwell's! A security guard was clubbed down, trampled to death and the shop was looted while Montrose and his men waited – just waited! – a couple of streets away. After the damage had been done, they moved in. It was deliberate, and it could happen to me. If there was ever a time to stop Montrose, it was before the attack on Maxwell's. Now there's blood on his hands, and he can't be stopped."

"But he must be! Surely there is some corner of the St David's security forces which hasn't been contaminated!"

Khanna shrugged. "Perhaps there is, but I don't know where it is and nor do you. I can't afford to take a chance on being wrong – not on my own, anyway. If enough others were prepared to stand up with me, maybe it would be a different story."

"How many others?" Wallace was challenging.

Khanna considered the matter. "Six," he said. "Me and five others. You get them and I'll come out in public. I'll also make you a partner in my business, that's how sure I am it can't be done."

Wallace finished his tea. "How often does Montrose come for payment?"

"Once a month."

"What do you give him? Do you mind my asking?"

"Not at all. If you quote me, I'll just deny it. He gets $150 a week."

"Six hundred dollars a month!"

"That's right," Khanna said calmly. "In cash."

"Jesus. He must be making a fortune!"

"Oh, he is. That's another reason he can't be stopped. There's too much in it for him."

"Does he come on a particular day? Or at a special time?" Wallace asked.

"No. He just turns up. He was around a few days ago, so I don't expect him again until next month. But from the beginning of the month, I'll have his money ready and waiting in my safe. I don't want him hanging around my office for longer than I can help it. He's usually in and out in two minutes."

"Any idea what he does with the money?"

"None at all," Khanna said. "I presume he calls on a few of his victims at a time: maybe all of them, for all I know. So he must have a lot of cash on him. I suppose he puts it in the bank, or hides it under his mattress."

Wallace stood up to leave. "I'm really grateful to you, Mr Khanna," he said earnestly. "Thank you for squaring with me."

"It's a pleasure. But you realise it's all off the record. If you ever mention my name, I'll swear on the Bible that I never spoke to you."

"Yes, I understand. I'll see if I can rake up another five to stand up and tell their stories."

"Tell me when you reach four, and I'll start preparing the partnership documents."

Wallace grinned and Khanna's thin, heavily veined hand reached out to grasp his. "Good luck," Khanna said. "And for God's sake, be careful. Montrose is not a man to play around with."

Out in the street, his shirt still damp with sweat, Wallace began the painstaking business of going from store to store, trying to see the owners. None of them were in to him.

Finally, Wallace headed for the Democratic Front offices, now almost deserted because of the Jubilee Park rally.

As he was eating his sandwiches, he heard the rifle shots in the distance, echoing explosions.

Montrose.

Chapter Twenty-four

Joe Rana sat waiting for the telephone to ring. His stomach was in tight knots of tension and his mouth was dry. Even continual sips of hot, sweet tea did little to help.

The list was in front of him: the ten names provided by the American. It was ironic: their meetings on the beach had always been a routine of him talking, and the other listening. Suddenly last night, it was as if he, Rana, was the control, getting a report from his agent. But of course, it ended with instructions, and the illusion was gone.

He had to give the names to Daniel Moorhouse. The Prime Minister must somehow be told what was going on – and the Americans were not to be mentioned under any circumstances.

The "non-aligned" course onto which Moorhouse had swung the island after the expulsion of the CIA men remained very strongly the new foreign policy. Effectively, it meant closer ties with Russia, coupled with official indications that the Soviet navy would soon be regular callers at Port Lombard and that the Americans might find themselves having to renegotiate their defence agreements on St David's.

Meanwhile, a number of new Moscow-backed projects had been announced for the island, and Russia's aid commitment had trebled overnight. Because of this, the Americans felt their motives would be misunderstood if they were associated with the list of names. The Prime Minister would be tempted to dismiss it as a ploy.

Joe Rana, as Cabinet Secretary, understood this perfectly. What he wasn't so clear about was how he should present the list to Moorhouse. His control had not been helpful: the decision on presentation had been left up to Rana himself, with the proviso that it be done quickly – preferably the following day.

After a sleepless night, Rana had tried out the only story he was able to concoct on Kataria, and it had gone down badly.

Tilak Kataria was still sitting in the armchair on the other side of his desk, looking at him doubtfully. He had agreed to go into the meeting with Moorhouse for moral support, on condition it was understood he would take no part.

Rana wondered what he was letting himself in for.

He gave a nervous start when the phone rang and Bob Sehai asked them to come through. The men walked the few yards down the corridor to the Prime Ministerial suite, and were ushered straight into Moorhouse's presence. He greeted them cordially: an unusual attitude for him.

"Please sit down, gentlemen," Moorhouse said. "I haven't had a chance to tell you how grateful I was for your intervention in the unfortunate case of Stephen Ayer. It was a grave injustice. I hope that soon, I will have a clearer picture of the position of the other detainees. This island owes you both a debt of gratitude."

"Thank you, sir," Rana said. "It was a difficult decision to make, whether to confront you, busy as you are, or whether to tell our suspicions straight to the Commissioner of Police. I think we made the right decision."

The Prime Minister smiled slightly. "Yes, I think so too," he said. "Well, gentlemen, what can I do for you?"

Rana cleared his throat. "It's been an even more difficult decision to make coming to you this time, sir," he began. "And I think I should tell you right away that I'm here by myself, as an individual. Mr Kataria is my moral support." He looked helplessly at Moorhouse, and the Prime Minister nodded encouragingly.

"Go on," he said.

"I have no evidence," Rana admitted, "only suspicions, and a list of names. But the case is sufficiently important – grave – for me to bring it to you directly at this early stage. Normally I would not have dared. But I think the situation on the island is sufficiently unusual for me to take the liberty."

"For heaven's sake, Mr Rana," the Prime Minister said, his old asperity returning. "Get to the point. What is it you want to say?"

Rana took a deep breath. "My informant has sworn me to secrecy over his own identity, although I'm convinced personally of his bona fides. Basically, there is reason to suspect that Mr Montrose himself may have been behind the violence on the island."

Moorhouse's eyebrows shot up. "Why do you say that?" he asked incredulously.

"I have been given a list of names – ten men – who have been drawn from both the police and the army, and who form a special squad, answerable to Montrose. They have been taught the principles of crowd disruption. In a nutshell, they start riots."

Rana leaned forward and passed the piece of paper over to the Prime Minister. It was in Rana's own writing, copied the night before from a list supplied by the American.

Moorhouse glanced over it. "Doesn't mean a thing to me," he said. "Never heard of any of them."

"No, sir, nor have I. Apparently each of them has committed some crime: rape or robbery or something like that."

"Rape? Robbery?" Disbelief was in the Prime Minister's voice.

Rana nodded. "That's right, sir. They were given the choice of being prosecuted and kicked out of the services, or joining Montrose's private army."

"I've never heard anything so preposterous in my life," Moorhouse said shortly.

"That's what I thought at first, sir. But we all know there's something rotten in the St David's police department. This is a suggestion about what it might be."

"You haven't offered a shred of proof," the Prime Minster said. From the corner of his eye, Rana could see Kataria shifting uncomfortably, wishing he had stayed behind. Unsupported allegations – particularly serious allegations – were not the sort of thing Moorhouse viewed in a kindly light.

"But let's put all that aside for the moment," the Prime Minister said. "Forget about anything as inconvenient as proof. Let's just look at the question of motive. Why would Mr Montrose, the most senior policeman on the island, do something like that?"

"According to my informant," Rana said, sticking doggedly to the brief given by his control, "Mr Montrose is running a protection racket on St David's."

He watched Moorhouse's mouth drop slightly open. "Mr Montrose demands money from the major store-owners in return for guaranteeing their security," he explained. "If they refuse to pay up, then a riot occurs conveniently close to their premises, and the looters go to work, led by the ten gentlemen whose names you have there."

"I don't believe I'm hearing properly," the Prime Minister said faintly.

"Look what happened to Maxwell's, sir," Rana continued in a desperate rush. "Martin Maxwell refused to pay, and his store was smashed and looted. A security guard was killed. You must have heard the criticism on the island about how long it took Montrose to get his men into action. They just stood waiting a few blocks away, and let the wreckers go in."

"It could equally easily be explained," Moorhouse said in a reasoning tone, "by the fact that the Commissioner of Police was holding back in the hope of avoiding a confrontation which could lead to a loss of life. These things happen so quickly, as you know. Of course, if you're actually under attack, it seems like hours, but in fact only minutes have gone by."

"That's what he told you?" Rana asked.

"That's what he told me," the Prime Minister confirmed.

"Well, sir, all I can say is that this information suggests an alternative reason. Right at the beginning I said I didn't have evidence. These are allegations, made by someone I believe could be in a position to know what's going on."

"You won't tell me his name?"

"No, sir. I'm afraid I can't."

Moorhouse grunted.

"What I'm suggesting, sir, suggesting strongly, is that somehow these should be investigated. Obviously, a way must be found to do it without alerting Mr Montrose."

"What way would that be?"

Rana's mind went blank. "There must be something we could do," he said. "Swear his Deputy to secrecy and ask him to look into it perhaps."

Moorhouse leaned forward and his voice was not unkind: a headmaster speaking to a wayward but promising child. "Let me make my position clear," he said. "I would not even think of instituting an inquiry into the Commissioner of Police unless I had some solid evidence to go on. Even one piece. You have made serious and totally unsupported allegations. I don't want to hear any more of them unless you can come to me with proof." He paused. "The only thing that might change my mind is if I knew who your informant was. If I was convinced he, or she, was really in a position to know, it would add weight to your story. Weight which, I must say, it badly needs."

For a moment Rana hesitated, feeling the Prime Minister's eyes boring into him, and the sense of stillness from Kataria's chair. The seconds ticked by as his mind raced through the implications of naming the Americans. But his contact had been right: if Moorhouse even smelt CIA involvement, he would be laughed out of the office. Also there was the small matter of explaining how they came to give him the information.

Rana stood up slowly. "Thank you for your time, Prime Minister," he said. "I understand your position, and I hope you understand mine. Perhaps we can both keep a watch for signs that might prove, or disprove, the suspicions."

Moorhouse nodded curtly. Rana felt a wave of relief that the ordeal was over: he had failed, of course, but he hardly cared about that. He had done what they asked, and that was enough.

As he walked through the double doors into Bob Sehai's office, he was suddenly aware of a bulky figure blocking his way, but it was a second before his eyes focused on the fat, smooth face of Montrose two feet from him, and he felt himself give an involuntary gasp. Montrose's eyes were bright and hard, and for once his forehead was dry. Rana wondered frantically how long he'd been waiting in the outer office, whether he'd heard anything, whether the Prime Minister had somehow summoned him to listen to the allegations.

Montrose pushed past, almost as if he hadn't noticed he was there, and the double doors closed firmly.

Rana, his face ashen, looked across at Tilak Kataria and rolled his eyes, but Kataria was expressionless. They walked quickly away.

As Montrose entered the Prime Minister's room, Moorhouse opened a drawer and dropped into it the paper containing the names of the ten.

"Prime Minister," said Montrose, his large hands gripping the edge of the fragile gilt chair. "I have come straight from the Democratic Front meeting in Jubilee Park. Bad news, I'm afraid."

"You may as well tell it to me sitting down, Commissioner," Moorhouse said dryly.

"Thank you, sir." Montrose settled himself. "More violence, more looting, around the Imperial Hotel this time," he said. "My men spotted a group of troublemakers carrying off television sets and electrical equipment – bold as brass, right in the middle of the street. We recognised them from other demonstrations. We challenged them, of course, but they paid no attention, so I gave the order to open fire."

"How many?" Moorhouse's voice was quiet. "How many dead?"

"Nine of them. Three other rioters caught in the firing. Forty or fifty arrests on charges of looting, unlawful assembly, disturbing the peace, and so on."

"Well, Commissioner," said the Prime Minister. "What was the cause this time? Not the CIA, surely?"

Montrose flushed pink. "I wish I knew, sir. We'll be interrogating those under arrest, so perhaps a clue will emerge from that quarter. My own view is that it might be a secondary infection."

"A secondary infection? What does that mean?" The Prime Minister's voice held a hint of derision.

The Commissioner's colour mounted. He said defensively: "After all, they've been watching the CIA gangs in operation all these weeks. They must have learned something from that. And as I said, we spotted some familiar faces in today's mob. But," he gave a tight, grim smile, "we shan't be seeing them around again."

"Good for you," Moorhouse said flatly.

The Commissioner mistook it for a compliment. "Thank you, sir," he replied.

Moorhouse lapsed into silence. Finally he asked: "Who were these people, the ones you killed? Have they been identified?"

"We don't have all the names yet, sir."

"Well, I'd like a full written report as soon as possible please. I'd also like to remind you that it was to end incidents like this that I agreed to the detentions. Nothing has improved since then. Indeed, everything is a lot worse."

Montrose made no response, but stared impassively at the edge of the Prime Minister's large, solid oak desk.

Moorhouse continued: "Which reminds me: what progress have you made on the cases of the detainees?"

"Slow but steady, sir," Montrose replied. "We should be in a position to make recommendations in two or three days."

"*Two* days is your limit, Commissioner," Moorhouse pointed out. "I thought I'd made that very clear yesterday."

"Yes, sir, you did. Two days. But at the moment, there's nothing which persuades me to recommend the release of any particular individual. It could be that Ayer was just a freak case."

"You still haven't told me how it happened."

"I still don't know for sure, Prime Minister," Montrose said steadily. "I don't want to go about making unsubstantiated allegations. I don't think that would be helpful."

"Indeed not," the Prime Minister said.

"So I'll hold my counsel for the time being, if you don't mind."

Moorhouse shrugged. "Not for too long, however," he said. "Unless I get action from you quickly, I will have to consider setting up a Commission of Inquiry to look into the matter. I might ask the Chief Justice to head it."

If he expected to explode a bombshell under the Commissioner of Police, the Prime Minister was disappointed.

All Montrose did was to murmur: "Quite right, sir!" and smile in a way which struck Moorhouse for a second as being insolent. But then the moment was gone, and he was uncertain whether he had imagined it.

The Commissioner of Police stood up to leave. "I think I'll have some action for you sooner than you expect," he said. "We're working on it day and night."

"I hope you are," the Prime Minister said.

After Montrose had gone, he sat thoughtfully for a long while, ignoring the pile of folders awaiting his attention on his desk.

At one point, he picked out the list of names Rana had left with him and re-read it, as if seeking a clue. Then he locked it away again.

The memory of that instant of insolence – did he imagine it? – kept

160

returning. The Commissioner had always been proper and courteous in his behaviour. Overly courteous sometimes. Some people would have said sycophantic.

But now the man was causing him uneasy stirrings and he wasn't sure why. Rana's allegations, perhaps? The Prime Minister knew he had been leaning very heavily on Montrose recently. For the Emergency, he had relied on his advice, and on the information of his man at the United States Embassy, of course. As a direct result of this, they'd purged the island of the influence of the CIA. But to what avail?

Nothing had really changed. The expulsions had not brought peace, nor had the detentions and the State of Emergency. They had simply caused injustice in Ayer's case and brought about another riot. Twelve more people dead. More international headlines to keep tourists away.

Yet Montrose was quite calm. Calm and . . . and insolent.

And there was Rana's incredible story that Montrose was to blame for the violence: he and his private force of ten. That he was running a protection racket.

They'll have to prove it, Moorhouse thought decisively. It's easy to make allegations, but let's see the evidence.

Then he remembered the $10,000 that had been given to the Commissioner out of the Special Contingencies fund: the incident just came into his mind without him being sure exactly why. The money had been to pay Montrose's American informant. It had been handed over to the Commissioner against his signature in two instalments, but of course, there was no receipt from the American.

Yet this was surely the sort of trust due a Commissioner of Police, Moorhouse thought. There was nothing unusual in it. No reason to suspect the money hadn't gone to the person for whom it was intended.

But no way of knowing that it had, either.

Corrupt.

He couldn't shake the word: it stayed in his mind along with Montrose saying: "Quite right, sir!" in that faintly insolent tone.

Acting on impulse, the Prime Minister pressed the buzzer on his desk and waited until his PPS came through.

"Mr Sehai, I want you to make an inquiry with the Paymaster General's office, if you would, and I'd like an answer quickly."

Bob Sehai nodded, his notebook and pen ready.

"It's very simple. I just want to know what bank we pay Mr Montrose's salary into."

"What bank, sir?"

"That's what I said. What branch."

Moorhouse forced himself to begin work on the pending files on his desk while his PPS was away getting the information. When Sehai came in, holding a piece of paper, he made a conscious effort to continue working as if the matter was of scant importance. He gave a curt "Thank you," and kept writing in the margin of a document until the PPS had left.

Then he looked at the paper. National Bank of St David's, High Street Branch.

Moorhouse smiled slowly. He flicked through the telephone directory for the number, then picked up his direct line.

It was answered after half a dozen rings.

"National Bank, good afternoon."

"Good afternoon. I'd like to be put through to the manager, please."

"Certainly, sir. May I know who's calling?"

Moorhouse hesitated. "It's a personal matter," he said. "We're old friends."

Chapter Twenty-five

Gordon Macgregor was reading carefully through the balance sheet of a company which had applied for a substantial overdraft: one of the many firms badly hit by the recession. It was debatable whether it would be able to survive, with or without an injection of capital. He would later dictate a letter sending it into bankruptcy.

Macgregor's office was walnut-panelled, but essentially austere. It signalled the fact that money was not to be spent carelessly, and that this was no centre for dispensing largesse, but was rather a hard-headed place of business.

The manager was a Scot who seemed to embody many of the generalisations made about his race, although those who knew him intimately claimed that it amused him to play up to people's preconceptions. However, he was undoubtedly a good businessman.

Macgregor had come to St David's shortly after his twentieth birthday, and had joined a local Barclays branch as a clerk. Twenty years later, and with the granting of independence to the island, he was offered a senior appointment with the National Bank, and a seat on the Board.

Although he was theoretically answerable to the Board, he was answerable also to the Prime Minister.

Moorhouse had never called on him before, leaving such matters to his officials and, in particular, the Ministry of Finance. But he was calling now, and his breezy manner and apparent deference masked the reality.

"Macgregor," the manager said into the telephone, his voice neutral.

"Good afternoon, Gordon," the Prime Minister replied. "Daniel Moorhouse here."

The manager sat upright, half wondering if it was a joke.

"Good afternoon, Prime Minister," he said cautiously. "This is an unexpected surprise."

"Yes indeed. I was wondering if you could spare me half an hour. I know how busy you are, but I'd appreciate it."

Now Macgregor was sure it was no joke. He recognised the tone.

"Certainly, Prime Minister," he said, pulling his diary towards him. "When would be convenient?"

"What about right away?"

Macgregor was startled. "Now?" he asked.

"I'm sorry, I realise you must have a dozen other appointments waiting."

"No, no. Nothing I can't cancel," Macgregor said. "I presume you'd like me to come round to you?"

"Yes please. My office in the Cabinet building, if you don't mind. Ask at the desk for my PPS, Mr Sehai."

"Very well, Prime Minister. It will take me ten minutes."

Moorhouse said warmly: "I appreciate this, Gordon. Thank you very much."

Macgregor hung up the phone, bemused. He had seen Moorhouse a couple of dozen times during his career, at official functions, but he'd never been on "Gordon" terms before. He calculated correctly that the Prime Minister wanted something, and it was pointless to speculate what it might be. He would learn soon enough.

He called his secretary and told her he was leaving for the afternoon. Then he collected his car from the private park behind the bank, and drove carefully towards Constitution Avenue.

Bob Sehai fetched him from the foyer and took him directly through to the Prime Minister. A tray of tea was waiting, and the PPS poured cups for them both. Then Moorhouse dismissed him.

As soon as they were alone, the Prime Minister got down to business. "The Commissioner of Police banks with you?" he asked.

"Mr Montrose? Aye, he does."

"You are aware of the state of his account?"

Macgregor looked at him shrewdly. "In broad detail," he admitted. "For specifics I would have to consult the records."

"In broad detail, how would you describe it?"

"It is not in credit."

Moorhouse raised his eyebrows. "Overdrawn? By how much?"

"He has an agreed overdraft. It currently stands at about $12,000 if I remember correctly, and I think I do."

The Prime Minister gave a low whistle. "That is a lot of money," he said. "Six months' salary. What did he borrow it for?"

"House improvements, so he said."

"You sound as if you don't believe him."

"I don't. Not now."

Moorhouse opened a large carved wooden box and pushed it across the desk. "Cigarette?"

"No thank you. Don't use them."

Moorhouse took one himself and lit it. "Why don't you believe him?"

"Because he's a gambler."

"Is he?" The Prime Minister was incredulous. "You don't mean the $12,000 represent gambling losses?"

"I couldn't say for certain, but it looks that way. He says he's having a winning streak at the moment, and that's certainly reflected in his account. His overdraft a few weeks back was as high as $30,000."

Moorhouse stared at him, shaking his head in disbelief. "He gambled away $30,000?" he asked faintly. "The Commissioner of Police did that?"

Macgregor shrugged. "Well, as I say, I don't know for sure that he gambled it all away. He certainly borrowed the money for his house. Naturally I wouldn't have lent him a penny if I'd thought he was a gambler, and I won't lend him a penny again after he's paid off what he owes. Not now I know what's going on. But he's certainly settling his debts through gambling. Or that's what he tells me."

Moorhouse was curious. "What does he gamble on?"

"Horses, apparently. The St David's races. And he plays poker every week. Seems to be part of a pretty big school. I told you he'd reduced his overdraft by about $18,000 in the last three weeks."

"That's impossible!" Moorhouse said faintly.

Macgregor smiled thinly. "He's done it though. All in cash, deposited with me in my office, every week."

The Prime Minister felt the blood had been slowly draining from his face. Perhaps Montrose *was* a compulsive gambler. But perhaps he was just – that word again – corrupt.

It was certainly a coincidence that his massive wins should dovetail so neatly with the allegations that he was running a protection racket.

Either way, he would have to go. Resign his office. But it was important to know whether the Commissioner of Police simply lacked moral fibre, or whether he was criminally involved.

"Tell me, Gordon," he said. "Between ourselves now. Do you believe his story about gambling?"

The manager looked at him candidly. "Speaking professionally," he said, "there's no reason for me to disbelieve him. He volunteered the information."

"He admitted to you he was gambling heavily?"

Macgregor nodded. "It is not our custom to ask depositors where they get their money," he said. "In this case, Mr Montrose told me himself. I think he wanted to explain where so much cash was coming from. As you know, his official salary is paid direct into his account by the Paymaster General's office."

"But you believed him?"

"Speaking professionally, yes."

Moorhouse stared at him shrewdly. "And speaking as a man?"

Macgregor grinned. "Ah now," he said. "Now you're asking."

"Yes," the Prime Minister insisted. "I am asking, Gordon."

The manager took a deep breath. "As a man," he said finally, "I think he's a liar. I have nothing specific to go on, of course. I just don't believe him."

"Why not?"

Macgregor shrugged again. "Instinct," he said. "Instinct developed over years of dealing with the public. I fancy I can tell when someone is lying. In the Commissioner's case, it was none of my business. He was paying money in, after all: not drawing it out. So it wasn't necessary for me to enquire further."

"Where do you think he's getting all this money?"

But Macgregor's face was bland. "That, Prime Minister, is something I'm afraid you'll have to tell me."

"You've heard rumours, of course? A man in your position would."

"I hear a lot of things. I only talk when I'm sure."

Moorhouse sighed. "One last thing, Gordon," he said. "I want to know about two specific deposits." He consulted a piece of paper. "I don't have precise dates, but one would be sometime after June the twelfth, and the other would be about a week later. Each would be for $5,000."

Macgregor thought for a moment. Finally he said: "May I use your phone?"

"Of course." Moorhouse motioned to his direct line. "That one goes straight out."

He watched as the manager dialled the number of the bank, and was put through to the Ledgers Department.

"Who is that?" he asked. "Oh, Mr Johnson, this is Gordon Macgregor. I'm out of the office at the moment, but I require some information quickly. Get out the latest statement of Mr Claud Montrose ... that's right, the Commissioner." There was a long pause. Finally Macgregor said: "Okay, that's fine. Now have a look at all deposits from June the twelfth and read them out to me. I'll tell you when to stop."

Macgregor's gold fountain pen scribbled dates and figures and he muttered "Uh-huh" from time to time. At last he said: "Right, that's enough. Thank you for your help. See you tomorrow."

The manager hung up and pushed the paper across to the Prime Minister.

"As you can see," he said, "$5,000 was deposited on June the fourteenth and a similar amount on the twenty-second."

Moorhouse scanned the figures and nodded. There was the proof he had wanted. "It all becomes depressingly clear," he said slowly.

"I'm sorry if I'm the bringer of bad tidings."

Moorhouse smiled wearily. "Don't worry. I make it a policy never to blame the messenger," he said.

"I'm glad to hear it. Is there anything else I can do?"

"Yes please. I want copies of Mr Montrose's bank statements going back two years."

Macgregor nodded. "When do you want them?"

"Tomorrow morning will be fine."

"I'll bring them round myself."

Moorhouse rose to signal that the meeting was at an end. He held out his hand. "I'm grateful to you, Gordon," he said. "You have been a great help."

He pressed the bell for Sehai to show the manager out, and when the PPS entered the office, he carried with him a "Confidential" folder, which he placed in front of Moorhouse without comment.

As soon as his visitor had left, the Prime Minister opened it, to find Montrose's preliminary report on the rioting.

It was typically terse and not particularly informative, ending with a list of the dead. Moorhouse scanned it quickly and was about to close the folder when it occurred to him he recognised some of the names.

He went through it carefully, and when he had finished, he discovered that his hand was trembling. He unlocked his desk drawer and pulled out the list of ten names given to him earlier in the day by Rana.

Nine of them were among the dead.

Moorhouse did not know what precisely this meant, but it chilled his blood. He closed his eyes. It was like lifting a rock and finding underneath it a human skull, with worms eating out the eyes.

He had discovered the rottenness which was infecting the police force where he least expected it: right at the top.

Montrose would have to be suspended, there was no doubt of that. He could no longer continue as Commissioner of Police. An official inquiry would have to be held, almost certainly *in camera*. Then there would be charges, and a trial, also in secret. Whatever the sins of the Commissioner of Police, the identity of his American contact still had to be protected. Moorhouse was convinced that the basic information naming the CIA agents on the island had been accurate. The absence of an American response had proved that: it was tantamount to a confession.

The Americans had now been dealt with, and their special relationship was coming to an end. It was a bad moment to discover corruption in the top ranks of his administration. This was a time when it should be presenting a solid and steadfast front.

Yet there was no alternative. The Commissioner of Police was a thief, and he might also be something infinitely more dangerous.

Why had nine of the men who made up his so-called private army been shot dead? Why would Montrose kill his own people?

The more the Prime Minister thought about it, the further away from the truth he felt he was.

Two men would know. One was Montrose himself: and he was unlikely to make a clean breast of anything. The other was ... who? Moorhouse compared the lists again, and at length underlined the name of the missing man.

Molvi. Offer him a pardon in exchange for turning state's evidence, he thought. Molvi would tell the truth.

In the margin, Moorhouse wrote "Find Molvi", and after a second's thought, he put an exclamation mark beside it.

Chapter Twenty-six

Clive Lyle was not there. Montrose could hardly believe it. He and Alec Clifton walked cautiously up to the sea wall, but the familiar silhouette failed to appear out of the darkness, and there was no red glow from the tip of a cigarette.

Montrose called softly: "Lyle! Lyle!" It was high tide and the waves crashed onto the sand beyond the wall. He stared deep into the black shadows of palm trees, and walked to the pitch edge of the overhanging bougainvillea in case the American had seen the approach of two men, and had hidden through fear.

But he remembered he hadn't seen Lyle's car parked off the road either.

"Lyle!" Louder this time.

He could sense the disapproval of Alec Clifton in the blackness near him, and the triumph too. Clifton had virtually called him a liar when he'd told them about the names, and his only function now was to check on Montrose. He was secretly laughing.

"LYLE! YOU BASTARD! LYLE!"

"There's no point shouting, Claud," said Clifton primly. "He doesn't appear to be here. Perhaps he thinks it's tomorrow."

"He knows it's not fucking tomorrow," Montrose said savagely. "I'll have that little bugger's balls. I'll send the photographs around to the Ambassador by special messenger!"

"Oh really, Claud!" Clifton was becoming irritated. "You don't *have* any photographs. It's all in your mind."

"I've got the dossier!"

He could almost see Clifton shrugging dismissively. "Oh God. Another dossier."

Montrose was nearly overwhelmed by an urge to squeeze Clifton's scrawny black throat in his fingers and smash his head against a rock until the rubbish that passed for his brain spilled onto the sand, and his miserable shrimp body . . .

Headlights.

A flash of illumination against the wall and the twin spears along the dirt road. The vivid red glow at the rear of the Chevrolet, and finally lights out blackness.

Montrose felt exhausted with hatred, and relief.

Clifton's voice, calm and disinterested: "Either this is him, or we'll be able to spy on a courting couple."

Montrose spoke in a tone more civil than he imagined possible: "I know what you'd sooner have, Alec."

The interior lights of the car flashed briefly. One person in it. The slam of a door. And then, inexplicably, silence. No one approaching.

Montrose's eyes were used to the dark now, but whoever had got out of the car was waiting beside it, unmoving.

The minutes passed. Montrose felt a growing unease. Perhaps it wasn't Lyle after all.

Clifton said softly: "Shouldn't you blow him a kiss or something, Claud?"

"Fuck off, Alec." A note of warning in Montrose's voice.

The Deputy Commissioner half-muffled a laugh and Montrose ignored him, alert as a panther, eyes boring into the darkness for the slightest movement: ears straining for the faintest whisper of sound.

Should he go up to the car, see what was going on? He was the Commissioner of Police, after all.

Then a movement, but no sound. A silhouette coming towards them, approaching swiftly, sure of the ground, closer and then upon them.

"Good evening, Commissioner." Lyle's calm, self-possessed voice with the hint of the American South. "I see you've brought a friend."

"You're late."

"Mmmmm. Sorry about that, Claud. I was having a drink with someone. It went on a bit longer than I'd expected."

Montrose suppressed a wave of anger. "This is Alec Clifton," he said gruffly. "He's my Deputy."

"Good evening, Mr Clifton."

"Good evening, Mr Lyle."

They did not shake hands.

Lyle said conversationally: "I was having a drink with one of the new CIA guys."

"Did he have anything to say, or was it just girl talk?" Montrose asked offensively.

Lyle glanced across at Clifton, and even through the darkness, the Deputy would have sworn that he was amused. But Lyle's voice was even. "This and that," he said vaguely. "Some bits that might interest you."

"Such as?"

"Such as Moorhouse was being told today. No confirmation yet, but that was the plan."

The news had no effect on Montrose: it was what they had anticipated.

"That's all right," he said, offhandedly. "It couldn't matter less now."

He noted the surprise in Lyle's voice. "I'm glad to hear it," the American said. "Why couldn't it matter?"

"Because they're dead. They were shot while looting a shop this afternoon."

"You killed them? All ten of them?"

"Nine. One got away. Fuck knows how."

There was a silence: Montrose's brooding, Lyle's thoughtful. Then the American said quietly: "You know better than that, Claud. Ten out of ten's a pass. Anything under that is failure. My mother used to tell me that frightened canaries sing louder than any other sort."

"Let *me* worry about that, if you don't mind."

"With pleasure."

Clifton asked: "Were you able to find out whose names were on the list?"

"Yes," Lyle confirmed. "Just as Claud suspected, they were his ten heroes. I've got the other names if you want them."

"I know who the hell they are," Montrose said.

"Any idea how your boys got them?"

"None," said Lyle. "It's all under wraps. I might be able to find out later, but at the moment, no one's saying a word. I get the impression it's a pretty senior source."

"A senior source?" asked Clifton cautiously. "Are you sure?"

"Not a hundred per cent," Lyle admitted. "But surely it must be pretty senior."

"Not necessarily," Clifton answered. "It could have been one of the ten blabbing to a friend of his. It doesn't have to be anything higher than that."

"Well, I'll let you know if I find out."

Clifton pulled out a box of cigarettes and pushed it forward in the darkness. "Smoke?" He felt Lyle fumbling for one, and then the exaggerated flame of a Zippo flared.

"Sorry, Claud," said Lyle apologetically, although they weren't his cigarettes. "Do you want one?"

"No."

Clifton said: "So Moorhouse knows."

"Apparently."

"When was he told?"

"Some time today. I don't know exactly."

Clifton turned to the Commissioner: "When did you see him, Claud?"

"After the demo. It would have been about three, I suppose."

"Notice anything about him?"

Montrose shrugged. "He was as arrogant as usual. On my back about the investigation into the dossiers. Nothing else."

Clifton asked: "Mr Lyle, do you know *who* told the Prime Minister?"

Lyle puffed his cigarette. "Yes," he said. "It's a guy called Joseph Rana."

Montrose growled the name: "Rana!"

"He's the Cabinet Secretary."

"I know who the fuck he is," Montrose snapped. "He's the bastard who started the problem about Ayer."

"Are you saying, Mr Lyle, that Rana is a CIA agent?" Clifton asked.

"It looks that way," Lyle said. "His name wasn't on the list I got earlier from Berenson, but he might have been part of the secret cell."

"I see," said Clifton softly.

"I saw him there," Montrose remembered suddenly. "In Moorhouse's office this afternoon. He was leaving as I came in, and that idiot Kataria was with him."

Clive Lyle said: "Then you must have spoken to Moorhouse immediately after he was told about the list. Didn't he seem any different to you?"

"Just the same."

"Well, maybe you're in luck, Claud," Lyle said lightly. "He might just ignore the whole thing: convince himself it's a vicious rumour or something. Why not take a chance? Maybe the whole problem'll go away."

"And maybe not," Montrose said churlishly.

"Well that is a risk," Lyle admitted. "You *could* end up with egg on your face." There was a long silence, which the American seemed to enjoy. "Or a rope around your neck," he said. Finally he asked: "What are you going to do?"

Montrose said slowly: "We're going to make sure it doesn't matter, that's what we're going to do. We're going to show that bastard Moorhouse who runs this fucking island."

Lyle dropped his cigarette onto the ground and stepped on it. "Well good luck," he said. "Watch out for your canary, though. They can be heard a long way off, I'm told. Which one is it, by the way?"

Clifton replied evenly: "Molvi."

"Molvi. Sounds like a singer, doesn't it? Castrato, probably. Well if I can't help you gentlemen any more, I'll be off. I'm expected at dinner."

"Nice to meet you, Mr Lyle," said Clifton.

"And you."

Montrose growled: "See you keep in touch."

"Of course, Claud," Lyle said. "I wouldn't forget a thing like that."

They waited until the American reached his car and the engine started. Then Montrose asked aggressively: "Satisfied?"

"Yes, thank you, Claud," Clifton said civilly. "Perfectly satisfied. Now I think it's about time we made a move. There's a lot to be done tonight."

When the Chevrolet was out of sight, the two men walked to their vehicle and, with Montrose driving, headed for the house of General Stephen Luther.

There was no sign of Priscilla. God knew where she was: perhaps her husband had strangled her, the Commissioner thought with grim longing. At least she wasn't lounging over the carpet doing her pussy-cat act.

Luther himself was dressed in jeans and a black turtle-neck sweater, exuding controlled, muscular tension. The pastel portrait of his second wife had been removed from its dominating position in the middle of the midnight blue wall, and in its place, the General had Sellotaped a map of St David's.

Montrose noticed that none of the photographs of Luther himself had been disturbed. The fact amused him. Montrose's mood improved.

Clifton quickly filled Luther in on what had happened, and the General nodded. "So we go into stage two of the plan, then. Agreed?"

"Agreed."

"Yes."

"What time is your briefing, Claud?" Luther asked.

"Eleven p.m."

"Good. What about police arms?"

"They've all been called in. Should have been handed in by six this evening. I haven't had confirmation, of course, but I don't imagine there'll have been a problem. They'll all be locked in the armouries by now. Everything will be sealed off by dawn."

"That sounds fine. Special Battalion again?"

"And General Headquarters. They're a pretty dozy lot, but they'll do as they're told."

"Excellent. What about the rest of the island?"

"I've called the Chief Constables to Port Lombard. They're on their way now, and I'll brief them at six a.m. With them away from base, there won't be any trouble in their areas. No one's got enough balls to take an initiative. They'll wait and see."

Luther nodded. "Good enough. I'm briefing the Commandos at 2230. They've got to get over to the barracks at Galloway and Aberdeen, so I've laid on air force transports and helicopters. My men have taken over guard duty at the armouries, and I'll reinforce them from midnight. Any problems?"

He looked from Montrose to Clifton. There were none.

"Okay," he said at last. "To make sure there are no mistakes, let's go over the whole thing from the beginning."

For the next hour, the men discussed the details of the operation, and then dispersed: Luther driving to the military base near the Port Lombard airport, and Clifton and Montrose to Police Headquarters.

By midnight, their men had been briefed: it had been surprisingly easy. No murmurs of dissent were heard, although some surprised glances had been exchanged, and there was a sudden buzz of conversation, quickly quelled. It was, as Luther had assured Montrose and Clifton, merely a matter of taking the initiative and holding it, brooking no argument. At the first sign of trouble, he said, shoot to kill. You have the guns, they have not.

But there was no trouble. Men trained to obey orders tend to accept them, whatever they are, from the officers they know.

At one point, Montrose launched into a patriotic speech he had prepared, but half way through, he decided from the baffled faces of his men that it wasn't necessary, and so brought it to an abrupt and unceremonious end.

By midnight, the Security Battalion and General Headquarters men were armed and deployed in the areas around the radio station, Cabinet Offices, and the large gracious Prime Ministerial residence which Moorhouse had been planning to leave in favour of his new white house on the hill. The Prime Minister was asleep inside.

Because the army would play the major role in the operation, Luther's commandos were trucked in to secure the primary objectives.

Just before they took over Moorhouse's residence, Montrose went to the commander of the guard, and relieved his platoon of duty. There was surprise but no argument, and the guards went unquestioningly back to their barracks to sleep.

Then the commandos were in place, submachine-guns at the ready, ringing the darkened residence.

In the distance came the throb of diesel motors, and Centurion tanks rumbled through the pre-dawn streets to take up positions. It was a nice touch: Montrose watched with satisfaction. It showed they meant business, and it implied they had rather more support for their actions than was the case. But support would come quickly, if only because everybody had been taken by surprise, and there were no alternatives immediately available.

The tanks outside the Prime Minister's residence swung their gun turrets until they pointed in through the wide wrought-iron gates at the house itself, half-hidden behind trees, and the engines fell silent.

It was 2 a.m., and the night for once was cool, with low humidity and a light breeze off the sea.

Luther arrived at the main gates in his official chauffeur-driven car. He was dressed in crisp khaki uniform with rows of medals on his left breast.

A commando ran forward to open the door for him while the others snapped to attention. Luther emerged grim and businesslike, returning the salute.

"Take up positions!" he ordered. "The men in Number One platoon form up over there on the lawn!"

Darkened figures moved quickly and silently.

Luther noticed Montrose and Clifton watching a few yards away and walked over to them.

"Everything all right, gentlemen?"

The Commissioner of Police was starting to feel outranked and inferior, and resentful that General Luther was coming across as being so obviously in charge, although this had been implicit in their plan. It had been easy enough to make a leadership decision in theory the night before, but Montrose was finding the practice galling, and he knew the feeling would not get better as time went on.

So he snapped at Luther: "Of course everything's all right. We're just waiting for you to stop playing toy soldiers so we can get this show on the road!"

If Montrose had expected the General to back down, he was mistaken.

Luther kept his voice low, but there was no mistaking the determination. "Get a grip on yourself, Claud," he said. "I'm not going to put up with any fucking rubbish tonight, understand?"

He turned away, not waiting for a reply, and issued instructions to the men guarding the gates. Montrose felt his face burn, and heard the slight shuffling of Clifton beside him. Clifton, he knew, would have enjoyed that.

There was nothing Montrose could do. Not now. But he would keep score, and the day would come when things would be evened out. Montrose waited sullenly in the shadows.

When Luther rejoined them, it was ten minutes after two, and the moon had risen, full and yellow, over the buildings and the palm trees of Port Lombard.

"Shall we go?" Luther said. It was more an order than a question.

The three men began walking, shoulder to shoulder, up the drive leading to the residence, boots loud on the tarmac. From the corner of his eye, Montrose could see commandos falling silently in behind them, submachine-guns ported. In the trees, an owl hooted mournfully, and a bat flickered and dodged overhead.

Commandos peeled off to surround the house, covering doors and windows in case anyone should try to escape.

The main party paused at the large oak front doors and Luther glanced around him. "Everyone ready? Right! Go!"

Three commandos stepped forward, one pushed his finger onto the doorbell and held it there, while the others hammered at the door with batons. The sound seemed obscenely loud in the still night, but there was no immediate response. No lights clicked on inside, no voices called to find out what was happening. The hammering stopped and the commandos waited for orders.

"Keep it going," said Luther.

The men beat at the doors with all their power, beginning to sweat slightly now, and Montrose and Clifton exchanged uneasy glances.

The light on the veranda flicked on, and from the other side of the oak doors there was a scraping of bolts and the sound of a key turning. The commandos stepped back, and others took their place, weapons ready.

The doors opened a timid inch, and the men launched themselves forward, shoulders heaving against the wood. They swung open, the force knocking a servant onto his back, hands flailing to protect his face from the men who burst in, hunched low over their Sten guns.

The commandos spread out through the gracious wood-panelled lobby, more pouring in the doors. Lights came on.

Luther ordered: "This way!" He raced up the stairs, three at a time, his pistol drawn. Behind him came the commandos. Montrose and

Clifton brought up the rear. Montrose had decided that if Luther was intent on the glory, it was right that he should accept whatever dangers might occur. Maybe the Prime Minister would be waiting in his bedroom to brain him with a poker.

Luther's previous visits to the residence had been for official functions which were always held on the ground floor, or under marquees in the garden, but at the top of the stairs he did not hesitate. He knew from the plans where the bedroom wing would be.

He brushed past a small table, knocking over an ancient Chinese vase which rolled slowly to the edge and smashed down onto the wooden floor, but Luther heard the crash only dimly.

His men grouped round him by a door, and he inclined his head towards it. Light showed through the gap at the bottom. The next second, it crashed open and three commandos raced into the room, fingers on the triggers of their Stens. Luther followed with his pistol.

Daniel Moorhouse stood open-mouthed, frozen in the act of tying the cord of his silk dressing-gown. His wife lay in bed, sheets pulled half way up her face in an instinctive combination of fear and modesty, and her eyes stared brightly out.

Moorhouse was the first to speak, although he remained motionless under the threat of the submachine-guns.

"And just what are you doing, General?" His voice was dry and calm.

Luther saluted. "I'm sorry to have to tell you, sir, but, in the national interest, I have taken over the country."

Still no movement from Moorhouse. The Stens were pointed at his chest. "Oh have you?" he said, casually interested. "May I ask why?"

"This place is a mess, Prime Minister. Economically and politically. Now you want to drive us right into the arms of Russia. We're not going to put up with it. The people don't want you any more. So we've taken control. We're going to get the island back on a reasonable footing, and when that's done, we'll hold free and fair elections."

Moorhouse's hands began moving slowly to complete tying his dressing-gown cord. The commandos watched him.

"Historically," Moorhouse observed, "that is extremely unlikely. Armies hardly ever voluntarily hand back power to the people, whatever their intentions at the beginning. St. David's will slide into violence and chaos. I take it that this is a responsibility you accept?"

"There is violence now, Prime Minister," Luther pointed out. "There's certainly economic chaos. We want to sort it out ourselves before the Russians get here."

"Your arguments are too simplistic," Moorhouse said dismissively. "You don't know what you're talking about." He was gaining confidence now. "And can you please ask your men not to point their weapons at my wife and myself. As you can plainly see, we are unarmed."

Two more figures appeared in the door, first hovering indecisively and then moving into the room: Montrose and Clifton.

Moorhouse saw them and his lips curled. "I should have known, Commissioner, that you would be somehow mixed up in this," he said.

Montrose ignored him and his eyes focused on the Prime Minister's wife. She tossed her head – black and silky hair – trying to look as composed and dignified as possible, drawing on her training of years of being First Lady.

Luther spoke: "Get dressed please, Prime Minister."

"What about my wife?"

"We have nothing against your wife. I suggest she goes back to sleep."

"Where are you taking me?"

"To a place of safety."

Moorhouse snorted. "Safety for whom?" he asked. "You or me? I really cannot abide the terminology of revolution. It's as disgusting and sneaky as the act itself." He was beginning to feel reckless. He pushed past the first commando, paying no attention to his Sten gun, and walked towards an adjoining dressing-room.

"Leave the door open," Luther ordered.

"With pleasure," Moorhouse snapped. "It will give me the chance to speak to you meanwhile about the meaning of treason, and the penalties it attracts."

Suddenly Claud Montrose spoke, slowly and lazily. "If you don't shut up, Moorhouse, we'll take you out now and kill you."

"That would be just your style, wouldn't it . . . Commissioner," the Prime Minister almost spat out the last word. "First corruption, then treason, and finally murder. And all of it in the national interest, no doubt."

"Daniel!" His wife's voice, speaking sharply from the bed. "There is no point in provoking Mr Montrose at this stage. He has a gun."

Montrose turned to her with a thin smile. "We should make you Prime Minister, Mrs Moorhouse. Your husband has a big mouth and no brain."

"Dress please, Prime Minister," Luther broke in sharply. "We can do without the debate for the time being."

"Where is my husband being taken?" Mrs Moorhouse asked, her composure regained despite the continuing psychological disadvantage of still being in bed.

"To the Central Gaol, Mrs Moorhouse."

"But why?" she demanded. "He is not a criminal. Might I remind you he is still the elected leader of this country. He deserves better treatment than that!"

Luther replied coolly: "He *was* the Prime Minister, Mrs Moorhouse. He's no one now. Just a private citizen like all the others. I'm afraid he warrants no special treatment. Besides, the gaol is the only place we can guarantee his safety."

"Safety!" Moorhouse interjecting angrily again. "You keep using that word! Are you suggesting I'll be attacked by the people of this island? The people who owe their independence to me? Who voted my administration into office and kept it there?"

"I don't wish to discuss it," Luther said. "You're not as popular as you seem to think."

Moorhouse made a scoffing noise. He was almost dressed, and the commandos were beginning to relax, feeling the air of unreality. Clifton, who had watched silently, thought: *is this all there is to overthrowing a government?* It seemed too easy. The great edifice was crumbling at the first blow.

When the Prime Minister was ready, they escorted him out. His parting from his wife had been perfunctory, as if neither wished to make any display in front of their enemies. Moorhouse went across to the bed and touched her hand briefly. They stared at one another for a moment, and then he turned and walked briskly out.

Luther's car had been brought up to the front door, and the Prime Minister got into the back, squashed between the muscular frame of the General and the fat bulk of Montrose. Clifton sat in the front with the driver. They completed the drive to the gaol in silence.

Moorhouse was stripped of his personal belongings and made to sign a receipt for them. The men watched him being led away and the steel gates crashed shut behind him.

Then he was gone. They exchanged glances. They had done it: taken over the island.

It would be dawn in an hour, and Luther, the newly proclaimed head of the Revolutionary Council, would be making his first broadcast to the nation.

Broadcasting House in Port Lombard was in darkness, except for the dim lights inside the entrance hall. Commandos guarded the doors and the tanks waited squat and black in the street. The nightwatchman sat scanning the visitor's register at his desk with eyes that refused to focus, trying desperately to appear busy and unconcerned and somehow still in charge, to combat his uneasy impression that he might in fact be a prisoner.

He became aware of new activity outside the main entrance, the shapes of men gathering round and voices raised. Then into the gloom of the entrance hall came four commandos escorting a young man who looked more puzzled than scared.

The nightwatchman found himself being shouted at.

"You over there!" a commando yelled. "You know this man?"

The watchman answered quickly, springing to his feet and trying to appear as helpful and agreeable as possible. "Yes, he's one of the engineers here. Mr Sampson, if I remember correctly."

"Let me go," the young man said angrily, shrugging away from the two commandos who held him by the arms. "What the hell's happening here?"

The commandos released him and he stood defiantly a step or two away, glaring at them. They ignored him.

"The others will be in any time now," the nightwatchman offered. "Is there anyone special you're looking out for?"

"Only essential staff are being allowed in," the commando corporal said. "Is he essential?"

"Of course I'm bloody essential," Sampson retorted. "If I'm not there to press the buttons, nothing goes out of this place."

"Then go and press your buttons, sonny," the corporal said. Sampson walked quickly through swing doors leading to the lifts. "How many others are going to be in over the next hour or so?" the corporal asked.

"Twelve or fifteen," the nightwatchman said.

"You able to recognise them?"

"I've worked here for twenty years," the nightwatchman said, an edge of pride in his voice. "If I don't know them, no one does."

"Well you can screen them for me," the corporal said. "And you'd better not make any mistakes."

The nightwatchman sank back into his chair and waited. The staff began trickling in, some staring curiously at the soldiers, others pretending the military presence didn't exist and even ignoring the tanks which could now be seen clearly in the lightening streets. Not one asked the nightwatchman what was going on, each apparently feeling sure that those inside would have full details, and that it was unwise to linger in the foyer. They'd know in the Newsroom.

But those people who gathered in the bleak editorial office on the second floor, surrounded by newspaper files and ancient typewriters, had no information either. They were hoping that one of the new arrivals would come in with an explanation.

While they speculated on what was happening, the automatic drinks dispenser stole the coins of people wanting coffee, but managed to produce thin plastic cups of hot chocolate.

After a while, everyone went about their business, preparing for the day's transmissions of Radio St David's. Typewriters in the newsroom began to clatter as the first bulletin of world news was prepared from agency tapes. The military presence outside was almost forgotten.

The Sten guns had been trained on the three journalists on duty for two or three seconds before the first man glanced up and stiffened. Five commandos were standing to the left of the doorway and others were filing in, moving along the right-hand wall – walking quietly, not running. One after the other, the typewriters fell silent and the journalists stared, baffled and beginning to be frightened.

Then General Luther entered briskly, taking in the scene at a glance.

"Good morning, gentlemen," he said.

The journalists watched in silence for several seconds before one replied: "Good morning, General."

"What are you men doing?"

"The morning news bulletin."

"It's been cancelled," Luther said flatly. "Nothing's going out over this radio that I don't personally authorise. But we will need a news bulletin later, so hold yourselves ready for that, please."

From the back of the room, a journalist took a quick drag at his cigarette and said: "May we ask what the hell's going on?"

"Certainly," Luther replied. "There has been a coup d'état and the security forces – police as well as army – have taken over. I now head the Revolutionary Council of St David's."

The journalist said softly, almost to himself: "Oh for Christ's sake."

Luther ignored this. "I intend broadcasting to the nation in a few minutes," he said. "I need one of you gentlemen to take me to the appropriate studio."

The journalist at the back was the first to get to his feet, not smartly as if he was afraid and wanted to ingratiate himself, but lazily and with what seemed to Luther like a flicker of amusement.

"Allow me, General," the journalist said. "I'll give you a guided tour. There's not much point seizing power if you can't tell the people what you've done. You'd like martial music too, I take it? Perhaps I can direct you to the record library. There's not much time before we go on the air."

His voice faded away as he moved out of the newsroom and down the corridor, followed by Luther and most of the commandos.

Two men with submachine-guns remained behind. Although their early bulletin had been cancelled, the typewriters of the other journalists were soon clattering again, for the distraction as much as anything else.

Luther was led down corridors to Studio 1A, followed by his armed guard. The General was beginning to feel ill at ease. This was not a role he had been trained for, and in the quiet gloom of Broadcasting House, it seemed unlikely that anything as significant as a nationwide broadcast could possibly take place there.

The control-room of 1A was cool and brightly lit. Beyond it, through a double-glazed window, was the studio itself: two chairs, a brown desk on which was a tray with paper cups and a pitcher of water. There was a thick grey carpet and cream acoustic tiles covered the walls and ceiling. An old-fashioned-looking microphone hung down over the desk.

Three people stared at the armed men filing in to the control-room. The producer – a middle-aged woman with glasses and a permanently anxious expression – let her mouth drop open, and her knuckles whitened around a reel of tape which she held tightly against her stomach and breasts, as if it might offer protection.

The journalist spoke first, unable to resist the temptation to break the news. "There has been a coup," he said, trying to keep his voice suitably grave. "General Luther here has taken over. He wants to make a nation-wide broadcast."

"When?" asked the producer faintly. "We're on the air in . . ." she glanced at the wall clock " . . . eight minutes thirty-five."

Luther said: "Normal programmes are cancelled. Nothing goes out without military clearance."

"And we need some music," the journalist said. "Military marches, that sort of thing."

The producer looked around, wild-eyed. "I think we might have something here," she said finally. She put the tape down and sorted through a pile of discs. "The Band of the Coldstream Guards," she said, reading from the record sleeve.

"Sounds just the sort of thing," said the journalist.

Luther took the record and glanced at it. " 'Great Film Themes'," he said. "Hopeless. We need something martial. Royal Marines. Something like that."

"There's not much time," the producer said nervously. "We're on the air soon and you won't have time to get anything from the record library."

"Then we'll start late," Luther said crisply. "The world won't crumble if you're not on the air at six."

The journalist said: "I'll scuttle down and see if I can pick something up in time. We can't start off the island's first coup with the theme from 'Love Story', can we?"

Luther glared, aware now that he was being made fun of. But the journalist had already gone.

The General went through to the studio, and settled himself at the wooden desk. From his pocket, he pulled a sheaf of folded paper and smoothed it out. Peering through the glass, the producer could see that it was handwritten on thin paper which would crinkle when he turned the pages.

"Oh dear God," she said faintly. The wall clock showed two minutes and fifteen seconds to go.

Luther read through his speech, frowning slightly. He pulled a ballpoint pen from his pocket and made a correction. In the control-room, one of the commandos stirred restlessly, and shifted his Sten gun onto his other shoulder.

When the door swung open and the journalist reappeared, the soldiers instinctively braced for action.

"Relax, men," the journalist said breezily. "It's only me: the bringer of music." Then to the producer: "I picked up three military bands. God knows what they're playing."

She seized the records and flipped through. "I don't know any of these," she said despairingly. "What if they're not appropriate for a coup?"

The journalist drew a finger graphically across his throat.

"Thirty seconds," the studio manager said.

The producer flicked down the button to talk to Luther in the studio. "Are you ready to start, General?" she asked.

He shook his head. "I want to go through my speech again," he said.

"Fifteen seconds." The red light above their heads flicked on, signalling that the transmissions were about to begin.

The producer pulled a disc from the sleeve and almost slapped it onto a turntable, and pressed a button to set it revolving. "Console two!" she shouted. "No time for levels!"

"Five, four, three . . ."

She lowered the arm onto the disc. As the second hand flicked across to the minute, the band struck up a march. It was "Colonel Bogie", but it was better than nothing.

The producer felt a wave of relief and jubilation. "We did it!" she said. "Right on the second! It couldn't have been better."

The journalist grinned at her. "What a pro," he said. "That BBC training shows through every time."

The producer flicked the button to talk to Luther again. "General," she said. "We've started playing martial music. I can put it on the studio loudspeakers if you like."

"No thanks."

"Well, just let me know when you're ready to go, and I'll cue you in at the end of a cut."

Luther nodded abstractedly, and the woman turned to light a cigarette, back in charge of her studio, triumphant that something was filling the seconds allotted to her.

After several minutes, Luther looked across and nodded.

"Ready?" the producer asked.

"Yes, I'm ready now," he confirmed.

"Then will you read a couple of sentences so we can get a voice level, please?"

Luther cleared his throat. "Good morning," he intoned. "I am General Stephen Luther, Chief of Staff or the Armed Forces of St David's, and I am speaking to you on a matter of national importance. Please give your full attention to what I have to say now."

"That's fine," the producer broke in. "Try and put a bit more expression into it. Don't start until you see the green light."

Luther waited, his throat becoming dry. He sipped the water. Over the studio loudspeaker came the sound of the military band. Suddenly it broke off and a voice said: "Stand by."

The green light glowed in front of him. Was he supposed to start now? He glanced through to the control-room where the producer was nodding vigorously at him, her face grimacing enthusiastically.

"Good morning," Luther said at last. "I am General Stephen Luther, Chief of Staff of the Armed Forces of St David's, and I am speaking to you on a matter of national importance." He felt he was choking, and he cleared his throat loudly. In the control-room, the producer groaned.

"I beg your pardon," Luther told the microphone. "Please give your full attention to what I have to say now. During the night, there have been a number of important changes. The armed forces of St David's, together with the island's police force, have combined to take control of this nation's destiny.

"It is not a step that we have taken lightly, or without due thought, but we were convinced that grave national issues were at stake, and we had to move before it was too late.

"Daniel Moorhouse, the Prime Minister of this island until last night, is no longer in control. Instead, you are being governed by a Revolutionary Council comprising myself as head, and with the other members being Mr Claud Montrose, the Commissioner of Police, and his Deputy, Mr Alec Clifton.

"The Revolutionary Council will naturally be expanded, and other names will be announced soon. Meanwhile, I ask you all to remain calm and patient.

"The reason your security forces have taken command of St David's is simple: under Daniel Moorhouse, the island was being moved, like it or not, into the hands of the communists. Our American allies and our British allies, on whom our overall security depends, were being brushed aside. In their place, Moscow was stepping in.

"Daniel Moorhouse had no mandate from the people to do this. We, your security forces, were being constantly approached by concerned and patriotic citizens who asked what we thought of this: whether we felt it was a good, sensible and *safe* thing to do. We had to answer honestly: no.

"We thought it senseless and dangerous. We frequently warned Daniel Moorhouse against it, but he brushed our advice aside.

"Then people began asking us: 'But isn't there something our security forces can do to stop us being driven, willy-nilly, into the arms of Moscow?'

"From those pleas, those calls for help from many of the most trusted men and women on the island, has come the action which took place last night.

"Not one life has been lost. The situation on the island is completely calm and orderly, and we are determined that it shall remain calm and orderly. If there are any anti-social or unpatriotic elements thinking of fomenting trouble, I warn them here and now to think again! We do not want violence, but we shall not shrink from it. Our duty is, and always has been, to protect the inhabitants of St David's from danger. That is what we are doing now.

"The danger is both internal – the misguided, dangerous and arrogant actions of Daniel Moorhouse; and external – the approach of the Russian bear, arms open to seize another victim, this time an apparently willing one.

"But we are not willing, ladies and gentlemen. We are of the Western bloc, not of the East. We do not want to be swallowed up by the Russian bear. We fought for our independence, and we will not abandon it lightly.

"We of the Revolutionary Council, backed by the officers and men under our command, are sworn to protect this island's sovereignty and integrity, and this we will do.

"You may be wondering how long we intend remaining in control. I can assure you: not one day longer than is necessary. There is important work to be done. The nation has to be set back on its feet. Properly thought out policies must be implemented. Then elections need to be held.

"Politics is for the politicians, not for the military or the police. We recognise that, but Daniel Moorhouse has betrayed the nation's trust and put its constitution at risk, and the people must now be given a chance to elect new civilian leaders.

"That is what we intend giving to St David's: fair and free elections so that we can tell Daniel Moorhouse, and show the Soviet leaders, that we are not as easy to subjugate as they thought! We are a proud people, an independent people. We fight for what we believe is right.

"We may be small, but my God we are tough! We will fight them for every inch of this territory, if it ever becomes necessary.

"But we believe that our action last night has forestalled such a possibility. A new day has dawned on St David's, and a new era has begun.

"The Revolutionary Council asks for your prayers and co-operation during this testing time. I will speak to you again shortly. Meanwhile, go about your normal business in a peaceful way, and no harm will come to you."

Luther leaned back, glancing through the window into the control booth both to show that he was finished, and instinctively for approval.

The producer half-turned to the studio manager, and he saw her lips moving, and then the military music was back on the loudspeaker.

Luther shrugged and stood up.

Out in the street a few minutes later, surrounded by his commando bodyguard, Luther noticed that very few other people were about.

He looked at his watch. It was coming up to seven o'clock. Although this was early, the streets should have been fuller than they were.

As he was about to climb into his car, he glanced about him again, and this time the thought suddenly struck home so that he smiled broadly: *now this is mine.*

Chapter Twenty-seven

Claud Montrose, with his feet up on his desk and a cup of coffee growing cold beside him, found it difficult to shake the feeling of anti-climax. Surely there was more to it than this?

His briefing of the Chief Constables of the island had gone without a hitch, and at the end, they had all pledged loyalty to the new regime and its objectives. Montrose was surprised to find there existed a genuine groundswell of opposition to Moorhouse's new foreign policy. Luther had forecast this – he probably felt it himself – but the Commissioner had been too concerned with the protection racket and his own future to care particularly about overtures to Russia.

In his view, the Soviets were a long way from making any fundamental difference to the island's way of life, and he did not care whether a realignment damaged Western security plans. That was a problem for Washington or London, and not for Claud Montrose.

But now it was ten o'clock in the morning, and he had become a member of the Revolutionary Council, with tanks in the street and the Prime Minister in gaol, yet he was dogged by the uncanny feeling that nothing really had changed. Surely he should feel different? Shouldn't things *be* different when he walked along the corridors of the Police Headquarters and spoke to people? Yet it all seemed unsettlingly routine.

Montrose supposed his senses had dulled because he was tired. None of them had slept the night before, and there was little chance of rest for many hours.

The Revolutionary Council was due to hold its first meeting at midday, basically to decide what to do next. They had taken over St David's to save themselves, and having done that, it was necessary to formulate policies, choose Ministers and make sure the country kept running. The thought made Montrose uneasy. When he began to consider the ramifications, they stretched out endlessly.

But no doubt there would be compensations. They would probably be able to abandon the protection racket in favour of something which was both more lucrative and easier to collect. They were in the big money now.

His telephone rang. "Yes?" said Montrose.

"There's a Mr Clive Lyle on the phone for you," his secretary said. "Shall I put him on? He says it's personal."

Montrose lifted his eyebrows in surprise. What the hell was Lyle doing telephoning him? What about the CIA circus sniffing around for their security leak?

"Put him on," Montrose said. He waited for the click, then said abruptly: "What the hell do you want?"

"Good morning, Claud," Lyle replied, his voice calm and friendly. "I gather it's a busy morning for you."

"It is. What do you want, Lyle? What about your fucking security?"

"Oh I'm not phoning from the office, if that's what you're worried about," Lyle said. "I'm in a call-box in the High Street. I wondered if I could see you at the same time tonight?"

"Tonight?" Montrose was cautious. He wasn't sure he wanted to meet the American so soon, and perhaps not ever again. Lyle's usefulness seemed to be at an end. They were in charge now. "I don't think I can make tonight. What's it about?"

There was a silence, and he could feel the American's surprise. "I can't talk about it over the phone, Claud," Lyle said firmly. "But it is important. I'll tell you at 7.30."

Montrose was still reluctant, although in the end curiosity got the better of him. "Okay," he said grudgingly. "Same time, same place. It had better be good."

"It is good. Why not bring your friend along?"

"Alec? I didn't think he was your type."

"He's not, Claud. You are," Lyle said with a hint of anger. Then the phone went dead. Montrose shrugged.

At twelve o'clock, the Commissioner and Clifton drove along to the Cabinet Offices, where Luther now had his headquarters. It was here that the first signs of increased deference were obvious. Men sprang forward to open the car doors. There were stares and bows from officials as they walked through the foyer. Someone murmured to Montrose: "Good morning, Excellency." It was a term he felt went down rather well.

In the anteroom, nothing had changed. The PPS, Bob Sehai, had always been deferential, and the atmosphere of air conditioned calm and quiet power was still there. Montrose didn't like being made to wait while Sehai checked whether Luther was ready for them, but the doors swung open quickly and there was the General, just on the other side, a broad smile on his face and his hand extended in greeting.

Sehai left them alone and they went to the long oval table at one end of the room where Moorhouse had held discussions with cabinet ministers.

Luther had prepared an agenda, together with a list of suggested names of members of the Revolutionary Council, and the portfolios which could be assigned to them. Montrose glanced quickly through it. He saw he was down as Minister for Industry. Clifton was supposed to be in charge of Tourism, and Luther himself had taken Finance.

A mixture of senior police and army officers were suggested for the other portfolios.

As Montrose read, the list assumed new significance for him. Each portfolio had its own implications. If you wanted to make money, you were better off in charge of the Ministry of Finance, where permissions were handed out or refused, than you would be if you had Industry. With the depressed state of the St David's economy, there weren't as many opportunities with the Industry portfolio. And poor Alec Clifton: there'd be even less going for him with Tourism, and hardly any tourists.

Luther grinned boyishly at his colleagues. "Well," he asked, "how does it look?"

There was a long silence from Montrose and Clifton, during which the General's smile became strained and finally faded completely.

It was Clifton who spoke first. "Tell me, General," he said, apparently casually. "What's going to happen to our – what shall I say? – *unofficial* sources of income?"

Luther selected a cigarette and lit up. "That's over," he said briefly. "We run this country now, and we don't need to be involved in some small-time protection racket. We just let it lapse. We don't need to say anything to our clients. They'll get the picture soon enough. It would be demeaning for members of the Revolutionary Council to go around collecting a few dollars here and there. I think you'll find that your assigned portfolios contain sufficient opportunities for making a bit of extra pocket money. Besides which" – he took a drag on his cigarette – "as members of the Revolutionary Council, we have new responsibilities so it's not unreasonable that we vote ourselves extra money for it."

"And you, as Chairman of the Council, will get the most?" It was Clifton again who posed what should have been a question, but turned out to be a statement. Montrose sat silently, surprised at how his Deputy was going straight for the jugular.

"That's what usually happens," Luther replied carefully. "Yes, I'll get the most. But precisely what the figures are, we can argue about later."

"And as Minister of Finance, you'd also have a larger number of opportunities for making what you call pocket money?" Clifton persisted.

"I don't know about that, Alec," Luther said, his voice still even. "*Some* opportunities. But so will you."

"As Minister for Tourism?"

"Why not? There's still an industry there. It needs building up, I admit."

Montrose joined in: "It certainly does," he said. "From scratch. And what about the Minister for Industry? There's not much industry around as far as I can see."

Luther was starting to get angry. "Oh yes there is," he said. "Open your eyes, Claud. There's gemstones, tea, rubber, coconuts. A hell of a lot."

"Not as much as the Minister of Finance," Montrose pointed out.

"Every bit as much. Maybe more."

"Okay, then you take it."

"What we're getting at," Clifton said patiently, "is that until now, we've all been making just about the same amount of money. There's been a couple of dollars difference, I agree, but it's literally been a couple of dollars. You remember how we sat down and worked out how much every one of us would earn, and we split our clients accordingly? Now that's changed. You'll be getting far more than Claud, and Claud will be getting far more than me. But the risks we all take are the same."

"Alec's right," agreed Montrose. "We have to even it out."

For the next two hours, the Revolutionary Council debated how the spoils should be divided. In the end, it was agreed that Luther would take Industry, giving Montrose Finance, and Alec Clifton would be Minister of Tourism and Ports. Development projects had been planned for Port Lombard, and these ought to provide extra opportunities.

The PPS brought sandwiches and coffee and, over lunch, they quickly agreed on the other members of the junta. The meeting broke up at 3.30, and Montrose and Clifton were once more bowed out of the Cabinet Offices and into their car.

As they drove down Constitution Avenue, Montrose remembered the meeting arranged for that night.

"Lyle telephoned me this morning," he said. "You want to come along again tonight?"

"What's it about?"

"He wouldn't say. I'm rather inclined to tell him to fuck off. We don't need him any more, and he's getting to be a pain in the arse."

"You could be right," said Clifton. "But it wouldn't do any harm to get along and see. If he's wasting our time, we can tell him then."

At 7.30, Lyle was waiting in his usual place, not apparently in the least put off by Montrose's reluctance to meet him. As they gathered, Clifton wished there was more light so that he could watch the American's expressions. Lyle's voice was always very careful, but occasionally there seemed to be something behind it: not exactly humour, not exactly spite. It would be interesting to see his face and his eyes, Clifton thought.

He could understand Lyle's secret glee when he thought that Montrose, who was for him no more nor less than a blackmailer, was about to take a tumble. But why was he keeping the relationship going now? The coup had succeeded, and Montrose had won. The American could once more fade into the background and let the Embassy security check go on around him without fear that any move of his would give him away.

But the bonds between spies and their masters are complex things, and he decided it would need a psychiatrist to sort Lyle out.

"I believe congratulations are in order, gentlemen," Lyle said softly. "So congratulations."

"Thank you," Clifton replied courteously.

"I hope you didn't call us all the way here for that," said Montrose. "You could have sent a greetings telegram."

The American sighed. "Claud, you are such a bum," he said. "All conversations – even the ones we have – start with pleasantries. That's the way our society is structured. Think of it as sex. You don't just walk into the bedroom and start pumping away, do you? You work up to it."

"I don't," said Montrose.

Lyle stared speculatively at his silhouette in the darkness. "Hmmmmm," he said. "Come to think of it, you probably don't. But you should try it. It's nicer that way."

"The day I need sex lessons from you, you creep, is the day I'll cut my throat," Montrose said flatly.

"That may not be necessary," Lyle answered, heaving himself up to sit on the sea wall. "Other people may cut your throat before that. And yours too, Mr Clifton."

"Oh yes?" Clifton followed his example, and pulled himself up onto the wall. Montrose stayed where he was, a fat, hulking shadow moving restlessly.

"What the fuck do you mean, Lyle?" snapped Montrose.

The American had their attention, and he pulled out his pack of cigarettes and offered them around. Montrose waited impatiently for him to begin, but he knew the bastard would make him wait until they had all lit up.

"Can I start by asking you a question?" Lyle said.

"Please do," replied Clifton.

"What have you done with Daniel Moorhouse?"

"He's in the Central Gaol," Clifton said.

"And that's where he's going to stay," Montrose added churlishly.

"But what exactly are you going to do to him?"

There was a silence. Finally Clifton said: "Well, we're going to keep him there."

"I was surprised you didn't shoot him when you took over," Lyle observed. "That would have been the obvious thing to do."

"That's what *I* wanted to do," Montrose said. "Alec and Luther voted against it."

"Why?"

"It was mainly Luther," Clifton explained. "He wasn't sure he could get his junior officers to go along with him if we were going to kill Moorhouse. He thought it might be too drastic a move."

Lyle inhaled thoughtfully and blew the smoke out into the darkness. "I can understand that," he said. "It might have been difficult. But what about now?"

"What are you driving at, Mr Lyle?" Clifton asked.

"Just this: Daniel Moorhouse must be a danger to you – the biggest danger you face. He knows too much. While he's kept alive, there's always the chance that one day he'll be free, and then he'll come after you. You know what a vindictive son-of-a-bitch he is. And it won't only be the coup he'll pay you off for. It'll also be the protection racket and the violence. I wouldn't give two bits for your chances."

"Forgive me for asking, Mr Lyle," Clifton said, "but what is your interest in this? Surely if our friend Claud Montrose ended up with a rope around his neck, you'd be out opening a bottle of champagne?" He felt Montrose glaring at him. "After all, Claud has been blackmailing you because of your homosexual activities. I hope you don't mind me bringing this up again? So why should you want to keep him out of harm's way?"

"Well put, Mr Clifton," Lyle said equably. "Claud would dump me if he thought there was a dollar in it for him. I know that. But you can imagine how I feel about what *I've* done to my Embassy. It's not very nice knowing you're responsible for getting rid of a whole batch of your colleagues, including someone who was very close to me." In the darkness, Montrose snorted. "In a way, this is my chance to make it up. It's in the United States' interests that this island doesn't swing towards the Soviets. As you know, it's very much in our defence interests. But if Moorhouse comes back – and particularly if he comes back with a vengeance – we may be in bad trouble. So we want you to succeed."

"Jesus!" Montrose exclaimed. "How can you say that? Only yesterday, your buddies were busy selling us down the river, making sure Moorhouse had evidence to put us away for life!"

"Ah yes," Lyle agreed. "But yesterday you were a bunch of small-time crooks."

"Thanks."

"And now you're a bunch of big-time crooks. In fact, the sort of people we do business with every day. And your foreign policies are exactly in line with our own. You should have been at the Embassy this morning. First everyone was shocked. Then there was triumph. It was like the fourth of July. The Russians had been kicked in the balls, and the Americans were safe again in St David's. Has the Ambassador been to see you yet?"

"He may have seen Luther this afternoon," Clifton said. "I hadn't heard."

"Well he won't lose much time going along to wring the General's hand," Lyle predicted. "But what we're all worried about is Moorhouse. What if he gets out?"

"*We* won't let him out," Montrose promised. "Not ever."

"You won't be in power forever, Claud. Sooner or later, like all military dictatorships, you're going to have to hand over or you'll be pushed out. Military men usually screw things up – I hope you don't mind me being frank – and the people are bloody glad to see the back of them, whatever they thought at the beginning. Add to that Moorhouse still in prison, and possibly a martyr. You know how fickle the public are. And the fact that he's got the goods on you, and it could end up with Russian warships anchored in the port down there, and the 'Battleship Potemkin' showing at the local Odeon."

"The United States wants us to kill Moorhouse?" Clifton asked, thoughtful and subdued.

"Jesus, I can't say that," Lyle laughed. "I don't have any authority. But I do know our Government is afraid of what might happen in future if Moorhouse is released. All I'm doing tonight is putting to you a scenario. What you do about it is up to you."

"But if you were us," Clifton persisted, "what would you do?"

Lyle pondered for a moment. "It's difficult," he admitted. "The time for just shooting Moorhouse out of hand was last night. It's the sort of thing you can do during the coup, and no one minds much, but if you do it the following day in cold blood, you run into trouble. Have you been through his papers? Maybe there's something there you can get him on."

"I don't think anyone's worried about that yet," Clifton said.

"Well, maybe you should. Never know what you might turn up."

"What if we found nothing?"

"If I were you?"

"Yes."

"If I were you," said Lyle, "I'd invent something. Do it the easy way, the way they teach us in Washington. Take a situation that already exists and adapt it. Now here on St David's, what have we got? Well, for example, we've got your ten heroes. Moorhouse was going to get you on that, Claud, wasn't he? He'd have charged you with having a private army and sending them in to start riots, which led to people being killed. That fits in okay with what we know about Moorhouse. It's a good scenario if you turn it round and use it against him. Why don't you say Moorhouse controlled your heroes and *he* sent them in to cause trouble so he could blame the CIA, kick the Americans and move towards Moscow? Simple, isn't it? Now if my arithmetic is right, four members of the public were killed in the first two big riots. Forget about the latest one for the moment. That's four charges of conspiracy to murder you can have Moorhouse on."

"But how?" Clifton asked. "How do we make it stick?"

"Surely that's easy enough?" Lyle said. "You get people to stand up in court and confess. What's the canary's name again? Molvi? Find Molvi. Put a vice-like grip on his balls, and he'll sing a different tune just as sweetly. He'll swear before a judge that Montrose was Moorhouse."

Montrose was standing very still now. "Yes, he would too," he said thoughtfully.

"Of course he would. You just give him a private guarantee that whatever sentence he gets from the court, you'll set it aside a few weeks later, and he can go off with a pocketful of money and start life somewhere else. After all, there's not much left for him here, whatever happens."

Clifton broke in: "But Molvi by himself isn't enough."

"No he isn't," Lyle agreed. "You need others to give your story some weight. Now, Claud, this is where your astonishing brain comes in. Who else can you blackmail? Think about it. And don't look at me, please. It has to be someone close to Moorhouse."

They waited for an answer. At last Montrose gave a short laugh, and, for the first time, it had a trace of humour in it.

"Rana," Montrose said softly. "That fucking Rana."

"Well done, Claud," Lyle approved. "Rana is a CIA man. Offer privately to forgive him for spying, and he'll do as he's told. You'll have a man's balls in each of your hands. There are some who would envy you that."

"Rana," Montrose repeated, an edge of anticipation in his voice.

"And Kataria, too. Those bastards work together."

"What do you have on Kataria?" Lyle asked. "I don't know that he's CIA."

"I'll find something," Montrose promised grimly.

Lyle shrugged. "Well, good hunting," he said. "I must be off."

"And someone else as well," Montrose said.

"Don't get carried away, Claud," Lyle cautioned. "Remember the more people you involve, the bigger your chance of error. You don't want it all collapsing around your ears."

"Stephen Ayer."

"Mr Lyle's right, Claud," Clifton added. "We don't want to make it more difficult than it already is. This isn't the time to go round paying off old scores."

"Fuck it!" Montrose said savagely. "We're in charge now. We don't have to act as if Moorhouse is watching over us any more."

"But the *world's* going to be watching you, Claud," Lyle reminded him. "You put an overthrown Prime Minister on trial for his life, and you've got everyone's attention. So your case has got to be a good one. Otherwise you're better off just going down to the Central Gaol tonight and blowing Moorhouse's brains out. But then you risk a murder charge later."

"We can use Ayer," Montrose insisted. "That bastard's pretty broken down already. And he was close to Moorhouse. He was the bloody PPS! We need Ayer."

"Well, you gentlemen decide amongst yourselves," Lyle said, hoisting himself down to the ground. "The United States wants no part in these matters. Drop a note in my mailbox if I can be of further use, Claud. Goodnight, Mr Clifton."

"Goodnight, Mr Lyle."

"Claud."

"Night."

"Thanks for your help, Mr Lyle," Clifton said. "I'm sure you're right."

Clifton watched him go through the darkness. He was surprised at how swiftly and silently the man moved.

Chapter Twenty-eight

Joe Rana was arrested in a pre-dawn operation a few hours later. He seemed unsurprised.

Tilak Kataria's house was in darkness and there was no response to the persistent banging on the door, or the doorbell, which melodically chimed the quarter-hour every time a commando pressed it. The arresting party shot away the lock and burst in, running from empty room to empty room, crouched low, as if armed desperadoes might be holed up there.

Kataria, his middle-aged wife and their twelve-year-old son had gone to stay with friends. His wife and child returned the following morning to a scene of devastation.

Their belongings had been thrown out of drawers and cupboards and were lying in heaps on the floor. Mattresses had been dragged off the beds and ripped open. Books were torn and strewn about.

As it seemed to be the work of vandals, Mrs Kataria telephoned the police to report it, and then called the Cabinet Offices to leave a message for her husband when he arrived.

Tilak Kataria never returned the call. He was arrested as he parked his car in the space reserved for him.

Rana and Kataria were locked away in separate cells, without explanation, or even knowledge that the other had been detained as well.

Daniel Moorhouse's wife was unceremoniously evicted from the official residence at 8 a.m., shortly after she rose for breakfast. She was forbidden to go to either of the homes owned by the family in Port Lombard or in Aberdeen on the east of the island, and so she moved in to stay with friends.

The preliminary search through Moorhouse's papers was a long one, undertaken by Montrose and Clifton working at the family houses and the official residence, while General Luther scrutinised the documents in the Cabinet Offices. The work could not be entrusted to others. Only the top three members of the Revolutionary Council knew what they were looking for, and why. Apart from finding papers which might convict Moorhouse in a court of law, it was also necessary to track down any embarrassing documents which related to the three of them. These were to be taken away and destroyed.

Luther started by going through the drawers of Moorhouse's desk. One of the first things he found was the official report submitted by Claud Montrose on the riot near the Imperial Hotel, when twelve people were killed. With it, was a hand-written piece of paper containing the names of Montrose's ten men. Luther had no idea whose handwriting this was, but he recognised the note in the margin as being the work of Daniel Moorhouse.

"Find Molvi!" Moorhouse had written, and the name itself was underlined with the distinctive broad fountain-pen nib he always used.

Luther smiled to himself. That was certainly capable of more than one explanation, he thought. He put it to one side.

The United States was the first country to recognise the new government, and the Ambassador, Freeman Leister, requested an appointment with Luther. This was followed by a similar British announcement. Moscow, however, recalled its Ambassador for consultations, and there was no indication when, or indeed if, he would return.

Luther was seeing no one at that stage. He recognised the potential danger posed by Moorhouse, and that whatever action was to be initiated against the deposed Prime Minister ought to be started soon. As a military man, he realised he could never guarantee tomorrow's situation. If any papers were lying around incriminating himself, Montrose or Clifton, they had to be found and destroyed before others had the chance to see them.

There was very little. Rana and Kataria's evidence discrediting the dossier on Ayer was on file, and Luther fed it through the shredder himself.

He sent two of his men in plain clothes to the St David's Club with orders to seize the Members' Register and bring it to him. As usual, the porter who ought to have been on duty in the club foyer was nowhere to be seen, and the men were able to pick up the Register and take it away, unnoticed.

Luther ripped out the pages and shredded them. He was loath to send the leather binding to be burnt: it was a beautiful piece of old leather, soft and supple and smelling of nature. The Register had only been in use for three or four years, but it was clearly decades older than that. Obviously the club had a store of these books somewhere and used them as a reminder of the past. Luther put the leather binding in the desk drawer, feeling sure he'd be able to find a good use for it later. It was a shame to waste it.

From the archives, Bob Sehai brought Luther copies of all reports submitted to Moorhouse on the violence and its causes. The Prime Minister's habit of making notes in the margins, and of underlining passages which caught his eye, was particularly useful, and Luther was able to set aside several examples which might help a prosecution.

The preliminary search took two days. When it was over, Luther turned his attention to the ordinary work facing a ruler of a country, whether he be elected Prime Minister or military usurper. His In-tray was full, and Bob Sehai had a pile of files needing attention in the anteroom.

Luther worked slowly and was surprised and, in spite of himself, admiring of the volume and scope of subjects Moorhouse dealt with daily.

He received daily security reports from all over the island, but apart from a short spontaneous demonstration by workers at a clothing factory in Albany which broke up immediately the military arrived, there was complete calm.

In accordance with instructions issued by Luther, the *Herald* and the island's other smaller newspapers made no mention of Daniel Moorhouse, while Radio St David's had returned to normal state-controlled programmes after the initial day when martial music was interspersed with repeats of the General's nationwide broadcast. The radio bulletins now concentrated on positive aspects of island life, particularly the

Anglo-American decision to recognise the new revolutionary government, together with negative aspects of life in other countries.

Luther was ready to consolidate his hold. The United States Ambassador was granted an appointment four days after the overthrow of Daniel Moorhouse.

The relief felt in the Embassy when Bob Sehai telephoned Freeman Leister's private secretary was profound. With the passing of the days speculation had mounted that the revolution had hit trouble. What other explanation could there be for the silence of Luther, and the failure of the three main Revolutionary Council members to appear in public? The United States' decision to recognise the regime had been acknowledged by a brief note from the Foreign Affairs Ministry – and then silence.

It was strange, even discourteous. Yet the Americans knew they were the nation who would benefit most from the overthrow of Daniel Moorhouse, so they waited with as much patience as they could summon up.

Freeman Leister's airconditioned black Cadillac drew up at the steps of the Cabinet Offices five minutes before the appointed time, and the Ambassador was ushered immediately into Luther's office.

Leister had met the General only once before, although he had seen him at a distance on many official occasions. The confidential Embassy biography described Luther as "a man who makes up in machismo what his nation lacks in weaponry". It went on to list a number of rumours concerning his rather active sex life, particularly when he was between wives, and added that he was thought to maintain several extra-marital liaisons even now. He drank, smoked, but kept himself rigorously fit.

Leister had to admit there was a dynamism and confidence about the man, as Luther came out from behind his desk to greet him warmly and usher him into a chair. The contrast with Moorhouse was marked. Moorhouse was arrogant where Luther exhibited a bluff, muscular charm. Shaking Moorhouse's hand, you noticed how cool and soft it was: Luther's was hard and assertive. Moorhouse's eyes were watchful and assessing: Luther's frank and friendly.

Yet Leister felt rather like a doctor who knows that his healthy-looking, athletic patient is actually being destroyed by cancer. The confidence of the new military leader would evaporate as the months passed, Leister thought. The problems which to a soldier seem so simple to resolve, providing he can impose a little discipline, contain snares which entrap the amateur.

Luther would be caught and dragged down. At length, people would blame him, and not Moorhouse, for the island's problems.

Feeling would grow until it seeped through even the *cordon sanitaire* which most leaders erect around themselves, and the depth of the nation's hatred would one day shock Luther.

"I bring the congratulations and good wishes of the United States Government," Leister said. "You have our assurances that the traditional friendship between our two nations is of the highest consideration. We will do all we can to see it grow from strength to strength."

Luther grinned across at the Ambassador, seeming suddenly boyish and disarming. "Thanks very much," he said. "You know what *we* think about the links between us. We're part of your defence strategy, and you are part of ours. We're not going to let the Russians screw that up, that's all there is to it."

"I'm glad to hear it," Leister smiled.

"But we need help, and I'm now going to ask you for it."

Leister raised his eyebrows politely. "I'm sure my Government will do everything it can. What did you have in mind?"

"We haven't had a chance to go through the books properly yet," Luther said, "but it's no secret this island is in a hell of a mess and we all know basically why. Tourism was very important to us, and we have to build it up again, but we can't while we've got a water problem. We need a new water system in Port Lombard and we need to fix up the sewage."

"I understood Mr Moorhouse – er, the previous administration – had taken that in hand," Leister observed.

"As far as I can tell, Moorhouse ordered a few patch repairs. I'm not interested in that. I'm not interested in that sort of rubbish. I want experts to come out here and make a proper assessment, and then I want a totally new system installed. There's got to be good, clean water for people to drink, and when they go to the lavatory, they don't want it pumping straight into the sea."

"That would be a very expensive undertaking," Leister warned. "I'm not saying it wouldn't be worthwhile, but can St David's afford it at this stage?"

"Let me be frank with you, Ambassador," Luther said. "This island will never be able to afford it. I want it as a gift, from the Americans."

Leister sat silently. At last he said: "Well, of course I will put your request to my Government, and I will relay their reply to you immediately I receive it."

"I should also say," Luther continued, "that I expect the answer to be Yes."

"We're talking about a lot of money," Leister said cautiously. "Many millions of dollars. Much more than the total United States aid budget to St David's at the moment. And of course, we ourselves don't have unlimited resources. You are aware of the cutbacks we've had to make because of the recession. It might not be possible for the United States to meet the entire cost."

Luther smiled at him. "I'm sure it will be," he said, "when your government thinks what it's getting in exchange: virtually unlimited defence facilities on the island, the Russians kept out. That's worth a lot. And don't forget, we have to make this revolution work if we're going to consolidate this. We don't want people looking back on Moorhouse as 'the good old days'. We want a strong, pro-Western government here, and so do you. You have to help us get one, and to do that, you've got to dig deep into your pockets."

Leister was startled at the General's frank and realistic assessment of the situation. There was obviously more to Luther than met the eye.

"All I can say, sir," he replied, "is that I will send a message off to my Government today, and I will repeat to them what you have told me."

"Will you give it your personal backing?" Luther asked.

Again Leister was startled. After a pause he agreed. "Yes. Yes I will."

"I imagine you'll have some terms of your own. Don't hesitate to bring them to me. You'll find me very accommodating to my friends."

And what about your enemies? Leister thought. But he said: "I wonder if I may be permitted to enquire what has happened to Mr Moorhouse?"

"What had you heard?" Luther asked, with another quick grin.

Again the Ambassador was thrown off balance. "Oh," he said, confused. "Not much. Nothing, in fact."

"Oh, come on, Ambassador. What are the rumours? That's the trouble with this job: you never hear any good rumours."

Leister scratched his head, bemused. "Well," he admitted. "I have heard that he is being held in Central Gaol."

"Your information is correct."

"What is to happen to him? I take it this is preventive detention?"

"It is at the moment," Luther confirmed, "but I expect that to change within a few days. Criminal charges are being prepared."

The Ambassador's face was impassive. He waited for the General to continue.

"The charges will be conspiracy to murder four citizens of St David's. The state will be seeking the death penalty."

For all his years of training, Leister found himself taking a deep breath. "The death penalty," he said softly.

"You may tell your government, Ambassador, that since taking power, my colleagues in the Revolutionary Council and myself have been going through records and documents, and what we have found has shocked us deeply. Daniel Moorhouse is a criminal. When the full story is told in court, you will see what I mean. Of course, it will be up to the courts to decide on his guilt, and as you know, we have an impartial judiciary here. We will not seek to interfere with this. His trial will be open and fair. We will abide by the court's decision."

"Whatever it is?" Leister asked.

"Whatever it is. If they say: release him, then I'll release him. But if they say: hang him, I'll hang the blighter."

Chapter Twenty-nine

The climb to the top of the Loop Head cliffs had exhausted him, and Stephen Ayer's legs ached with the effort. The weeks of imprisonment had left their mark, not only on his body which had always been lean and was now painfully thin, but on his mind. He found it difficult to concentrate for more than a few minutes. His brain seemed to tire and his thoughts became distracted.

On the day after his release, Ayer, Nora and the three children had driven to the fishing village of Galloway on the north of the island, where, at Moorhouse's insistence, they stayed at the official government guest-house.

Moorhouse had done what he could to make them comfortable. Bottles of champagne and imported French wines had been provided, and a large staff waited on them.

Ayer hated it. Almost every room had a framed photograph of Moorhouse. The man's vanity was insatiable. Ayer was presented with constant reminders of the Prime Minister, and, with them, the fact that it was Moorhouse who had sent him so unjustly to gaol.

And then the other memories tumbled in unbidden: the darkness and the stink, the harsh, loud noises of prison, and the long aching silences. The food: its foul smell and hateful taste. The withdrawal of human dignity.

Ayer had not spoken of his ordeal to Nora. He could not find the words, and he did not yet have the heart to confront what had happened to him. He tried to deny it. And yet in the guest-house, there were always the Prime Minister's portraits: stern, smiling, triumphant, jocular, serious, as Ayer passed from room to room, each stabbing him with the memory of the other world from which he had been released.

After two days, Ayer could stand it no longer and the family moved out.

Nora drove their car along the winding, rutted roads around to the east of St David's, and they rented rooms in an isolated farmhouse near the cliffs and the lighthouse of Loop Head.

The track to the farmhouse was appalling. It had rained overnight and the surface was muddy and treacherous. But at the end, it all seemed worth it.

The farmhouse itself was a double-storied stone building covered with white plaster. Inside, it was dark and cool, and the walls were of wood. Old copper pots and buckets, mellow with age, reflected the warm flickering light of the fire which burned every night. The furniture was solid, heavy wood. There was no newspaper delivery, and no telephone. Ayer felt as if a weight had been lifted from him.

Here was calm, country peace. The pace was measured and natural, the food simple. He and Nora had a feather bed in which his body sank gently, relaxing as it went, and on which for the first two nights, he left wet patches from the tears which came as he slept and dreamed. Whether he spoke or cried out in the darkness, he did not know. Nora never mentioned it if he did.

On the third night, he slept calmly. Each day, the family would go out for walks, although Ayer found he could not manage more than a mile, and he would sit by a river bank, or lie on his back in a grassy field staring at the sky, while Nora and the children went on to explore.

It was taking him longer to get his strength back than he had thought, and he was beginning to feel particularly sensitive about the fact that he and Nora had not yet made love. He held her warm soft body at night in the old feather bed, but he felt only exhaustion. It seemed impossible that his body had ever known desire, and unlikely that it ever would again. What he craved was sleep and no dreams.

When the coup d'état was staged, no ripples spread to Loop Head, and those at the farmhouse remained unaware of it.

Then it rained, a grey deluge beating against the windows and the slate roof, hour after hour, with drops tumbling down the chimney to hiss into the fire.

The children were fretful, arguing with each other and complaining to their parents, until the farmer brought a new-born lamb into the kitchen and it claimed their complete attention.

Ayer, made drowsy by the sound of the rain and exhausted by the children's earlier demands, went to the bedroom to rest.

He curled into the feather bed, between the crisp, fresh-smelling sheets, and felt more secure and relaxed than he could remember since childhood. The curtains were shut and the room was dark. Outside the storm raged and there was a boom of thunder.

In the warmth of the bed, Ayer shivered and closed his eyes.

How long had he slept? It was hard to tell if it was still afternoon, or whether it had become night, but the soft warmth of Nora's nakedness pressed against his back.

Ayer rolled over and brushed his lips against her hair. She raised her head and they kissed lightly. Then softly, with hardly any pressure at all, Nora's tongue licked slowly up Ayer's cheek and across his closed eyelids. The sensation was electric.

His hands went down over her smooth body and cupped her breasts and he found her nipples were hard.

Ayer felt a stirring, the feeling of strength returning and he thought: oh, thank God.

The rain stopped during the night but heavy clouds covered the sky.

In the morning, the children were still preoccupied with the lamb, but Ayer felt a restless energy. He and Nora left them in the farmhouse and went for a walk up to the cliffs.

They strolled for a long time, holding hands. The earth smelled fresh and the clouds scudded low overhead. They followed the path towards Loop Head lighthouse, past bushes of yellow gorse and clumps of wild flowers. The path rose gently at first, towards the cloud ceiling, and then they were shrouded in grey mist, able to see only a few feet ahead.

Ayer was getting tired, but for once his mind urged him to go on. The day was so fresh and clean that he did not want to stop. The wind blew cold against his cheek, but his chest and arms were protected by the thick fisherman's jersey he had borrowed from the farmhouse.

The path disappeared: perhaps it ran out naturally at that point, or they may have missed a turning in the mist, so they threaded their way through rocks and thorn bushes, climbing all the time. It was almost ghostly. The grey veils of mist floated towards them, sometimes obscuring everything so they had to pause, and occasionally clearing a path of twenty or thirty feet so they could plot precisely where they should head.

Finally they turned back, retracing their steps through the mist until they broke cloud and the panorama of the rich countryside and the farmhouse lay beneath them. A second car was parked outside the farmhouse. Nora spotted it first. If they were wanting to stay, they were out of luck, she thought. The Ayers had taken all the available rooms, and did not intend moving out for some time.

She pointed it out to her husband. "Visitors," she said.

Ayer stood very still, staring down and his grip tightened on her hand.

"What's wrong?" Nora asked. "Who are they?"

Ayer shrugged. "I don't know." But still he did not move. They watched for several minutes. Whoever it was had gone into the house.

At last Ayer said to her simply: "Thank you for these few days. I'll never forget them."

She felt panic rising. "What do you mean?" she asked. "There'll be other days. We've got the rest of our lives!"

"Of course we have," Ayer said in a voice which lacked conviction.

"You *do* know who they are!" Nora accused.

"No. It's just a feeling I have. We'd better go down and see."

Ayer led the way back towards the farmhouse, feeling suddenly numb.

Chapter Thirty

The nightmare that had once been endured by Stephen Ayer began for Rana and Kataria with some significant changes.

Ayer had been taken simply to be taught a lesson by Montrose, and nothing had been required from him: hence there had been no interrogations and no tortures. Rana and Kataria were needed for the plot against Moorhouse, so they were to be broken for a purpose.

Montrose was not entirely sure what it was he would require them to say publicly: the details still needed to be worked out. Meanwhile, the prisoners had to be prepared so that they would accept whatever it was.

Rana and Kataria were housed in adjoining cells in the prison basement without being aware of the other's presence. The walls were thick and of stone. High up, a small barred window gave out onto what looked like a ventilation shaft. Both men had the merest glimpse of it before the cell doors were slammed shut and locked, leaving them in pitch darkness with only the momentary picture of the cell layout fading on their retinas. A steel-framed bed with no mattress or blankets on the right. A bucket in the corner on the left. Was that all there was?

Both men, their arrests separated by hours, had reacted in the same way. They stood frozen in the darkness, hearing the receding noise of the prison warders' boots on the concrete and the loud thumping of their own hearts. Then slowly, inch by inch, they shuffled forward, hands out, palms raised, finding their way to where they thought the bed was, fearful of crashing into a blank wall. When their shins hit against the steel of the bed and their hands tentatively groped down to investigate, both were surprised at how low it was. Without a mattress, there was just the criss-crossed wire for them to lie on and it cut into their flesh.

Gradually their eyes became accustomed to the darkness, but only enough to make out the perimeters of the bed frame, and the darker shadow of the bucket. The silence was total.

Montrose had left orders that the two men were to be disorientated. Rana, arrested before dawn, was given breakfast in his cell: Kataria was brought in just after nine.

Both should have been fed lunch at midday, but in fact no one went near them for nearly twenty-four hours. Without watches, or any method of telling time, they were lost.

Rana developed a raging thirst during the afternoon which signalled to him that something was wrong, that he had been forgotten down in this dungeon. The thirst became worse during the night, and in the lonely silence of the adjoining cell, Kataria felt it too.

They would also have been hungry, except that fear had killed their appetites. Both men tried to doze, but steel wire of the beds dug painfully into them.

At 7 a.m., the boots of the warders rang down the corridor, alerting them both so they sat upright and still, listening to the approach.

Rana's door was unlocked first and swung open, the electric light flooding in, dazzling him so that he covered his eyes with his hands, and a voice shouted: "Lunch!"

Lunch! Christ, what time was it? It couldn't be lunch! Rana stumbled forward to take the tin plate and the mug of tea. There were no knives and forks, only a spoon. He was sipping greedily at the cup when the cell door slammed shut and he heard the boots moving further down the corridor.

The same shout: "Lunch!", then, after a pause, that door slammed. The warders went back to their stations and the silence closed in. From the noise of the boots, which echoed deceptively, it seemed the other prisoner was two or three cells away from Rana, rather than right next door.

It took only a few seconds for Rana's eyes to readjust to the darkness and he walked back to the bed carrying his food, with some confidence. He perched on the edge with the tin plate on his lap and pushed the food around a bit with the spoon: dark, unidentifiable mounds. It was impossible to guess what they were. Rana remembered seeing potato and some gravy. He scooped something up and smelt it tentatively.

It smelled of nothing. He was reminded of a game he had played when a child, and hated. He had been brought into a room blindfolded and made to feel certain things. He remembered it was called the Lord Nelson game. Some guided the blindfolded child's hand up to a person's face, making him feel the mouth, the ears, the nose, and then took the victim's index finger and plunged it into a hole made in a squishy tomato, held at face level, shouting trimphantly that this was Nelson's eye. Rana remembered the disgusting feeling of that warm, wet pulp, and not knowing, until he had ripped off his blindfold and looked, exactly what it was.

He felt the same with the prison food. What was it he was eating? He expected it to be pretty horrible but he found it difficult to tell when he couldn't see what was on his spoon.

He ate cautiously. There was definitely potato, because it wasn't properly cooked, but he ate it anyway. Also vegetables of some sort: peas or carrots, or perhaps both. And some peppery meat, much of which was gristle. The gristle was the only thing he left on his plate.

The tea slaked his thirst and he was feeling very tired. It was impossible that this should be lunchtime. The prison schedule was obviously running late. It must, at least, be late afternoon. It seemed a week since his arrest.

Time was dragging in a way he had never imagined possible. He spent hours thinking about his own position. Did they know about his link with the CIA? He would have sworn he hadn't been followed to any of his meetings, but no one could be a hundred per cent certain about something like that.

It was also possible that Montrose was just paying him back for exposing the Ayer dossier as a fraud.

Christ, it was all such a mess. Who would have thought that Moorhouse would be toppled in a coup? A coup on St David's! Even now, after the event, it seemed a ludicrous idea.

Rana debated with himself what Montrose's likely moves would be, but could reach no conclusion. His concentration seemed to be slipping away from him, so he found it increasingly difficult to focus on any subject and, besides, he did not yet have enough information to go on. Maybe, like Ayer, he would just be left to rot.

When midday came, neither Rana nor Kataria were fed. Their next meal was at 3.30 p.m., the time prisoners are normally given their dinner prior to the 4 p.m. lockup.

Two days had passed, but to Rana and Kataria, it seemed like one endless day.

They were not served breakfast until lunchtime the following morning, and lunch came at ten o'clock that night. Dinner was served the following midday, and then no food or water were given through the afternoon and the whole of the long night until 7 a.m., when their breakfasts again coincided with the prison routine.

The men were starting their fifth day of solitary confinement, but according to the cycle of meals – their only way of telling time – they had merely completed two, and were beginning the third.

After breakfast, Rana broke down and wept. The cell was stinking from the bucket in the corner, and the ordeal seemed unending.

Kataria was, if anything, in worse shape. His thoughts, racing in panic, were of his wife and children, and the fact that they had no savings and the mortgage needed to be paid. Kataria had no illusions that Montrose would immediately order the cutting off of his salary, and once the small amount of money owing was used up, his family would be destitute. His wife had never worked, and had had no useful training. She couldn't even apply for a job as a secretary. He hoped friends would help out, at least for a while. But how long did Montrose intend keeping him there? It was impossible to say. It could be months, although his mind rejected the thought that it might just as easily be years.

He wouldn't be able to cope with that, he was certain. He would have to kill himself, find a way of committing suicide in this bleak, empty cell, before he went mad, and so give his wife the opportunity while she was still comparatively young of finding a new husband.

Kataria was already instinctively writing himself out of the picture. The loneliness and desperation which now overwhelmed him in the dragging hours was like a physical presence.

Kataria tried to pray, kneeling on the floor, feeling the concrete hard and uncomfortable under his knees. *Our father, who art in heaven* ... saying the words left him with a sense of piety which quickly turned into self-pity and anguish at the fragility of his position.

Was his life now effectively over? Would he be kept here, day after empty day, until he could find some way of putting an end to his misery? He started to sing, hymns at first and then songs of love and loneliness, singing in a soft voice, little more than a whisper, because more than solitary confinement, he found he feared bringing attention to himself. If the guards were to come, what would they do? He felt they might find some new way to punish him. But he also felt, strangely, that his dignity as a man was violated every time one of the warders opened the heavy steel door and saw him suffering. They looked at him, in his stink, as if he was an animal, and he hated that deeply.

Kataria began thinking he would do anything – almost anything – to get out and relieve the distress to his family and the pain to himself. The silence stretched into eternity.

Daniel Moorhouse was also in the Central Gaol, but in comparative luxury. He had been given an ordinary cell, with an adjoining ablution block to himself. In addition, there was a bed, with mattress, sheets and blankets, a small table he used for writing a book on foreign policy and the non-aligned movement, and shelves on which he kept volumes of reference works and a small transistor radio which picked up foreign news broadcasts.

The Prison Superintendent, Simon Norwood, was doing what he could to make the deposed Prime Minister comfortable. Moorhouse had food brought in from home, or from restaurants of his choice in Port Lombard, and he was allowed alcohol. His wife visited him daily, spending two or three hours at a time with him in his cell.

Norwood was not noted for his humanity, but he could sense when he should keep an eye on the future.

Britain's record of decolonisation contained lessons for all gaolers, the most important of which was this: be kind to the politician in your cell. Things changed so quickly, you never knew when he'd be back in a position of influence, or even absolute power.

So Norwood *was* kind, and personally treated Moorhouse as if he was still a man of importance and dignity. The Prison Superintendent gave no hint of this to Montrose who would, he realised, insist on a tougher regime for the deposed Prime Minister if he knew what the actual conditions were. And Montrose, too, was more influential than ever and had to be watched.

It was a delicate tightrope Norwood was on, but he had walked it before and he did not feel particularly worried.

Montrose had given no special orders concerning Moorhouse, so Norwood was within his rights interpreting the prison Regulations as liberally as he cared to.

The only orders given had concerned the treatment of Rana and

Kataria, and it was clear they were being softened up for something. Norwood, with natural caution, had not enquired what, but had simply passed on the instructions.

Two weeks went by, although as far as the prisoners in the basement were concerned it had been less than one. Kataria, whose prayers had become almost constant, felt he was being given a sample of what hell must be like: a man suspended in an eternity of loneliness, silence, filth and stink.

The metal buckets in the corners of their cell overflowed, and the cement floor was patched with excrement and urine.

The warders who brought their meals did so in silence now. There was not even the shout of "Lunch!" or whatever the meal was, because they seemed to be holding their breaths when they opened the doors and if the prisoners were not right there to take the plates and mugs, and return the empty ones, the warders merely dropped them quickly on the floor and got out.

At the end of the fortnight, Montrose drove round to the gaol to begin the interrogations. He had decided to start with Kataria, since Rana's CIA involvement virtually guaranteed co-operation.

Kataria might be a harder nut to crack.

Stephen Ayer was also in the prison, back in his old cell in the same conditions of solitary confinement. Montrose had initially intended putting him in the basement with the others when he was tracked down to the farmhouse near Loop Head and brought back to Port Lombard under arrest, but he decided against it at the last moment. The more prisoners there were in the basement, the more noise would be made by the warders delivering food and the prisoners might get a feeling of solidarity in numbers and begin trying to make contact with each other.

Silence and loneliness were the essential ingredients for breaking Rana and Kataria, and these could not be risked by adding Ayer to their number.

Ayer was, in any case, half broken already and Montrose judged it would not need much to push him over the brink.

The room where Montrose carried out interrogations was also in the basement, but along a different corridor. He usually worked with teams of three or four men if a prisoner needed to be physically softened up, but now he was alone. The original members of the Revolutionary Council had decided at the beginning that no one else should be involved in their plan against Moorhouse, unless it was absolutely necessary and agreed upon in advance.

The room was brightly illuminated with strip lighting and the walls were painted grey, but because it had no windows, a flick of a switch could plunge it into total darkness. There was a simple wooden desk and two hard, upright chairs. On the desk was a reading lamp.

Montrose waited for the knock on the door.

Kataria's eyes were bright with fright: that was the first thing Montrose noticed when the prisoner was brought in and made to sit in the chair while his wrists were handcuffed behind the wooden back. The second thing was the disgusting smell which clung to the man: a nauseous mixture of body odour, excrement, urine and fear. Kataria seemed hardly to know where he was.

Montrose considered briefly ordering the warders to take him out and get him showered and cleaned up, but decided this would be bad tactics. He would just have to steel himself to the smell.

When Kataria was properly secured, staring about him in panic, Montrose switched off the strip lights and stygian blackness closed in. The warders left quietly and, after a moment, Montrose turned on the reading lamp and shone it straight into Kataria's face. The man strained his head away from the glare, his eyes screwed up.

Montrose pulled the other chair close in front of Kataria, trying to breathe normally, to accept the stink, and then, gently at first, he closed his knees around one of the prisoner's thighs.

Kataria's head turned towards him again, and his eyes opened, uncertain, blinking in the light. Montrose's face was half in shadow, but Kataria could see the whites of his eyes gleaming. There was a long silence – two or three minutes; just the thigh pressure.

At last Montrose spoke, in a low, loving voice: "I've been seeing quite a lot of your wife, Tilak. I hope you don't mind." The knees tightened around his thigh. Kataria felt his pulse racing. He did not know how to react to the contact, or what to say. He was completely thrown.

"She's a good-looking woman," Montrose observed seriously. "What's she like in bed?"

Kataria felt his breath had been stopped.

"I've been watching her. Thought I might go around there some night. Slip her a length, know what I mean?"

Long silence. Just the pressure on his thigh. Kataria sat motionless and appalled.

"Some of my men were saying last night they wouldn't mind going round themselves. You've been away a long time. Someone's going to be moving into your bed soon, especially if they think you're never going to come back." Montrose's voice was almost crooning.

In the silence, Kataria spoke, his voice shaking, although not with anger. "My wife's not like that," he said.

"All prisoners say that," Montrose answered easily. "It's never true. Not in my experience, and I can tell you, I've had quite a bit of experience." Even with his face in shadow, Kataria knew Montrose was leering.

"I'd put money down that if I sent my boys around to your house tonight, five or six of them, they'd all shoot their loads."

Kataria was almost whispering, on the verge of tears: "But that would be rape!"

Montrose shook his head slowly. "I don't think rape would be necessary," he said confidentially. "She must be randy by now. If I sent round some of my men – young ones, tough, good looking, you know the sort – she wouldn't need much persuading. A bit at the beginning perhaps, but once the first man gets inside her, she'll be shouting for more."

A whisper: "It's rape!"

"Oh, now you're being technical," Montrose mocked, shifting his bulk in the chair. "A lot of women like being knocked about a bit first. It's part of the fun. Anyway, my men wuld be happy to pay. A couple of dollars each, that sounds fair. More if they keep her the whole night." A pause. "She could do with the money. Did you know she was short?"

Kataria shook his head in silent misery.

"Oh sure," said Montrose. "You didn't leave her well provided for, you know that? Where's the mortgage coming from? Or the food for the kids?"

Kataria's voice was hoarse: "There should still be money from my salary."

Montrose shook his head again. "No my friend," he replied. "No money."

"But my salary!"

"It's been frozen."

"Well, what about the government retirement annuity? She should collect that," he said desperately.

"I confiscated it."

Montrose let the silence drag out, while Kataria digested this information. Then he said: "She's going to have to get out of the house in two or three weeks. She can't pay the mortgage."

"That's robbery," Kataria burst out. "It's *my* money!"

"Then why don't you go and get it?" Montrose asked simply.

Kataria sat impotent, and felt a tear welling out of his eye. With his arms handcuffed behind the chair, he tried to wipe it away on his shoulder.

This time the silence lasted several minutes. Montrose sat comfortably, the pressure of his knees unwavering against Kataria's thigh.

"What do you want?" he burst out. "For Christ's sake, Montrose, what are you holding me for?"

Montrose considered the question. "I'm holding you because I think you're a spy," he said.

"That's ridiculous."

"Why? Your friend Rana is a spy."

"Rubbish!" His voice stronger now, and scornful.

"No, not rubbish. He's admitted it himself. Made a full confession. And told us about Moorhouse. How the violence on the island was started by Moorhouse and his ten troublemakers."

Kataria said flatly: "I don't know anything about that."

"Ayer does," Montrose pointed out. "So does Rana. It's just you who's playing the hero, refusing to co-operate. Well, play it that way if you want. As far as I'm concerned, you can spend the rest of your life in that cell. As for your wife: she'll soon have other things to occupy her mind. I'll see to that myself."

Montrose started to get up, but Kataria said urgently: "Please – you must believe me! I'm not a spy! I don't know anything about Moorhouse."

Montrose was standing now, his face totally in darkness. The pressure was gone from Kataria's thigh and, stupidly, he felt naked and alone without this contact. Between him and going back to his cell was just this big, fat man looming threateningly in the blackness.

"Moorhouse had a gang of ten men," Montrose explained quietly. "Moorhouse, not me. *He* picked them from the police and the army, and turned them into his own private force. Then he sent them into demonstrations, with orders to start trouble. They did as they were told: the riot at Maxwell's was one of theirs. The other riot in the High Street a few days earlier was another. Total number of dead: four. Moorhouse tried again around the Imperial Hotel just before we took over, but this time we caught his gang." Montrose paused. "Well, when I say 'caught', I mean we saw them carrying off looted televisions and that sort of thing, and we shot them. Nine of them. The tenth we arrested, and he told the story. Ayer and Rana have now backed it up. They're being helpful and co-operative. We're working out a special deal with them. They'll be free men soon. I'm sorry about you." Pause. "And your wife."

Montrose moved away into the blackness. Kataria was desperate to stop him going.

"I don't know anything about that!" he cried. "I've never heard a word of it before! You have to believe me!"

From the darkness, Montrose answered coldly: "I don't believe you."

"You must!"

"*You* must," insisted Montrose. "*You* must co-operate."

"There's nothing I can say!"

"Then you'll have to think of something."

The door opened, and he could see Montrose's bulky silhouette walking out into the corridor. It closed and there was silence.

Kataria was left weeping and confused in the interrogation room, handcuffed to the chair, for an hour. *What did Montrose want?* At last the warders came for him.

The strip lights flashed on, and his hands were freed. Kataria was led back along the corridor and pushed quickly into his cell. The stink overwhelmed him and he felt he would throw up. Jesus, was that what he had been living in?

He moved tentatively towards the steel bed but it wasn't where he thought it would be and even though he was moving slowly, he crashed against the cell wall with such force that he hit his forehead and the pain exploded in a red flash.

Kataria sank to the cement floor, sitting against the wall with his knees drawn up and his lungs breathing in the foulness of the air, and waited for his eyes to become accustomed to the gloom.

After ten minutes, he realised what they had done. They had taken away the bed.

His shoulders slumped in defeat.

In the prison car park, Montrose waited for his driver to open the door for him. It was lunchtime and he would eat in the Cabinet Offices with Luther, to fill him in on how the first interrogation had gone. Montrose was satisfied with the progress he had made. He would see Kataria again in a week. Leave him to stew until then. And Rana would be a problem to cope with after lunch.

Montrose stepped into his new official Mercedes and settled back in the seat.

It was all going to plan, he thought, except for one thing. They hadn't yet been able to find Molvi. The man who was the linchpin of the plot, the one who could tie Moorhouse directly into the scheme. The others would simply add the authenticity which would convince a court.

But Molvi had disappeared, as completely as if he had never existed.

He lived alone in a room, but he had not been near it, not even to collect the few hundred dollars the police had found hidden under a floorboard. Montrose was convinced he was still on the island, and it was only a matter of time before he was found. But not having him in their hands was unsettling.

In the Prime Minister's office, Luther had taken to drinking bottles of chilled French wine with his sandwiches, and refused to serve Montrose whisky. Montrose particularly disliked the way Luther was growing into the job, and the deference it commanded, accepting it as his due as if he had been swept into power by popular acclaim, rather than coming in at midnight with a gun.

Montrose thought he would choke with derision and fury the first time he heard Luther refer to the population of the island as "my people". But instead, he had managed to grin thinly. They had been at a cabinet meeting and army officers headed most of the ministries. Montrose knew he had been outflanked, and there was nothing he could do immediately about General Stephen Luther.

But it was interesting to see the grand mask disappear whenever Luther was confronted with a problem concerning his own survival.

The whereabouts of Molvi was one of these. Luther had initially blamed Montrose for bungling the operation, and had imperiously directed that his troops take over the manhunt. They had, but to no effect. Now Luther had handed the operation back to Montrose and it was clear that he was badly worried.

After lunch, Montrose returned to the Central Gaol to begin work on Joe Rana and, despite the gloom which lunching with Luther had inspired in him, he felt he would enjoy this interrogation.

But that bloody stink! Montrose smelt it as soon as the warders brought Rana into the room, and he wrinkled his nose in disgust. Jesus, he would be glad when they'd progressed far enough to order the bastards to have a bath and be given some fresh clothes.

He waited while Rana's arms were secured behind the chair and the desk lamp was adjusted so it shone directly into his face. Then the warders left, and Montrose moved in close.

Rana's thighs were together and he sat bolt upright as if waiting to be shot. His eyes were not fearful like Kataria's, but were glazed with dullness and, Montrose thought, acceptance.

Rana would be easy.

Montrose spread his legs wide so that he would grip both Rana's knees with his own, and he saw with satisfaction the startled expression on the prisoner's face.

It was a tactic which seldom failed. The teasing physical contact threw everyone off balance: this almost sexual intimacy first made the prisoners think that their interrogator was making a pass at them, and then realise they would be powerless if he did. Most men were mentally dominated from the beginning. Some resisted, of course, and then it became necessary to try other methods, but all of them would listen apprehensively to what he had to say.

Montrose leaned forward, sliding his knees further up the sides of Rana's thighs, and increasing the pressure slightly.

His voice was confidential: "I bring you greetings from the CIA," he said softly.

Rana's eyes met his own and looked away, guilty.

"You did some good work for them. They were glad to have a spy like you, working away in the Prime Minister's office."

Silence.

"Did they pay you well? I hope so, Joe. I hope it was worth it." His tone was silky, almost loving. Montrose's big hands moved slowly, very slowly forward and his fingertips lightly touched Rana's ears and then down the two-weeks' growth of beard to his neck where they stopped, and drifted over his Adam's apple until they were encircling his neck, not squeezing, but just there. Rana found his eyes drawn back to Montrose, and saw his interrogator's expression, intense and concerned.

"You realise what the penalty for spying is, Joe my friend?" He waited. Then quietly: "The rope around the neck, just where my hands are."

Montrose removed his fingers slowly and he saw Rana was watching, frightened like a rabbit, still feeling the touch.

"But we all have to go sometime, don't we, Joe? And this way is quick. Snap! That's all there is to it. Usually anyway. We don't like to make mistakes nowadays."

He paused as if in thought.

"Well you can understand why. It's unpleasant for everyone. Messy.

You'd be surprised how blokes can struggle when they're dangling, even with their hands and legs tied and that fucking rope round their neck. There's not much sound of course, 'cos the rope's so tight, and it's throttling them. A bit of gurgling sometimes. It would be better if they just held still and waited to die, but they never do. I don't know why. They all struggle."

Silence.

"I was watching a bloke in this very prison, end of last year. You remember Gerald Witt, who murdered his mother-in-law with a shotgun?"

He could see from Rana's expression that he did.

"Well, Jesus, the hangman got that one wrong. The drop was nowhere near long enough. Witt was going at it, struggling away, for twenty fucking minutes! Can you imagine that? I thought we'd have to start from the beginning again and give him another drop, but the hangman said no. So eventually he climbed down into the pit and swung on his legs. Then you heard the neck snap. Jesus, yes! Like a pistol shot."

Montrose's hands went out again, and delicately touched Rana's neck. An involuntary shudder went through the man.

"They set you up, Joe, you know that?" Montrose said. "The CIA set you up. There you were, taking that list of ten names through to Moorhouse, claiming they were my men, and all the time they were Moorhouse's."

Rana stared at him incredulously and he knew he'd hit home.

"Sure," Montrose said calmly. "Nothing to do with me at all. Shit, coincidentally, my men shot dead nine of those bastards that same day. Luckily the tenth one lived to tell the story. Moorhouse is going on trial for his life. Four people died in those riots, you know that? That's conspiracy to murder. Moorhouse is going to swing, no doubt about it."

He paused.

"But you'll be going first, my friend," he said lazily. "I'm sorry to have to tell you."

Another pause.

"Unless I change my mind. But that depends on you."

Rana had not made a sound so far, but finally he spoke, almost in a whisper. "What do you want me to do?"

Montrose looked doubtful. "It's not going to be easy," he said. "It depends on what sort of co-operation I get from you."

"Please."

"I don't know if I can trust you."

"You can trust me! Jesus, ask anyone!"

Montrose smiled thinly in the darkness. "Who whould I ask?" he wondered aloud. "Moorhouse or the CIA? They both trusted you. It was just me. I didn't trust you one bit, and anyway, I'm not sure I wouldn't rather see you dangling at the end of a rope, you load of shit!"

His voice was hard and contemptuous. "I think I might see if you can beat Gerry Witt's record. I'll make bloody sure no one goes down to swing on *your* legs."

Rana made a sobbing intake of breath. "Jesus, Claud, don't do that to me! Help me!"

"Help me, *sir!*"

"Help me, sir!"

"*Please* help me, Mr Montrose, *sir!*"

"Please help me, Mr Montrose, sir!"

There was a long silence. Finally Montrose said: "Why in fuck's name should I help you? Are you going to help me?"

"Yes! Yes!"

"How? What the hell have you got that I want?"

Rana, broken: "I don't know. Anything!"

Montrose moved away slightly, releasing the pressure of his knees against Rana's thighs, leaving the man isolated. But his voice when he spoke was friendly. "Well," Montrose said, "let's see how I feel *after* you've made a statement. A *full* statement, do you understand? You hold back one fucking thing, Joe my friend, and you're going to feel what it's like to hang . . . by the neck . . . *until you are dead.* Those judges know what they're talking about, don't they? There's none of this crap about your neck being broken is there? That's just a modern refinement to show we're not barbarians. The sentence is that you hang by the neck *until you are dead.* And I'll see that you do. Understand?"

Rana's voice was barely audible. "Yes."

"Right," said Montrose softly. He walked to the door and called for a police stenographer, a young constable whom he had ordered to wait in the administration block. When they were ready, Montrose said: "Let's start from the beginning. What's your full name?"

"Joseph Montague Rana."

"Jesus. Montague. What's your address?"

"Seventeen, Ocean View, Port Lombard."

"Do you make this statement voluntarily?"

"I do."

"What is your occupation?"

"I am – I was – Cabinet Secretary to the Government of St David's."

"When were you recruited by the CIA?"

"Four years ago. In March. I don't remember the date."

"Where were you recruited?"

"In Washington. I went over there with a cabinet delegation."

"Did you have a control here in Port Lombard?"

"Yes."

"What was his name?"

"Clive Lyle."

Montrose felt his heart lurch and he knew the blood was draining from his face. There was a stunned silence. "What did you say?" he asked incredulously.

"Clive Lyle," Rana repeated. "He's a First Secretary at the American Embassy. He was my control."

Montrose stared at him in disbelief. Without being able to help himself, he said tonelessly: "Oh Jesus Christ Almighty. That fucking Lyle."

Chapter Thirty-one

"Lyle! You double-crossing bastard!"

Montrose was still in a fury hours later when he and Clifton walked across to the sea wall where the American waited, a cigarette glow pinpointing his position.

Montrose had telephoned the Embassy from the prison immediately Joe Rana was taken back to his cell. He no longer cared about any of Lyle's security considerations, even though he had not worked out the full implications of Rana's confession. He wanted to see Lyle, and quickly.

Now he was shouting at him from yards away. Lyle watched the approach in silence.

"You fucking double-crossing fairy! I'll make you sorry you were ever born!"

Clifton, cautioning and restraining beside him: "Calm down, Claud, for heaven's sake."

Montrose brushed him aside. "I'll break the bastard's neck!"

If Lyle was apprehensive, he gave no sign. He stood his ground and his voice was calm and casual. "Good evening, gentlemen," he said pleasantly. "I see that Claud hasn't yet learned the language of diplomacy. How would it be if delegates at the United Nations went about calling each other double-crossing fairies? It wouldn't do at all. No one would get any work finished."

Clifton couldn't help liking the American's style, despite the unease he also felt at Rana's revelation. But it was good to see someone standing up to Montrose.

The Commissioner went straight up to Lyle, his shoulders hunched for attack and his huge body looming out of the darkness, yet there was something about Lyle's stance which indicated he was ready for him.

"If you're thinking of trying to hit me, Claud," Lyle said, "I'd advise against it. I was an instructor in unarmed combat for a while, and I might have to break your arm."

"Claud! For Christ's sake!" Clifton grabbed at Montrose and was shaken off, but the Commissioner paused, glaring at his enemy.

"That's better," said Lyle unperturbed. "Now settle down, Claud, and have a cigarette. Then you can tell me what's on your mind." Lyle did not offer his box. He watched, weight evenly distributed on both feet, body alert for action and his eyes not moving from Montrose. His half-smoked cigarette lay on the ground where he had dropped it.

"Here, Claud. Have one of these." Clifton thrust his open box towards Montrose and, after a second, the Commissioner grudgingly took one and waited for a light. His breathing was short, as if he had been running.

Clifton's lighter flared. "Were you really an instructor in unarmed combat?" he asked.

"I sure was," Lyle said. "At Fairfax. I did it for a year. It's one of my many accomplishments. I gather from Claud's behaviour you're now aware of another."

"You bastard," Montrose rasped. "I want an explanation."

"Well, you tell me what it is you need explained," Lyle said, "and I'll see what I can do."

"What sort of game have you been playing?" Montrose demanded. "Why didn't you tell me you were Rana's control?"

Lyle sighed regretfully. "Ah, poor Joe Rana. You've been doing him over today, I suppose?"

"I bloody well have."

"He was a good man." Clifton noticed Lyle's use of the past tense: the acceptance that Rana was finished, a pawn given up.

"You're not denying you were his control?" Clifton asked curiously.

"No. He was mine all right."

"So what was your game, Lyle?" Montrose said. "Playing me against him, not telling me you were CIA. What for?"

"Isn't it obvious, Claud?" Lyle answered. "It was in my interests to get you sacked. I owed you nothing. You were a blackmailer, nothing more than that. So when I found out certain things, I did what I could to make sure they got back to Moorhouse. You'd have done exactly the same in my position."

"I'd never have been in your position, you shit," Montrose said.

"If anything, Claud, youd've been worse off," Lyle pointed out. "Think about your ten heroes. The moment there was a chance Moorhouse might make a few inquiries, you gunned them down. That was gangsterism, plain and simple. Now I never told you any lies. I just didn't tell you the whole truth. That's what being a diplomat is all about."

Clifton laughed briefly, then he said: "But you pretended to be on our side, and you weren't. And you're still pretending to be on our side."

"There's an important difference, Mr Clifton," Lyle said. "It wasn't *your* side at the beginning. It was Claud's. Claud was a blackmailer and I was within my rights seeing that he got his. The three of you only came in later, and by then the whole game had changed. As I told you before, it's in America's interests to make sure our defence arrangements here are maintained, so naturally I'd do what I could to help. They're two totally separate issues."

Montrose stared at him angrily, saying nothing. Clifton thought for a moment, then asked: "But it was you who turned in the names of the other CIA agents at the Embassy, wasn't it? Why did you do that?"

"Claud wanted me to," Lyle explained simply. "I didn't have much choice."

"But you didn't bloody tell me about yourself!" Montrose accused.

"Why should I, Claud?" Lyle asked evenly. "What difference would it have made? Would you have expelled me along with the others? Would you hell. You wanted me around, to act as your eyes and ears in the Embassy."

"So the names of the ten, it was you who got hold of them, and not any of the new CIA agents?" Clifton probed gently.

"That's right. I got them."

"Who from?"

In the silence, Lyle shook his head. "That I won't tell you."

"You bastard!" – Montrose again – "You tell us who your informer is, or I'll take those photographs around to the Ambassador myself!"

"What photographs would they be, Claud?" Lyle asked innocently.

"The photographs of you screwing with those other pooves! I've got a stack of them in my office."

"I'd like to see those myself," Lyle said pleasantly. "Maybe you could drop by a set of prints for me at the same time."

"They wouldn't go down well with your Ambassador, or with the CIA," Clifton reminded him. "It would be the end of your career."

"Tell me something, Mr Clifton," Lyle said. "Have you seen these phtotgraphs yourself?"

Clifton paused a fraction of a second too long. "Yes," he lied, "I've seen them."

"Are they good?"

"It depends what you like, Mr Lyle," Clifton said stiffly.

"Well you see," Lyle replied thoughtfully, "I just don't believe they exist. I'm prepared to call your bluff. Show the Ambassador the photographs if you've got them. Bring them round any time."

"It isn't only the photographs," Clifton said, edging off the ground crumbling around him and onto something more solid. "There's also the matter of the list of names of CIA agents, including your friend Mr Berenson. You supplied that to Claud, and Claud gave it to Moorhouse. They were all expelled. Now that's the sort of thing your government would take a very dim view of, don't you agree?"

Lyle sat quietly for a moment. Then he said: "You're right, they wouldn't like it a lot. But again, I'm going to call your bluff. You want me to tell you who my agent is, and I'm not going to do it. No matter what it costs me."

"Is he the last of your lovers, Clive?" Montrose sneered.

"Think what you like," said Lyle evenly. "This is not a negotiable position. But before you go to the Ambassador, you also ought to do some thinking. If you did tell him, there's bound to be an inquiry. They'd want to know why I acted like that, and I'd answer all their questions. They'd find out that one of the heads of the Revolutionary Council, with whom they are now so cosy, blackmailed a US official to get the names of CIA agents on the island, and then made sure these men were expelled. They'd learn that it was Claud who played a major role in pushing St David's towards Moscow, and, of course, they'd want to know why. So then I'd tell them about the protection racket the three of you were running. I think you'd find relations with Washington cooled off a bit after that. Besides, other governments would get to hear. Everyone would know what sort of people were running the revolution and why. So bang goes your prestige. I wonder what General Luther would think of that? I hear he rather likes being Prime Minister. It's a post which commands respect, usually. I don't think he'd find himself getting a lot of respect once the story got out. And of course, there's the other aspect to consider: when the diplomatic community knows about it, it'll only be a matter of days before the story is circulating round the island. In a fortnight, it will be common gossip. Now what you have to decide is this: is it worth that, just to pay me back?"

Clifton and Montrose stood silent. At last Montrose said: "I don't give a shit what diplomats think."

"No, I'm sure *you* don't," Lyle agreed. "But what about General Luther?"

"He can screw himself too, as far as I'm concerned," Montrose said dismissively.

"Bravely spoken, Claud," Lyle applauded. "Well, you must do what you think is best."

Clifton said: "What I don't understand, Mr Lyle, is your double standard."

"I thought I'd explained that," Lyle answered. "At the beginning I was dealing with a blackmailer. At the end I was involved in something that was in the interests of the United States."

"No," said Clifton, "not that. The double standard I'm talking about is the one you apply to your agents. You are their control, yet you betray Rana without turning a hair. In fact, you offer him to us on a plate. But you're prepared to risk your career for another agent. You won't tell us a word about *him*."

Lyle said calmly, "But that's the game, isn't it? Sometimes you have to give up a pawn as part of the general strategy."

"But what are you aiming for?" Clifton asked. "What's the object of the game?"

"The same as you," Lyle replied. "Getting rid of Moorhouse. Advancing United States interests."

"Yet you won't give up another pawn to save yourself?"

"My other agent?"

"Yes. Are you . . . emotionally involved with him?"

Lyle shook his head. "No," he said. "And anyway, he's not a pawn. He's my King. I give him up and the game's over."

Clifton considered this for a moment. Finally he shook his head. "I don't understand you at all," he admitted. "And I don't understand the game you're playing. I don't think it's chess. It sounds to me like Liar Dice."

Lyle laughed. "That's half the fun," he said, "not knowing exactly what the game is, just realising what you've got at stake. It keeps you on your toes, don't you think? Makes life interesting."

"You're a very complex man, Mr Lyle," Clifton said. ("Fucking fairy!" Montrose muttered in the background.) "I wonder how much of what you've told us is the truth."

"It's all the truth," Lyle said. "That's one of the rules."

"But not the whole truth?"

Lyle lit himself another cigarette. "Who of us in the world can say we know the whole truth about anything?" he asked.

"I'm not speaking in any philosophical sense," Clifton replied, "but in practical terms. You're withholding important information, are you not? How do we know that we're right to go ahead with the trial of Daniel Moorhouse, for example? Maybe we should just let him go."

"Sure," agreed Lyle readily, "you could do whatever you liked. You have to decide what road you're going to take. I've pointed you in the direction of the action against Moorhouse because it's in the interests of my country that he doesn't come back. Ever. But you don't have to agree with me on that. Maybe you'd like to have Moorhouse in power again. So be it. You're in charge. You can do whatever you like. If you think your own necks will be safe, let him out of gaol tomorrow. I'm not authorised to commit the United States to anything. I'm just speaking as a citizen of my country. Washington certainly doesn't want to be part of anything messy. We get into enough trouble as it is already, without being accused of backing a crooked revolution in St David's. So it's up to you what you do. And good luck. I'll watch with interest."

"See you at the Embassy tomorrow," Montrose warned.

"Maybe," said Lyle, and Clifton could see the glint of his teeth as he grinned. "Don't forget my copies of those photographs, Claud. Blow them up to eight by twelve if you can. I'd like to pin them on my office wall." He started to move off, then paused. "By the way, have you found Molvi yet?"

"No," said Montrose shortly.

"That's not very good is it?" Lyle reproved. "You can't have been looking very hard."

"Don't try to tell me my job, you prick!" Montrose snarled. "We've been everywhere. He's just disappeared."

"Maybe he sneaked onto a ship and got away?" Lyle suggested.

Clifton said: "We don't think so. That was the first door we shut. The guards at the port have been doubled, and no one goes on board without being fully checked. We think he's just lying low somewhere. He'll turn up sooner or later."

"If you're going ahead with the case against Moorhouse, it had better be sooner," Lyle said. "He's the pivot of the whole thing, isn't he?"

"We'll get him, thank you," Montrose replied, flatly.

"Have you tried the meat market area?" Lyle suggested innocently.

"What? In the bazaar?" asked Clifton, pricking up his ears.

"That's the one. He's got some friends there, apparently. It might be worth a try."

"You've heard something?" Clifton again.

"A whisper. Have a look around Grant Street. No guarantees, though."

"Thanks, Mr Lyle," said Clifton. "We'll do that."

As they watched him go, Clifton wondered aloud: "Where the hell does he get his information?"

Montrose replied sourly: "From his boyfriends."

"It can't all be that, Claud," Clifton said. "He's obviously got an extraordinary network of his own. I wish we knew who was on it."

"We don't know if he's right about Molvi, do we? It might be bull-shit."

"It might," Clifton agreed. "We'll soon find out." He lit himself another cigarette and stared thoughtfully at the tail lights of the Chevrolet, heading towards the Coast Road. "What are we going to do about Mr Lyle?" he asked.

"Turn him in to the Ambassador," Montrose said flatly.

"I wonder if that would be wise."

"What do you mean, wise? We can't let this bastard get away with it."

Clifton moved restlessly. "We'd better discuss it with Luther anyway," he said finally. "I wouldn't be surprised if he didn't agree with Lyle's assessment. We don't really want word about our dealings to get round the island, do we? Not just so you can pay Lyle back."

"It wasn't only me," Montrose pointed out. "He was dropping all of us in the crap, whatever he says."

"Even so," said Clifton. "What I really want to know is where he gets his information. Surely it would be better for us to let him go on as usual, and keep a close watch on him. See if we can't track down who his agents are."

Montrose grunted and Clifton knew the point had not been lost.

The men moved towards their car, then drove to see Luther.

The General was no longer in his suburban house. He had moved into the Prime Ministerial residence the day after the eviction of Mrs Moorhouse. Priscilla Luther's pastel portrait was now looking incongruous in the large, gracious living-room.

As Clifton suspected, Luther came down unhesitatingly on his side. There was to be no action against Lyle, at least until surveillance on him had been completed, and the identity of his agent, or agents, discovered. Then Luther himself might drop a word to the Ambassador that it would be better if Lyle was withdrawn. No mention would be made of his homosexuality, as this was certain to provoke the American into retaliation, and news about the protection racket would be out.

Luther was determined that his position as military ruler should not be undermined.

Montrose argued briefly, but without conviction, as if he knew he had no hope of success.

There was no difference of opinion, though, on Lyle's tip-off about Molvi. A close watch was ordered on the bazaar, and particularly the Grant Street area.

Later that night, plainclothes men moved in and loitered round the coffee and tea stalls which stayed open until after midnight, and in the shacks selling the rough, potent Arak made from the sap of palm trees, where drinking continued illegally until three or four in the morning.

The taverns were tiny rooms, usually with mats spread on hard dirt floors. Some had walls of matted coconut fronds, others planks nailed haphazardly together, so it was possible to see through the gaps into the narrow streets, and smell the faint odour of rotting meat and vegetables and the smoke from wood fires.

Except for the taverns and the tea and coffee stalls, all other shops were shuttered, and presented blank, brown wooden faces to the almost empty streets.

The customers in the Arak taverns were men and a handful of women in grubby, brightly coloured clothes who were prepared to go into quiet alleys nearby in exchange for a drink and three dollars, and always returned alone and sullen ten minutes later, to lounge about on the mats.

Occasionally voices were raised in argument or a group would give a sudden shout of laughter, but mostly there was a subdued buzz of conversation. Everyone knew the police would turn a blind eye to the illegal drinking only while things were quiet. Those were the terms on which they accepted their weekly payoffs. A fight, or rowdiness, meant they were entitled to claim an extra payment, or take everyone to gaol. The cost either way was high and tended to guarantee good behaviour.

The taverns were lit by dim oil lamps or candles which guttered when a customer moved past, or a breath of wind blew through a suddenly opened door. Occasionally, the air was rich with the aroma of marijuana, and doped cigarettes were passed leisurely between customers. No one cared about that either, not in the bazaar.

The plainclothes police, working in ones and twos, visited the taverns for a drink and a few drags on a shared marijuana cigarette, offered with the easy comradeship certain kinds of dope kindles among users. In the gloom, they scanned shadowy faces for Molvi.

A man on the run would probably not go out much during the day. He would feel safer at night, emboldened by the shadows and the half light. But it would be a phoney security, because there were fewer people about after dark and it would be easier to spot him.

This was the theory behind the late-night surveillance, and the plainclothes men, squatting on the mats, did not argue with it. It was a good way of spending their on-duty hours: preferable by far to waiting out-side, watching a house or following a car.

The palm toddy burned in their throats and warmed their bellies, and the marijuana made them feel at peace.

Seven Arak taverns were open in the bazaar area, and a pair of them were in each, waiting, talking idly, watching.

The men in the tavern nearest to Grant Street saw him coming first. Through the gap in the wooden boards of the wall, they glimpsed his figure. It was too dark, and he was too far off, for a positive identification, but his behaviour was so furtive they were sure it was him.

There were a few street lights along the way, and he hurried past each into the next patch of shadow where he paused, staying close to a wall, checking that everything was still clear. If he had walked normally, like anybody else, the chances were the men in the tavern would hardly have given him a second glance, and he would actually have had to enter the shack before he came under close scrutiny.

But Molvi was scared, a man running for his life, and he lacked the ability to hide this.

The plainclothes men swallowed the small glasses of Arak and stood up, pushing a handful of small denomination notes towards the owner. Molvi would be going past the tavern door, if in fact he wasn't planning to come right in, and they stepped into the darkness to intercept him.

He was on the other side of the street, ten or twelve feet away, and he looked back at them scared as they came out of the shack, but they could tell he was calmed when he saw no uniforms.

Molvi paused to let them get ahead of him, and they closed the gap, sauntering like men who have just ended a pleasant evening, until suddenly the saunter became a run.

A cry of terror escaped Molvi's lips as his body launched itself for flight, but the iron-hard arms were already locked around his chest and his neck, strangling, and then he was on his knees and a shoe was coming, driven up into his stomach just below his rib cage, pushing the wind from his lungs and collapsing him, gasping, onto the road, his arms twisted painfully behind him.

Molvi waited for death, sobbing.

Chapter Thirty-two

Clive Lyle poured himself a breakfast cup of coffee and stared thought-fully out of the window.

The car was still there, parked a hundred yards down the road. One man was sitting in it, obviously bored, while the other ambled aimlessly along the grass verge, stretching his legs. Lyle could see him yawn, and he wondered how long the surveillance had been going on. Presumably Montrose had ordered it soon after their meeting at the picnic site to find out who Lyle's remaining agents were, but it was professionally disappointing to see them making such an amateurish job of it.

Lyle shook his head sadly. St David's had a lot to learn about surveillance techniques, among other things. He went to get ready.

An hour later, he reversed his Chevrolet out of the garage and into the street. He knew he could shake them off fairly easily, but he had no wish to do so. He drove at a moderate speed, checking the rearview mirror to make sure they stayed behind him, all the way to the American Embassy.

Lyle flashed his pass at the gate, but instead of driving down to his reserved space in the underground car park, he turned into the small parking area at the side. As he locked his car, he could see the surveillance men pulling off the road underneath a tree a short distance away.

Lyle fiddled with the door handle until he was sure the men had seen him, and then he carried his black briefcase into the Embassy.

The Marine guard on duty greeted him laconically and pressed the button which unlocked the heavy door separating the foyer from the Embassy offices. Lyle walked through and the door closed swiftly behind him.

The Embassy carpets were thick and gold coloured, stretching along the corridor on both sides and up the circular staircase.

Lyle went quickly to the first floor, where another security door barred the way to the offices of most of the diplomats and CIA men, and the Ambassador himself. He pressed the number code on the buttons inside a small box placed at shoulder height, and the door unlocked.

Lyle's office was next to the Ambassador's, and he went there first to instruct his secretary to get him a ticket on the midday flight to London, with a connection to Washington.

From his safe, he fetched an envelope, security sealed and addressed to Freeman Leister. It had lain there for two years awaiting this moment. Lyle carried it through to the Ambassador's suite, and told the secretary he needed an uninterrupted talk.

Freeman Leister was frowning over a pile of documents when Lyle walked in, and he glanced up.

"Morning, Clive. Take a seat. I won't be a moment."

"Good morning, Ambassador."

The office had an open view over towards the road, and Lyle could see the car waiting under the tree. Presumably that team would be relieved later in the morning.

Freeman Leister signed his name at the bottom of the letter, closed the folder on his work and pushed it aside.

"Sorry about that," he said. "What's the problem?"

Lyle handed over the sealed envelope and said: "I think you'd better read that first, sir."

Leister's eyebrows raised and he turned the envelope over in his hands, studying the seal. "I haven't seen one of these in a long time," he said softly. "Whoever would have thought." The Ambassador reached for his thin steel letter opener and slit the brown paper.

Inside was a single thick sheet, with three paragraphs of typing, an assertive signature, and another seal.

"I should keep this for framing," Leister said with a smile, but Lyle knew he was less than pleased.

"Okay, Clive, I understand. You can do what you like. I can't over-rule you, and you're responsible only to your masters. What is it you want to do?"

"I've done most of it already," Lyle admitted. "May I smoke, by the way?"

"Please do. Have one of these."

Lyle accepted a cigarette and both men lit up.

"I'm booking a seat on the midday plane to London," he said, "and then on to Washington."

"Will you be away long?"

Lyle shrugged. "Forever. I won't be coming back, I don't think. I'm finished here now, and it wouldn't be smart to stick around. See that car out there on the other side of the road, just under the tree? The blue Toyota. That's my tail, as from last night."

Leister craned round. At last he asked: "What's it all about? They're friends now. Luther wouldn't do anything to damage relations, I don't think."

"They're trying to find out who my local agents are," Lyle explained. "They're making a pretty amateurish job of it at the moment, but I can't take the risk that the others will be as bad as that lot. I haven't got many agents left and I don't want to lose them, so I'm pulling out and handing them on."

"Yes I understand that. Do you think they'll try to stop you leaving the country?"

"I don't know," Lyle said. "Montrose might. But I'm not planning to give him much opportunity. My cases are packed and sitting at home. I'll send someone around to pick them up and take them to the airport. Those guys out there are watching my car – I've parked where they can see it, by the side of the Embassy. I'll go out as a passenger in someone else's car out of the underground park, and just keep my head down for a couple of blocks. That ought to do it."

"I'll drive you out myself," Leister offered. "What time do you have to be at the airport?"

"That would be kind, sir. Eleven o'clock. Two hours from now."

"Well then, we'll leave at ten-thirty if that's agreeable. If there is any trouble at the airport, I'll contact Luther myself and sort it out."

"Thank you."

Freeman Leister looked at Lyle shrewdly. "I realise I shouldn't ask what you've been doing on the island, but are there any aspects you think I ought to know about?"

Lyle nodded. "There are some, Ambassador. There's a chance you might hear about them from others, so you ought to be forewarned. Claud Montrose has been blackmailing me. Or anyway, he thinks he has."

Leister looked startled. "Good heavens," he said. "What for?"

"Homosexual activities," Lyle said easily. "He claims to have photographs."

The Ambassador's face assumed a look of professional caution. "*Does* he have them?" he asked.

"No. He might have a stab at faking some up, in which case he'll deliver them round to you. I've asked for a set of copies, eight by twelve, for my office wall. It would be just like Claud to let me have them, too. If he does, perhaps you could put them in the Bag and send them across to me in Washington."

"If they do arrive, I take it we'll be able to see they're fakes?"

"I imagine so. They're not very professional around here. You should be able to see the join if you look closely." Lyle grinned disarmingly. "He'll also tell you that I gave him the names of the CIA men Moorhouse went and expelled, and that I was having an affair with Charlie Berenson."

"Good Lord. Where did he get that idea from?"

"About Berenson? Oh, I told him that. And he'll be right about the names. I did give them to him."

"*You* did?" The Ambassador was incredulous. "Why on earth . . . ?"

"I think I'd better explain what it is I've been trying to do," Lyle said, then corrected himself: "No, hell, what I actually *did* do. You're not going to like it much, I'm afraid, so if you'd rather not know, speak now."

"If what you've told me already is any sample, I'm sure I won't like it, Clive," Leister said frankly. "I don't approve of covert activities, I'm afraid."

"Not many people do, but that's my job. It's what I'm good at."

"No doubt. Well, I might as well hear what you've got to say."

"My brief here," Lyle explained, "was to make sure that United States defence interests were not compromised by any change in island policy. As you know, Moorhouse had been dropping hints for a couple of years that he was unhappy with the present arrangement. When he visited Moscow in May last year, he had a few sessions with Kosygin and he pretty well spelled out his intention to ditch the treaty. Our guys in Moscow got a full report of the talks. You can imagine the reaction in Washington. A good chunk of our defence strategy is posited on exclusive staging rights at Port Lombard, plus of course the communications centre we've set up here. The feeling was that Moorhouse couldn't be allowed to do it. First we tried diplomacy and sweet talking."

"I remember that," Leister said. "I saw the Prime Minister several times but I couldn't get a straight answer out of him. He did deny he intended major changes, though."

"We didn't believe that," Lyle said. "It didn't square with what we had from Moscow. We were sure he was lying. So Washington took a policy decision and asked me if I thought I could stop him. I had a look around and said it was possible. So I did it. I stopped him."

"Wait a minute!" the Ambassador exclaimed. "It was the coup that stopped him! Luther and Montrose and Clifton."

Lyle smiled and offered another cigarette across the desk. Leister declined.

"*I* stopped him," Lyle said quietly, then, seeing the look on the Ambassador's face, added: "Oh, don't worry, we weren't actually involved in the coup. That was a homegrown thing. But I did set it up." His lighter flared. "I guess I'd better start from the beginning.

"If you have a look at Claud Montrose's file, you'll see he was operating a small-time protection racket when the island became independent. So were Luther and Clifton: the three of them were partners. Well, as the years went by, it all faded away. There was peace, perfect peace on St David's, and those aren't the conditions where people are frightened into parting with their money. We kept an eye on what was happening, of course, and we heard that the three of them were going pretty badly into debt. Well in that sort of situation, something's got to give, sooner or later. My guess was, the three of them would try to restart the protection racket. But to do that, they had to have the conditions in which people were so frightened, they'd be prepared to pay for protection."

Lyle drew deeply on his cigarette. "They're such a bunch of wankers," he said, "you can't trust them to do anything properly.

"After the cholera scare, when Moorhouse became unpopular, they thought that might do it. No luck: there were demonstrations but no real trouble. Then the three of them got the bright idea that they might help things along by pandering to one of Moorhouse's pet bogies – the American threat. According to the Moscow reports, he'd had quite a bit to say about that to Kosygin, and presumably he'd been dropping the word around his office as well. Claud Montrose was the brains behind that idea, and as far as it went, it wasn't too shabby either. Claud thought: let's cause trouble in Port Lombard, punch a few heads and blame the CIA. He knew Moorhouse would go big on the idea that the CIA were destabilising his government. He was paranoid anyway, because he wasn't the beloved leader any longer and he couldn't understand why. So it was just a question of Montrose playing on that, and he'd be able to persuade Moorhouse to declare a state of emergency without much trouble, kick out a few Americans and lock up some locals. After that, the shopkeepers would start paying up."

"Good heavens," the Ambassador said, surprised. "That's a long, complicated way round."

"Not really," Lyle replied. "Once you start along the road, things just happen. They fall into place."

"Wouldn't it have been easier for Montrose just to send his men along at night to break up a few stores?"

"In theory, yes, it would. But then everyone would be wondering what the hell was going on. Even Moorhouse would be wondering. There has to be an explanation for the trouble, and unless the political conditions were right, and there was general uncertainty, it would be easy for some shopkeeper to blow the whistle on Montrose and the others."

"Oh, I see."

"So I knew all that before I started. It made my job pretty easy really. I just had to work within the format that was already presented. I knew Claud was trying to get a line into the Embassy. He made a pretty crass attempt to recruit one of the junior officers – Milward, down in ciphers. Milward told him to go to hell and came to me. So that was the way in.

"I got one of my local guys to pass the tip to Montrose that I was homosexual and hung out at the Jack Tar."

"What's the Jack Tar?" the Ambassador asked.

"It's a Gay bar down in the docks area."

"I didn't even know it existed," Leister said.

Lyle grinned at him. "Oh it exists all right. There's a heavy scene there on Saturday nights. So I went along the next Saturday, and sure enough, suddenly whistles were blowing and cops were everywhere. Next thing, I found myself in front of Montrose, pleading with him not to say anything to the Embassy. Jesus, you should have seen his face. He thought he'd struck oil. So that's when the blackmail started. I gave him the names of the CIA men, and Moorhouse kicked them out."

Leister frowned. "I must say I think that was a pretty irresponsible thing for you to do," he said. "I don't know what they're going to say about it in Washington."

"They won't care," Lyle prophesied. "You have to give up a few pawns every so often. They know that better than I. The trick is to judge when and which ones. Moorhouse would have chucked them out sooner or later anyway."

"Well, what happened after that?" the Ambassador asked.

"After that, I saw things weren't going very well. Montrose didn't know how to cause crowd disturbance any more than he knew how to fly to the moon. He'd got himself ten thugs to start trouble during demonstrations, but they were hopeless. So I gave him a couple of lessons on how to start riots."

"Great God. What sort of lessons?"

"Just basic stuff. The things they teach at Fairfax. It really opened Claud's eyes, though. And it worked too, as you saw."

The Ambassador's face was a mask of disapproval. "I hope it wasn't your idea that he open fire on innocent men and women," he said stiffly.

"That *is* part of the lesson," Lyle replied. "Pawns again, unfortunately. So for Montrose, Luther and Clifton, things started going really well. The money was rolling in again, the emergency was in force and the island was in a mess. That's when I had to get to work again. It wasn't my brief to make money for Claud and his buddies, but to get rid of Moorhouse. This meant giving them a bit of a push."

"What did you do?" Despite himself, Leister was fascinated, rather as birds are with snakes.

"Again, Claud gave me the opportunity. He's a pretty nasty, vindictive little man. He'd asked me to let him have a list of local CIA agents to give Moorhouse, so I weeded out the ones who weren't much use to us any longer and handed them over. This was before the emergency."

"More pawns?" Leister asked, with distaste.

"More pawns," Lyle agreed. "But Claud couldn't resist adding a name of his own and making up a phoney dossier. Stephen Ayer, Moorhouse's PPS, had got in his way apparently, so he had the Prime Minister order his detention. Now I knew the dossier on Ayer would have to be phoney, so I tipped off a friend of his – Joe Rana. Rana's one of ours, too."

"Isn't he under arrest now?"

"That's right."

"Another pawn."

"I'm afraid so."

"You're getting through pawns pretty fast, aren't you, Clive? You can't have many left."

"One or two. The thing is, you have to decide how badly you want something. Now we want to stay on St David's very badly indeed. Our vital defence interests are involved. So we want Moorhouse out of the way very badly, too. We have to be prepared to make bold sacrifices."

"We're certainly boldly sacrificing other people," the Ambassador said sourly.

"That's what they teach us at Fairfax. Rana is a good man. He and Tilak Kataria, the Cabinet Secretary . . ."

"Also in gaol."

". . . as you say, now also in gaol, they got to work and proved to Moorhouse that the dossier was a load of lies. So suddenly Claud found himself with some explaining to do, and his own position crumbling around him. He had to fight back. But by itself, that wasn't enough. I had to get the other two involved as well, Luther and Clifton. They also had to be battling for their lives. So I did a bit of digging around, and got the names of Montrose's ten thugs – the ones who start the riots. I passed them on to Moorhouse, via Joe Rana. Then I told Montrose what had happened. And that was that. Claud, Luther and Clifton couldn't take the chance of being found out, not with four people already dead. So they had to move fast. You know the rest."

Leister sat silently, deep in thought. "What happens to Moorhouse now?" he asked finally. "You know they're going to charge him."

Lyle shrugged. "Moorhouse will hang," he said simply. "I'd put money on it."

"What about the others?"

"They're not important. I mean, I'm not actually involved any more. But I gather they'll give evidence against Moorhouse and later they'll be pardoned and set free. It's Moorhouse they want to get rid of. He knows too much about them now."

"Another pawn."

"No. A knight, at least. Or a bishop. But that's what my target was: get rid of Moorhouse, and I've done it. I know you don't like the means, but what do you think of the end? Pretty satisfactory, I'd say."

Leister inclined his head reluctantly. "I suppose so. The defence agreement is certainly safe for the moment. But how long do you think this regime is going to last?"

Lyle shrugged again and grinned. "Well, that's another problem," he said. "We'll deal with it when it arises. Now if you'll excuse me, Ambassador, I've got a few things to settle in my office."

"Of course, of course. Come back here when you're ready."

Lyle strolled down the corridor. His secretary said: "Clive, I had a bit of trouble getting you a seat on the plane. Economy's on wait-list, apparently. I've had to get a First Class ticket."

"I guess I'll just have to grit my teeth," he said cheerily. "Try and make it First all the way through to Washington."

"Not a chance," she said. "Not unless you pay the difference yourself."

"Spoil sport."

At 10.20, Lyle went back to Leister's office, and the two men took the lift down to the basement car park. Lyle had the distinct feeling the Ambassador was sorry he'd offered to accompany him to the airport. The revelation of how Moorhouse had been ousted had disturbed and depressed him, and Lyle was sensitive enough to realise that, but professional enough to feel no pain.

Lyle ducked down behind the front seat, with Leister sitting stiffly upright next to him, and the chauffeur drove up the ramp into the daylight.

The surveillance men gave the Ambassadorial car, flying the Stars and Stripes, a cursory glance, but did not move. Two blocks away, Lyle felt it safe to get up and back onto the seat.

They drove in silence. In a way, Lyle was sorry to be leaving St David's. It was a good little island, he thought. Picturesque. And he'd made some good friends. But it was time to move on.

Just before they reached the airport, Leister said: "You're a strange man, Clive. I thought I knew you and now I realise I don't know you at all."

"Does anyone ever really know anyone else?"

"I've just had a look at your personal file. There's hardly anything on it."

"I don't suppose there's very much to say."

"What will you do when you get back to Washington?" the Ambassador inquired.

"I'll have to go into the office and tie up bits and pieces," Lyle said. "Then I think I deserve some time off."

"I expect your family will be glad to see you back. It must be hard for men like you who are always sent out by themselves."

"My family?" Lyle said. "Oh, I'm not married. It's not my sort of thing. And my parents are dead."

He could see the brief, speculative look Leister shot him and he knew the question which was forming in his mind and which he would be too much of a diplomat ever to ask.

Lyle grinned at him. Leister looked away.

Chapter Thirty-three

Daniel Moorhouse stared thoughtfully at the wall opposite, at the slightly lighter rectangle of cream paint where his official portrait had once hung.

The courtroom was full as usual, and even now, after the trial had been going on for three months, the queue for seats always began forming more than an hour before the doors opened. Moorhouse had never seen the queue, of course: He was brought in alone in a closed van and held in a cell beneath the gloomy High Court building until the judges were ready to resume.

He hardly saw his four co-defendants either: not in the prison, where their cells were corridors apart, nor in the musty-smelling Court basement. Whenever he was taken up to the dock, they were already seated and they avoided his eye.

The seating arrangement for prisoners was such that he could leave a gap of two or three feet between himself and the others – a physical separation which suited both sides. Moorhouse was sickened by their treachery and had no wish to be associated with them more than was strictly necessary.

Ayer, Rana and Kataria sat in a huddle, frequently whispering to each other. Moorhouse saw them as conspirators, and had no way of knowing the burden of guilt and fear they shared.

Only Molvi, from whom even the three kept a small but noticeable distance, was unaffected by his actions.

When he had found out he was not going to be killed, he was overwhelmed with relief and gratitude. He owed nothing to Daniel Moorhouse and so did not care whether Moorhouse lived or died. There had been only one cloud on Molvi's horizon – and it had finally been resolved. It was over Montrose's promise that any sentence he received from the judges would be commuted as soon as Moorhouse was hanged, and Molvi quite simply did not trust the Commissioner of Police. He could not forget the day of the Democratic Front demonstration, when he heard Montrose ordering his men to shoot looters on sight, and the sounds of the rifles, killing.

Molvi often relived that day in dreams which left him whimpering and sweaty. But he was canny enough to realise that Montrose needed him alive now, and that he still had cards to play, so he told Montrose his promise wasn't good enough.

One night, a car arrived at the gaol, and Molvi was taken off to the official residence of General Luther himself for iced beers, whisky, snacks and a man-to-man talk.

Luther told him that the role he had been asked to play was crucial to the defence of the free world, and that at the end of it, the rewards would be good. Molvi would have a First Class air ticket to anywhere in the world, and $50,000 would be paid into any bank account he cared to nominate. If he didn't like banks, he could have the money in cash. It was a chance for a new start.

After an hour, they shook hands on the deal. General Luther saw Molvi to the car, and even held the door open for him.

When he remembered it, months later, Molvi could hardly stop himself grinning.

From then on, Montrose and Clifton just needed to coach him on what to say, as they did with the other three.

The trial opened at the end of October, and the co-defendants pleaded guilty to four counts of conspiracy to murder. Moorhouse, of course, maintained his innocence.

Slowly the trial moved into gear. After the opening addresses of the prosecution and defence counsels, a long list of witnesses was called. Policemen told what had happened during the riots: demonstrators who had been caught up in them gave their versions. Some identified Molvi. A Government pathologist based in Port Lombard gave details of his autopsy findings, and a ballistics expert matched the bullets to rifles issued to members of the Security Battalion.

Then Montrose was called. For two days, he gave State evidence of the events leading up to the riots, and how he had handled them. He was the first possible chink in the prosecution's case, and when the Attorney-General had completed his questions, it was late in the day and the court adjourned.

Now, this morning, procedural arguments held up cross-examination and there was a feeling of restlessness. Moorhouse scanned the rows of spectators again, identifying the faces of friends and foes, and the strangely pathetic group of relatives. The wives and close friends of the co-accused sat together for support. Moorhouse wondered how much they knew of what was really going on, and he felt a strange compassion for them. They, more than anyone, were innocent bystanders. Their numbers had grown and shrunk during the trial as close friends and relatives came to show solidarity, and then drifted away after a few hours, seemingly disappointed that there wasn't more drama and emotion and that the evidence and questioning plodded dully on, sifting and resifting the same events.

Today there was at least the promise of action, and the group swelled once more.

Moorhouse's own wife sat alone in her usual seat, just behind the row of defence attorneys. She was quietly attentive to the proceedings. Occasionally she tapped one of the counsel on the shoulder and whispered some comments or suggestions and when she caught the eye of a supporter, she smiled graciously, as she had learned to do over the years.

She and the other wives never spoke to, or greeted each other. It was as if the public gallery contained two alien worlds which could never meet, or touch, and were even unaware of the other's existence.

There was a sudden stillness in the court. The procedural arguments were over and Montrose was again making his way to the witness stand. Moorhouse watched him with a stab of bitterness. *He is almost my creation,* he thought. *I kept him on as Commissioner after Independence when many advised me to sack him. I leaned on him and trusted him, and never saw the corruption. I made him what he is.*

Montrose was reminded that he was still under oath, and Moorhouse's counsel rose ponderously to his feet.

Charles Rupa was the most senior advocate on the island: a large, fat man whose skin was deep black and whose jowls hung heavy over the collar of his black legal gown, while his eyes dolefully regarded the world and its works.

Rupa shuffled papers on his desk and failed to find what he was looking for. Then he stood in silence, as if trying to recall some information or collect his thoughts. Montrose gave a thin, scornful smile and his eyes were bright. *Bloody local,* he thought.

"Mr Montrose," Rupa began, "how well do you know my client, Daniel Moorhouse?"

"Very well indeed. I met him regularly in his office, and of course I saw him at other functions."

"What about Mr Ayer?"

"I *saw* a lot of Ayer, whenever I went to the Prime Minister's office. But I don't *know* him."

"And Mr Rana?"

"I've seen him around, that's all."

"What about Mr Kataria?"

"The same thing."

"You haven't spoken to him?"

"Not much, no."

"And the last defendant, Mr Molvi. How well do you know him?"

"Not at all."

228

"Not at all? Are you sure of that?"

"Perfectly sure."

"Perfectly sure," Rupa repeated. "What about during the riots?"

"No."

"Not even a glimpse of him?"

"No."

"Didn't you tell Daniel Moorhouse that you had recognised some troublemakers from previous riots?" Rupa persisted.

"I think I might have said something of that sort," Montrose admitted.

"But Mr Molvi was totally new to you?"

"Yes."

"You said, if I remember correctly, that you knew Mr Ayer only slightly."

"I'd seen him around many times."

"But you didn't know much about him?"

"That is correct."

"Then why was it you recommended to Daniel Moorhouse that Mr Ayer be served with a detention order and taken off to gaol?"

"Oh, that's different," said Montrose. "I know a lot about what Mr Ayer was up to, what he was doing. We'd been keeping a close watch on him. But I didn't know him personally. That's what I meant."

"And what was it that Mr Ayer was doing?"

"He was up to no good," Montrose replied shortly. "We had reason to believe he was passing confidential information to the government of another country."

"Which country was this?" Rupa asked, raising his eyebrows.

Montrose looked towards the bench of judges. "Do I have to answer that, your Lordships? I don't think divulging this information publicly is in the national interest."

The Chief Justice leaned forward. "Is it relevant, Mr Rupa?"

Rupa backed down. "Perhaps not," he said. "Perhaps for the moment, we can call it Country A." He smiled agreeably at Montrose. "Well then," he said, "so you thought Mr Ayer was spying for Country A, did you?"

"That is what the information indicated," Montrose said stiffly.

"And so you had him locked up. But then he was suddenly released. Why was that?"

"Moorhouse ordered his release."

"Yes, but why?"

The prosecutor was on his feet. "Objection," he said. "Inadmissable speculation."

"Let me put it another way," Rupa said soothingly. "Did Daniel Moorhouse indicate to you what his reasons were for releasing Mr Ayer?"

"He did."

"What did he tell you?"

"He said the information in the dossier was wrong."

"Did he order an inquiry?" Rupa asked.

"No, he did not," Montrose said, looking him straight in the eye. "He just wanted Ayer released, that's all."

Surprised: "You're saying that he did *not* order an inquiry into the cases of the other detainees?"

"No."

Rupa frowned again slightly and rummaged through his documents again. He pulled out a copy of a newspaper. "This is the *St David's Herald* of July the second 1977, and here on the front page there is a report headlined 'Ayer Release Sparks New Probe'. Let me read you the first paragraph: 'The Prime Minister, Mr Daniel Moorhouse, has ordered a thorough investigation of the cases of all those detained on the island, following the release of his former Principal Private Secretary, Mr Stephen Ayer, official sources said today.' I'd like to hand this in as an exhibit, M'lords."

The newspaper was taken by a court official and passed up to the Bench. The judges perused it silently.

"Do you recall seeing that report?"

"No, I don't think I do," replied Montrose sullenly.

"And you say that no such inquiry was ever ordered?"

"That is correct."

"Let me put it to you, Mr Montrose, that you *were* ordered to inquire into the case of every single detainee, and you were also ordered to find out what had gone wrong with the Ayer dossier."

"That is not true."

"Daniel Moorhouse will give evidence on oath that he personally gave you these orders."

Montrose shrugged. "I can't be responsible for what Mr Moorhouse says, either to this Court or to the Press."

"You were not ordered to investigate why Mr Ayer's dossier was so inaccurate?"

"No I was not. There was nothing wrong with Ayer's dossier."

"Oh come now, Mr Montrose," Rupa said scornfully. "You are well aware that the dossier was a pack of lies."

Calmly: "I disagree."

"And that on a number of occasions when Mr Ayer was supposed to be meeting his contact from Country A, he was in fact enjoying a quiet drink at the St David's Club!"

Montrose stared smugly at Rupa. "That is not correct," he said.

"The Members' Register at the St David's Club has his signature as going into the club on those days and at those times!"

Claud Montrose failed to suppress his triumph. "I'd like to see proof of that," he challenged. "Show me the Members' Register!"

Rupa turned away, busy at his papers again. "Unfortunately," he replied quietly, "the Members' Register covering the period in question has disappeared from the club. It has been stolen. As you are probably well aware, Mr Montrose."

"Objection!" called the Attorney-General.

"Sustained," the Chief Justice said, and Rupa let the matter drop.

The rest of Montrose's cross-examination on that day, and on the two which followed, failed to budge him. But although no one knew it then, buried in Montrose's evidence was a piece of information which would rebound on him and shake the foundations of the prosecution case.

It was Molvi who unwittingly provided the ammunition.

Ayer, Rana and Kataria had each been called to the witness stand, and had recited their evidence, unshakeably. The Defence counsel was beginning to despair.

Ayer claimed to be the direct link with Moorhouse in the management and tactics of the gang of ten, and Rana and Kataria told of meetings with Ayer to plan individual attacks.

Their evidence on dates, times and places agreed exactly. The case against Moorhouse began to look bad.

And then it was Molvi's turn, and for two days, he was taken through his story.

He described the riots in the High Street and at Maxwell's and how he'd been told what Moorhouse wanted done. He had never actually spoken to the Prime Minister himself, he agreed. All instructions had been passed on by the three civil servants.

Then Rupa began questioning him on the events of the afternoon of the last Democratic Front meeting and the violence round the Imperial Hotel.

"We picked up the van from the car pool in the morning and parked it just round the corner in Connaught Street," Molvi said.

The words slipped out, irretrievably.

"You got a car from the car pool? What car pool?" Rupa asked.

Molvi felt a brief wave of unease. He had been told not to mention using vehicles, but there was no going back now, and Molvi thought it wouldn't make any difference. He could talk his way out.

So he said: "The car pool at the police station. I used to work there."

"The Central Police Station?"

"Yes. We took it early and parked it while there were still a lot of spaces."

"You had free access to the Central Police Station?"

"I've got friends there," said Molvi evasively. "People remember me. I don't get asked questions."

"What sort of car was it?"

"It was a closed van. No windows."

"Do you remember what colour it was?"

"It was grey colour," he said.

"What make was it?" Rupa asked.

"Ford Transit."

"That was one you'd used before, of course," Rupa ventured.

Back came the admission: "Yes, that's it."

"Oh? How often had you used it?"

"Once I think."

"Now, can you tell me, how precisely did you get it out of the police car pool?"

"What d'ya mean?" Molvi asked cautiously. "We drove it."

"Yes, I'm aware of that," Rupa said calmly. "But whose permission did you get to take it away?"

"We didn't get anyone's permission," he said. "We just took it."

"No one tried to stop you?"

"No."

"No one wanted to know what you were doing?"

"No one."

"No one saw you driving this grey Ford Transit van out of the police car park, right under their noses?"

"No. As I said, we took it early."

"Surely there was somebody in charge?"

"There may have been. I don't know. I didn't see him."

"And, of course, no one missed the van in the hours it was away, did they? It had simply vanished, but no one noticed, or cared. Is that what you're asking us to believe?" Rupa demanded.

"I dunno," Molvi said, his eyes darting over to the Attorney-General for help, but the prosecutor's face was impassive.

"Didn't you think about that? Didn't you wonder what the police would say about one of their vehicles suddenly going missing? And then, just as mysteriously, coming back?"

"If we got into trouble," Molvi offered, "we'd just tell the Prime Minister. He'd fix it."

Rupa grimaced and moved onto another tack. "Let's get back to this vehicle," he said. "Was it you who drove it?"

"Yes, I was the driver."

"And it was you who actually took it from the police car pool?"

"Yes."

"Are there many grey Ford Transits there?"

"Hell yes. Nine or ten."

"But you chose this one?"

"That's it."

"And you'd chosen it before."

"Yes, I'd driven it before."

"It was a good car?"

"Not bad."

"Reliable, would you say?"

"Yes."

"Well maintained?"

"Same as the others."

"But anyway, you preferred it."

"Yes."

"Why was that?"

"I dunno," Molvi said easily. "It was lighter on the steering than the others, I suppose. And it always started first time."

Rupa stabbed in the dark: "So you'd know what the licence number was, wouldn't you? To choose it out of nine or ten identical grey Ford Transits?"

Molvi hesitated, and then thought, *shit, it can't make any difference.* "It was KP620," he said.

Rupa turned to the Bench of judges. "M'lords," he said, "the vehicle Log Book of KP620 is obviously a document concerned with this case and should be admitted as an exhibit. I would certainly like to study it myself."

Molvi shifted uneasily. Rupa glanced at his watch.

"I see that it is nearly time for the lunch adjournment. Perhaps it would be convenient to your Lordships if we adjourned at this point. If the court could summon the authorities to produce this Log Book in the meantime, I will be able to take up my cross-examination on this matter when we resume."

The Chief Justice glanced across at the Attorney-General. "Any objection, Mr Zanja?"

The Attorney-General rose. "Is this necessary?" he asked wearily. "It is the witness' evidence that he took the vehicle without permission, so the Log Book will scarcely assist the court. Yet if it is held here for the duration of the trial, this might hamper the police. It would mean a vehicle was effectively out of commission during a time of national emergency."

Rupa replied evenly: "With respect to my learned friend, we won't know how to deal with this witness' evidence until we see the Log Book. No one can speculate what it will contain. We just don't know. And if the police are short of grey Ford Transit vans, perhaps they can just drive this one without completing the usual formalities. There appear to be precedents."

The Chief Justice observed: "I think the court ought to see the Log Book, Mr Zanja. If it does not assist us, we could agree to return it to the police immediately, rather than entering it as an exhibit. So, Mr Zanja, perhaps you would ensure that the Log Book is produced before the court by the end of the lunch adjournment."

The Attorney-General bowed. "As your Lordship pleases."

In the cells below the courtroom, Molvi ate alone. The food was good. Ever since his agreement with General Luther, he had been treated well. The warders brought him cold beer at night, as much as he wanted, and his meals were sent in by a restaurant. There was none of the muck the prison kitchen served up, except breakfast, and there was nothing anyone could do about that.

Yet Molvi did not feel hungry today. Some distance away, he could hear the murmur of voices as Ayer, Rana and Kataria ate together. And

Moorhouse would be around too, by himself as usual, out of sight.

Molvi could not shake his sense of unease. He had no idea what was in the Log Book, but he had a hunch something might be. He knew Montrose would be furious, but hell, it was only one mistake after more than two days in the witness box. Two words out of place, that was all: car pool.

He wished he knew what was in the Log Book. At least then he could plan what to say.

When the normal time came for the court to resume, no one arrived to take the prisoners up. The Log Book had not been produced and the court was waiting for it.

Finally, at 3.10, prison officers came to get Molvi and he walked up the stairs leading straight into the dock. Behind him, he could hear the echoing footsteps of the others.

Molvi could see Rupa and his assistants at their table, poring over something, but he could not tell from their faces if they were pleased or disappointed.

"Silence in Court!" called the usher. Everyone rose as the three judges filed in and took their places. The wooden door at the side of the dock was unlocked, and Molvi was led back to the witness stand and reminded he was still under oath.

The Chief Justice said: "Yes, Mr Rupa?"

Rupa stood up. "May it please your Lordships," he said formally. "Now, Mr Molvi, let's go through the sequence of events leading up to the last demonstrations of the Democratic Front in Jubilee Park."

"Again?" Molvi asked, surprised.

"Yes please, if you don't mind. Who was it who first told you there would be a demonstration?"

Molvi went through his story again, feeling happier, more relaxed. There couldn't have been much in the Log Book. It looked as if Rupa had dropped that line.

But, at length, they got back to the question of the van, and Molvi was on his guard again. They had decided among themselves to get hold of a vehicle big enough to carry all of them and their loot, he said.

"Did anyone else know you were planning to take a police van?" Rupa asked.

"No."

"Did anyone else help you get hold of the Ford Transit?" Rupa circled slowly back to the point.

"No," said Molvi firmly.

"So how did you manage to take it from the police car pool?"

"I just went and got the keys and drove it out."

"No one stopped you?"

"No."

"And no one helped you?"

"No."

234

"You certainly didn't fill out any information on the Log Book, did you?"

Molvi grinned. That was one thing he was sure about. "No, I didn't fill out the Log Book," he agreed.

"What time did you take the van?"

Molvi thought. "It must have been about eight in the morning," he said. "Eight-fifteen, maybe."

"Have you ever drawn a police car using the normal procedures?" Rupa asked.

"Yeah," replied Molvi.

"What exactly happens? Describe it to the court, please."

"Well, you get a chit saying you can have it, and why, and you take it down to the transport offices. They fill out part of the Log Book, and they give you the keys."

"Do they write the time in the Log Book as well?" Rupa inquired. "The time they hand the keys over?"

"Yes."

"So you take the keys and off you go. The car is then your responsibility. Isn't that so?"

"Yes," Molvi confirmed.

"Now, on the day of the meeting in Jubilee Park, you say you just went and helped yourself to the keys?"

"That's right. That's what I did."

"Where were they?"

"Hanging on a hook in the transport office."

"Are you sure about that?" Rupa asked sternly. "You took them from the hook?"

"Yes."

"No one handed them over to you?"

"No one."

Rupa picked a cardboard-bound book from his desk and held it thoughtfully. Then he gave it to a court official to pass across to Molvi.

"This is the Log Book for Vehicle Number KP620, is it not?"

Molvi inspected it. The registration number was written on the cover in thick black pen.

"Yes," he agreed.

"And KP620 is the grey Ford Transit you used on the day of the Jubilee Park meeting. It's the one you parked nearby to carry your loot."

Molvi felt strangely reluctant, as if a net was closing in on him. "I suppose so," he said finally.

"You only suppose so? Well, was it, or was it not the same van?"

"It was," Molvi admitted.

"Open the Log Book, please, and find the entry for the date of the Democratic Front meeting, July the fifth, 1976."

The court waited expectantly. Molvi glanced nervously across at the

235

Attorney-General, and then over to the doorway.

The fat figure of Montrose stood there, face pink and his small eyes furious. Someone must have passed the word.

A black-gowned attorney whispered in Rupa's ear, and they both looked briefly around at the entrance.

Rupa cleared his throat. Molvi dragged his eyes away, and hunted through the pages.

"Have you found the place?" Rupa asked.

"Yes." Molvi's voice was subdued.

"Then perhaps you can read to the court what is written in the vehicle Log Book for July the fifth."

Molvi read: "0700 . . . Commissioner of Police . . . Special Duties . . . 21,836 . . . 21,845 . . . 1330."

"Thank you," said Rupa. "Now what you've read us is information which comes under particular column headings, is it not?"

"Yes."

"What does 0700 refer to?"

"The time the van was signed out."

"And 'Commissioner of Police'?"

"The person it was signed out to." There was an edge of defiance in Molvi's voice now.

"What about 'Special Duties'?"

"That's what it's being used for."

" '21,836'?"

"The mileage on the clock when it was taken out."

"The mileometer? What about '21,845'?"

"The mileage when it was brought back."

"And, finally, '1330'?"

"The time it came back. Half past one." A picture flashed through Molvi's mind of the grey van being driven into the police car pool while he was running up the street, hulking Montrose's portable television and searching for it, and Montrose's men were advancing with rifles ready to kill. Molvi stared angrily at the menacing figure in the court-room doorway. *Thank God for a gentleman like General Luther,* he thought.

"So," Rupa said, "the grey Ford Transit which you claimed you *just took* from the car pool at about eight o'clock on the morning of July the fifth, had in fact been signed out to the Commissioner of Police an hour earlier and the keys handed over. Perhaps you could explain that to the court?"

Molvi stared blankly. Finally he admitted sullenly: "I dunno."

"You have no explanation?"

"No."

"Let me suggest one to you, then. You're lying about *just taking* the van, aren't you? It was *given* to you, wasn't it?"

Molvi shook his head dumbly.

"The keys were in the possession of Mr Claud Montrose, and *he* gave

236

them to you! You were getting your instructions from *him*, and not from Mr Ayer, or Mr Rana, or Mr Kataria."

"No." Molvi's voice was low, but he was determined not to budge. If he told them what really happened, he would be dead. He felt the eyes of the three judges unwaveringly on him.

"Claud Montrose was your boss, wasn't he?" Rupa accused. "You and the other nine! You'd never even *seen* the other defendants before! Except for my client, Mr Moorhouse – and then only in photographs!"

"No."

"Then offer an explanation, Mr Molvi. Tell this court how you came to use a van which was actually in the possession of the Commissioner of Police!"

Silence.

"Do you deny that the van was in Mr Montrose's possession?"

Jesus, Molvi thought, his mind confused. *What should I say to that? Yes or no?* "I had the van that day, Mr Rupa," he insisted. "I dunno about anything else."

"Oh, I'm not saying you didn't *have* the van," Rupa replied. "I am suggesting you didn't go down to the car pool and *just take it*. I'm suggesting you were *given* it by the Commissioner of Police himself, for your 'Special Duties'!"

"No," Molvi shook his head.

The moment had passed. Rupa entered the Log Book as a court exhibit, and gave notice that he would want to recall Claud Montrose. He glanced over his shoulder again, but Montrose had gone. Still, Rupa knew he had scored his first success. He had put doubt in the minds of the judges, and in a case carrying the death penalty, this came close to negating the whole thing.

But Molvi was still on the stand, looking sullen and shifty, and Rupa decided to have another stab at him.

"As a policeman," he said, his voice suddenly relaxed, "you'd naturally have come across the Commissioner of Police quite a bit, wouldn't you?"

"Some," Molvi agreed doubtfully.

"You'll have seen him around, I suppose?"

"Sure."

"Whereabouts?"

"Where what?" Molvi asked, not giving an inch.

"Where had you seen him around?"

"Oh, in corridors, briefings, that sort of thing."

"Briefings? What, for operations?"

"Yeah."

"Special Operations? Ever been on any of those?"

Cautiously: "Sometimes."

"Only the best policemen go on Special Operations, isn't that so?" Rupa asked flatteringly.

"If you say so."

"Do *you* say so?"

"I suppose that's right," Molvi shrugged.

"What exactly *are* Special Operations? Give me an example."

"Well, surveillance is a Special Operation," Molvi explained. "Following someone around, seeing where he goes."

"And you've done that?"

"Oh yes, lots of times."

"Not many men would be involved in something like that, would they?" Rupa inquired, still with a trace of admiration in his voice. "It's something rather special, isn't it?"

"It's not bad." That shrug again.

"How many people would go on a surveillance mission? Two or three?"

"Sometimes. It depends."

"When you did it," Rupa persisted, "how many men were with you?"

"A few usually. Sometimes up to a dozen. As I say, it depends."

"But *hand-picked* men? Not just anyone."

"I s'pose so."

"Have you ever been on any important surveillance missions? Small but important ones?"

"Yeah," Molvi agreed.

"Important enough to be briefed by the Commissioner of Police himself?"

"Sometimes."

"When was the last Special Operation you went on?"

Molvi looked furtive. "Long time ago," he said vaguely. "Last year. Before I got mixed up in this other thing."

"What other thing?"

"With Mr Moorhouse."

"But before that, you were picked for Special Operations?"

"Yeah."

"Ever been picked by the Commissioner of Police?"

"Probably."

"Don't you know?"

"No. Your name just gets called."

"But you've certainly been briefed by Mr Montrose?"

"Oh yeah."

"Often?"

"Quite often."

"Always with a lot of you around, or only a few people around?"

"A bit of both."

"So in fact he knew who you were?"

The silence stretched out. *Jesus,* Molvi thought, *he's doing it again!* At last he said: "I don't know if he did."

"Surely he must have known who you were," Rupa insisted in a jocular tone. "He may have picked you himself for certain operations.

238

He certainly briefed you in the company of only two or three others. So you must have been familiar to him."

"I dunno." Molvi's back was against the wall, and he knew it.

"The reason I ask," Rupa said, "is that Claud Montrose has told this court in evidence that he had *never seen you before in his life!*" Rupa's eyebrows almost vanished into his hairline in astonishment at the claim, but his eyes looked sad and disappointed. "Now from your own evidence, we hear quite a different story. Which one is true? Yours? Or the Commissioner's?"

"Objection!" The Attorney-General was on his feet. "Counsel is leading the witness."

"Sustained."

Molvi stood in confused silence. He looked around him for a friendly face, but he encountered only stares.

"Maybe he forgot," he said lamely.

Chapter Thirty-four

Montrose's forehead glistened with sweat but his small eyes were cold and his mood belligerent. From the dock, Daniel Moorhouse stared at him intently, as if the force of his personality could somehow drag the truth from his former Commissioner of Police.

Montrose's big hands held the rail of the witness stand, the knuckles white.

Rupa was at his most charming, trying to put him at his ease in the hope that he would lower his guard sufficiently to allow a knife to be slipped between the ribs.

But Montrose was not taken in by the affability of the moment. He had his own men posted in the courtroom, and each day they brought him reports of the trial's progress, whether any of the judges showed signs of favouring one side or the other, and what, broadly, was the evidence.

In addition to this, the Attorney-General made regular and more informed reports direct to General Luther, including courthouse gossip about what the judges were saying privately to one another during adjournments, or at the afternoon sessions when they reviewed the day's evidence.

The combination of these sources gave the Revolutionary Council a clear insight into the progress of the case: and it was clear that the prosecution had taken a sudden and serious knock.

It was not a fatal blow – not yet. Much depended on Claud Montrose's evidence.

"I do apologise for asking you to return, Mr Montrose, and the Court is obliged to you," Rupa said smoothly. "We know how busy you must be in these disturbing times."

Montrose inclined his head slightly in acknowledgment, and his piggy eyes glared back. Rupa had an uncomfortable sense of the repressed violence in the man and he wondered suddenly if he would have to pay for this day, whether he lost the case or won it.

"A question has come up, and we hope you will be able to assist the court in clarifying it." Rupa gave an encouraging smile. There was no response from Montrose. "How well do you know the defendant, Mr Molvi?"

"I've told you before," said Montrose shortly. "I don't know him at all."

"Perhaps *know* is too strong a word," Rupa suggested. "But do you know *of* him?"

"No."

"Have you ever *heard* of him then?"

"Not until this case, no."

"Had you ever *seen* him before this case?"

"Not that I'm aware."

"Do you have a good memory for faces, Mr Montrose?" Rupa asked.

"I have an excellent memory for both names and faces. And events. I never forget."

"But Mr Molvi's face has escaped you?" Rupa ignored the implied threat.

"Totally."

"Would it surprise you to hear that Mr Molvi has told this court that he knows *you?*"

"A lot of people know me, but I've no idea who they are. It's a hazard of the job."

"Quite so. But Mr Molvi was a policeman, was he not?"

"So are six thousand five hundred others on this island."

"Not all of them at the Central Police Station in Port Lombard, though," Rupa observed wryly.

"No. There are four or five hundred at the Central Police Station itself. I come into personal contact with all the officers, of course, but very few of the men."

"But you do brief the men, don't you?"

"Occasionally."

"How often is occasionally?" Rupa asked.

"Impossible to say. Once a month perhaps. Once every two months. It depends what's happening. I only brief men before major operations in which I myself am involved."

"Would you normally brief large numbers of men, or small numbers?"

"That also depends. Usually large numbers."

"But sometimes only two or three men?"

240

"Hardly ever. I can't think of an example: at least, not in the last few years."

"Mr Molvi has said in evidence that on several occasions he was in a group of two or three men being briefed by you."

"That is not correct."

"How can you be so sure, Mr Montrose?"

"I'm sure, because I would have remembered. And I've never seen Mr Molvi before." Montrose stared across at the dock. Molvi met his gaze and quickly looked away.

"Was it a surprise to you when Mr Molvi said he had been working at the Central Police Station until last year?"

"Yes, it was."

"Why?"

"Because I should have seen him before. I would have recognised him in the crowd."

"The crowd at the riots?"

"Yes."

"But when you actually saw him in the riots, you didn't think 'there's a familiar face'?"

"That is correct."

"Which riots did you see him in?"

Montrose paused, uncertain. "I didn't say I'd seen him in any riots," he said.

"I thought you did. I thought that's exactly what you said."

"No."

Rupa turned to the official stenographer and asked him to read back the last few questions and answers.

Montrose had said: *"I would have recognised him in the crowd."*

Rupa: *"But when you actually saw him in the riots, you didn't think 'there's a familiar face'?"*

Montrose: *"That is correct."*

Rupa turned back to the witness box.

"Your answers clearly imply that you *did* see Mr Molvi in the riots, and that if he had been a policeman based at the Central Police Station, you would have recognised him."

Montrose conceded grudgingly: "I didn't say I *did* see him. But I *may* have seen him."

"What does 'may have seen him' mean, Mr Montrose?" Rupa asked scornfully. "Either you did or you didn't. By your own admission, you have an excellent memory for names and faces. Not to mention events."

"I don't have a clear impression of Mr Molvi in the crowds," Montrose hedged.

"Do you have an unclear impression, then?"

"I have no impression at all."

"Yet first you say you *saw* him, and then you *may have* seen him."

"I didn't though, did I?" Montrose snapped. "I didn't see him. I've never seen him before in my life."

Rupa sighed and switched tack. "Let's turn now to the morning of July the fifth 1976. That was the morning of the Democratic Front meeting. Did you requisition a vehicle from the police car pool?"

"Yes I did."

"Which vehicle was it?"

"I can't remember exactly. It was a van though."

"What did you want it for?"

"If I remember correctly, it was for a Special Operation."

"What do you mean, 'If I remember correctly', Mr Montrose? Of course you remember! You were standing in this very courtroom yesterday, listening to Mr Molvi read from the vehicle Log Book, were you not?"

"I may have been."

"Another *may have been*, Mr Montrose?"

"I was for part of the time, not all the time."

"But you heard Mr Molvi reading from the Log Book?"

Pause: "Yes."

"So you know the Log Book has the van marked out to you personally, for Special Operations?"

"Yes."

"What was this Special Operation, Mr Montrose?"

Montrose looked defiant. "I'd rather not say," he replied. "It's an on-going operation, and to talk about it here would jeopardise the island's security. But it's nothing to do with this case."

"Nothing at all to do with Daniel Moorhouse, or the charges being heard in this court?"

"No."

"Was it anything to do with the Democratic Front rally? Or the riot which followed?"

"Nothing to do with either of those."

"So the van was taken out of the police car pool for something else entirely?"

"That is correct. It shouldn't have left the police station at all," Montrose said. "In the end, I didn't use it."

"But you had the keys."

"Yes."

"In your possession?"

"In my pocket, actually."

"Did you give them to anyone?"

"No."

"So how did Mr Molvi come to take the van out of the car pool at about eight o'clock on the morning of July the fifth?"

"I've no idea. You'll have to ask him."

"I did. He says he got the keys from the transport administration office. At the very time you say they were in your pocket, Mr Molvi says they were hanging on a hook in the administration office."

"I don't know about that. There may have been a spare set," Montrose offered.

From that point, Montrose would not be budged, although Rupa went back time and again, worrying away at small points, trying to force contradictions. In the end, the best he could do was to leave a question-mark over the issues. It seemed clear either Molvi or Montrose was lying, and with Molvi already pleading guilty, there seemed little reason for it to be him: at least not on this point. And Montrose's suggestion that a spare set of keys might have been hanging on a hook in the administration office was not a question for the defence to settle. That was the prosecution's task.

A hole had been left in their case, and it was up to them to mend it. If they failed to do so, Rupa would be able to point to it as an important issue on which the benefit of the doubt ought to be given to the accused.

Late that afternoon, General Luther was visited by the Attorney-General and given a report on the day's events. Luther had already heard Claud Montrose's version, in which Rupa came off badly, but Herbert Zanjo had a different tale to tell.

Luther leaned back in Daniel Moorhouse's chair, gazing at the ceiling as Moorhouse had often done, and listened with growing disquiet to the Attorney-General.

Behind Luther's head, in the place where the deposed Prime Minister once hung a large colour portrait of himself addressing a rally, there was an even bigger official photograph of the General, stern and bemedalled.

"Our system of justice," Zanja explained, "is based on the Anglo-Saxon model as you know. It's not the task of the defence to prove innocence. The prosecution must prove guilt. If there's any doubt in the court's mind, they usually come down on the side of the accused, particularly in a capital case such as this."

"Well then," Luther said evenly, "you're the prosecution. Let's see you prove guilt."

"It's not as easy as that, sir," Zanja replied. "We can't patch up our case as far as Molvi's taking the van is concerned. Mr Montrose suggested to the court today that there might have been two sets of keys hanging on hooks in the administration office. That would have been a full explanation. But one of my staff has been down to the police car pool, and that simply cannot be so. The spare keys are locked away, in a safe. They don't hang on a hook."

"And we can't get anyone to say otherwise?"

Zanja glanced quickly at Luther to see if he was joking. Then, deciding he was not, replied quietly: "Well, *I* can't, anyway."

Luther took a cigarette and lit it. "What do the judges say?" he asked.

"I get the feeling that their confidence has been shaken. Don't forget, the nub of the defence submissions is that this is a fraudulent case launched against Mr Moorhouse personally for political reasons, that the co-accused have been hired for the job, and that when it's over, they'll be rewarded and freed. If a link is proved – or even strongly suggested and not effectively disproved – between Mr Montrose and any of the co-accused, particularly Molvi, then the defence thesis is given weight."

"And that's what the judges say?" Luther asked thoughtfully.

"Not all of them. Mr Justice Kaye still seems on our side. But the Chief Justice and Mr Justice Wigram have definite suspicions. Apparently they were talking about it in the robing room just after the adjournment. Wigram said: 'Well, that's the end of that, then.' And the Chief Justice said something like: 'Unless Zanja can come up with an answer to this lacuna, I don't see we have any choice but to consider acquittal.' "

"What did Kaye say?"

"He just made a scoffing noise. He doesn't like Moorhouse of course. Kaye should have been Chief Justice, but Moorhouse superseded him and appointed Martyn in his place. So there's bad feeling there. I think the case for Moorhouse would have to be very strong indeed before Kaye could find it in his heart to acquit."

Luther smiled. "So," he said, "one down, two to go."

"A lot depends on Moorhouse's own evidence," Zanja said. "The defence should start its case tomorrow or the next day." He looked diffidently across at Luther. "I understand they've been having a bit of trouble getting witnesses."

"So I hear," Luther said, seemingly uninterested. He had no intention of discussing the intricacies of the case with Zanja, although he knew the Attorney-General must have his own suspicions. Suspecting was one thing: knowing was quite another.

Yet Zanja needed some reinforcement. He was treating the case too much like an academic exercise for Luther's liking. He lacked the killer instinct and now, more than ever, this had become an essential quality.

Luther said emphatically: "This trial is vital to us, Mr Zanja – to the island as a whole. I can't stress that strongly enough. Moorhouse can't be allowed to escape on a technicality. I want you to do whatever you need to do to get a conviction. If you succeed, there's $50,000 as a bonus for you, tax free, on the day the judges pass the death sentence. Do I make myself clear?"

Luther waited for Zanja to show some emotion, to argue, at least to be startled, but nothing showed on the man's face. After a pause, he merely asked: "What about a conviction without a death sentence?"

"Nothing," said Luther. "You just get your normal fee. I want that death sentence. I won't settle for anything less."

They stared at each other in silence.

Then Luther brought the meeting to an end. "Thank you for coming around, Mr Zanja," he said. "I won't detain you any longer. If you hear anything fresh, please let me know right away."

"I will, sir. Thank you."

244

Luther waited until the Attorney-General had left, then phoned Montrose on the secure line, but he was not in. Luther dialled Clifton. It was better to discuss the matter with Alec anyway, he thought. Claud was too emotional and unreliable.

Luther outlined his conversation with Zanja, and Clifton listened without comment. At the end he merely said: "Well, we'll have to do something about the judges then, won't we?" And he hung up, promising to call again in ten minutes.

When Clifton did phone, it was to say he had dug out the personal files on Chief Justice Martyn and Judge Wigram, and that they contained information which might be useful.

"Didn't Moorhouse have his own personal dossiers on people?" Clifton asked. "He was supposed to keep them on his friends and enemies, just in case they came in handy one day."

Luther said: "That's right – they're in the strongroom next door, I think. I had a look at them to see what they said about us."

"Anything interesting?"

"Not too bad," Luther replied. He saw no reason to tell Clifton that his own personal file, which he had destroyed, contained detailed information about his tangled private life which was all too accurate, but gave no indications of Moorhouse's sources. Clifton's though, was scanty, and Montrose's contained some information about questionable tactics he used in getting confessions, and nothing much after that.

Luther called a meeting for that night with Clifton and Montrose, and then walked through to Bob Sehai's office and got him to open the strongroom.

Luther went in alone, and found the files on the three judges: Martyn, Wigram and Kaye. He was glad to see that they were all bulky. He shut himself in his office and settled down to read.

In the Central Gaol at about the same time, Stephen Ayer heard with relief the cell door slam shut and the boots of the warders fading into the distance. There would only be one more check on him; at nine o'clock, someone would peer through the spy-hole in the door to make sure he was all right, and then the light would be switched off.

The conditions for Ayer and the others had improved immediately they agreed to go along with the plot against Moorhouse, but there was still a dreamlike quality about life.

In some ways, it didn't feel as if they were telling anything other than the truth, even when they were telling lies. When you are held in solitary confinement, in darkness, and disorientated by people like Montrose, what after all is the truth? Is today Tuesday or Thursday? Or Sunday? Is your wife going to be raped by Montrose's goons? Are you ever going to get out? Are you going to die in a stinking hole? Is the hand of friendship which Montrose suddenly held out, and which you seized with such obvious relief that day in the interrogation room, a ploy, or was he really your ally?

And anyway, isn't it necessary to make some concessions to let yourself, and your family, waken from the nightmare?

So perhaps it was true what Montrose said, that Moorhouse was really the villain.

If you thought about it long enough in the right conditions, you could convince yourself that the plot had existed, that you had really met Molvi and the others, and had organised riots.

Was that any more unreal than the cell, and the fear, and the overwhelming stink, and the silence?

But now his conditions had improved and Ayer was stronger. He knew the time, and the day. He saw his wife and she was well. His official salary had been restored, with back pay. The food he ate came from a restaurant, paid for by the Government, or from home if that was what he preferred.

He opened a can of beer, still cold from the prison refrigerator, and his hand trembled as he drank.

He could fool himself no longer. *Oh Jesus, it's such a mess,* he thought.

He remembered Montrose's face in the court when he had stared over at the dock with such undisguised hatred. Of course, he was looking principally at Molvi, but Ayer had felt the effect as well.

And that afternoon, when Montrose suddenly appeared in the doorway of the court, to listen to Molvi. His face! Such hardness, such contempt.

But now the case was crumbling around them, held up only by the lies of himself, Rana and Kataria. And Ayer knew that, whatever the consequences, he no longer wanted to be part of it.

He took another long swallow of beer, picked up a pen and began to write:

To the Chief Justice of the High Court of St David's, The Hon. Mr Justice C. V. Martyn.

My Lord,
I am one of the co-accused with Daniel Moorhouse, and I beg your Lordship's indulgence in reading this letter.

I pleaded guilty to all four charges, and gave evidence, under oath, that I carried out Mr Moorhouse's orders in organising riots in Port Lombard which resulted in the deaths of four people.

I must now tell you that I perjured myself. Daniel Moorhouse is innocent of these charges, and so am I. To my knowledge, Joseph Rana and Tilak Kataria are also innocent.

We were forced into taking part in this plot by Mr Claud Montrose, the Commissioner of Police and now a Minister in the Revolutionary Council. I myself was kept in solitary confinement in conditions amounting to mental torture, and was told that my wife would be sexually assaulted unless I co-operated. I eventually agreed to do so.

Mr Rana and Mr Kataria could tell similar tales, but I fear they are still too scared to do so.

We have all been promised that, whatever the verdict and sentence of the court, we will be pardoned and released. The target of the Revolutionary Council is Daniel Moorhouse. They want him hanged. I feel that I can no longer be part of this despicable plot, whatever the cost.

I therefore request that my plea be changed to Not Guilty.

I should be glad of the opportunity of taking the witness stand once again, and of telling the truth in public.

Yours faithfully,

Stephen Vincent Ayer

Ayer folded the letter, sealed it in an envelope and put it in the inside pocket of his suit jacket, which hung in a plain wooden cupboard.

He opened another beer, and noticed that his hand had stopped trembling. But just then, without warning, he felt the tears running down his face and his body shook with violent sobs, totally out of his control, and he could not be sure whether they were tears of relief, or fear of the uncharted path onto which he was setting himself and his family.

At last, exhausted, Ayer fell asleep.

The following morning, he found he was calm, as if the act had already been done and the crisis passed. He dressed and breakfasted as usual. At eight o'clock the warders escorted him to the prison van, along with the others. Except for Moorhouse, of course.

Moorhouse was always kept out of their way, in case he tried to speak to them in private. Ayer desperately wanted to see Moorhouse now, although he knew he would have no chance until they were in the dock under the eyes of prison and court officials.

The drive and the wait seemed interminable. The letter in his jacket pocket was almost a physical presence. He could feel its hardness, its angular edges, pressing against his chest.

When they were taken up, Ayer manoeuvred to make sure he would be sitting nearest Daniel Moorhouse.

He could hear Moorhouse's feet coming up the stone steps leading to the dock, and then his head and shoulders appeared and he was taking his seat, face impassive, ignoring his fellow-prisoners and looking quickly into the body of the court to see who he knew, and if his wife was there.

Ayer leaned across: "Mr Moorhouse," he whispered.

Moorhouse looked startled, as if a toad had spoken. "Yes?"

Whisper: "I've written a confession."

A snort: "Another one."

"The real one this time. I can't go along with this any more. I've written to the Chief Justice, telling him the truth."

For an instant, there seemed to be hope in Moorhouse's eyes. "What have you done with it?"

"It's in my pocket."

"It would be best if you gave it to my lawyer," Moorhouse instructed. "He'll see that it's passed on safely."

"All right."

The fact that Moorhouse and Ayer were talking in low voices – the first time exchanges of any sort had been seen between the deposed Prime Minister and his co-accused – attracted some attention in the court. The Attorney-General, Zanja, noticed it and doubted that it boded any good for the prosecution case, or for his $50,000. Moorhouse's counsel, Charles Rupa, also watched, but with interest, and when his client signalled him to come across, he moved with a speed surprising in a man so obese.

Moorhouse leaned forward to whisper: "Ayer says he has made a full confession. The truth this time. It's in his pocket. He wants to give it to the Chief Justice."

Rupa nodded, and anyone watching his face would not have seen the slightest change of expression.

"Can you take it?" Moorhouse asked.

"No," Rupa whispered in return. "He can't be seen giving me anything. It might be confiscated, and we'd have a devil's own job getting it back. Wait till after the tea adjournment. I'll bring over a case file for you to look at, and you can slip it in there and hand it back to me."

Rupa was scarcely back at his place before the court was called to order, and the three judges filed in, scarlet-robed and bewigged, professionally impassive.

Ayer's heart was thumping so loudly he felt it could be heard throughout the chamber. Moorhouse turned away, ignoring him again. There had been no word of thanks, and he had expected none: the Prime Minister – for Ayer still thought of him in that way – accepted the change of heart as a fact and as no less than Ayer's duty. But for his part, Ayer felt gratitude towards Moorhouse, and a closeness, almost a conspiracy between them. He was aware of stirrings on his right from Rana and Kataria, but he paid no attention.

The morning passed slowly, again taken up with procedural arguments, supported by references to piles of law books, stacked on the clerk's tables in the well of the court. It became clear that Rupa was in no hurry. He went out to the High Court library for other authorities, and the clerk's messengers returned, their arms high with old volumes.

Ayer lost track of the arguments and finally stopped listening. He stared at the public benches, sorting out who he knew and trying to decide whether they were on the side of the prosecution or the defence, or neutral. Rana and Kataria's families were there, whispering furtively to one another. Nora, his wife, was staring intently at Rupa's back as he addressed the court, and he felt his stomach contract. He wished he could let her know what he was doing, and he felt overwhelming gratitude and love for her. Watching her profile from the dock, and her auburn hair which shone, Ayer wondered what she would think of him retracting his confession, whether she would be pleased with him or angry, and consider that she and the children had been placed in jeopardy. But he did not believe Montrose would dare harm her now. Things had gone too far.

However, Ayer's salary would probably be stopped once again, and Nora would have to live on their savings. There wasn't much: but enough for six or seven months, if used carefully.

And long before that time, the High Court should have thrown out the case and declared them all free men.

Ayer hesitated to think what might happen if the court rejected his evidence and found them guilty. He blotted this possibility from his mind. The judges were trained to discover the truth and administer justice, and this they would do. The courts remained impartial and independent, even after the coup.

But whatever happened, he could no longer be part of the plot against Daniel Moorhouse. His conscience lay too heavily on him, and now he was stronger, it would not let him rest.

When the tea adjournment came, Rupa was still dealing with procedural matters, arguing in that dry, scholarly manner judges appreciate, but without obviously playing for time. He knew that if they became bored, or he moved too far from the point, they would cut him short and move on to hear Moorhouse's evidence.

And Rupa was anxious to postpone this, at least until the Bench had seen Ayer's confession, and had called the defendant for re-examination.

That would be the moment for Daniel Moorhouse to take the stand, and complete the demolition of the state case.

No one, except Moorhouse himself, noticed the casual way Ayer slipped the letter from his inside jacket pocket and onto his lap below the level of the wooden partition, out of sight of the prison officer escorts alongside. Ayer left it there for several minutes, before inching it along towards Moorhouse.

Moorhouse saw it from the corner of his eye and shifted position, stretching his arms out beside him as if he was becoming stiff with the hours of sitting. His right hand fell on the envelope and, in one movement, scooped it along the bench and under his thigh. Ayer dared not watch.

Moorhouse once again became attentive to the proceedings, making occasional notes on the pad before him as he had done throughout the long weeks of the trial.

Moorhouse glanced towards the prison officers, but they looked bored and unconcerned. He took his notes from the wooden ledge in front of him and studied them closely, shuffling through the pieces of paper.

At one point, Ayer's letter joined the pile and quickly became buried in its midst.

Moorhouse did not look at Ayer.

After the tea interval, in the few minutes before the court resumed, Rupa came over to the dock as he had promised, bearing with him a file of case notes, and he embarked on an earnest discussion with Moorhouse concerning some minor points. Their voices were low and did not carry. Court officials and prison warders watched without interest.

At one point, Moorhouse took the file and leafed through it, and this was followed by a further discussion. Then he shrugged dismissively and handed the file back. Rupa carried it away.

Ayer's confession sat safe between the pages of the file throughout the morning, while procedural arguments continued. It was extraordinary how Rupa was able to string them out, without apparently repeating himself, although at the $500 a day he cost not only Moorhouse but all his other clients, this was a device he had used many times when a trial was drawing to a close without him having another case in immediate prospect, and when his clients could afford the fees.

As soon as Rupa had the letter, Ayer sat tensely, waiting. He kept expecting the lawyer to produce it with a flourish, stopping the case in its tracks. He thought he might be immediately summoned into the witness box to give fresh evidence. He wasn't ready for the fact that nothing would happen.

Rupa did not read the letter, or glance at the case file into which it was supposed to have been slipped, or make an announcement of any sort.

He wished he could ask Moorhouse what was going to happen, but when the lunch adjournment came, the deposed Prime Minister was hustled away first as usual, and did not even look across at Ayer.

Ayer had an acute feeling of anti-climax, which without warning sent him spiralling into a depression so deep that he found it difficult either to move down the stone stairs to the cells, or to talk. The confession which he had made after agonised soul-searching and at considerable personal risk, suddenly seemed a shabby thing of no particular consequence.

Rupa had not been bothered to read it. The trial had not been dramatically halted. Moorhouse was as silent and alone as he had been throughout. No one had thanked Ayer or seemed in the least grateful, and he did need to be thanked and praised for the sacrifice he was making.

Yet no one seemed to care.

Ayer could not eat lunch. He lacked the energy or the will to swallow, and the food seemed dry in his mouth and totally inedible. He spat it back onto the plate.

Rana and Kataria, who were in the holding cell with him, were first curious and then anxious about him, but he felt too sad and betrayed to talk. Ayer shook his head slowly at their questions, and took himself off to the bed in the corner where he sat as motionless as if he had been turned to stone.

He rallied slightly when they were escorted back to the courtroom for the afternoon session, thinking that probably Rupa had waited to see the judges during the lunch break, and that an announcement would be made immediately they resumed.

But Rupa continued with the procedural arguments as if nothing had happened, and the long afternoon dragged on. No one looked at him with special interest. Indeed, no one seemed to be looking at him at all.

At the end, Ayer and the others were returned to the Central Gaol. Still he could not eat: but he could drink, and he persuaded the warders to bring him half a dozen beers – he had asked for twelve but they refused – and he drank his way steadily through them and fell into a dreamless sleep.

Rupa had in fact handed the confession in to the court at lunchtime, after reading it first to make sure of the contents and then transferring it to a fresh envelope.

The original envelope had in any case been slit open by the time he got it: Moorhouse had obviously been making sure of the contents too.

As procedure demanded, he took the letter round to the Registrar of the High Court and asked that it be given urgently to the Chief Justice. This the Registrar promised to do.

Chief Justice Martyn was, however, entertaining a guest to lunch. A visiting British jurist had come to observe a few days of the trial, but was having to return to London the following morning and so would miss Moorhouse's evidence.

Martyn put the letter aside, meaning to read it before the resumption, but it slipped his mind until he and his brother Judges were actually taking their places on the Bench, and he had to save it for later in the day. It was not a *habeas corpus* application, and it would surely keep.

Later in his Chambers, stirring a cup of tea automatically as he read, and the old, dry skin on his slightly skeletal face wrinkling as he grimaced and frowned, Martyn wondered where this latest twist left the prosecution. Did Zanja know what his prime witness – the only man alleging a direct link with Moorhouse in the organisation of the riots – had done? Probably not, as the new confession had been sent via Rupa.

Martyn decided to call in his brother Judges, Wigram and Kaye, to inform them of the development, but before he could, his telephone rang and he was speaking to General Luther himself.

"Chief Justice, I'm sorry to bother you at this time of day, but I wonder if I could possibly impose upon you?" Luther said, his voice suitably respectful because, after all, the judiciary was independent and traditionally kept its distance from the Government.

"If I can help you, General Luther, I shall do my best," Martyn replied in his clipped, precise tones.

"A matter of national importance has suddenly arisen and I would dearly like your guidance on it," Luther said. "Do you think it would be possible for me to call on you at your earliest convenience this evening? I could come round to your residence."

"Good heavens no, my dear General," Martyn replied, flattered by the military ruler's tone. "Let me come round to see *you*. What time will you be at home?"

"I'll be there in thirty minutes," Luther said, and it suddenly seemed to have become a firm date.

Martyn hesitated briefly before agreeing. "I'll see you then," he said.

In fact it was almost an hour before Martyn's chauffeur-driven car was admitted through the gates of the Prime Ministerial residence, and he was ushered into Luther's study, where the General shook his hand warmly and offered him a fine malt whisky.

Luther settled back in a big leather armchair. He reminded Martyn that the President of St David's was reaching the end of his term of office in four weeks, and it had now been established that he did not wish to be reappointed, so Luther himself had decided to assume the Presidency and leave vacant the post of Prime Minister. He would rule under martial law, with executive powers.

The Chief Justice observed: "No constitutional challenge to your administration has been brought before any court on the island, General – at least, not so far. We have not been called upon to pronounce on the issue."

"But between us," Luther said, "if a challenge was made, what would be the likely outcome?"

Martyn sipped his whisky in the flawless uncut crystal glass. "In a specific instance, it is impossible for me to say," he replied primly. "But in general, there are a number of precedents. Usually the doctrine of necessity is invoked."

"What does that mean?" asked Luther.

"It means that the court gives you the right to continue with your administration, usually within specified broad limits, because if they rejected you and you resigned, there would be a governmental vacuum, and if they rejected you and you stayed, the judiciary would not be able to countenance prosecutions brought by you. So either the rule of law would break down, or you would appoint your own courts, with your own judges and rules, and the result might be the gravest injustices."

"So that's what your finding would be – that we should continue in office?"

"I doubt that it would be *my* finding, General," Martyn said, giving a smile which reminded Luther strongly of a death's head. "The High Court would probably not be called upon to decide. It would be a matter for our brothers in the Supreme Court, I should think. But the outcome would almost certainly be as I have sketched."

"Splendid," said Luther charmingly. "I must say it is gratifying to see how well the judiciary operates on St David's. It's exactly as it should be, learned, fair and, above all, independent. Beyond reproach really. One hears so often criticisms of various sectors of society, particularly in government, but none about the judiciary. Well, virtually none. The judiciary is one of the cornerstones of our civilisation, and we must ensure that its status and reputation are not eroded. Remind me, Chief Justice, how long have you held your present position?"

"Six years now," Martyn said, a slightly reproving edge to his voice.

"That long!" Luther sounded shocked. "A man of your calibre! You should have been moved up to the Supreme Court by now. Surely you ought to be next in line as Chief Justice of that court!"

"It's kind of you to say so, General," Martyn replied. "However, my days in the High Court are certainly busy and full of interest."

"I daresay. But nonetheless, can the island afford to let talent such as yours be spent there when the Supreme Bench – and the nation – could derive far more benefit from it?"

Martyn laughed deprecatingly. "That is for others to decide," he simpered. "Luckily it is not a judgment I am called upon to make."

"No," Luther agreed. "But I am. I shall be here for at least another year, probably two, and in that time, I intend making changes."

"That is your prerogative, General."

"For example, there will be two vacancies on the Supreme Court Bench within eight months."

"Ah yes," Martyn said, "but both the retirements will be junior judges."

Luther had to stop himself grinning. So the talking skull was keeping a close watch on the job prospects above.

"One of the appointments could be of a senior Justice," he pointed out. "That also is my prerogative. And it could be on the firm understanding that the person concerned would be the next Supreme Court Chief Justice. The present incumbent retires in twelve months."

"It would mean superseding the others!" Martyn replied, the corners of his mouth twitching as if undecided whether or not to smile again.

"Exactly."

Martyn did smile then. "That would not make you very popular," he said.

"We military men are used to unpopularity," Luther said heartily. "It's like water off a duck's back to us. Another malt whisky, sir?"

"Thank you." His bony hand held out the crystal tumbler and Luther poured a generous measure.

The General raised his glass in a toast: "To the next Chief Justice of the Supreme Court of St David's!"

Martyn lifted his glass. "Yes indeed," he murmured. They drank, and Luther looked frankly across at his guest.

"May I speak candidly, sir?"

"But of course, General."

"It has been a busy and, in many ways, confused time for my colleagues and me over the last few months. So much to do: so much to find out. The previous administration left some extraordinary messes, as we both know. And it had started some actions which had not yet become public, but which were of vital importance. One of these concerned the judiciary."

"Oh?" Martyn was listening with close attention.

"I don't want to mention any names at this stage, you understand. In fact, I hope I won't ever be obliged to mention any names. But briefly, the previous administration had been investigating land deals undertaken by certain judges. This concerned valuable sites which were allocated to the judges by that administration at a price which I'm sure everyone would agree was derisory. One per cent of the real value."

"It wasn't only judges who benefited from this," Martyn put in swiftly. "Others did as well. Senior civil servants. And members of the military."

"Quite so," Luther replied smoothly. "However, it was not the military nor the senior civil servants who were under investigation by the previous government. It was the judiciary. We can only speculate on the reasons for this. Now according to the documents we saw when we took over, the allocated sites were resold by certain judges after two or three years in direct contravention of the terms on which they had been given. As we both know, the land was for the judges themselves to live on, and specifically not to make an enormous financial killing on the open market. The sites could not be resold for twenty years." Luther sipped his malt whisky. "In one case . . ." he said ". . . and again, no names . . . the judge concerned first transferred the land to his wife, and *she* sold it. It was a prime site in the diplomatic quarter of Port Lombard, and the profit was something like $100,000. Not bad by any standards."

Martyn sat silent and uncomfortable. As they both knew, General Luther was talking about him.

"The terms of the allocation are capable of more than one interpretation," the Chief Justice put in quietly, breaking the silence.

"No doubt. And the previous administration was preparing to let the various interpretations be argued in open court. Can you imagine what they would have done to the prestige of the judiciary?"

Martyn could imagine only too well. "It would have been ruinous," he admitted.

"Exactly! Whatever the rights or wrongs of the case, there would have been an unwarranted scandal. The careers of talented and dedicated men would have been destroyed, tainted by the actions of the previous government."

Luther rose and walked across to the large windows which looked across the acres of trim green lawn, shrubs and trees.

"You know, Chief Justice," he said. "I sometimes lie awake at night and I thank God – I thank God! – that we acted in time to save this island. Heaven knows what would have happened otherwise! Our security would have been put at risk: our friends in the Western alliance would have been compromised. Men who have dedicated their lives to the service of this island would have been pilloried, their reputations besmirched by scandal. There *was* a plot, Chief Justice. It was aimed at you. At many of your brother judges. At me. At many of my senior officers. We caught it just in time. And now, thank God, it is running its natural course through our courts."

"But not doing very well," the Chief Justice observed.

"Oh? Why is that?"

"There's the matter of the police vehicle which was used on the day of the Democratic Front meeting, and the Log Book marked out to Mr Montrose. There are contradictions in the evidence of Mr Montrose and the defendant, Molvi. And now, the letter from the defendant Ayer."

"What letter?" Luther asked cautiously.

"I don't have it with me or you could read it. Ayer has retracted his confession and changed his plea to one of Not Guilty."

Luther managed to hide his shock. "For what reason?"

"He says there is no truth in the state case. He says he was made to suffer mental torture which is why he agreed to perjure himself. He asks to be recalled to give fresh evidence."

"And will you recall him?" Luther asked quietly, standing very still against the window.

"I imagine we will be obliged to. I have not discussed it with my brother judges. I read the letter only a few minutes before coming here."

Luther sighed, and returned to his leather armchair. He opened a box of Havana cigars, offered it to the Chief Justice and took one himself. The rich blue smoke wreathed around their heads.

"The previous administration still moves like a phantom on this island," Luther said softly. "Not content with the dangerous mischief it indulged in while in power, it tries to carry on, perverting, misrepresenting, and no doubt now bribing poor Ayer into agreeing to a set of fantastic lies. But thank God for our judiciary! That is where I set my hopes." Martyn was watching him intently. "That is where this island looks for justice."

"What can the High Court do?" Martyn asked, his voice neutral. "Our hands are tied by the facts of the case."

"Of course they are. No one would have it any other way. If you are convinced that the man is innocent, that he is being framed by my government" – Martyn made a dismissive gesture – "then certainly you must acquit him. But please do not acquit him simply because such and such a thing did not happen, such and such contradiction is there. If there is a mandatory provision in the law which vitiates the trial, then we cannot help it and he must be set free. We cannot expect the courts to lay down new principles of law to apply only to Moorhouse. But what I mean is, this country after all is ours too. Let us not therefore do anything on mere technicalities that will have the effect of further destroying it. Do you understand what I'm saying?"

"Perfectly," the Chief Justice said.

"If the judges were to take a *technical* view of the Moorhouse case, then as hard as I tried, I would find it extremely difficult to persuade my own colleagues not to use this as a precedent and, in their turn, take a technical view of certain other investigations which are pending before us. Who knows where it would all end? Judges in the dock! Certainly not in the interests of the nation."

"Quite."

Luther refilled both their glasses. "What do you think will happen about Ayer?"

"I don't know. Really, it's too early to say. I will have to consult my brother judges. We work by consensus in these matters."

"Mr Justice Kaye is on our side, isn't he?" Luther asked bluntly.

Martyn was flustered, slightly off-balance. "Broadly speaking, yes," he admitted finally.

"And you are on our side."

It was a statement rather than a question, but Martyn knew it required a reply. He nodded slowly. "Yes," he agreed.

"Which leaves Mr Justice Wigram."

"My brother Wigram is strongly against."

"So I hear. Of course, he's the same Wigram who had two plots of land allocated to him."

"Two?" Martyn had known only of one.

"Certainly. One in Port Lombard, and the other in Galloway. According to Moorhouse's information, he netted $93,000 on both deals."

"Even so. I am not sure whether my brother would be inclined to take a broader view of the issues involved in the case," Martyn said thoughtfully. "He insists on a rigorously technical view."

"But it's still two to one, isn't it?" Luther pointed out.

"Yes, that's true. There would be a majority against him. Providing of course, that the case is sustainable in law."

"Oh, of course."

"And that isn't yet clear."

"Naturally not."

"We have yet to hear Moorhouse's evidence. And then there's the problem about Ayer."

"Yes. Will you hear him again?"

"I think we will have to."

"When?"

"I'm not sure. The defence will probably try to recall him before Moorhouse gives evidence, so it could be as early as tomorrow."

"I think," said Luther slowly, "that it would be better if Mr Ayer's performance was delayed. If he was given a chance to consider his actions, perhaps wiser counsels would prevail. We don't know what sort of pressure Moorhouse has put him under or what promises have been made. Ayer is the real weak link in the chain, isn't he?"

"That is the way it appears at the moment. His testimony would be crucial. He is the only defendant who alleges a direct link between the plot and Daniel Moorhouse."

"Then please give Mr Ayer a few days to think, Chief Justice. Is that an unreasonable request?"

"Not at all, General. It seems perfectly proper."

"Will you have a word with Justice Wigram and Judge Kaye? Or would you prefer me to?"

"I will speak with them. If it is necessary for you to see my brother Wigram, I will so advise."

"Excellent." He raised his glass again. "All hail to thee, Chief Justice of the High Court, soon to be Chief Justice of the Supreme Court!"

Luther laughed. "That sounds like a quotation from something."

"*Macbeth*," said Martyn. "Not a happy choice."

Chapter Thirty-five

They moved along Nelson Avenue, six of them, their faces occasionally lit, then shadowed, by the street lamps on the way, walking purposefully although not aggressively.

There was no one else on the road, not at ten o'clock at night in suburban Port Lombard. Most of the servants had gone off down to their quarters at the ends of the gardens, this being a Thursday night.

The men were young and, from the way they moved, fit. The night was cool: the sultry, humid air of summer had given way to the pleasanter temperatures of winter.

The man in the lead, a pace ahead of the rest, wore a white cotton shirt, half-unbuttoned to show off the thick bush of black hairs covering his chest and hard belly. The trousers he wore were tight around his buttocks and thighs and flared out over his shoes, and, because he wore no underpants, the material bulged obviously over his crotch. He had a strong, handsome face and his full lower lip seemed almost to pout.

Behind him, the others were also casually dressed: jeans, flared trousers, leather belts whose big buckles fastened around waists on which there was no fat. Their chests were broad and strong under their open-necked shirts.

They walked quietly, rubber-soled shoes making no sound on the concrete pavement or the tarmac street, and turned in to Number 34. There was a light on in one of the front rooms, probably the living-room, and it glowed dully through the drawn curtains. One of the windows there was open too, and was not burglar-barred.

257

Four of the men peeled off and headed for it.

The leader and a short, stocky man with a thick bull neck walked to the front door and rang the bell. They grinned at one another.

In the hallway, a light clicked on and they could see a figure through the frosted glass panel on the door, but it was difficult to tell immediately if it was a man or a woman.

Nora Ayer called out: "Who is it?"

"Mrs Ayer?" The leader's voice was respectful.

"Yes. Who is that?"

"I'm a friend. I've got some news about your husband. It's important."

They heard her fumble with the safety chain on the door, and then the key turned and she stood silhouetted against the light.

"We're very sorry to disturb you, Mrs Ayer," the leader said. "We're friends of your husband. May we come in?"

They could see her hesitate.

The leader smiled charmingly. "It's a bit conspicuous out in the open. We'd be in trouble if anyone saw us."

"Oh of course," Nora said, flustered. "Please come in."

She closed the door behind them and led the way through to the living-room, but, even as she did so, a faint sense of unease overcame her, and she wasn't sure whether it was because of the men, or because of what they might have to tell her about Stephen.

"Won't you sit down?" she invited.

The leader smiled. "Thank you," he said, and, as he did so, Nora Ayer had her first chance for a good look at him and his friend, and she didn't like what she saw. But it was too late to go back.

She settled herself on a chair on the other side of the room and became determinedly businesslike. "You say you have news about my husband," she prompted.

"Yes we do. But excuse me, would you mind telling me if there's anyone else in the house?" He looked boldly across at her. Nora became alarmed, but she kept her voice calm.

"As a matter of fact, there is," she said.

The man grinned. "Your kids, right? Two boys and a girl. Unless you're hiding a man down there in your bedroom."

Nora Ayer stood up. "If you have something to tell me about my husband, please say it now. Otherwise there is no point continuing this conversation."

"Sit down, Mrs Ayer." The man's voice was flat. Neither he nor his friend had stirred but they watched her intently and she was very conscious of the strength and the menace in their bodies. "Please."

"No," Nora said firmly. "Tell me what it is you've got to say, and then you must leave at once."

"I'll tell you when you sit down," the man replied. They stared at each other in a battle of wills. Finally she sat.

Behind her, the curtains moved as in a breeze, and if the men noticed it out of the corner of their eyes, they did not shift their gaze from her face and breasts.

"Well," she said aggressively. "I'm sitting. What is it?"

"Your husband's worried about you."

"There's really no need."

The curtains moved again and, through the opening in the centre, the first man appeared.

"Well there is, really," the leader said easily, rising from his chair but not moving nearer, just standing. "I can understand why. You're a beautiful woman, Nora. You know that?"

"Get out of here!" Her voice was determined, yet for some reason she found she suddenly lacked the strength to stand.

"Oh don't get mad, Nora honey. We just want to get to know you."

She saw, with sickness in her throat, that the obscene bulge in his trousers was swelling, thrusting large against the material. She thought she should scream, but then she thought of the children.

Still he made no move towards her.

"If you don't get out of here this minute, I'll scream the place down," she threatened.

He grinned, and his hand lightly touched the bulge of his crotch. "Sure you'll scream, honey," he said softly. "But when it's in, you'll love it."

"GET OUT OF HERE!"

His laugh was gentle. "I like a woman with spirit," he said. "We don't mean any harm, baby. We've just come to give you a bit of what you've been missing." His eyes looked lazily past her. "All six of us."

Now she leapt from her chair and whirled around.

The young men waited in a row, thumbs in the waistbands of their trousers, and they were all smiling insolently at her.

"Silence in court!"

Everyone stood silently as the judges filed in, bowed and took their places. For a minute, they arranged papers, put on spectacles and stared quickly round to see who was present.

The Chief Justice said: "Before we begin, I think I had better inform the court that one of the defendants, Stephen Vincent Ayer, has written to me asking that his plea be changed from Guilty to Not Guilty. This should so be entered in the record."

There was a surprised buzz of conversation from the public benches and, in the dock, Rana, Kataria and Molvi stirred restlessly.

"Mr Ayer has also given some reasons for this and has asked that he be called for re-examination. It would not be proper for us to discuss the reasons at this stage, and we are all agreed" – he glanced at the judge on each side of him for confirmation – "that a decision on recalling Mr Ayer can be held in abeyance for the moment."

Rupa was on his feet at once. "My Lord," he said, "with respect I should like to apply that the defendant be called for re-examination immediately. The evidence he will give is likely to be of vital importance to this case, and to my client, Mr Moorhouse."

"Will it be of less importance if it is heard *after* Mr Moorhouse has been examined?" the Chief Justice asked.

"No, my Lord, not in the sense that it is vital to this case and will remain so. But it is my client's right to hear the evidence ranged against him before making a full and complete reply."

Martyn smiled indulgently down at the senior counsel. "That would be correct if Mr Ayer was pleading Guilty. But he is not. He now says he is *Not* Guilty. He has exactly the same rights as Mr Moorhouse and it is our decision that we will not hear him at present. We are ready to hear *your* client next, Mr Rupa."

Rupa protested further, saying that Moorhouse's case would be prejudiced, but the judges were unbending.

Ayer anxiously scanned the public benches for his wife. She usually sat as near to the dock as she could get, in the hope of snatching a word with him, or of being close enough to hear a request he might make, although sometimes if the queue outside formed early she would be forced to take a seat on the other side of the room, and they would stare helplessly but lovingly at each other.

On this day of all days, when his change of plea was announced and he needed her desperately, to tell from her face whether she supported him still, she was nowhere to be seen. It was bad enough not being able to discuss things with her. He was allowed only one visit a week, and it was not due for another three days. He had not been able to speak to her in court either, except to say hello, and that he loved her. And now she was not there.

Ayer felt acutely disappointed and, when it became clear he was not to be called immediately to give evidence, he lost interest in the proceedings and fell to worrying.

Nora had never been late before. One of the constant things about walking up those stone stairs from the cells was that at the top, within seconds, he would see her, fresh and beautiful and smiling a welcome. Even if they could not speak, they would look at each other for minutes, trying to exchange loving thoughts and wishes, and share fears. She always looked so good, and he knew she dressed every day for him, to show how much she cared.

Ayer was becoming so distracted that he scarcely noticed Moorhouse leaving the dock and walking solemnly over to the witness box to take the oath. It was only after Rupa was into the first few minutes of the Examination-in-Chief that he forced himself to concentrate.

Moorhouse's evidence was essentially the case against Claud Montrose. Moorhouse said he himself knew nothing about the disruption of opposition political rallies, or of a gang of men recruited to start riots. He had never heard the names of the ten until shortly before nine of them appeared on the police report as having been shot dead while looting. Moorhouse testified that he had been given a full list of this gang by Joseph Rana, who had told him they were controlled by the Commissioner of Police. He had been reluctant to believe this without clear evidence, and so did nothing about it. And then, within hours, he had been overtaken by the coup.

There were two important omissions from Moorhouse's Evidence-in-Chief: the first was he did not mention Montrose was suspected of running a protection racket on the island. Rupa had tried vainly to find a shop-owner prepared even to admit privately that such practices had taken place. This meant they were unable to produce independent evidence and it had been judged better to leave the matter alone, thus saving Moorhouse from being publicly pulled to pieces by the Attorney-General.

The second omission was the proof that Montrose had personally pocketed the $10,000 meant to be paid to his American informant for the list of CIA agents, and that unexplained amounts were constantly being deposited in cash into the Commissioner of Police's personal account. This evidence, even more damning in the light of Molvi's admissions about the van he had used and the implied links with Montrose, was simply unobtainable. Gordon Macgregor, manager of the National Bank of St David's, had been requested to produce Montrose's bank statements for the past two years, and a court order was obtained for this. But the statements showed Claud Montrose as having a current credit balance of $1,456.11, and that he had not once been overdrawn. The only payments into the account were regular transfers of salary from the Paymaster General's office.

The bank statements were lies from beginning to end, forgeries especially prepared for the occasion. Macgregor had new masters, and he was dancing to their tune.

Moorhouse's evidence continued throughout the day, and it was clear Rupa planned taking a good piece of the following week before handing his client over to Zanja for cross-examination.

By late Friday afternoon, the defendants were all back in their cells. In the van on the way, Ayer was closely questioned by Rana and Kataria about his change of plea, and urged not to be a fool. But he would not be swayed, and the others finally accepted the change. After all, they reasoned, it would do them no harm.

Montrose could hardly be angry with them: they were sticking to the bargain. Yet if the court accepted Ayer's version, it would be obliged to acquit everyone. Perjury charges might follow, of course, but Montrose had promised they could ignore any sentence passed by the court. They would be released, whatever happened. So whichever way they looked at it, it seemed they could not lose. They admitted it would be good, though, if somehow Daniel Moorhouse managed to win.

In the cell, Ayer asked the warder to bring him a couple of beers, and was told there were none left. Dinner that night, instead of being sent in by a restaurant, came from the prison kitchen and was inedible. Ayer had almost forgotten how vile the ordinary food was. It seemed this would be the price he had to pay for bucking Montrose.

He found he cared little about that, but he *was* becoming seriously worried about Nora. She had not been in court at all that day, and his own counsel, an ineffectual man clearly stung by the fact that the first news of his client's change of plea had come from the judges them-selves, had shrugged and said unconvincingly that he would make inquiries.

Ayer had no idea whether he had actually done so or not, although the man claimed later to have phoned their house and received no reply.

Perhaps the telephone was out of order: sounding as if it was ringing, but not actually doing so. Nora could be ill, down with a virus perhaps. Or it could be worse than that: she could have had a car crash, Ayer thought, his imagination working fast, and be lying unconscious in a hospital. Perhaps someone had broken into the house and murdered her. Perhaps . . . the more Ayer thought about it, the more upset and tense he became.

Montrose arrived unexpectedly at his cell that evening, carrying a bottle of whisky, two glasses and a brown paper bag.

Ayer started nervously when he saw him, but Montrose was in a strange, hyped-up mood and didn't seem concerned about the change of plea or the confession. Ayer became more confused and frightened.

Montrose sat on the bed beside him and poured two generous measures of whisky. He clinked glasses and murmured: "Good health!"

Montrose inquired about prison conditions, and how Ayer felt these days.

The man's eyes were shining, alive with some marvellous secret. He was nearly, Ayer thought, in ecstasy, as if he had suddenly discovered God. They had a second whisky and, as Ayer poured it, Montrose moved closer and a large, muscular hand touched Ayer's thigh. When he put the bottle down, Montrose did not move away, and Ayer felt his alarm growing: the hand stayed on his thigh.

Montrose spoke, soft and cajoling, ready now to tell his joke, share his secret: "Hey, Steve. Hey, come here."

"What do you want?" Ayer was feeling embarrassed.

"Come on. Bend your head closer. I want to whisper in your ear."

There was the hint of bubbling laughter in his voice. The hand caressed Ayer's thigh, going higher now.

"Oh shit, Claud. What are you doing? Listen, you're not my type," Ayer protested, trying to turn it into a joke.

Montrose's hand slid down between his legs and his lips brushed Ayer's ear, following even when the prisoner leant away in protest.

Montrose's voice was husky with, what? Humour? Lust? "Hey, big boy," murmured Montrose. "I got a surprise for you. You know what's in this packet?"

"Jesus, Claud, stop doing that! No I don't know. Look, for Christ's sake take your hands off. I'm not into that sort of thing."

262

Ayer tried to move away. Montrose kept his right hand where it was, but reached over with his left to put his whisky glass out of the way and pick up the packet. He wiggled it in front of Ayer's face.

"Surprise for you," he said archly. "Bet you can't guess what."

"Claud, I've no idea what. Tell me." Ayer tried to control his anger. He was not in a position to kick Montrose out.

"Open it and see," Montrose teased.

Ayer accepted the packet and pulled out what looked like a small bundle of material, stained brown and stiff in places, but soft and delicate in others. Montrose's hand had stopped rubbing.

"Shit, Claud, what is that?"

"What do you think?" Montrose's laughter could barely be suppressed. He leaned over and his tongue flicked into Ayer's ear.

Ayer jerked away, head twisting. It wasn't a joke any longer. "Fuck off, Claud," he said harshly. "What the hell is this?"

And suddenly there it was before him, making a slight ripping sound as he pulled it into shape and whatever had stained and stuck the material together gave up its hold: a pair of women's pants.

Ayer was shocked: "Christ, Claud. You really are a pervert. Where the hell did you get this?"

Montrose started to giggle and his eyes were aglow with delight. "You know what those stains are?" he asked confidentially.

"No. What?"

"Blood! And semen!"

"Oh Jesus." Ayer tossed the pants onto the cell floor in disgust.

"And guess whose they are?" Montrose was leering now.

"I've no idea. Whose."

Montrose began to laugh and he lay back on the bed, his hand sliding up to pat Ayer's stomach, and his fat body shook with mirth.

At last he recovered himself, although his voice was weak.

"Ah me!" he said, standing up and collecting the whisky bottle and the glasses. He sighed with the exhaustion of laughter. "Don't you recognise those, Stephen? I must say, you can't have been very observant."

A cold band of fear gripped Ayer's chest. "What do you mean?" he asked softly.

"I brought those panties from the emergency ward at the General Hospital. They belong to your wife. It seems she was dispensing her favours rather lavishly last night. Six blokes, one after the other. Bang, bang, bang. Some of them had her two or three times, I'm told. They call it stirring the porridge, apparently. Well, you can understand why, can't you?"

Ayer watched him, transfixed. "You're lying," he said, his voice hoarse.

"You think so? As your wife. Not now, I mean, but when she gets out of hospital. Seems some of the blokes were pretty big. They split her a bit. Maybe she wasn't really ready to take them. A few painful stitches

I'm afraid, and maybe even a new addition to the Ayer household in nine months' time! Who can tell with these things?"

"You're a liar, Montrose!"

"It's always so troublesome when guys like you suddenly shift from one camp to another, don't you agree, Steve? Innocent people get hurt sometimes. Sad really."

Whispering: "You're a fucking liar!"

"And you've got a little girl too, haven't you. Laura, isn't it? A pretty little thing if I remember. Can you imagine, there are some bastards I know in this town who get hard-ons when they think about little four-year-old girls. No, don't laugh." Ayer's face had gone chalk white. "They lure them away, lift their little dresses and – Christ, it's a mess."

Montrose was suddenly grim and his small eyes stared.

"Mostly kids that age don't survive," he said coldly.

He walked towards the cell door. " 'Night, Steve. Pleasant dreams. See you in court next week. I'll be looking forward to hearing your new evidence: me – and a couple of friends I know. 'Night."

The cell door slammed with a dull metallic bo-oom. Montrose was gone.

Ayer sat motionless, his breathing so shallow it seemed to have stopped, and he stared at the bloodstained material crumpled on the cell floor.

Tentatively he picked it up to inspect it, studying the label and the size, and recognising the small embroidered flowers on the side. He held it against his cheek and the cake-hard blood rasped against his skin.

Ayer began to howl, to howl like an animal, not screaming or crying, but baying his grief and anguish.

He charged the steel door, smashing his fists against it.

The sound echoed hollowly in his cell. Through the night Ayer howled. No one came.

Chapter Thirty-six

Sentences of death on Daniel Moorhouse and his four co-accused were passed by Chief Justice C. V. Martyn at midday on Wednesday 16 March 1977, after taking two months to consider the facts of the case and the points of law involved. The verdict was unanimous.

The Chief Justice recalled that only Moorhouse had entered a plea of Not Guilty, although during the trial the defendant Ayer had altered his original plea of Guilty for a period of four days before changing it back again, and unreservedly retracting his new confession.

The essential facts had been proved, and what confusions there were on some issues were not enough to cast doubt on the final outcome, let alone vitiate the trial. The Chief Justice chastised Moorhouse for betraying his position of high trust on behalf of a hidden political cause. This was a case, he said, which clearly called for exemplary punishment. No one could be above the law, and there were no mitigating factors. The plot had been ruthlessly conceived, and ruthlessly carried out. No words of remorse for the four murdered citizens had been uttered by any of the accused. They had shown no mercy, and they deserved none.

Chief Justice Martyn motioned to a court attendant, who stepped forward and held a stiff, black square of material over the judge's powdered wig.

The accused men stood, squashed into the dock, each with a prison warder escort in case they fainted or tried to escape. Ayer glanced across at Nora and made a wry face. She stared numbly back.

Physically, she had almost recovered from the attack, although she had lost weight and lines of tension now marked her face. Emotionally, Ayer dared not speculate but he knew instinctively the scars went deep. She had not blamed him, not when he had been taken to visit her in hospital – his price for retracting the second confession – nor at any stage afterwards. In the private hospital ward, they had been able to talk freely for the first time in months. His prison guard stayed outside the door. Ayer told her everything then, and she, haltingly, described her ordeal. They both wept.

Emotional energy, like courage, is an asset which reduces with expenditure and can be renewed only if the circumstances are right and time is available. The Ayers had run their reserves down to a dangerous level.

But still Nora remained the stronger of the two, and Stephen Ayer relied heavily on her for support.

Waiting for the Chief Justice to pronounce the sentences – a surreal prospect – Nora Ayer felt a shiver of apprehension and the skin on her arms prickled into goose pimples.

"Daniel Moorhouse," the Chief Justice intoned, his voice grave and ponderous, "it is the sentence of this court that you be taken to a place appointed, and there that you be hanged by the neck until you are dead. May the Lord have mercy on your soul."

The silence in the courtroom was utter and complete. Moorhouse's face was a mask of disdainful calm.

"Stephen Vincent Ayer." Ayer involuntarily held his breath and he knew his legs were trembling. "It is the sentence of this court that you be taken to a place appointed, and there that you be hanged by the neck until you are dead. And may the Lord have mercy on your soul."

Ayer found himself nodding. Out of the corner of his eye, he could see Joe Rana swaying slightly as his turn came.

"Joseph Montague Rana. It is the sentence of this court that you be taken to a place appointed, and there that you be hanged by the neck until you are dead. May the Lord have mercy on your soul."

Why are we taking this seriously? Ayer wondered suddenly. *The sentences will never be carried out. Moorhouse, yes. He's the one who will hang. But we will not.* Yet inside his brain, a voice said: *Who says so?* And Ayer answered: *Montrose has promised.*

Montrose has promised! Jesus, what a guarantee! Ayer felt a cold sweat break out on his forehead.

But then he remembered. Luther had also given an undertaking to Molvi. Luther was involved up to his neck, and he was not in the same category as Claud Montrose.

Ayer knew what they had to do: they must get a message to Luther, to make him repeat his solemn assurances to their families. That would settle things, and everyone could rest easy and wait it out. Except for Moorhouse.

The Chief Justice had passed the death sentence on Tilak Kataria and was doing the same on Molvi. Ayer looked down at the prisoner standing at the end of the dock, and he saw Molvi grinning foolishly at the judge, although it was impossible to know whether this was involuntary from nervousness, or whether he was remembering his evening with General Luther and was amused by the grim charade they were now going through.

The court attendant removed the black square from above the Chief Justice's head and Rupa was on his feet at once, his face angry but his manner continuing courteous.

"If your Lordships please, I request leave to appeal on behalf of my client."

Chief Justice Martyn nodded. Appeals against death sentences were automatic. "Of course," he said, and looked over at the counsels for the other defendants. "I presume you all require a similar order? Yes?" He held a quick conversation with Judge Wigram on his right, while screwing the top on his fountain pen. Judge Kaye collected up a small bundle of papers he had brought in with him.

"Silence in court!"

Everyone stood as the judges filed out and immediately they were gone, the prisoners were taken down to the cells.

Each was allowed to see his family before being returned to the gaol. Ayer held Nora wordlessly in a tight hug in the middle of his cell, his face buried in the soft freshness of her hair, until he became conscious of the physical reserve which she had shown since the attack: he tried not to think of it as a gang rape. It was as if she was forcing herself to accept this contact with him, her husband, and was trying desperately but unsuccessfully to relax into it.

"I love you," Ayer whispered. "I don't know what I'd do without you." Her hand patted his back automatically, as if he was a baby being comforted.

She pulled away from the embrace and avoided his eye.

They sat on the edge of the steel-framed bed while the prison escort officer watched from a chair on the other side of the bars.

266

"How are you feeling, Steve?" Nora asked, fumbling for a cigarette with hands which shook slightly.

"Fine. A bit numb."

"I didn't expect it to be a death sentence," she said bitterly. "I know they'd been talking about one, but it seemed impossible to believe. And now they've gone and done it. You could just feel the shock-wave going through the court. It was incredible."

"It'll never happen. Not to us, anyway. They just want Moorhouse."

"Yes."

Ayer felt alarmed that she did not sound as convinced as him. "You think there's something wrong?" he asked anxiously.

"I don't know. What do you think?"

"Montrose gave his word," Ayer offered.

Nora smiled at him. "So he did," she said brightly. "That's all right then."

"And Luther gave *his* word to Molvi."

"But not to you."

"No. Listen, I think that's something that's got to be rectified quickly. I'm sure all the other families will come in on it. Can you see Luther and get his firm assurance that everything's still okay?" Ayer asked.

"Will he see *us?*" Nora wondered.

"I don't see why not. We still hold some cards, after all. There's an appeal to be got through yet, and if we don't get proper guarantees from Luther himself, we could all change our pleas to Not Guilty. Then they wouldn't have a case at all."

"I suppose that's right. Fine, I'll see about it this afternoon. Everyone's here, so I'll get them to come home now and we'll talk about what to say. A big family pow-wow." She looked at him with sudden compassion. "I'm afraid it's going to be a long time yet," she said, her voice soft.

Ayer nodded reluctantly. "God knows how long the appeal will take," he said. "Probably another year. Then it should be over."

The prospect of twelve more months seemed intolerable, and Ayer felt his spirits sag.

The families were allowed half an hour with the condemned men and Nora Ayer left immediately this was up, as she wanted to catch the other wives before they left the court precincts.

By the time the prisoners were locked back in their cells, the families were seated at 34 Nelson Avenue, being served tea and biscuits. Everyone had been shocked at the sentences, and with this came new uncertainty. It was quickly agreed that Nora Ayer should write a letter to General Luther requesting an urgent and private interview, and that they should all sign it.

The letter was sent by Registered Post the following day, and they waited for a reply.

The days dragged on. At the end of the first week, everyone was becoming nervous, although in their prison visits, they glossed over the lack of response.

By the end of the second week, however, Rana's wife was in a state approaching hysteria. She had tried to telephone Luther's office and had got as far as his PPS, Bob Sehai, where she had come up against a blank wall. The General's calendar was full for several weeks, Sehai told her. It would not be possible to arrange a meeting. He also wondered aloud if such a thing would be proper anyway, as the case was under appeal and was, therefore, *sub judice.*

Nora Ayer summoned a second council of war, which agreed on the wording of a new letter, couched in blunt terms. Unless the families were seen quickly, it said, they would issue statements to the local and overseas press detailing the assurances that had been given to their husbands by senior officials of the military administration, and announcing that these were no longer acceptable. All the co-accused would apply to the Supreme Court to change their pleas to Not Guilty.

Nora Ayer marked the letter PERSONAL AND PRIVATE, and sent it Registered to Luther's official residence. She also telephoned Bob Sehai to inform him that it was on its way. She felt this would give Luther the opportunity to intercept it himself if he preferred not to have it read by members of his staff.

The effect was gratifying. Within three days, General Luther himself was on the telephone to Nora Ayer, inquiring solicitously after her health and wondering if it would be convenient for the families – one representative of each – to come to his residence for a private talk the following evening.

Face to face, Luther was even more charming than he had been over the phone. He served the three women drinks and offered them plates of canapes: Beluga caviar heaped on crisp biscuits and topped with tiny slivers of lemon, fresh shrimps on rye bread, stuffed mushrooms, imported cheeses and chunks of fresh pineapple; and gins and tonics, or Pimms No. 1, served in long crystal glasses.

Luther was in his uniform, giving the occasion an official air.

After the preliminaries, he apologised for not seeing them earlier. "You'll never believe how busy I'm being kept these days" – and they got down to business. Nora Ayer had been appointed spokesman for the wives. She took a place on the sofa next to the General, summoning all her reserves of energy to be pleasant and remain calm, reminding herself that this assured man with the firm handshake and the calm, steady eyes had the power of life and death over their husbands.

But it was Luther who took the initiative. "I imagine you ladies are worried about the sentences passed on your husbands," he said. "I can understand that. But you realise that the matter is out of my hands, for the moment at least. The courts of this country are independent: totally beyond the command of any man, least of all me. I cannot interfere. However, once the judicial process has been completed, then I can step

268

in. I now combine the functions of President and Prime Minister, and so all petitions for mercy come before me. Mercy is a Presidential prerogative."

"Yes, General," Nora said. "I think we all understand that. But what we want is your personal assurance that you *will* exercise your prerogative of mercy, and set our husbands free immediately it is in your power to do so."

"I can't anticipate the findings of the court, Mrs Ayer."

"I'm not asking you to. I'm asking you to promise that once the courts have finished with the case, and you as President are able to consider the question of sentences, that you will do so – favourably."

"Oh, I'll certainly do that," Luther agreed. "There's no question of it. Assurances have already been given, and they will be carried out in full."

"So you'll free our husbands?" Nora persisted.

"If that is the assurance, that is what will be done."

"But is it the assurance?"

"Mrs Ayer, I have given no personal assurances myself," Luther reminded her gently. "Others have, however. And they will be carried out."

"You gave an assurance to Molvi," Nora pointed out. "Or at least, he believes you did."

Luther said thoughtfully: "Mr Molvi. Yes, that's true enough. I did see him myself. What holds true for him holds true for everyone."

Nora had the uncomfortable feeling that Luther was ducking the issue, and she was not prepared to let him escape without being unequivocally nailed down, despite the slight restiveness already being shown by the other wives, who clearly thought she was being pedantic and even rude to a charming and civilised man who had already made it perfectly clear what he planned to do.

"We'd like to hear the assurance from you, if you don't mind, General," Nora said firmly. "I'm sure you'll appreciate our positions. Our husbands have gone along with a deal which allowed you to sentence Mr Moorhouse to death, and they themselves have been condemned to hang along with him."

"They won't hang with him, Mrs Ayer."

"Well then, perhaps they'll hang separately. Unless you give us your categorical assurance that you will pardon them and release them."

Luther sighed: "I've done that already."

"With respect, General, no you have not. For my peace of mind, please spell it out."

Luther smiled at her, a respectful, friendly smile. "Very well," he said. "I will see to it that your husbands are returned to you . . ." he caught Nora Ayer's expression ". . . in good health and unhung. Unhanged I suppose it should be. I will do this as soon as I am able to. On this you have my word as an officer and . . ." he grinned around the room ". . . as a gentleman. Will that do?"

"That will do very nicely thank you, General," Nora said.

"Now what about you ladies?" Luther looked at each encouragingly. "I know what a strain all this must be on you and your families, and I want to do what I can to ease it. How are you off financially, for example? I hope you don't mind my asking."

For the next half hour, Luther heard detailed complaints about their family finances and problems they were experiencing with their husbands away. He promised to give each of them $10,000, in addition to their husbands' salaries which were still being paid into family bank accounts.

Nora Ayer was on the point of refusing the money – she needed it all right, because with legal fees, their savings were almost exhausted and she would soon have to get a job, which in turn meant having to leave the children with friends during the day, but it was tainted money and she hated to touch it. In the end, she smiled and inclined her head gratefully. Even if she didn't use it, she felt, it might be useful to have the evidence of the $10,000 payment.

Luther was off at the cocktail cabinet preparing more drinks for everyone when Nora heard the dull click from inside her beige straw handbag. She glanced around guiltily in case anyone else had noticed it, but no one had.

It was a cassette recorder that had switched itself off at the end of the tape. It had been concealed in her handbag on the floor between herself and Luther, and she thanked God the General had not still been sitting there or he would surely have heard it.

All she had to do now was pray that the voices were audible.

For the rest of the meeting she was determinedly charming, and when she returned home and wound the tape back she found that, except for most of the comments by the other wives, her conversation with Luther and the final assurances had come through loud and clear.

Nora Ayer almost wept with relief and exhaustion.

Chapter Thirty-seven

The shockwave that swept St David's on the day Daniel Moorhouse was sentenced to die was more profound than Luther, Montrose and Clifton ever recognised.

It was not easy to detect. It did not manifest itself in violent demonstrations or strikes, because martial law was in force and harsh penalties would have been imposed.

But there was a change in the hearts of the people, a stiffening of resolve which, as the months passed, could grow to become obstructive and violent.

Until that point, the coup d'état had been something of a joke for many people, while being regarded as a good thing by others. It was time Moorhouse was kicked out, they argued, and it was certainly in the island's interests that the Russians be kept at bay. Who could say: it might do the place a bit of good to have army discipline imposed for a while. And in any case, elections would be held at some stage, so it wasn't as if Luther was planning to remain in charge forever.

But from the day of the verdict, the people began to distance themselves emotionally from the military. Moorhouse's popularity increased. Opposition parties, like the Democratic Front, were shaken from their lethargy and began working doggedly for the restoration of democracy.

No one wanted Moorhouse dead, and few people could be found who actually believed the state case against the deposed Prime Minister.

By common consent, Moorhouse was regarded as having been framed, although no one was certain quite how, and the benevolent paternal image which Luther had carefully fostered was destroyed.

The Democratic Front, which because of the anonymous letter and Sam Wallace's investigations in the High Street had more background information about the regime's leaders than anyone else in political life, felt the injustice, and their own impotence, most strongly.

By themselves, these facts were bad enough, but on a local level, the repercussions could be electorally disastrous. Moorhouse would become a martyr, and although the man himself might be gone, his Popular National Party would remain. The possibility of a sympathy vote for it could not be discounted. All the tremendous gains made by the Democratic Front could be totally negated. The PNP, under a new leader – God knows who – might then be swept back to power.

That was a prospect to be avoided at all costs. Albert Francis held lengthy talks on strategy with Sam Wallace, and decided that the only way to stop a sympathy vote for Moorhouse was for the Front itself to mount a vigorous campaign against the hanging.

In addition to attacking the basic injustice, this campaign – if sufficiently determined – would probably confuse many voters, especially if the Democratic Front outdid the PNP in its battle for Moorhouse's life. This should not be difficult. Moorhouse had run his party as a one-man operation, and now the one man was in gaol, it was in disarray. Most of his senior colleagues seemed to have been chosen for sycophancy rather than ability.

However, the Front would have to start quietly. Because of the Appeal, the conspiracy to murder trial remained *sub judice*, and the Front would risk legal action if it said too much, too early.

But there was nothing to stop Albert Francis from seeking an interview with General Luther. This took place the day after the General gave his personal assurances to the wives of the co-accused.

Francis took Sam Wallace with him, and made a strong plea that if it ever came to the point, Luther should not hesitate in using his Presidential powers to reprieve the former Prime Minister.

Luther asked, rather tartly, why the Democratic Front did not seem similarly concerned about saving the lives of the other four as well, and after toying for a wild instant with the idea of telling the General bluntly he did not think it necessary to worry about the regime's co-conspirators, whose necks were almost certainly in no danger, Albert Francis merely replied that, naturally, his remarks covered them all as it would surely be impossible to reprieve Moorhouse and execute the rest.

Luther merely grunted. At last he declared that he would abide by the decision of the courts. If the Supreme judiciary upheld both verdict and sentence, the General believed it would be improper for him then to intervene.

"Our courts have a proud tradition of freedom and independence," Luther lectured his visitors. "If the honourable Judges in their wisdom, having considered all the circumstances, say 'hang him', then I'll hang the blighter."

An hour after this meeting, Albert Francis addressed a press conference and repeated Luther's words. The representatives of the local radio and television stations, the *St David's Herald*, as well as other island magazines and newspapers, scribbled furiously in their note-books, but Francis doubted that much would survive the censorship. He was far more interested in the two foreign journalists present – one from United Press International, the other from the BBC in London – who sat silently at the back.

Of these two, the BBC man was the most important because almost everyone on the island now listened to BBC bulletins and to programmes like Radio Newsreel to find out what was going on in their own country. They certainly were not getting the information from local sources.

Later that night, the Francis press conference was the second item on the world news, and a more detailed account led Radio Newsreel.

Francis congratulated himself on a good start.

Among those who heard the broadcasts was Martin Maxwell, wondering slightly at the Democratic Front's motives, but applauding their action. From then on, Maxwell kept a close watch on the Front's campaign.

In the months that followed, the Front maintained its indirect pressure, through statements and appeals to the President, and Albert Francis went personally to see several days of the Supreme Court hearing of the appeal.

This was a much less dramatic affair than the original trial. None of the accused were permitted to attend. Lawyers had to confine them-selves to arguing questions of fact and of law, arising out of the High Court transcript of evidence and the judgment itself.

Behind the scenes, General Luther established regular contact with the Chief Justice of the Supreme Court, and organised several personal meetings with the three other judges who constituted the full Bench.

The dossiers Moorhouse had kept on those around him proved to be invaluable sources of information. In the end, only one judge could not be relied upon to reach a non-technical verdict, a fact which did not unduly worry Luther. Indeed, he felt rather pleased. The presence of a dissenter tended to prove the independent-mindedness of the St David's judiciary. In a case as controversial as this, unanimity between seven judges in two courts would have had the hollow ring of one of those elections in Third World states where 99.9 per cent of the electorate apparently vote for the ruling party.

The Supreme Court did not hurry, as befits a cautious, thorough and independent body, although from time to time, rumours of angry exchanges between the majority judges and the single dissenter filtered out from the private chambers of the gloomy Gothic structure, and increased everyone's sense of unease.

The decision, when it came, surprised few people, but dismayed many. By a three-to-one majority, the Supreme Court upheld the convictions and sentences passed on Moorhouse and the others, and with that, the senior judiciary's seal of approval was placed on a case which stank in almost everyone's nostrils.

However, martial law remained in force and the people stayed silent: a silence Luther mistook for consent.

For Martin Maxwell, the appeal verdict was the last straw. He telephoned Sam Wallace.

Wallace was deep in paperwork when the call came through, and on top of that, he had a slight hangover, so at first Maxwell did not receive his full attention.

"Good morning, Sam. It's Martin Maxwell here. I hope I haven't disturbed you?"

"Oh no. Not at all, Mr Maxwell. What can I do for you?" Wallace thought: *silly old fool.*

"The consignment you were inquiring about has just arrived. Perhaps you'd like to come around to my office to see the samples."

Wallace's face furrowed in puzzlement, and he stared into the mouthpiece as if Maxwell had gone senile. "I'm not with you," he replied after a pause. "What consignment was this?"

"When you came to see me at my office the last time? Do you remember?" Maxwell's tones were guarded.

"Yes. Yes, I remember." His face was still blank.

"You wanted some information about a consignment, and I said I couldn't help you. Well now I can give you the information you want. In fact, I can show you some of the goods."

Recognition dawned on Sam Wallace and he flushed with embarrassment at his obtuseness. "Of course, Mr Maxwell," he said apologetically. "Oh yes, I'm sorry. It was so long ago it slipped my mind for an instant. Well, it's good news that it's arrived. When shall I come round?"

The relief was evident in Maxwell's voice. "Why not right away?" he suggested.

"I'll do that. Be with you in fifteen minutes."

Albert Francis was in conference with several others, so Wallace left unnoticed.

Maxwell had obviously been watching for him, because no sooner had he stepped out of the lift and begun walking towards the nubile receptionist, who looked even better than he remembered, than the old man appeared in his office doorway, calling him in.

Maxwell closed the door behind them and they took armchairs facing each other.

"I'm sorry I was so dense when you called," Wallace said. "I'm not usually as bad as that. I suppose I ought to blame a party I was at last night. More of a wake, really."

"Please don't apologise. It is I who should be asking your forgiveness. I told you some untruths last time you came round, as I'm sure you are aware." Wallace nodded, encouragingly. "The point is, I was desperately afraid of what Montrose might do if he discovered any of us were talking. He is a vicious man: a killer. I am still afraid, perhaps even more so now. But things have changed. What's happening to Daniel Moorhouse is shocking: a travesty of justice. We have all stood by for too long. We can't watch silently while an innocent man hangs. We must do something."

"I'm glad to hear that," Wallace said evenly. "I wish I knew what, though. And I also wish I didn't think it was too late."

"It can't be too late! Luther still has the power to commute the sentence – at least that. We must force him to do it."

"How?"

"I understand that my colleague Stephen Khanna promised that if you could find five people apart from himself willing to stand up publicly and denounce Montrose, he would join them."

"You have good information," Wallace conceded with a smile.

"In this case, it's from the horse's mouth. I had lunch with Mr Khanna on the day you made your record-breaking sprint down the High Street."

"Oh I see. He told you everything."

"I believe so. Well what I'm saying, Sam, is that I am prepared to be Number Two. That means we're a third of the way to Khanna's target of six."

Wallace felt a faint surge of optimism which quickly died. *Does any of it matter any longer?* he wondered. *Wouldn't we just be putting a whole lot of other innocent people in jeopardy without having a hope of saving Moorhouse?*

But he said: "That sounds very good, sir. Who else do you think will go in with us?"

Maxwell rubbed the side of his face thoughtfully with an old, veined hand. "Any one of a dozen possibles," he answered. "Sam Laksha is closest to us now in terms of distance. We could try him. Or Luke Davies. I understand he's having a lot of trouble with Montrose holding up imports."

"You're still paying Montrose?"

"Oh, not the protection racket. That's closed down. For the moment. But he's Minister of Finance, and he takes a cut of every item that comes into, or goes out of, this island."

Wallace whistled. "I'd heard the odd rumour," he admitted, "but I'd no idea it was as extensive as that."

"I'm sure it goes a lot further," Maxwell said contemptuously. "Everything the Minister of Finance touches turns to gold – for him, that is."

"Well," said Wallace discouragingly, "if that's so, I wonder if it doesn't make our job totally hopeless. I think we might have left it too late."

"Don't say that, Sam!" Maxwell begged. "It can't be too late. While Moorhouse is alive, there must be hope. We have to make it impossible for Luther to hang him."

"But you see," Wallace pointed out, "proving Montrose ran a protection racket last year isn't going to save Daniel Moorhouse now."

"It damages the state's case!" Maxwell was becoming excited, trying to infect Wallace with his own enthusiasm. "It adds weight to Moorhouse's contention that Montrose *was* involved in the street disturbances. It gives him a motive! And then we can call for the case to be reopened to hear the new evidence," Maxwell pressed his point. "And once a skeleton like this comes out, who knows? Other people may find they still have tongues and be prepared to speak out against injustice."

That was certainly a heady prospect.

Suddenly Wallace grinned. "Right," he said, "let's give it a try. See if we can't get our half-dozen. Are you going to come and help, sir?"

"I certainly am. If you went by yourself, I don't think many of them would agree to speak to you."

Old man Maxwell and Sam Wallace spent the morning in the administration offices of major stores down the length of the High Street, starting well with Samuel Laksha, owner of Pioneer Stores, who agreed to become Number Three after less than ten minutes of discussion. But diagonally across the road, Luke Davies, President of the Port Lombard Suppliers' Company, was an impossible nut to crack. He was not convinced anything either could, or should, be done to save Moorhouse – at any rate, not by the business community. He agreed that official corruption was now costing an extra ten per cent, but the sheer scope of it, and the amount people like Montrose and Luther must be making, convinced him that they would not stand idly by watching their investments destroyed.

They would attack without mercy. For the same reason, Davies did not believe military rule would be a short-lived thing. The more money they made, the more they would want, he argued. The longer they remained in power, the more difficult it would be for them to relinquish it, and not simply because of greed, but because once they handed over the reins of government, they would no longer be able to protect themselves from prosecution.

Sam Wallace could see the force behind Davies' arguments. They were similar to his own thoughts earlier in the day. But Wallace was now persuaded that at least they should try something. The attempt should be made. At any one of a dozen points along the road of preparation, they would be able to reconsider, and call a halt if necessary.

And anyway, he had an idea for another line of inquiry.

Wallace was not surprised when Luke Davies flatly refused to have anything to do with the scheme, although he could see Martin Maxwell was profoundly disappointed.

They drew a blank on the next one, too, but just after 11 a.m., Brian Philips, generally regarded as the most important store-owner on the island, agreed to become Number Four.

And although they worked through the remainder of the day, arguing their case with all the persuasion at their command, they were unable to convince another businessman to join them in denouncing the protection racket.

Two-thirds was just not good enough. Khanna was insistent that the full number be reached. For self-preservation, there had to be so many of them that the military would be dissuaded from the temptation of launching a pre-emptive strike.

And without Khanna's co-operation, the other three felt their positions even more exposed. They too were reluctant to go ahead.

Sam Wallace watched the brave edifice they were erecting tremble and begin to collapse, and he realised some sort of holding action was needed. Martin Maxwell, who had started the day so full of enthusiasm, looked defeated and depressed.

Wallace adopted a note of cheerful optimism which he did not feel himself. "Look, sir," he said, "don't be despondent. I think we've done a bloody good job so far. This is only the beginning. After all, we've spent the day walking – without notice – into people's offices, asking them to take a massive risk, both business and personal. *And* we've got Sam Laksha and Brian Philips to come in with us! I think that's bloody marvellous. Now what we need to do is give people a bit of time to think."

"Time is one thing we don't have much of," Maxwell observed.

"Oh, I don't know. We've got a few weeks, surely. Don't forget, every condemned man gets a statutory thirty days to file a mercy petition with the President. Then Luther's still got to consider the petition, and that'll take another few days at least. And if he turns it down, there could be anything between five days and five months before the hanging."

"But if we're going to move, we really need to do it before Luther comes to decide on the mercy petition, don't we?" Maxwell said. "Once he's committed himself, it'll be too late."

"Yes, I think that's right. But even so, we've got enough time. It's important not to force the pace at the beginning. Let your colleagues think about it for a few days. Then perhaps you can call them to a private meeting in, let's say, one week's time? We can discuss it again, altogether, and maybe when others are around them, a couple will feel more courageous. What we need is the bandwagon effect. As long as the plan has a fighting chance and the bandwagon begins to roll, people will climb aboard."

Maxwell brightened up. "I hope you're right, Sam," he said. "Yes, I'll certainly call a meeting. I can't guarantee everyone will come, but I'll try."

Back at the Democratic Front headquarters, Wallace went straight to the office where Albert Francis was completing the last of the day's paperwork.

"Where the hell have you been all day, Sam?" Francis asked tetchily.

"Out hunting," replied Wallace with a grin.

He described the day's events, leaving out nothing, and when, while he was still talking, the party President quietly fetched a bottle of Scotch from the cupboard beside his desk and poured large measures into glass tumblers, he knew Albert Francis was pleased.

What a gamble it would be! Francis thought. *A selection of the most respected businessmen on the island publicly confronting the might of the armed forces and announcing details of large-scale corruption by the very leaders of the revolution. If enough of them would agree to take the risk!*

But, even as he thought of the dramatic scene – perhaps in the Democratic Front headquarters – the uneasy feeling grew in him that, unless they were crafty, they might all be on a suicide course. There seemed only one solution.

Albert Francis said quietly: "You realise we'll have to absolve Luther from any blame."

"Oh? Why?"

"Because we need him. If we back Luther into a corner and there's no escape, he has no option but to fight. He has guns, we have not. What we need to do is pin the blame on Montrose. Maybe Alec Clifton as well, I'm not sure. But we heap the shit on that fat pig Commissioner in such a way that Luther has a clear choice: either he sides with Montrose, in which case he risks smearing himself with muck, or he keeps his distance and lets the evidence pull Montrose down. I think he'd sooner say: Goodbye, Claud. But if he does, we have to make it clear he can't have

Moorhouse as well. At the very least, he must sign a reprieve. Better still, he can order a retrial."

Wallace raised his whisky glass with a smile. "Cheers," he said. "Let's get our half-dozen brave men and true. And that's easier said than done."

Francis refused to have his enthusiasm dampened. "I've got a feeling about this, Sam," he said. "We're going to knock the hell out of this lot."

The two men stayed late in the headquarters, discussing possible strategies and it was nine o'clock before they left.

Wallace intended going straight home, but instead he found his thoughts wandering to the other possible line of inquiry. It was a long shot, he had to admit, and would probably be a complete waste of time. But even so . . .

Wallace turned right at the next street, and headed for Nelson Avenue.

He saw the police guard outside the gate of Number 34 when he was still a hundred yards away, and wondered whether he should simply drive past and go home. But presumably the guard was there to protect Nora Ayer after the rape, rather than to stop people going in to see her.

Sam Wallace knew Stephen and Nora Ayer only slightly. They had met at parties of mutual friends, but the Prime Minister's PPS and an official of the opposition Democratic Front were not natural soulmates, and, apart from casual greetings and general conversation, they had treated each other with reserve.

Wallace was very attracted to Nora Ayer, though. She embodied most of the things he admired in women. Apart from her warmth and obvious attractiveness, she managed to combine feminity and independence. She had a good sense of humour, a sharp brain, and – as she had now proved – natural dignity and courage.

Wallace parked his car outside the house and went up to the guard. "Is Mrs Ayer home?" he asked.

The policeman looked at him without interest and jerked his head towards the building. "Inside," he said curtly.

"Thank you."

Wallace walked up the paved pathway to the front door, surprised that the man had not even asked his name, or what his business was. It was not very efficient.

He rang the bell and saw through the opaque glass someone's approach.

"Who's there?"

Wallace could detect the edge of fear in her voice. Perhaps it had started just like this, he thought, the night of the rape. He corrected himself: the rapes. He felt suddenly foolish and gauche to have come un-announced to her house after dark.

"It's Sam Wallace, Mrs Ayer," he called through. "I really am awfully sorry to disturb you, but I wondered if I might have a word."

The figure on the other side of the glass did not move.

"What do you want, Mr Wallace?"

"To talk. If I may."

There was silence for a few seconds, then she said: "Do you have a card?"

He felt in his pockets. "Yes. Yes I think so," he said. "Hold on. I'll fish one out."

He slipped the small staff visiting card under the door and saw the figure stoop for it.

"Are you alone, Mr Wallace?"

"Yes, Mrs Ayer. There's no one else."

The chain rattled on the door and the key turned. He saw the blurred form behind the glass moving quickly back.

"Come in slowly, please."

He turned the handle carefully and pushed the door open. Nora Ayer had backed against the far wall, with her hands straight out in front of her, pointing a revolver at his chest.

Wallace halted in shock.

"Close the door behind you, and lock it."

He did so, and the hairs on the back of his neck crawled. No one had ever pointed a gun at him before, and he was sure the safety catch was off. He wondered whether Nora Ayer had been unhinged by the attack, and if so, what his chances were of getting out alive. Wallace turned around slowly and, without being asked, put his hands in the air.

The gesture made Nora Ayer smile suddenly, and relax. She lowered the revolver.

"I'm sorry to do that to you, Sam," she said. "It is Sam, isn't it?" He nodded and his hands dropped to his sides. "It probably seems insane to you. It even feels ridiculous to me, but not quite as ridiculous as I felt when I'd opened the door to some men who . . ." she broke off and made a helpless gesture.

"Please don't apologise," he answered. "It's a sensible precaution. My own fault for not arranging this with you in advance." They walked through to the living room. "I can't say how sorry I was – we all were – to hear about that disgraceful . . . attack. I hope you've recovered.

"Recovering," she said lightly. "It's not the sort of thing you get over easily. A man probably wouldn't understand that." She placed the revolver on an occasional table beside her.

"I think I do .understand," he said sympathetically, but then he grimaced. "Only, of course, I obviously don't, otherwise I wouldn't have dreamt of knocking on your door late at night when you didn't even know I was coming. I'm so sorry about that. It was stupid and thoughtless."

She approved his honesty. "Have a drink," she invited.

"Thanks. I've been on whisky, so I'd better stick to that if you've got it."

"Certainly. Water or soda?"

"Soda, please."

Wallace watched her at the cocktail cabinet. "What news of Stephen? How is he?"

"He's fine, in the circumstances. They're not treating him badly any more, but you can imagine what sort of strain he's under."

"When did you last see him?"

"Last Friday. I'm due for another visit tomorrow morning."

"Please give him my best wishes. He is – they all are – in the thoughts and prayers of a lot of people on the island."

She handed him his whisky and sat opposite.

"What can I do for you, Sam?"

"I really don't know, Nora. I'm wondering rather why I came, except of course it's good to see you again. But this wasn't a social call. More of a step into the dark."

"You're talking in riddles."

"Sorry. I came to talk about Stephen."

Her face was guarded. "What about him?"

"And about Daniel Moorhouse. You know they're going to hang Moorhouse?"

"They're going to hang my husband."

"Are they?" Wallace's voice was quiet, and a silence fell. Finally he said: "You're thinking I'm presumptuous and hurtful and that I've no right to be talking like that."

"Correct."

"But that's my awful dilemma. There's no really tactful way I can think of to say what it is I want to say."

"I appreciate honesty. It's one of my failings," Nora replied. "So just talk. But before you do, let's be clear that all this is entirely off the record. Agreed?"

"Agreed." She really was a remarkable woman: he stared at her with new respect. "We think Claud Montrose, General Luther and the whole bunch of them are crooks," Wallace began. "We think they framed Daniel Moorhouse because he knew too much about them and the protection racket they were running. If they hadn't staged the coup, he'd have slapped them all into gaol. We believe Moorhouse's story that he'd been framed."

"Which means you believe Stephen was perjuring himself to get Moorhouse hanged?"

A pause: "Yes. Yes I do believe that," he said. "I'm sorry."

"Please go on." Nora Ayer leaned back in her chair and sipped her gin and tonic. Wallace could see that her hand was shaking slightly. He could also see the revolver was within easy reach and he hoped, uneasily, that he had not miscalculated about her.

"I don't know why Stephen lied, but I can imagine. Montrose is one of the most vicious men in the island's history. I've never been down in one of his dungeons, or been interrogated, ever, although I've heard enough to convince me I wouldn't last down there either. No one would. It's no reflection on Stephen."

"Thank you."

"In fact, he's obviously made a brave fight of it, otherwise why would he have changed his plea and written a new confession? We never heard what was in it, of course."

"But he changed back," Nora pointed out.

"Yes. God knows why."

She laughed humourlessly and Wallace could see her face going pale, emphasising the stress lines.

"I was why," she said simply.

Wallace looked stunned: "You?"

"After this . . . this thing happened to me, Stephen had to get back into line."

"But what did that have to do with it? The attack happened before the confession."

"No. The confession was already in. The Registrar of the High Court had it by lunchtime. The . . . the men came round that night. They just didn't announce it until the next day."

"Jesus Christ. So you think the two things are related?"

"I don't *think*, Sam, I know."

"But how do you know?"

She shrugged. "Montrose told Steve. He went round to the cells especially to tell him. And he threatened the same thing would happen to Laura."

"Laura?"

"Our little girl. She's four."

Wallace stared at her, disbelieving. "That's disgusting! But it couldn't happen again. They've put a police guard outside," he burst out finally.

"Oh that." Nora shrugged dismissively. "They'd probably use it to stop people coming to our aid. That means nothing. Anyway, it could be withdrawn tomorrow."

"And they've still no idea who the men were?"

"Oh they know all right," she said flatly. "You can bet on that. They chose them. One of Claud Montrose's Special Operations, I suppose." She smiled without humour.

"Listen, Nora," Wallace said urgently. "There's a way of short-circuiting this whole thing, of saving Moorhouse and Stephen and everyone, *and* putting Claud Montrose behind bars."

"I'd love to hear it."

Wallace told her of the proposal to have senior businessmen swear affidavits about Montrose's activities, and pointed out that if this was bolstered by declarations from the condemned men, Luther would be obliged at least to order a retrial.

"And that would take another two years," Nora Ayer pointed out quietly.

"No. If our case was strong enough, we think Luther would ditch Montrose immediately," Wallace argued. "In that case, Montrose would be in gaol, and the others would be let out. And we'd certainly arrange that the families were safe. We'd get you off the island if necessary."

Nora Ayer shook her head. "Nice try, Sam," she said, "but it's no good. We won't play."

"Why not?"

"Because if it goes wrong, our husbands will be hanged. Because Montrose would never let us get away with it. Because there are too many vested interests. And also..." she hesitated, then stopped. "There are other reasons as well," she said, "financial ones. But I won't go into them now. It's just not on."

"So Claud Montrose wins?"

"Unless you can stop him."

"And if I can't, are you sure Stephen and the others will live? That they'll be reprieved?"

Nora Ayer nodded silently.

"Jesus, Nora!" he said. "You can't be sure. That's a terrifying gamble! Apart from the morality of the thing, what if Montrose double-crossed you? What if they hang everyone?"

She smoothed her auburn hair away from her face.

"Leave that to me," she said, tonelessly. "I'll see to it that it doesn't happen."

"I hope you do," Wallace replied. "But Montrose is a crafty and ruthless man. For God's sake, don't underestimate him."

"Thank you, Sam. I have already had some experience of Mr Montrose."

"Oh God, I'm sorry. Of course you have."

"Another whisky?"

Wallace left the house half an hour later, having failed to make any impression on her. She simply would not countenance joining any attack on Montrose, and she knew the other wives would not either, and, listening to her argue, Wallace began to feel his own enthusiasm dampening.

Yet something had to be done. They could not sit around wringing their hands, while a possibility existed of saving the life of at least one innocent man – and of punishing at least one of the guilty.

Wallace spent a restless night, and in the morning he had no clearer idea of what they ought to do. So much depended on the private meeting Martin Maxwell was calling. Perhaps more businessmen would be able to summon up their courage in the presence of their colleagues, although it could just as easily go the other way: the doubters might persuade Maxwell's side that they were making a futile and dangerous gesture, and the meeting could end with everyone running for cover.

It was a chance they would just have to take.

*   *   *

It was a beautiful day. The palm trees were still, and the sun warmed wthout burning. The sea was a deep blue, with gulls, brilliant white, wheeling and mewling over the shoreline and plunging like arrows into the water to snatch a fish from schools just beyond the breakers.

From the air, St David's looked a tropical paradise. The Boeing 707 from London made its approach over the east coast fishing town of Aberdeen, clearing the majestic mountain range with a view of the rugged Mount Forel to the north, and then losing height when the terrain flattened into fertile plains and Port Lombard loomed on the port side, green with palm trees, hibiscus which would soon be in flower, and large, strong shrubs.

The airport lay dead ahead. Over the landing lights, the Boeing flared out and floated into a stall. Puffs of blue smoke marked where the tyres thumped home on the main runway, and the engines roared into reverse thrust.

There were forty passengers on board, only four of them tourists. The rest were returning residents, businessmen and one American carrying a diplomatic passport.

Clive Lyle walked with a casual, easy gait to the immigration hall and joined the queue. But his stomach was tight with the tension he always felt when an operation neared its climax.

Chapter Thirty-eight

The United States Ambassador, Freeman Leister, was less than pleased to see Lyle return to the island, although for a foolish instant he had entertained a hope that there had been a change of heart in Washington, and that an operation was being mounted to save Moorhouse. But he regretfully dismissed this as a pipe dream.

The United States regarded the deposed Prime Minister as an enemy, and it was more likely Lyle had been ordered in to make sure he was hanged.

"Good to see you again, Clive," Leister said, shaking his hand with professional insincerity.

"And you, sir."

They sat in the Ambassador's office, looking out over acres of palm trees and fruit orchards towards a distant sea.

"What brings you to these parts again? Am I allowed to inquire?"

Lyle smiled briefly, and offered his pack of cigarettes. "One or two small points need to be cleared up," he replied, an evasion so obvious that Leister feared the worst.

"Have you not seen a hanging before, then?" the Ambassador asked, still fishing for a hint.

"A couple of times," Lyle admitted, offhand. "It's not too bad. Not as messy as a beheading."

"You've watched a beheading?" Leister was appalled.

"Only once, and that was enough. You've got to stand well back or you get splashed."

Suddenly Leister was unsure whether Lyle was poking fun at him. It was difficult to be sure about anything with this strange, amoral young man. Christ knew where Washington had found him.

Lyle, correctly reading Leister's intentions in the original question, added: "But I'm not here to watch Daniel Moorhouse swing."

"Does that mean he won't swing? I mean, hang?"

Lyle drew deeply on his cigarette. "No it doesn't. As far as we're concerned, Moorhouse is a dead man," he said with finality.

"And the others?"

Lyle shrugged. "I don't know. I don't much care, actually. They're not important. In my terms, I mean."

"I daresay." The Ambassador looked away, angry.

"They sent you a cable about me?"

Leister nodded. "I got it last night. You have free run of the house."

"I'll try not to make a mess." Lyle smiled disarmingly.

"Please do. Any idea how long you'll be around?"

"No. A few months, I think."

"There's someone else in your old office, of course. I could move him out if you insisted." Leister clearly did not want to.

"That would be nice," Lyle said easily. "That office fits my bill pretty well. Janice still the secretary?"

"Yes. She's going on long leave in a few weeks, though."

"It would be good to have her for a while anyway. She understands the way I work."

"I wish *I* did," the Ambassador said sourly. "Well, I'll give orders for the move. They won't be very happy about it."

"Any chance of me moving in this afternoon?"

Leister frowned. Lyle really was carrying things too far. "That's pushing it, don't you think?" he said. "It's lunchtime in only two hours."

Lyle was unmoved. "Actually, sir, I would appreciate it. I am in a bit of a hurry."

For an instant, Leister thought of telling him to go to hell, but then he remembered the terms of the cable which had been decoded and rushed to him the night before, and he realised he had no choice. God, he hated being involved in covert operations.

"Very well," he said crisply. "I'll ask them to make sure it's ready for you by the afternoon. Do you need anything special?"

"Just the room. And the telephones, of course. I'll requisition anything else." Lyle rose to leave. "Thank you very much for your help, sir. I'm grateful."

The Ambassador grunted, and watched as Lyle crossed the carpet and let himself out.

It was astonishing that this sort of operation could still be mounted when there was supposed to be so much scrutiny by Congress and the media, Leister thought. But there it was – still going on unchallenged and unassailable. Until something went wrong, of course, and it blew up publicly in everyone's faces. Then there would be recriminations, and heads would roll, and rules would be changed. And, after a pause, things would go on pretty much the way they always had, of that the Ambassador had no doubt. Still, he supposed he should be grateful that there seemed to be fewer covert operations around these days, which on one level at least meant there was less to go wrong.

Lyle worked quickly and methodically. He spent the first two hours checking back copies of the island's newspapers and being briefed by the new CIA station chief about the situation. Neither of these exercises taught him much.

He got an Embassy chauffeur to drive him into town, where he hired a car. Port Lombard had not changed at all, he thought. It had the old deceptively sleepy air which even government by Luther and Claud Montrose could not alter.

Then Lyle, convinced he was not being followed, set about re-establishing contact with his few remaining agents. Although he had once told Leister he was handing them over to other CIA men at the Embassy, he had done nothing of the sort. He had merely stood them down for an unspecified time. He had recruited them, and they were his.

By the following afternoon, Lyle had learned enough of what was happening on St David's to be thoroughly alarmed. In particular, he did not like the proposed meeting of businessmen which would discuss blowing the whistle on Claud Montrose. He wasn't averse to the principle of getting Montrose, but the timing was critical.

On the other hand, he had learned positive things too. Corruption had grown faster than he had imagined and was public knowledge, and the death sentence on Moorhouse seemed to have made a deep, although still hidden, impression on the people.

It was, on the whole, fairly fertile ground for him to work in. The biggest problem was the question of time. By the most pessimistic estimate, he had just over a month before the execution of Moorhouse. It was not long.

Lyle set to work, arranging to collect the information he needed, and organising the first sensitive meetings of his new campaign.

Sam Wallace prepared for the private gathering of businessmen at Martin Maxwell's home. It was arranged for the following Friday night at eight p.m., with a buffet dinner afterwards – or during, if the discussions were prolonged.

Maxwell had invited the top twelve businessmen, and to Wallace's surprise every one of them attended, lounging on the gracious antique sofas and chairs, drinking out of the finest lead crystal glasses and listening with complete attention.

There was an economy of words which Wallace appreciated after the ritual verbosity of politicians. The store-owners were used to getting straight to the point.

Martin Maxwell made a short speech of welcome, laying down the ground rules of the discussion. Everything said there was to remain confidential. No attempt would be made to force anyone into a particular course of action. The meeting was simply to clarify a situation, and decide what, if anything, should be done.

He introduced Sam Wallace, and said that although the Democratic Front was taking an active interest in the affair, this did not mean it had become a party political matter. Wallace's involvement, he said, stemmed from an anonymous letter which had probably been sent by one of those present to the Front's President, Albert Francis.

The Front was prepared to help where it could, Maxwell said, but it had given a solemn assurance that no political capital would be made out of it. The issue was above politics and, in Maxwell's personal view, it was one which could not be ignored by the business community. Then he handed over to Sam Wallace.

It turned out to be a long, and at times acrimonious, evening. Despite Wallace's assertion that Moorhouse could be saved by their decisive intervention, many clearly did not believe him.

Luke Davies headed the antis' lobby. "This is politics!" he stormed at one point. "Why the shit should businessmen get mixed up in it? Worst of all, why get involved fighting a crooked General and a couple of killer cops? Sure, the present set-up is costing money. A lot of it. But we're surviving. And if we sit tight, we can see them off. If we stand up and fight, they might give us such a knock that we'll never recover. Don't forget what sort of money those bastards are making now! You add up what we're all paying! You think they're going to give it up just because we start shouting our mouths off? Jesus, the noise we make will be silenced pretty fast. Probably by rifle fire."

Brian Philips presented the most cogent arguments of the case in favour of intervention. It wasn't only a question of money, he pointed out calmly, but of morals. St David's had been a clean island, and it was turning into a corrupt one. While Luther, Montrose and Clifton were continuing to line their pockets unchallenged, there was no incentive for them to hand back to civilian government, and the longer they stayed in power, the harder it would be for them to leave. They weren't businessmen, they were criminals, and the economy was sure to suffer at their hands. It was true that Luther had the guns, but the business community had knowledge which, if used sensibly, was more powerful and could silence those guns.

To do this, they had to be smart, which essentially meant dividing and ruling. Wallace had been right when he advised them to focus their attack on Montrose, and leave Luther strictly alone. This would give him the incentive to ditch his colleague.

Sam Wallace listened anxiously. For a long time, he was sure they were losing. However, just before midnight, when a final vote was taken, half those present opposed action of any sort.

But six were in favour, and that was Khanna's magic number. Wallace felt a surge of hope.

He stood up quickly. "Gentlemen, are the six of you who voted in favour of action prepared to take it further? Will you swear affidavits so that we can stop Montrose and save Daniel Moorhouse? And before you vote on this, I'd just like to say that last year, when I was trying to start a similar operation, Mr Khanna kindly offered to make me a gift of a partnership in the St David's Provision Company if I could find six people willing to stand up against Montrose. I'd like to make it clear that, while appreciating his promise, I hereby release him from it. So he can vote without feeling he might be giving away millions."

This raised a laugh and a scattered round of applause, and Wallace found all six wanted to fight.

They agreed that, over the weekend, they would see their lawyers. Wallace reminded them that in less than two weeks, Luther could announce a decision on clemency for Moorhouse, so another meeting on tactics was needed urgently. They agreed on Monday night.

At last things were moving: Wallace could hardly believe it.

Lawyers spent Saturday and Sunday preparing affidavits, and Wallace and Albert Francis were sent copies of every one of them. All were lengthy documents, but the information they contained was dynamite. Montrose could never survive the cumulative effect.

Apart from the two Democratic Front men, the party headquarters were deserted at the weekend. Since the coup, much of the public excitement and activity had dissipated, and even on weekdays there were far fewer people around. So the men were able to discuss tactics and be as enthusiastic as they liked without fear of being disturbed, or of their secret leaking out.

But it had leaked out.

Late on Sunday night, when the last of the affidavits had been received and read, they were all locked into the office safe, to which only Francis and Wallace had the combination.

Clive Lyle sat in a car, parked in the darkness well off the road, and watched the party offices from a distance. Just after eleven p.m., the two men switched off the last lights and locked up. Lyle saw the night-watchman salute as they drove away in their separate cars, and then there was silence.

Two hours passed, with Lyle waiting motionless. At last, he opened the door quietly and stepped outside. He had switched the interior light of the vehicle so that it stayed off.

Lyle picked an attaché case off the seat, shut the door silently and locked it. He stood in the darkness, flexing his cramped muscles.

The new moon cast a glow so dull it hardly mattered.

Lyle moved forward cautiously, staying on his side of the road and keeping to the cover of trees and bushes. When he was directly opposite the entrance to the party offices, he waited for several minutes, staring into the blackness for a sign of movement. There was none.

A small wooden shack had been erected for the watchman next to the gate, and Lyle doubled back a few yards so he could cross the road and approach from behind.

He moved as silently as a hunting animal, crouching low as he passed one of the windows. This was the sort of operation he least enjoyed. It was when he was at his most vulnerable, and as Watergate had shown, discovery could have extraordinary repercussions. The important thing was to know when to take your time, and when to hurry.

He took his time, standing silently beside the open door of the shack, body pressed against the wooden wall. There was no sound from inside. It was impossible to know whether the nightwatchman was in there, or patrolling the building.

At last, the sigh of a man turning over in his sleep provided the answer. Lyle crouched again, soundlessly opening the black attaché case, and his hand reached unerringly for the small canister with its rubber covering.

Lyle peered around the bottom of the door and he could just make out a shape on the bed in the corner. He pulled the pin, and immediately rolled the rubberised canister across the floor, deep into the room.

Then Lyle stood, emptying his lungs of air and inhaling, again and again, until he was sure he would be able to work holding his breath for at least a minute and a half.

Inside the shack, the canister silently released its odourless gas.

Lyle took a small penlight from his case and closed the lid.

Taking one last deep breath, he stepped inside, shining the light directly at the watchman. The man did not move. Lyle closed the door to prevent the gas dispersing quickly.

The sharp slim beam of light flicked around the hut, taking in the old coat hanging from a hook, the table with the watchman's report book, and the old iron bed on which the man lay.

Lyle went across and gave his face a hard slap. No response. He lifted one of the eyelids and shone the torch into his pupil. The man could almost have been dead.

Lyle's hands went down the sleeping body, searching the pockets and quickly locating a bunch of keys.

He headed for the office building.

Lyle used a side door, and checked the first rooms briefly with his flashlight. Most had no curtains at the windows: an irritating factor. There is nothing as suspicious to a casual passer-by than a flashlight beam glimpsed inside a darkened building. It is preferable by far to turn on all lights and behave as if you owned the place, because that is not the way intruders are popularly expected to operate, and passers-by tend to take no notice.

Lyle was convinced the affidavits would be kept in the President's office, or perhaps in Sam Wallace's, if he had a safe. But the way to find out would be to check which office doors were locked. The documents were sure to be inside one of those.

Lyle was in luck. The only locked door had the sign "Albert Francis – President" on the outside. He was not surprised to discover the watchman did not have a key to this, but he had come equipped himself.

The lock was almost an insult to have to pick. It was the sort of thing students mastered in their first lesson at Fairfax. Inside, the room was quiet and carpeted.

As befits a party president, Albert Francis had curtains at his windows, and Lyle immediately closed them. They were thick, and after making sure no chinks of light would shine through, he switched on a small desk lamp which cast a low glow over the room.

The safe was an old, free-standing heavy steel job with a combination lock. From his attaché case, Lyle took a pair of Latex rubber gloves and pulled them on, and a small transistorised box which stuck, magnetised, to the steel beside the combination lock. Lyle switched it on, and a tiny light glowed. He moved the combination to the right, but nothing happened.

He moved it slowly to the left, and a second light flicked on. The first number was twenty. Then to the right. A third light came on at eight. Left again, twice round the dial to nineteen before the fourth clicked on, and right, once around back to nineteen.

That's all there was to it. Lyle turned the handle and the safe door swung open.

The affidavits were easy to spot: large, overblown documents of the sort beloved by lawyers, bound with red tape. He checked them through. All six were there.

Lyle was just about to fetch his miniature camera when he spotted the photocopier in the corner. It would be easier to use that and probably as quick. Also he'd be sure there were no mistakes.

It took Lyle almost forty-five minutes to complete the photocopying. The machine was slower than he'd thought, but, even so, he preferred using it.

When he had finished, he switched it off, packed his equipment and the photocopies into the attaché case, and returned the originals to the safe.

He left, remembering to lock the office door, and he used the watchman's key for the side entrance.

Outside, the night was dark and cool, and the stars shone dimly through a thin film of cloud. Lyle stood motionless, letting his eyes readjust while he listened for sounds.

He moved quietly back to the watchman's shack and, holding his breath once more, went inside to retrieve the canister which would have released its contents over a thirty-minute period, and to check that the man was all right. Not that there was anything Lyle could have done if he found him dying, for example, but it helped future planning to know as quickly as possible exactly what had happened.

Lyle felt the man's pulse and it seemed normal. The effects of the gas should begin wearing off in ten or fifteen minutes, although the tolerance of individuals varied widely, as did the size of the particular room in which the canister was used, and the ventilation. He replaced the bunch of keys in the watchman's pocket and covered him with a blanket.

The thin, sharp beam from his penlight located the empty canister and he stooped to pick it up.

It was time to leave. He was running out of breath.

As Lyle straightened up, through the open doorway he saw the approach of car headlights, and he flicked off his penlight immediately and froze in his tracks.

The car was moving slowly: that was the first thing to alarm him. A police patrol cruising? Coming to check on security arrangements? Perhaps someone had glimpsed the thin torch beam inside the building and reported it.

His lungs were sending urgent messages to his brain for oxygen, and he could feel his heartbeat speed up, pumping loud within his chest. But if he took a breath, he risked inhaling the gas and might be unconscious within seconds, to be discovered with his attaché case, the photostats and the tools of a modern burglar's trade. It would be Watergate all over again.

The car passed under a lamp post. Police. Still twenty yards away and cruising slowly.

Suddenly a spotlight cut through the blackness, lighting up the walls of the single-storied house which the Democratic Front used as its headquarters, piercing through the windows into the rooms and sweeping down to illuminate the inside of the shack as dazzlingly as if it were a magnesium flare, exposing the grain of the cheap wooden planking and the dust and dirt which lay about.

Lyle felt his lungs would burst. His face was suffused with the effort. He had only one chance: to get into the clean air, and flee or fight from there.

The spotlight went out. The shack was again pitch black and Lyle's eyes, dazzled, could no longer see anything inside, or even clearly make out the door, but he knew instinctively where it was and he moved fast, swinging to the right immediately he touched the ground and heaving in lungsfull of air. If the police had seen him, he knew he had only a second or two to recover, and even that would give them valuable time to close the distance between them.

Lyle's mind was sharp and perfectly cool. He wondered briefly whether they were armed. He himself was not, but in any case, a shoot-out between a United States diplomat and the St David's police force in the grounds of the Democratic Front headquarters was out of the question.

The police car had halted. Peering cautiously around the bottom of the shack, and trying to control his panting, Lyle could see the shapes of two men in the front seat, and he knew they were looking his way.

At first he could not understand why they were still in the car, but as he watched, he presumed there was uncertainty about whether they had actually seen anything. Lyle knew that, after a short debate, at least one of them would come across to investigate. That is, if they were any good at all.

He looked desperately around for escape.

If he moved in a straight line towards the main building, keeping the shack between himself and the police car, he would be able to make it to the shadows of the brick wall, and the shrubs planted against it. That would give him extra distance, but it would also leave him more exposed. A searchlight would pinpoint him in a second.

There was no alternative. Lyle crouched and ran, heading along an invisible corridor for a point which, he calculated, would keep him out of the policemen's sight lines. He threw himself down by the wall.

A car door slammed. Lyle could hear boots walking cautiously towards the entrance and the broad strong glow of a flashlight shone on the tarmac road.

A man paused at the entrance, directing his light against the main building and moving it slowly across. The focus of the beam was three or four feet above the ground, but even so, discovery might follow and Lyle tensed his body to run. The light need only flick down a little, and the policemen would be able to spot him.

The beam moved over to the watchman's shack and shone inside. Lyle heard the policeman's grunt of disapproval at the sleeping figure on the bed, and saw him enter the shack.

Lyle grinned. If the gas had dissipated, he would have his work cut out rousing the watchman. If it had not, well . . .

It seemed to Lyle that the flashlight had gone out. He shifted position slightly and saw that, in fact, it was still burning although it was on the floor and pointing under the watchman's bed.

One policeman down.

In two or three minutes, the other would become suspicious and come to investigate. Would there still be enough gas around to deal with him too? Lyle didn't intend waiting to find out.

He moved cautiously along the side of the house to the far end, away from the police car.

As soon as he rounded the corner, he straightened up and began to run, and vaulted the low wall marking the boundary.

He made his way silently through the grass and bushes to the intersection, and crossed the road at a point directly opposite the place where he had parked. A glance down the road showed him that the second policeman had left the patrol car and was presumably in the shack, although in what condition, Lyle had no idea.

Lyle stashed the attaché case under the front seat, and drove back to the United States Embassy, where he had been allocated one of the staff flats.

Lyle worked until dawn, going carefully through the affidavits.

They were quite something. Montrose would have a heart attack if he knew what was being planned against him, and if he could see the admirable detail into which the businessmen had gone.

Martin Maxwell's was undoubtedly the best contribution. It contained not only times and dates, but also accounts of conversations with Montrose both before and after the attack on the store.

Lyle made himself a cup of coffee.

It's all a question of timing, he thought. *It's a good idea, but they're moving too fast. We'll get Montrose in good time. I must slow them down.*

And that, he knew, was not a question of how, but of deciding whom. In the intricate game of chess he often imagined himself playing, it was time to move his King.

Lyle picked up the phone and dialled a number. It rang a dozen times before the sleeping man rolled away from the woman's warm body and fumbled for the receiver at his bedside.

"Uh?" he grunted. "What d'you want?"

"Sorry to wake you. It's Clive."

"Huh?" Already he could hear the voice struggling for alertness. "Clive? What the hell? Jesus, what time is it?"

"It's five past five. The sun's nearly up."

A groan: "Oh Jesus!"

"I'm coming round now, Steve. Leave word with the gatehouse to expect me."

"Shit, Clive, you're joking. Now?"

"It's important. You'll see why."

"Oh fuck. All right. See you soon."

General Stephen Charles Luther hung up on the man who, for four years, had been his control, and swung his legs out of bed with a sigh.

It had better be good.

Chapter Thirty-nine

Martin Maxwell felt younger and more hopeful than he had done for years. He was a peaceable, basically honest man, who had been deeply grieved at the growth of corruption on the island. His own involvement in it, the way he had felt obliged to co-operate, had left him feeling shabby and impotent. And old. Even though younger businessmen than he – Luke Davies for one – had also knuckled under, and come to that, still were – Maxwell regarded them as belonging to a different school.

They had not been trained in the old traditions of service and honesty as he had. He knew they cut corners, engaged in questionable business transactions and had been known to deal roughly with others. None of this was Maxwell's style. He had only knowingly cheated once, when he was still young, and these decades later, he could remember his humiliation and the shock on his father's face when it had been discovered.

Perhaps these disgraces became less important with repetition, but Maxwell had never put himself in the position of finding out. What he did know, though, was that paying protection money to Claud Montrose had not become easier for him, the more often he did it.

Maxwell had felt constantly degraded by Montrose's visits, each one worse than the last, and now, with much larger sums being demanded for the import of goods, and paid through third parties, the humiliation refused to subside.

Maxwell was furious with himself for not having called a halt to the protection racket at the very beginning. He should have gone directly to Daniel Moorhouse on the first occasion, and told him what the Commissioner of Police was up to. That was the time to say: "Enough!"

But now, at least, something was to be done, and there was the assurance of safety in numbers.

Maxwell finished his tea, and carefully replaced the bone china cup on the solid silver tray.

It was a glorious day in the best season of the year. In a month, it would be hot and humid again.

Maxwell checked his watch and saw that it was 7.55 a.m. He always left the house punctually at eight, driving himself to the office and arriving at 8.10. He took pride in being the first man at work each day, and found he got through a considerable amount before the others turned up.

The roads were never congested at that time of morning, which made the drive pleasant, and Maxwell let himself in through the rear entrance, using his own key, acknowledging with a nod the greeting from the security man outside.

Maxwell walked briskly through to his office, humming softly to himself, and was sitting down at his desk when a movement caught his eye and he stared, startled. For a second he froze, his hands on the arms of the chair, and his body half-way lowered, and then he stood up again, straight, and thin, and tall.

He felt no fear, although his mouth was going dry.

"What do you want?" Maxwell asked. "If it's money, you've come too early."

He must have been waiting behind the door, this young man with the strange-shaped gun and the impassive but not unpleasant face.

The blow came without warning and threw Maxwell against the wall, hard. He stood, as if pinned, staring at the young man. *It doesn't hurt,* he thought with surprise. He opened his mouth to speak, but something poured out of it suddenly, so he closed it again.

The young man was aiming once more. Maxwell wondered if he should try to move, but in an absurd way, he felt he ought not make it more difficult.

He thought: *God forgive all our sins.* And then: *I don't know his name.*

The silencer muffled the noise.

News of the murder spread throughout Port Lombard before midday, and Maxwell's was sealed off by police. Detectives went thoroughly through the building, looking for clues, but there were surprisingly few. The ejected shells lay on the carpet where they had fallen, showing the position of the gunman. There were no signs of forcible entry, so the man had either walked into the building with Maxwell – which the security guard disputed – or he had come in by himself earlier, using his own key.

The consensus in the city was that old man Maxwell had surprised an armed robber, who killed him either in panic or in anger, when he discovered hardly any cash was kept in the store overnight.

Maxwell's colleagues along the High Street, who were in any case paranoid about the plan to expose Montrose, were shocked and anxious, but it seemed impossible that it had anything to do with their private meeting or the affidavits. No one could know about the action six of them proposed taking. Or five, now.

But at eleven a.m., a telephone call was made to Philips and Company, and a softly spoken man asked to talk to Mr Brian Philips on a personal matter. He would not give his name.

"Mr Philips?"

"Speaking."

"When you signed that affidavit on Sunday, Mr Philips," the man said, "did you think you might be signing your death warrant as well? Maxwell was."

The man hung up, and Brian Philips listened, chilled, to the sound of the dialling tone.

After that, there was no question of going ahead. Everyone ran for cover.

Sam Wallace was bitterly disappointed at the retreat, although he appreciated the fear the remaining five men must feel. Somehow, Montrose had come to know of the plan, and that meant a spy among them. It was an uncomfortable thought. Was it one of the store-owners who had refused to sign an affidavit? Had one of them gone and made a full report to Montrose, soon after the meeting broke up? But it could just as easily have been a lawyer, or one of their clerical staff involved in the drawing up of the documents. It would be simple to slip in an extra carbon copy.

Wallace felt a little frightened himself. If Montrose knew about Maxwell and Brian Philips, he might just as easily have heard about Sam Wallace's part in the affair.

Although Wallace's instinct was to fight on, moving fast, and effectively to defy Montrose to kill them all, there was no question of doing this alone. Apart from being too exposed, there was a more basic issue: the affidavits were not his. They were the property of the men who swore them, and it had been agreed at the beginning that no one would be forced into anything.

At the request of the other five, Wallace returned the copies of the statement. But before doing so, he took the precaution of making photocopies, and these were locked back in the safe. Wallace told himself this was for the historical record.

But Claud Montrose had nothing to do with Martin Maxwell's death, and, in fact, he did not know of it until he and Alec Clifton assembled in General Luther's office for an emergency meeting at 10.30 that morning.

Montrose was first stunned at the news of the store-owners' plan, aimed specifically against him, more so because he realised instinctively that Luther would abandon him if necessary, and that he would then be killed. And when he had digested this, Montrose was fuelled by a calculating anger and a driving desire to get rid of as much human evidence as possible. Too many people knew some part of the story.

The performance Montrose gave impressed Luther and awed Clifton because of the depth of its violence and hatred. He was no longer the old Claud, blasting away thoughtlessly against his enemies, real or imagined, but he argued realistically and plotted logically.

They listened in silence and, in the end, agreed that Claud's plan would be for the best. As soon as the statutory period was up, they would hang everyone: Moorhouse, of course, but also Ayer, Rana, Kataria and Molvi. And they would do it quickly.

*   *   *

Clive Lyle felt that, at last, he was making progress. In the days since Maxwell's murder, the initiative had once again become his.

He had established contact with a group of dissident generals, and the initial meetings had gone well. There was no divergence of opinion on Western security interests, and the officers' disillusionment with their military government was satisfactory.

Lyle encouraged it by handing over photostats of the affidavits, and was gratified at the response. But the affidavits nailed Montrose only, and that was not enough. Lyle needed something else to tilt the balance, and he searched desperately for it.

A possible answer came from his own Embassy. Ambassador Leister had spent an hour with Albert Francis, during which time the politician spoke freely of the plot against Moorhouse, the affidavits and the murder, and the expectation that the deposed Prime Minister would be hanged within a week.

Leister listened with sympathy and with inner dismay, wondering how much was the responsibility of US covert operations.

Francis also recounted Sam Wallace's abortive meeting with Nora Ayer, and how she was totally convinced her husband and the others would have to be reprieved. She therefore had refused to take part in any attempt to save Moorhouse.

Reading between the lines, Wallace believed Nora Ayer had some independent evidence which would ensure Luther kept his part of the bargain, but he had no idea what this might be.

As soon as Francis left, the Ambassador called Clive Lyle and, controlling his distaste, repeated the gist of what had been said. That much was his duty. He doubted there would be anything in it to interest covert operations, particularly as Lyle seemed elbow-deep in blood already.

But Lyle *was* interested, particularly about Wallace's meeting with Nora Ayer.

He already knew the decision had been taken to hang all the condemned men, so, if Nora Ayer had evidence, the time for her to present it would be after her husband was served with the Black Warrant setting the date for his execution. And Lyle had to make sure he was in a position to see what that evidence was.

Lyle made contact with Sam Wallace, introducing himself as one of the Embassy's political secretaries, and inviting him to lunch.

They ate at Kay's. Lyle was both amusing and well-informed – he told Wallace a few things he hadn't heard before – and the two men struck up an easy friendship. By their second meeting, four days later, Wallace was recounting details of his talk with Nora Ayer, and what had happened during the store-owners' debate on confronting Claud Montrose.

Lyle was now constantly aware of the tightness in his stomach. The timing of this operation was being cut as fine as any he had ever been involved in, and the tension was beginning to tell. So many aspects were still beyond his control, or unknown to him, and the deadline was approaching fast.

Lyle calculated that if Nora Ayer wanted to publicise her evidence, she would probably come to Sam Wallace, at least for advice. He wanted to be sure that if she did, he would know about it quickly.

The last days before the expiry of the thirty-day period for mercy petitions were among the worst Nora Ayer had ever experienced, even though she tried to keep calm, reminding herself of the promise given by Luther, and sometimes taking the tape from its hiding place and listening to it for reassurance.

The condemned men, except for Daniel Moorhouse, addressed mercy petitions to the President. Moorhouse adamantly refused to do this, arguing it would amount to an admission of guilt. In any case, he was reconciled to his death, believing that nothing would sway Luther from his plan to kill him.

Claud Montrose visited the Central Gaol and, seeing spirits were low, casually mentioned the possibility of exile to the other four.

This was not something anyone except Molvi had given any thought to, although once the suggestion had been made, all the others felt their hopes lift. Ayer in particular realised what a trap St David's had become, and how he would find it almost impossible to pick up the threads of his old life. Somehow he would always be waiting for the police or the military to arrive a third time to take him to gaol. His stomach would churn whenever he saw a strange car parked outside his house. And the house itself, which he had once thought of as home, he had no wish ever to see it again, and he knew Nora would also turn her back on it without regret.

It reminded them both of police raids, of detention orders, of six thugs with hard muscled bodies . . . the more Ayer turned the matter over in his mind, the more convinced he became that happiness lay in another country: Britain, probably. He would elect to go there, and would fly out with Nora and the children. He tried to remember the days and times of the London Boeings, and suddenly it seemed that, at last, the end of the ordeal was in sight.

But even so, there remained the small core of fear in his belly. Until he was actually on that plane, something might still go wrong.

It did go wrong on a Tuesday morning at eleven a.m.

Ayer, Rana and Kataria were sitting together in a concrete court-yard, smoking and talking. Molvi was a distance away in the shade, writing a letter to a girlfriend.

The condemned men were allowed to spend most of their days together, sometimes playing cards or chess, and warders hardly ever came near them.

Daniel Moorhouse, however, was kept in a cell in another block, separated by two locked steel gates, and it was an open secret that his conditions were harsh.

The Superintendent, Simon Norwood, had been ordered by Montrose to withdraw all privileges, and one morning while the former Prime Minister was in the exercise yard, his cell was stripped. Everything went, except the bed and a mattress. He was not allowed a book, or a radio, or a newspaper. His food came from the prison kitchen. His exercise period was cut to twenty minutes a day, and then only on some days.

Moorhouse, a proud man, considered it a deliberate attempt at humiliation, and finally refused to go into the exercise yard at all. He remained locked in his stinking cell with only a once-weekly half hour visit from his wife to break the monotony. And even then, he was not taken to the visitors' room. Instead, Mrs Moorhouse was brought to the steel doors of his cell, where she spoke to him through the bars, touched his hand and tried to pretend she did not notice the overpowering stench from the slop bucket in the corner.

The whole prison knew this. Indeed, many people on the island had also heard it reported on the BBC, although some could not believe it to be true: Luther's government could surely not behave like that, they contended. No civilised government could.

Ayer was sprawled on a wooden chair, soaking up the sun and listening idly to Joe Rana explaining his decision to go to America – perhaps to settle in New York. The CIA would get him a Green Card without any problem, Rana said, and he was sure they'd help find him a job, just to get him on his feet.

They could hear the boots of the four warders on the concrete before they saw them round the corner and unlock the steel gate leading to the courtyard. The warders walked with grim official purpose and Ayer felt as if a hand was clutching at his heart.

The lead warder shouted: "Right you lot, back to your cells! Move!"

They stood up at once, bewildered, a bit scared, and with Molvi grumbling, were shepherded back into the small concrete-walled cells. The metal doors slammed shut behind them, with that solid, dull bo-oom sound that ex-prisoners hear in their sleep for years afterwards.

Ayer sat on the bed, waiting. He was aware of the approach of other boots, but they did not come to his cell. The minutes passed slowly.

Suddenly Ayer heard a sound – a cry of grief and fear, uttered twice. He recognised it as Molvi. The palms of Ayer's hands began to sweat and he rubbed them on the legs of his prison trousers.

He did not care how long the minutes lasted now. Every one of them kept him from . . . from whatever it was had made Molvi cry out.

The bo-oom of a distant door slamming. Silence again. They would be at Kataria's cell. Ayer waited. He found his hands were trembling.

Bo-oom. Boots, louder now, stopping at Rana's cell, just next door. Ayer strained his ears for the sound of voices but the walls were too thick. Time was speeding up, moving too fast.

Bo-oom. His turn. What had made Molvi cry like that?

An eye at the spy-hole, the key in the lock. Ayer sat on his bed, frozen.

In the doorway stood Simon Norwood, and behind him, the deputy superintendent. In the background were two warders. Norwood came in and positioned himself directly in front of Ayer with the others crowding behind. Ayer wished he had stood up because he felt at a psychological disadvantage with Norwood directly in front of him, making him crane his neck back to look into his face. But now it was too late.

"Stephen Vincent Ayer," Norwood said formally, "I am directed to inform you that your petition for mercy in the case of the State versus Daniel Moorhouse and others, has been placed before His Excellency the President of St David's for consideration. The President, taking account of all the facts and submissions, has not seen fit to interfere with the sentence of the honourable courts. Your petition therefore has been dismissed and your execution will take place at a date to be set by the Superintendent of the Central Gaol."

The chill hand was around Ayer's heart again.

Norwood held out a large thick piece of paper, bordered heavily in black. Ayer stared at it, mesmerised.

"Stephen Vincent Ayer, I have to inform you that, in pursuance of the sentence of the High Court of St David's, your execution by hanging will take place at 0600 hours on September the thirteenth, 1977." He paused and looked directly at the condemned man. "That is, at six o'clock tomorrow morning."

Ayer reached up automatically to take the Black Warrant, and read it, but the words blurred before his eyes. His lips moved and no sound came.

Norwood again: "I require you to sign that you have received and understood the terms of this Warrant."

The stiff parchment was laid upon the bed beside him and Norwood produced a fountain pen. Ayer found his hand had stopped shaking but his signature was smaller than usual and somehow this offended him as being improper for such a major document. He wished he could do it again.

Ayer found his tongue. "The others . . .?" he asked.

"The sentences on your co-accused will also be carried out tomorrow morning."

"Montrose said . . . and Luther . . . he promised my wife . . ." Ayer's voice trailed off ineffectually.

Norwood ignored this. "A priest is at your disposal should you wish to make use of him," he said tersely. "Your wife has been called to the gaol for a final meeting at half past two this afternoon. Is there anything else you want at this stage?"

Again Ayer tried to speak, but there seemed to be a blockage in his throat. He coughed to clear it. "At this stage," he said hesitantly, "I want justice. I want to see Claud Montrose."

"The Minister is a busy man. I doubt that he will have time to see you. However, I will convey your request to him."

The Superintendent left the cell, followed by his deputy and the warders. Ayer sat numbly on the edge of his bed.

They left the door open, and on the threshold stood a prison padre.

"May I come in, my son?" he asked.

Ayer nodded, unable to speak.

News of the rejection of the mercy petition and the setting of the execution date reached Nora Ayer at almost the same time it was given to her husband.

It came in an abrupt message from two policemen, telling her to report at the Central Gaol for the final meeting at 2.30 that afternoon, and that she could bring her children if she wished.

She stared at the policemen in disbelief.

"He can't do this to us," she whispered. "He can't do this."

As soon as the men left, Nora Ayer called General Luther's office and was put through to Bob Sehai.

"This is Mrs Ayer," she said, her voice straining for normality. "I need to speak urgently to General Luther."

"Ah, Mrs Ayer. I'm afraid the President is unavailable." Sehai sounded uncomfortable and evasive.

"He must speak to me! He must speak to me!" she burst out.

"I'm sorry, but I'm afraid it won't be possible."

"It bloody well will be possible, Mr Sehai! That man is going to hang my husband tomorrow morning! He promised us faithfully he would not. He gave his word as an officer and . . ." her voice faltered ". . . and a gentleman."

"I understand your distress, Mrs Ayer," Sehai said smoothly, "but I'm afraid I have strict instructions that the President is not to be disturbed today."

Nora Ayer found she was shouting again. "You tell that bastard that I've got a tape-recording of our meeting! You tell him that, Mr Sehai! I recorded everything – his assurances, the plot against Moorhouse, everything! And I'm going to hand it over to the press! He'd better not think he's going to get away with this! If he hasn't contacted me in the next ten minutes, I'm going to blow the whistle on this whole plan! Ten minutes, Mr Sehai!"

She slammed down the phone and stood in the hallway, shaking with anger.

Her next call was to Sam Wallace.

"Sam! They're going to hang them all tomorrow morning! They've just told me!"

Wallace was genuinely shocked and distressed. "Oh God, Nora, how awful. I'm so sorry. Is there anything I can do?"

"Luther won't see me." She was almost crying. "I've been called to the final meeting at half past two, and Luther won't see me. So I told Sehai I had a tape of Luther when he met the wives, and I'm going to make it public. He can't do this to us!"

"You've got a tape?" Wallace's voice was cautious. "You've actually got one?"

"Yes!" she said. "The whole thing! Luther admitting the plot, promising reprieves! I took a cassette recorder in my handbag when we went to see him. It's all there."

"And you told this to Sehai?"

"Yes. I gave Luther ten minutes to call me back."

Wallace spoke urgently. "Nora, when exactly was this? When did you speak to him?"

"Just this minute. I've just put down the phone to him."

"Now look, you must trust me. Please trust me. Have you got the tape at home?"

"Yes, it's here."

"Then for God's sake, get hold of it and leave that house immediately. This minute. Are the kids with you?"

"No. They're at school. And they're out this afternoon."

"Fine. You've got a car?"

"Yes."

"Well," Wallace urged, "take the tape, get into your car, and drive around to the party headquarters *immediately*. This minute. Do you understand?"

Nora was becoming frightened: "Sam, what's the matter?"

"If they know you've got a tape, they're going to come round to get it! Don't you understand? They'll be on their way now. For Christ's sake, Nora, get out! Bring it here. We can help you!"

"I will," she said. "Sam, I'll come now."

She slammed down the telephone and ran frantically to the book-shelves in the living room. The cassette was behind a set of encyclopaedias.

She dropped it into her handbag and dashed for the front door.

Wallace found two cassette recorders in the party offices, and set them up so that as they listened to Nora Ayer's tape, they would simultaneously make a copy.

His mind was racing. Christ, what could they do to stop the hangings? How does one blackmail a ruthless and corrupt military dictator, *and* get away with it? There was so little time to think or plan, and if they made a mistake . . . well, the consequences would be fatal, and not only to those already condemned.

For the first time, Wallace detected hesitation and fear in the response of Albert Francis when he told him that Nora Ayer was on her way round, and why.

"Sam," Francis said, "do me a favour and don't get us involved in anything we're not going to be able to handle."

"Jesus, Al, we've been involved for months!" Wallace reminded him.

"Yes I know. I'm just saying – move extra carefully."

Wallace returned to his own office and paced with impatience. It shouldn't take Nora more than another five minutes to reach the head-quarters. Unless she was stopped on the way.

Wallace badly needed to talk to someone else, to get advice. He thought of Clive Lyle.

The public executioner for the island of St David's was an unprepossessing man of fifty-one, with bowed legs. He might have been taken for a minor civil servant, perhaps a clerk in an office where he was kept away from the public. There was an air of submissiveness about him, a man who carried out instructions without complaint or question.

From the prison doctor, he collected the latest weights of each man and noted them carefully in a small dog-eared book. Then he went to the prison stores and requisitioned five lengths of new manilla rope, each sixteen feet in length and 2.5 centimetres in diameter.

The hangman made a series of calculations in his notebook, frowning with the mental effort, and ordered five large empty sacks, together with 1,323 individual bags of sand, each weighing one pound. The stores always had these in stock.

Within minutes, prisoners were carrying the sandbags and ropes and stacking them at the foot of the gallows.

The execution chamber was a drab, bare room on the first floor of the maximum security block. The corridor leading to it gives off to the condemned cells: the final holding rooms where those prisoners who can eat have their last food before dying.

The only windows in the chamber are high up on the walls and, until the fluorescent strip lights have been switched on, it is a place of half-light and shadow.

A stout oak beam runs lengthways between two walls at a height of nine feet, and without the lights it is difficult to detect the trap-door which falls away into another room. At the side is a large metal lever, of the sort used on railway lines to switch the points manually, and this springs the trap.

The hangman attached the five ropes to the beam, and began filling the empty sacks with sandbags. The equivalent of one-and-a-half times the condemned man's weight is used to stretch a new rope the day before an execution, and, at the same time, it allows the hangman to test the trap.

Two hundred and seventy-eight bags of sand went into the first sack. The executioner secured the mouth with the first rope and tied a label onto it: MOORHOUSE.

The second sack took 243 lbs of sand. He labelled it AYER. It was a lengthy task, and the hangman worked with absorption.

On the prison medical records, Joseph Rana's weight was down as 175 lbs, which meant that 263 bags had to be counted out and packed into the sack, name-tagged to represent his body.

Another 270 lbs for Kataria and 269 for Molvi.

The labelled sacks stood in a line on the scaffold and the hangman checked again they were properly secured.

He pulled the lever. The trap dropped with a crash and the five sacks plummeted, jerked and swung on the ends of their ropes, bashing together.

The executioner lit a cigarette.

Nora Ayer parked her car outside the Democratic Front offices and hurried in, her handbag tightly gripped as if someone might try to snatch it from her.

Sam Wallace, waiting in his office, noticed the high, nervous tone of her voice even before he registered that she had arrived, and he went out immediately.

He took her to the President's office and sat her in an armchair while Albert Francis offered her a cup of tea and Wallace wondered desperately how quickly he could get the tape out of her.

There was so little time: he had to come straight to the point.

"Nora, did you bring it?" he demanded.

"The tape? Yes."

"We have to listen to it. We can't decide what to do until we know what's on it."

She hesitated. "But I might not want it publicised," she pointed out. "If Luther agrees to stop the hanging, it must stay a secret."

"Oh of course," Wallace said hastily. "But if he doesn't – we have to move quickly. We'll need every minute we can get."

She reached into her handbag and pulled out the cassette.

"Thank you," Wallace said, taking it with a feeling both of relief and excitement – as well as a slight sense of treachery because he was surreptitiously re-recording it. But hell, he thought, this is war.

The beginning was indistinct, greetings being exchanged apparently, and some exclamations. Then there were noises as if heavy furniture was being moved about, and suddenly Luther's voice, loud and clear:

"I imagine you ladies are worried about the sentences passed on your husbands. I can understand that. But you realise that the matter is out of my hands, for the moment at least. The courts of this country are independent: totally beyond the command of any man, least of all me."

Sam Wallace snorted derisively.

"I cannot interfere. However, once the judicial process has been completed, then I can step in. I now combine the functions of President and Prime Minister, and so all petitions for mercy come before me. Mercy is a Presidential prerogative."

This was followed by Nora Ayer's interrogation, and at last Luther's personal assurance: *"I will see to it that your husbands are returned to you, in good health and unhung. Unhanged, I suppose it should be. I will do this as soon as I am able to. On this you have my word as an officer, and as a gentleman. Will that do?"*

Nora Ayer looked at the men questioningly. *"Will it do?"* she asked.

Sam Wallace grinned at her. "Perfectly," he said. "Better than I dreamed possible. Luther can't go ahead and execute Steve, not if he knows about this tape. It's out of the question."

"I hope you're right." She inclined her head in the direction of the cassette, which was playing on. "The rest is rubbish."

"Well," said Wallace evasively, "we may as well let it run through to the end. Just in case."

"What do I do now?" Nora asked, lighting a cigarette with hands that shook.

Albert Francis asked neutrally: "What exactly did you tell Luther's PPS?" Wallace could tell from the tone that his boss was less willing than ever to get involved.

"I told him that I had this tape, and that I'd release it if he didn't phone me back in ten minutes."

"Perhaps he's phoned," Francis observed reasonably, "and you weren't home."

"I asked Nora to come here straight away," Wallace explained. "I didn't think it was safe for her to be alone in the house, not with the tape. They might come looking for it."

Francis grunted. "It seems to me there's no alternative," he said. "Nora has to make contact with them again. She has to negotiate."

"I could go along with her," Wallace offered. "Make sure nothing happens."

Albert Francis shook his head decisively. "I think that would be absolutely the worst thing you could do," he declared. "It would tell them that other people already know about the tape. The secret would be out. They might not be as ready to negotiate. And in any case, unless you're going armed and ready for a fight, I don't think you'll be any match for Claud Montrose if he does decide to get tough."

Wallace felt a wave of disappointment.

"So Nora goes by herself?" he asked.

"I think that's best," Francis said. He turned to her: "How does that sound to you, Nora?"

She shrugged. "I'll do it."

Francis said: "Fine. The thing now is to find out whether Luther's been trying to get in touch with you. Phone him up from here – see if he'll speak."

Nora Ayer went across to the telephone and dialled the number she once used when she wanted to contact her husband in the Prime Minister's office.

"Mr Sehai? It's Nora Ayer. I've been out of the house for a bit. Has General Luther been trying to contact me?"

"Oh, Mrs Ayer. Thank God you've called. Hold on please."

She put her hand over the receiver and said: "It looks as if I struck a nerve."

Luther's voice, friendly and measured, came on the line. "Good morning, Mrs Ayer. Thank you for calling back," he said. "Look, I think there's been a terrible misunderstanding. We ought to clear it up at once. Can I come and see you?"

A look of hope lit Nora's face. "Certainly, General," she replied. "Whenever you like."

"What about right away? Where are you?"

"I'm ..." she hesitated. "I'm with friends. I'll be home in fifteen minutes."

"I'll meet you at your house then."

"Fine," Nora Ayer said. "Thank you."

She put down the phone and her shoulders slumped with relief. "He's coming to see me," she said. "Himself. He's coming to my house. I must get back."

Albert Francis was smiling now. "Excellent news," he said. "I'm sure it will all be sorted out."

"My tape. I must take my tape."

Sam Wallace went quickly across to the cassette and removed it. "Here it is," he said, "although if I were you, I'd leave it with us ..." he caught the party President's angry glance "... or with friends, or somewhere safe. Give it to them only when you're satisfied there won't be any funny business. You know what crooks they are," he said, staring directly at Albert Francis.

She put the tape into her bag and snapped the clasp shut. "I will," she promised. "I'll hide it somewhere."

"Good girl," Wallace encouraged. "If you hit any trouble, don't hesitate to give us a call. Isn't that so, Al?"

Albert Francis managed a smile. "Of course," he said insincerely.

Nora Ayer let herself into her house with her front door key, feeling better now, far more confident. Luther would arrive at any moment. She'd put on the kettle for tea.

She went through to the kitchen to arrange cups and saucers on a tray and to open a packet of biscuits. She switched on the kettle.

A terrible misunderstanding, he'd called it. It certainly was that. Now she would insist that Stephen was reprieved and pardoned before she handed over the tape. She wondered what states the other families must be in, if they had been victims of similar "misunderstandings".

Nora lit another cigarette and walked through to the living-room to make sure it was clean and tidy. She opened the door and stopped dead.

Claud Montrose was sitting on the sofa, smiling thinly, his face shining. "Good morning, Mrs Ayer."

She stood as if turned to stone. At last she recovered herself. "Mr Montrose. I don't recall inviting you in."

"You were out. I thought I'd take the liberty of coming in and waiting. I have my own key."

Nora glanced behind him at the shelves of books, tapes and records. It was clear he had gone through them, although some effort had been made to replace them in a rough order.

She stared at Montrose with contempt. "General Luther will be here in a moment."

Montrose shook his head and his small eyes watched her brightly. "No, Mrs Ayer. Unfortunately the General is not able to come after all. He has asked me to act in his place. Please sit down."

She did so, reluctantly. "What's happening about my husband?" she asked.

"That depends," Montrose replied, softly.

"Oh? On what?"

"On what there is on that tape. I have to hear it first before I make a recommendation."

"And you think I'm just going to get it and play it for you, and watch amazed when you snatch it away? You must think I'm very feeble, Mr Montrose."

"I don't think you're feeble at all, Mrs Ayer," Montrose said. "I think you're bluffing."

"I assure you I am not. I had a cassette recorder in my handbag when I went for drinks with General Luther. He will tell you that I sat right next to him and that I asked most of the questions. The quality of the tape is very good. There can be no doubt that it is his voice, and none at all about the assurances he gave."

"It's a bluff, Mrs Ayer," Montrose said. "A pitiful bluff to save your husband from hanging."

"Indeed it is not."

"Then go ahead and release it to the press. We don't care." Montrose stood up to leave. "See you at the funeral."

He walked towards the door and she watched with alarm. As he drew close to where she sat, his steps slowed.

"You don't have any choice, you know," he said. "Think about it. If you *don't* give me the tape, your husband hangs. If you do give it to me, he lives. He can go into exile for all we care. We'll even buy him an air ticket. You too. You can start a new life. There's a plane for London tomorrow morning, and you could all be on it. But only in exchange for that tape." He paused. "Now there's one other alternative. It's that you hand the tape over to the press. You know what'll happen if you do? We'll say it's a fake, of course. Luther will deny ever having seen you. On top of that, your husband will hang and I'll make sure he doesn't die easily. I'll see that he strangles at the end of that rope, and that's not a very nice thing to happen. And after that, then we'll come for you. There are six boys I know who are pretty horny and keep asking if they can come around again. They liked you, Nora, you know that? You made a real hit."

Montrose's fat hand reached out and touched some strands of Nora Ayer's hair. "I might come myself."

She wanted to scream; to order him out; to hit him. Instead she brushed his hand away and said bitterly: "Now you're the one who's bluffing, *Mister* Montrose. You wouldn't dare do any of that. Don't you think the world will be watching? Don't you think the whole island will be watching? And what about the army? You want me to believe that they're all as corrupt and vile as you and Luther? Not a chance! They'd know what happened, and they'd call you to account. The other families would back me up, too."

"I wonder," said Montrose dreamily. "When their men are actually hanged, I wonder if they would back you up? Think about it: what would they have to gain? It won't bring back the dead. Yet what have they got to lose? Well, there's the money we're paying into their accounts every month. That's mortgages, and food, and clothes for the kids. We'd stop that, of course, the moment there was trouble. We wouldn't arrange for anything unpleasant to happen to them, but then we wouldn't have to. By their own admissions, they would have been part of the plot to kill Moorhouse. The minute they agreed to the deal, they joined a conspiracy to murder. That's a crime punishable by death, as we all know, and they might be called to account when the government changes. Meanwhile, they'll have to live with their neighbours and friends. They'll have to explain how they came to have $10,000 paid into the accounts in one hit. Actually, you'd have to explain that yourself, Mrs Ayer – if you were still aroujd to talk. You really think we'd have trouble with the other families?"

Nora Ayer offered desperately: "What if I gave the tape to a third party? You free my husband and let us catch the plane tomorrow. When it takes off, you collect the tape."

Montrose shook his head. "We want to know what's on it first. I don't want to find I've got Mantovani and his Singing Strings when you're at 10,000 feet and still climbing, do I?"

Nora told herself: *I still have time. There's all today to get through. I mustn't give in right away. If their nerve is going to break, I need time.*

"Well, Mr Montrose," she said. "I'm sorry. We can't do business. You say I'm bluffing, but I'm not. I say *you're* bluffing."

"But I'm not either, " he said softly.

"I'll take a chance on that," she answered crisply. "I suggest you tell General Luther that unless he reprieves my husband today, and signs a paper agreeing to fly us all off the island on tomorrow morning's plane, I will release the tape to the world's press. The deadline is five o'clock tonight, and it is not negotiable. At five o'clock, the news goes out." She stood up to show him the door.

Montrose did not move, but stared at her with hatred. "I'm afraid we can't allow that," he said. "You have to change your mind." He turned his head to look out of the door. "You lot! Inside!"

Nora Ayer's fingernails dug deep into the palms of her hands. It was like a nightmare, seeing the six of them in her house again. The leader, the cruel, handsome man with the pouting mouth, grinned lazily at her. She knew the blood had drained from her face and she felt she might fall. She held the edge of the chair for support.

The men stood in line, watching her insolently.

Montrose looked on with evident enjoyment. "You see, Mrs Ayer, you can't win," he said. "Either you hand over the tape and your husband goes free, or you don't hand over the tape and he hangs, and we have ourselves an afternoon of fun and frolics. It'll mean you miss your final meeting with him, of course. Poor Stephen will be so disappointed. But I'll be sure to tell him what happened, just before they lead him away. It'll be a sort of going-away present for him."

Nora Ayer fought to stop herself being sick. Montrose was a sadist. How could any man behave like this? But she knew in her heart that even if she capitulated and gave him the tape, it would not save Stephen. The only hope – the most slender one – was to hold out and perhaps, at the last minute, fear of exposure would make *them* give in.

She could not trust herself to talk, but she shook her head firmly.

Montrose studied her for a second and gave a thin smile. "Well then, let's play a game," he said. "We're going to pull this house apart, room by room. The man who finds the tape gets a crack at you first. You just watch these boys at work, and you think about what they did to you last time. I'm sure you'll think it sensible to change your mind."

Chapter Forty

Sam Wallace was angry and disappointed at the reaction of Albert Francis. The fight was going out of him, just as it had suddenly gone out of the store-owners when they learned of Maxwell's murder.

Even if Nora Ayer gave the go-ahead for publication, and it was by no means certain that she would, Francis had said he was doubtful that the Democratic Front could take it on. He was careful not to rule it out entirely, but his reluctance was clear to see.

In years of working closely with him, Wallace had never before seen the party leader so intimidated.

It was almost lunchtime. Wallace phoned Clive Lyle and arranged to meet him at Kay's. He had to talk, and Lyle was the man to listen. He would probably be able to offer some suggestions on what to do.

Sitting on the veranda overlooking the harbour, Lyle did listen carefully, asking an occasional pointed question.

When Wallace was finished, the American said quietly: "I really need that tape."

"Oh, I've got a copy," Wallace replied, colouring slightly. "I forgot to tell you: I connected the recorder to another, so it automatically copied while we were listening to it. I can't use it, though."

Lyle stared at him and his face broke into a slow smile. "That's my boy," he said approving. "*You* might not be able to use it. But I can. I can use it."

Wallace was uncertain: "Hell, Clive," he said, "I don't know if I ought to give it to you. I don't mind letting you hear it, but you see, it's not really mine."

Lyle held up his hands placatingly. "Don't worry about it," he said. "It's not for publication. It's to save Moorhouse and the others."

"How?"

"I know some army officers, generals mostly, who are pretty unhappy about the way things are going. If they had proof Luther had given his word on something like that, they'd make bloody sure he kept it. The honour of the military, that sort of thing."

"And they wouldn't make it public?"

"Absolutely guaranteed not. They'd just see to it that Moorhouse and the rest don't hang."

"Well," said Wallace, still hesitating, "I suppose it'll be all right." Lyle immediately signalled a waiter for the bill.

"What are you doing, Clive?" Wallace asked, surprised. "We haven't eaten yet. The food will be here in a second."

"No time today, Sam. We've got to move fast. I'll buy you a celebration lunch tomorrow." Lyle was behaving with such determination that Wallace made no protest. They drove in the American's hire car to the Democratic Front offices, which, although Wallace didn't know it, were familiar ground to Clive Lyle.

The watchman saluted as they drove in, and Lyle waved cheerfully at him.

Albert Francis was out at a meeting, so they went to Wallace's office and listened, undisturbed, to the tape. Lyle had become very tense now, there was a sense of nervous energy being burned within him. He smiled wryly as the cassette wound through and Luther left unchallenged Nora Ayer's assertion that their husbands had simply gone along with a plot to kill Moorhouse; and then Luther's categorical assurance that the co-accused would not hang, and the offer of money.

It would, as Nora Ayer herself remarked on the tape, do very nicely.

Lyle took the cassette and slipped it into his jacket pocket. He put an affectionate arm around Wallace and gave a hard squeeze. "Sam, you're a friend," he said warmly. "Keep tomorrow lunchtime free."

Wallace rubbed his shoulder joints cautiously. Jesus, Lyle didn't know his own strength.

General Baxter, Lyle's contact at army headquarters, was cool. A direct telephone call, which bypassed the agreed security arrangements, surprised and angered him, but he suppressed this from his voice.

Lyle used the emergency code sentence for calling an urgent meeting – a simple invitation for a game of golf – and, after some hesitation, he was told this would not be possible for three days. The figure in days meant the actual time of the meeting: three o'clock, just over an hour away.

Lyle said that would suit him very well, and hung up.

He parked his hire car outside the suburban house, less than a mile from the army barracks and knocked at the door.

The atmosphere in the living-room was tense and expectant. Lyle apologised to the group for the breach in security, but said that when they had listened to a tape he had brought, they would understand.

Baxter was the head of the dissidents, and the others usually looked to him for a lead, but when the main part of the tape had run through, there was an immediate outburst from everyone.

Lyle switched off the machine. "That's about it," he said. "The rest is mostly inaudible – the wives talking about individual problems, I understand."

The voices rose again in anger and condemnation. Baxter stood up to take control.

"Gentlemen!" he said sharply, and the talking died away. "Gentlemen, I think we've heard enough. Do we agree that it's time to move?"

There was a buzz of assent.

Lyle grinned. It was working. It would take them a couple of days to get their final plans together, by which time Moorhouse would be long dead.

"When do you think you'll be able to do it?" he asked. "Two, three days?"

"No, Mr Lyle," Baxter said. "A couple of days will be much too late. They'll all be dead by then. We've got to move now."

Lyle felt his grin fade.

Moorhouse had to hang, whatever happened. The plan depended on it. Then a stable civilian government could be installed, giving the United States the long-term assurances it needed.

"What do you mean by now, General? Sometime tonight?"

Lyle felt he could persuade Luther to bring the execution forward a few hours.

"No, sir. Right now. This afternoon."

Lyle was no longer smiling, and his voice was cautious. "With respect, sir, is that wise? A coup in daylight? At almost no notice? Aren't you running the risk of it going off at half-cock?"

Baxter shook his head. "Mr Lyle, we've been ready to move for the last seven days. The preparations have been made. Our supporters command the most sensitive units. There has been considerable discussion among us about getting rid of Luther and his regime after the hanging. There was a general feeling that we should not move earlier in case the judiciary was brought into disrepute. But that tape changes everything. There can be no question now. The executions cannot be allowed to go ahead."

"But Moorhouse!" Lyle was almost shouting. "If Moorhouse lives, he'll take the island into the Soviet sphere! Think of the wider interests, for God's sake!"

Baxter cast a cold eye over Clive Lyle. "A new military government," he said, "will instal itself merely to hold swift general elections. Nothing more. We have no other plans. If Moorhouse wants to stand, he must bring before the people his foreign policy. If they vote for an alliance with Moscow, then so be it. But of course, none of us expect they'll do anything of the sort. The whole question is academic. Moorhouse will have escaped the noose, so he won't even get a sympathy vote. He'll have to fight for his political life, just like everyone else. We've seen what's happened to the island under military rule, and we don't like it one bit. We don't want to stay mixed up in this any more. And we're not going to start with civilian blood on our hands."

Lyle stared in astonishment. Jesus, Baxter really believed that, and looking around the room, so did the others.

Lyle shrugged in defeat. "Then, gentlemen, all I can say is, good luck. I'm sure the United States will look forward to welcoming your new government."

"Thank you, Mr Lyle. And thank you for the tape."

Lyle forced a smile. "It was my pleasure," he said.

Lyle raced back to the Embassy and telephoned Luther's office.

This was another breach of security, but there was no alternative. He had to tell Luther to order Moorhouse's execution to be brought forward, that it should take place without delay. If necessary, someone ought to go down to the cells and shoot him.

Lyle knew he could not explain why to Luther, or drop any hints about the impending coup, because the other part of the American plan was in complete accord with Baxter's – to get rid of the corrupt military administration, and let the St David's electorate vote into power a centrist, or right of centre administration such as the Democratic Front.

In fact, it didn't much matter which party came in: it was just Moorhouse himself who had to be out of the way.

Bob Sehai answered the phone. He regretted that the President was not in the office at the moment. He did not know when he would be back. He had been called away unexpectedly.

Lyle slammed down the receiver, cursing. Where in Christ's name was Luther?

The search of the Ayer house went on for nearly three hours. Nora watched from her seat in the living-room, cold with fear. Whenever the thug who was the leader caught her eye, he ran his tongue slowly across his lips and she felt weak with panic and uncertainty.

She knew also that it was past the time for her to be at the Central Gaol for the final meeting with Stephen, and that he would be sitting in the death cell, waiting, and not understanding why she did not come.

Nora Ayer prayed harder than she had in her life. *Please God, I need a miracle.*

The men found nothing. The family's possessions were heaped on the floor, books torn apart, clothes and letters jumbled into a pile, while the stereo player tested every tape cassette they owned in case the conversation with Luther should be on one of them.

Montrose himself went through these, leaving the general wrecking of the house to the others.

At last, Montrose went abruptly to make a phone call and, half an hour later, there in the doorway was General Luther himself, cool and unperturbed.

"Hello, Mrs Ayer," he said pleasantly. "You're causing us rather a lot of trouble today."

Even through her fright, the arrogance of the man left her breathless and angry. But at least he was here: presumably to negotiate.

The six thugs lounged around the doorway, staring. She avoided looking at them.

Luther said to Montrose: "Get them out of here," and Nora Ayer felt the relief flow through her.

Outside, she heard a vehicle start up and reverse out of the drive. She thought it strange she hadn't heard it come in.

She noticed another man in the doorway, and she recognised him from photographs as Alec Clifton, now the Minister of Tourism and Ports.

Luther sat opposite her and said evenly: "It's not very nice to tape record a private conversation, Mrs Ayer."

"It's not very nice to hang my husband, General Luther," she shot back, grateful that her voice sounded calm.

"Well, I'm sure we can make some arrangement about that," Luther replied with a laugh. "But I need to have the tape."

"You can have it when my husband is on a plane out of here," Nora said. "I will give it to you myself."

Luther sighed. "That's not acceptable." He turned to Montrose: "You've checked everything?"

"Everything."

"Inside the house, outside the house?"

"It's hardly likely to be outside, now is it?" Montrose snapped.

"What about the garage?"

"There isn't one."

"Well, the car then."

Nora Ayer felt her blood run cold.

Montrose paused. "No," he said at last. "Actually I'm not sure they did look inside the car."

"Oh fuck, Claud," Luther chided. "Why the hell not?"

Clifton offered: "I'll go and have a look if you like."

Nora Ayer waited in silent misery. Clifton was away ten minutes, and when he returned, she could see the triumph on his face immediately he came in the room. He held up a cassette.

"This was under the carpet in the front," Clifton said. "Recognise it, Mrs Ayer?"

Nora looked away. Her only bargaining card had gone. She felt her lower lip tremble and she knew that soon she would cry. She should have left it with Sam Wallace, but now it was too late. She thought in anguish: *I'm sorry, Stephen. I'm so very sorry.*

Luther, Montrose and Clifton listened to the first few minutes of the tape, then the General switched it off and ejected it from the machine.

He smiled amiably at Nora. "It would be a pity to interfere with the administration of justice, don't you think?" he said. "The majesty of the law and all that?"

She said, almost whispering: "You promised . . . you gave your word. . ."

"Ah," said Luther cheerfully, "but you didn't get it in writing, did you?" He looked at his watch. "My goodness, look at that. I think you've missed the final meeting with your husband. How time flies. Still, we're not barbarians. We'll take you to the gaol if you like. I'm sure you want a quick goodbye. Where are your children?"

"At friends. For the afternoon."

"Well never mind. No doubt he'd like to see you."

"I'll go by myself, if you don't mind."

"They won't let you in, Mrs Ayer," Luther warned pleasantly. "You're over your time. If you want to see Stephen at all, we'll have to see if we can get you in ourselves. A special concession to an attractive . . ." he smiled ". . . and courageous adversary. Shall we go?"

There seemed nothing for it. Nora felt her body slumping in defeat but she fought to straighten it and to hold her head high. She would not let these people see her beaten.

Luther escorted her into the front seat of the Land Rover. He drove fast, with Montrose and Clifton sitting behind.

Along the Coast Road, they passed the turnoff to the Central Gaol at sixty miles an hour, and Nora Ayer swung around in alarm. "Hey!" she shouted. "You've missed it!"

Luther grinned at her. "A short cut," he explained.

She subsided into silence, feeling once again through her pain and grief, the stab of apprehension.

They were out of Port Lombard now, still on the Coast Road and heading for Alden Cliffs, about thirty miles away, on the road to Aberdeen.

Finally Luther slowed down, and turned left onto a dirt track. Two hundred yards in, he braked and cut the engine.

Nora Ayer knew she was in trouble.

She grabbed the door handle, to open it and run, for she realised that something terrible was going to happen to her, but the muscular arms of Montrose came suddenly over the back of her seat and held her as she struggled, and then there was a smell, a sickening hospital smell, and something pressed down over her nose and mouth and her vision began to flicker. She tried holding her breath, twisting her face away, but soon she had to gasp in air and as she did so she felt herself falling ... falling ...

In Port Lombard, the takeover had begun. Tanks rolled into the streets again, but it was an hour before anyone realised there was more going on than an unpublicised army exercise.

Baxter had been right about the ease with which it could be accomplished. Luther's personal power base was small, based on greed and corruption spread around a limited number of officers, and once these centres were neutralised, the coup was a logistical problem rather than a physical one.

Except for Luther. The General had vanished, and with him, Montrose and Clifton.

For almost an hour, Baxter believed that they had somehow been given advance warning and had fled, perhaps to plan a counter-attack. If that was so, it could be serious, and the prospect of rival army units fighting on the island could not be dismissed, although Baxter couldn't imagine which units would align themselves with Luther now.

Still, you could never be sure. It was an anxious and uncertain time.

He put out a general alert for the three men, and within half an hour the driver of a police patrol car reported that he remembered seeing General Luther driving a Land Rover along the Coast Road towards Aberdeen. There was a woman passenger in the front seat with him, and two unidentified men in the back. They had passed his position at around five o'clock, driving fast.

Aberdeen? Baxter could not understand why Luther would be heading for a small remote fishing town, but he ordered paratroop reinforcements to be flown there just in case.

To Baxter, it seemed more likely that they had been heading for an intermediate destination, although heaven knew where. There were a few very small villages on the way – no more than half a dozen huts in a group, and otherwise nothing except beaches and beatuy spots, like Alden Cliffs.

And who was the woman?

It was Baxter's hunch that, within a few hours, they would return to Port Lombard along the same road. He ordered road blocks set up on all approaches, with the heaviest and most effective manning on the Aberdeen Road.

Luther, Montrose and Clifton were to be stopped and arrested. If they didn't have the woman with them, Baxter would order them shot out of hand. If they did, the law would take its course. No civilian blood must be shed.

Baxter settled down to wait. He thought with satisfaction: *we've done it. We've done it with clean hands. We've stopped the hangings. We'll give*

Moorhouse back to the country, if it wants him. And Ayer and the others can return to their wives and children and live as free men. We've given the island a new chance.

As he waited for Luther's Land Rover to appear along the Coast Road, it didn't seem a bad prospect.